W9-BUD-672

0 00 30 0459814 4

No Longer the Property of
Hayner Public Library District

RECEIVED

AUG 1 9 2008

By_____

· WASHINGTON'S LADY ·

HAYNER PUBLIC LIBRARY DISTRICT
ALTON, ILLINOIS

OVERDUES 10 PER DAY MAXIMUM FINE
COST OF BOOKS. LOST OR DAMAGED
BOOKS ADDITIONAL $5.00 SERVICE CHARGE.

BRANCH

Books by
Nancy Moser
FROM BETHANY HOUSE PUBLISHERS

Mozart's Sister

Just Jane

Washington's Lady

NANCY MOSER

WASHINGTON'S LADY

— *a novel* —

BETHANYHOUSE
PUBLISHERS

Washington's Lady
Copyright © 2008
Nancy Moser

Cover design by Lookout Design, Inc.
Cover photography by Aimee Christenson

Scripture quotations are taken from the King James Version of the Bible.

All rights reserved. No part of this publication may be reproduced, stored in a retrieval system, or transmitted in any form or by an means—electronic, mechanical, photo-copying, recording, or otherwise—without the prior written permission of the publisher. The only exception is brief quotations in printed reviews.

Published by Bethany House Publishers
11400 Hampshire Avenue South
Bloomington, Minnesota 55438

Bethany House Publishers is a division of
Baker Publishing Group, Grand Rapids, Michigan.

Printed in the United States of America

Library of Congress Cataloging-in-Publication Data

Moser, Nancy.
    Washington's lady / Nancy Moser.
        p. cm.
    ISBN 978-0-7642-0500-2 (pbk.)
    1. Washington, Martha, 1731-1802—Fiction. 2. Presidents' spouses—Fiction.
I. Title.

    PS3563.O88417W37   2008
    813'.54—dc22

                                                                    2008002533

F
MOS

b18172362

To my relatives who fought valiantly
for God and country:

To *Jonathan Tyler*,
my great, great, great, great, great grandfather
who fought at Ticonderoga,
was captured by Burgoyne's army, and escaped.

To *Solomon Young* and *William Chrystal*,
my great, great grandfathers.
One lost an arm, and one was made lame,
both in service to our country during the Civil War.

To my grandfather *Lester Young*,
who fought in France during the "war to end all wars,"
World War I.

And to my father, *Lyle Young*,
who carried on the family tradition
of honor and commitment
in the South Pacific during World War II.

Thank you for your courage, gentlemen,
and for your sacrifice toward so ably
planting and defending
our family's American roots.

NANCY MOSER is the bestselling author of eighteen novels, including *Just Jane*, the Christy Award-winning *Time Lottery*, and the SISTER CIRCLE series coauthored with Campus Crusade co-founder Vonette Bright.

Nancy has been married thirty-three years. She and her husband have three twenty-something children and live in the Midwest. She loves history, has traveled extensively in Europe, and has performed in various theaters, symphonies, and choirs.

PART I

· THE GOLDEN YEARS ·

— ONE —

Death mocked me.

Daniel's booming voice was forever still. Never again would I hear his explosive laughter, or his whispered, *"I love you, Martha."*

I walked away from the grave of my husband. Seven short years was not enough. Yet it was not just *his* death that scorned me. . . .

I was sick to death of death.

"Dow!"

I held little Patsy, but a toddling fourteen months, in my arms. "No, dear one. Let Mamma hold you."

Let Mamma never let you go.

I looked about the Queens Creek cemetery, at all who had come to offer their condolences. Their eyes revealed their compassion, their wish to help. But how could anyone help?

My mother approached, wearing the black of mourning that had become far too familiar within the Dandridge and Custis families. Patsy extended her arms to her grandmother. I relinquished her.

"Come, little one," Mother said. Her eyes included me. "Let us go back to the house. It is time for a nap."

A nap would be of great relief—though unattainable. For whenever

I attempted sleep I was greeted with the sight of my husband's eyes as he suffered. Although I had prayed for the best, he had expected the worst.

His throat thick with a virulent infection, he had struggled to speak. *"I am so sorry, Martha. So sorry to leave you."*

I was sorry too.

There would be no nap for a second reason: my son was still ill. Jacky, not yet three, lay abed, still holding on to a fever and the same swollen throat. For a month we had tried to make Jacky better, even bringing Dr. Carter the twenty-five miles from Williamsburg when my own medical abilities proved unworthy. Having just suffered the death of my second-born, Frances, three months previous, I would take no chances.

Nary a week ago Daniel had succumbed to the sickness. No treatment helped. And he died.

My Daniel died.

The doctor said his heart was weak and was further weakened by the fever.

It mattered not what took him, only that he was gone.

And I was left behind.

We reached the family home we used when in Williamsburg, and I put Patsy to bed and checked upon Jacky, who was better of body, though not of spirit. Then I took solace in the study, needing silence and solitude above social commiseration. It was startling to realize being alone was a permanent state.

Perhaps I *should* have sought the company of others. . . .

Perhaps I should have.

But I could not do it.

There was a soft knock on the door.

Before I could utter a response—tell the intruder to *please* leave me alone—the door opened. It was Mother.

She entered the room, closed the door of the study with a subtle click, then took a seat beside me on the settee, her black skirts touching mine. "What can I do to help you, daughter?"

Such a simple question, but one I could only answer in a most ungenerous manner. I sprang to my feet and faced her as though she were the enemy. "You can help me by explaining why our family is made to suffer so cruelly. Eighteen years of my life were passed with nary a sorrow, but in the past eight . . . First, my brother drowns in the river, then my father-in-law—after finally consenting to our marriage—dies before the ceremony. Daniel and I are blessed with his namesake—who dies at age three. And six months later my own father, your husband, dies from the heat at a racetrack and—"

"It is not wise to dwell—"

"I do not dwell! I speak facts. After Father died, three more children blessed us. Then death found us again—twofold in one year! My dearest baby Frances—only four years old—is ripped away from me, and now, but three months later, my husband?" My final words came amid sobs. "I am only twenty-six! How can I be asked to bear such grief?"

"You are not *asked.*"

Her words, so plainly said, stunned me to silence. No indeed, death had not asked my permission to inflict its wounds. For if it had solicited my opinion, I would have barred it at the door, saying, "Halt! You will not enter here!"

My vehemence fueled a new thought, more than a *mere* thought, a new resolve. I faced Mother and raised my chin with the tenacity that had become a necessary part of survival in these colonies. "I will not allow death to hurt me again! I will not!"

Mother opened her mouth to speak, thought better of it, then opened it again. "Then you best not love again."

I recognized the truth in her words. To love was to risk pain.

Then perhaps I would not love anew.

I continued my vow. "As God is my witness, I will protect what I *do* love. I will enshroud my two surviving children with constant attention, devotion, and protection. Death will not dare approach us, nor make any attempts to breech my fortification."

"But, Martha—"

I swiped away my tears. "I am done with death! And I swear, it is now done with me."

I strode from the room and hurried upstairs, pausing at the door that led to poor Jacky. I steadied my breathing as well as my hand upon the knob.

I entered the dim room, the draperies closed against the afternoon sun that scorned us with its brightness. I let my eyes adjust to the light and was about to seek the children's nanny—whom I had instructed to watch upon my son whilst I was gone. She was not there. How dare she leave him alone.

And yet . . . Jacky was not alone. For as I edged closer I saw that my dearest Patsy had left her room and climbed in beside her big brother. My two darlings lay snuggled in each other's arms, Patsy's head upon Jacky's shoulder.

I reached to lift her from his sickbed, then thought better of it. Jacky's breathing seemed easier. Perhaps the comfort of his little sister was a balm beyond the meager medicines Dr. Carter had offered. Brother and sister, bonded by their need as well as their love.

Gazing upon them, I put a hand to my lips, stifling a sob. For beyond my loss of a husband, my children had lost a father. There would be no more games of ride-the-pony or sitting in their father's lap by the fire as he told stories.

" 'London Bridge is falling down, falling down, falling down . . .' " The familiar song came to my lips unbidden.

I forced it to silence.

There would be too much silence in this house now.

The sobs threatened once again. Would they ever leave me alone?

I nodded once. They *must* leave me. I could not let them wield their power, for once unleashed, the sobs would lead to despair, which would lead to surrender and—

Death would claim further victory, not against the dead, but against those it left behind.

I moved a chair beside the bed, hoping the soft rustle of my skirts would not awaken my darlings.

This is where I belonged. This is where I vowed to remain, standing guard against all that dared come against my children.

So help me God.

‑‑‑‑‑‑‑‑‑

I stood in the parlour of our home at White House in New Kent, Virginia, and stared upon the portraits we'd just had taken. The painter, John Wollaston, had been here when Jacky had first fallen ill. I held nothing against him for his quick departure. A wise man knows when to run from illness.

My darling Daniel had commissioned the paintings soon after little Frances died in April. He knew how important it was for me to preserve the family I had left. Although children's portraits were rarely painted, Daniel insisted. At first Mr. Wollaston seemed a bit taken aback, but he agreed. So now I had a rendering of my two surviving children. Little Jacky with a hawk poised upon his arm, and my sweet Patsy, all dressed in hoop and silk, though barely old enough to walk.

I looked at the images. In truth, they were not good likenesses: their faces too adult and severe, their heads too large for the lengths of their frames. If Jacky had not taken ill, I would have asked Mr. Wollaston to change them.

If he had been able.

Which I was not certain he was.

I moved to stand before the portrait of my husband. His waistcoat clung too tightly to his midsection, as though he were a man more prone to drink and fine fare than the hard work of running a vast plantation.

And his face . . . I looked at my own portrait, then back again. Our features appeared too similar, as though the artist knew only how to paint one adult face and used the same for all, with a change in hair or jewel the only personal adjustment.

I cared not for my own portrait and resolved that it looked little like myself. But what did that matter? Who would care?

But the portrait of Daniel . . . I cared very much that it bore little likeness to the man I married. That I could distinguish the differences now was of benefit, but would my memories of his face falter as the months and years passed, so that I would someday look upon this portrait as his true likeness?

I shuddered at the thought. Yet what choice did I have? It was all that was left of him.

No. That was not correct. . . .

I left the portraits behind and ascended the stairs to our bed-chamber. I closed the door behind me.

I opened the armoire and was immediately assailed by Daniel's scent. I took a step back, my heart pounding as if he himself had appeared before me.

I put a hand to my bosom, allowing a moment to recoup. How odd that a scent unnoticed when its bearer was alive could find such life once he was gone.

I approached the armoire again. My fingers skimmed the lovely waistcoats that befitted my husband's status as the third richest man in all Virginia. His ancestors—on both sides of his family line—were the elite of the elite. Over seventeen thousand acres had been under his control, along with two hundred slaves. That he even looked at me . . .

I thought of our wedding and sought out the fine navy coat he had worn for that occasion—the occasion that had nearly not come about. I took it from its peg. Dust lay upon the shoulders and I brushed the offense of it away. The coat was smaller than those newer, for Daniel had prospered as a married man by readily partaking of the culinary delights I brought to our home—though certainly not to the extent Wollaston's portrait suggested. Before marriage, Daniel had lived as a bachelor far too long and was used to making do.

Making do would never do in my home. I had been raised to be the wife of a plantation owner, and my mother had trained me well. That the accoutrements of such a life brought me great joy was a benefit—though certainly not a requirement. Although these colonies were founded on a shared desire for independence and freedom, certain basics of life had to be maintained for the sake of continuity and a well-run passing of day to day. To find joy in the mundane was a gift I strived to keep.

I set aside Daniel's wedding coat and reached for one I had seen him wear far oftener and more recently. The brown wool flannel was his favourite, and no matter how I had his garments rearranged, no matter how I attempted to hide it, he sought it out and would invariably put it on. Nothing would be said between us, except for the wink he would offer upon his victory.

The memory made me smile and I held the coat to my face, its wool rough against my cheek. I closed my eyes and drank it in. Tears announced their intention to intrude, but I forced them away.

"No! I will not let you overtake me."

The tears wisely retreated, and once assured they were contained, I hung both coats upon their hooks. I quickly closed the door of the armoire and fastened its latch.

Keeping them safe. Keeping Daniel's scent contained until I needed it next.

⤛⤜

"Your husband had no will. He died intestate."

I gaped at our friend James Power in utter astonishment. James had been one of the friends who had tried to intervene on our behalf when Daniel's father had fought against our marriage, a friend then, and now. "How could Daniel have neglected such a thing?" I asked. "With all the trials and struggles we have had over his grandfather's and his father's wills, I would have imagined he—"

"Perhaps he assumed he had more time." James shrugged. " 'Tis a common misconception."

"My husband did not deal in misconceptions."

My statement spoke courageously, yet I knew I exaggerated for Daniel's benefit. His roots were so knotted with parental and grand-parental animosity that he plunged into our union as a means to finally escape the past and find happiness—and peace. If he neglected to make a will, I suspected it was because of a fear that thinking toward the day we would be parted would jinx the happiness he had finally accomplished.

My Daniel married late in life, at age thirty-eight, the delay not his choice, but caused by the exasperating interference—and contrariness and meanspiritedness—of his father. While living, John Parke Custis held the honour of being one of the most infamous and disagreeable men in Virginia. This was not only my view but one held by all who gained his acquaintance. He took great pleasure in these traits and oozed bitterness the way a wound oozes the poison that inflames it. He blamed his wife, Frances, for making him so. Apparently they fought hard and often, and though never divorced, they could have been. Perhaps should have been, if the desire for freedom from strife could have overruled the dictates of polite society.

Actually, the divorce issue became moot, as Frances died at the young age of twenty-nine, when my Daniel was but four years old. John all but rejoiced. He never remarried, acted as though all women were of the devil, and spent the rest of his life causing difficulties regarding his children's quest to find mates. Daniel's sister was disinherited for going against her father's wishes, and Daniel would have been too— if I had not won his father over. It seems his objection was rooted in thoughts I was not good enough for his son, my father having only five hundred acres.

Although I disliked even being in the man's presence, when the elder Mr. Custis began sharing nasty rumours about me, disparaging me and my family throughout Williamsburg . . . when he gave the Custis crested silver to an innkeeper's wife—stating he would rather toss it in the streets than let any daughter of John Dandridge have it—I could take it no longer. Daniel was so fearful of his father he could not go against him, even though we were engaged and friends urged him to do so. It was by my hand, and albeit by my charm, that the intractable Mr. Custis was won over.

I did so with great planning and without Daniel's knowledge. My father-in-law's only love and passion (since he found all humans deplorable and annoying) was the garden at his Six Chimneys home in Williamsburg. To his credit he was quite talented in horticulture and botany, coddling his plants and grieving over them when they died. I too was a gardener of some skill. So one day—without forewarning—I visited Mr. Custis at his home. A servant led me to the four-acre garden. Mr. Custis was barely civil, and only with God's help did I hold my tongue against his goading. But I soon won his favor by offering him some sage advice about his begonias. What you cannot fight, you flatter. Soon after, Mr. Custis gave his approval for our marriage.

There was marital disparagement on Daniel's mother's side too. When Daniel's mother, Frances, was young, her father, Daniel Parke, left her and her sister and mother in Virginia and went back to England, only to return a few years later with his mistress (whom he called his "cousin") and their illegitimate son. Soon after, he departed with the mistress but left the boy behind to be raised by his long-suffering wife! My head shakes in disbelief even now.

Eventually he had another family in the Leeward Islands (where he became governor), as well as some illegitimate children in other locales. Finally he was assassinated in Antigua. Rumour had it the motive (at least in part) involved his being intimate with women who were not his to have. He left behind a convoluted will we were still fighting forty-seven years after the fact. We fight because it threatens to disperse all the property my Daniel inherited to virtually anyone who claims this horrible man as their father. Which, considering his propensity to philandering, could be a copious number.

John Custis's will was no better. He died before we married, leaving part of his estate to a young man called Mulatto Jack, who, it is said, was his issue. Jack's mother was a slave, but with this will, John emancipated Jack. His freedom, and the inheritance he was promised, caused all sorts of problems that had the potential to extend beyond our family to the entire Virginia colony. A great fear within the Tidewater and beyond was that slaves would obtain power and revolt. To add to the complications, my father-in-law wished for Jack to live with us—in our home. This would never do. Beyond our own opinions, and his being a likeable sort or not, society would not permit it. In short, the law of the land made it impossible to execute the terms of the will. Being a slave, Jack could not own property, and because of the wording of John's will, even if free, he could not live on the property bequeathed to him. There seemed to be no solution.

But then . . . Jack died mysteriously before the issue was fully settled. Which, of course, settled the issue. I did not wish the boy dead, but I did acknowledge his passing allowed the difficulty to be set aside. As I was expecting our first child at the time, it was a relief.

The other requisite in my father-in-law's will was that only those who had "Parke" in their names could ever inherit. Thus our children all claimed that surname as a middle name. I would take no chances when remedy was so easily attained.

Yet, though hard to fathom, the difficulties in the will of John Custis were not caused by any error or omission but on purpose. To cause trouble. And he succeeded, for I truly believe a great part of my husband's death can be attributed to the pressures, peeves, and peculiarities of his family. Weakened by the illness that claimed Jacky for so long, Daniel's heart simply gave up and gave in to the stresses of being Daniel Parke's grandson and the son of John Custis.

I found this drama disconcerting, for I was raised in a happy home with loving parents. Poor Daniel. That I had been able to bring him some semblance of familial and wedded bliss was consolation. At least he had enjoyed seven years of peace.

"Mrs. Custis?" James queried.

My mind had drifted to past places that elicited cruel apprehension and anger. I could not change the past—nor the fact my husband had chosen not to think about the future. I had to deal with the present.

Presently.

I closed my eyes and opened them again, ready to look upon the subject at hand. "So, James. There is no will. Where does that leave us?"

"English common law says your husband's estate will be equally divided between you, Jacky, and Patsy. One third each."

"And how exactly is that done?"

"An inventory will have to be taken of each chair, plow, acre, and bag of seed."

With over seventeen thousand acres spread over five counties . . . the task was beyond daunting. It was too much. I could take no more.

"Are you unwell?" James asked.

That morning I *had* felt a bit feverish. It seemed as good a time as any to succumb. "I believe I am under the weather. Perhaps another—"

James rose and helped me to my feet. "Another day. Certainly. At your convenience."

He should not say such a thing. For dealing with yet another will—or lack thereof—would never be convenient.

I was genuinely sick; I did not playact the illness. That I chose to call it such upon hearing the latest news about the will was appropriate.

Did I not deserve to retire to my bedchamber for a few short days to rest and recover and let the world rush by without me? I had witnessed the effects of stress upon my husband's health. Was it not prudent for me to intercept such symptoms before I too suffered dire, unchangeable repercussions?

I heard a knock on the door. I adjusted the bed linens to make myself presentable. "Come in."

In preparation to accost my visitor, my eyes looked upon the spot far above the door's knob but quickly adjusted to a much lower level as little Jacky and Patsy came into the room. "Mamma?"

If anything could make me well, it was the sight of my children. "Come in, sweet ones." I sat against the pillows and patted a place on either side.

The children quickly accepted my invitation. Jacky lifted little Patsy to my right side, then ran round the bed to take his own place on my left. They cuddled close and I reveled in their huggable presence, their smell of the summer outside, and their mere *being*.

Once settled, Jacky asked, "When are you going to be well?"

"Mamma down," Patsy said.

Jacky nodded. "We want you downstairs. It's no fun without you."

Patsy nodded. "Papa."

I held them even closer. Yes indeed. By yielding to the sickness I had left them completely alone. I *was* feeling better. Not strong, but improved.

"You are right, little man. It is time I get up."

I was just pushing away the bedclothes when there was another knock on the door. "Yes?"

A servant, Amanda, appeared. "You have a letter."

"Bring it here." I broke the seal.

"What does it say, Mamma?"

It was from a dear friend, Robert Nicholas. I read silently:

> It gave me no small pleasure to hear with how great Christian patience and resignation you submitted to your late misfortune; the example is rare, though a duty incumbent upon us all.

Guilt assailed me. In the past few days I had set no example of any good kind.

"Mamma, down!" Patsy said.

Amanda shushed her. "Let your mamma read, little miss."

I went back to the letter. Robert further reassured me of his continuing friendship—and help. But he also offered a suggestion:

> I imagine you will find it necessary to employ a trusty steward; and as the estate is very large and very extensive . . . you had better not engage with any but a very able man, though he should require large wages, nothing appears to us very material to be done immediately, except what relates to your tobacco; if it is not already done, it will be necessary that letters be wrote for insurance and that we, or some other of your friends should be acquainted with the quantities of tobacco put on board each ship that we may get the proper bills of lading . . .

The tobacco! The mainstay of our plantation, and yea, most plantations in Virginia. I had grown up amid the growing, sowing, and selling of this crop. There were things to be done.

Immediately.

Yes indeed, it was time to get up. And be well.

Our lives and livelihood depended upon it.

I sat at Daniel's desk, in his study, and reread the letter I had just written:

Virginia 20th August 1757

Gent

I take this Opportunity to inform you of the great misfortune I have met with in the loss of my late Husband Mr. Custis, your Correspondent.

As I now have the Administration of his Estate & management of his Affairs of all sorts, I shall be glad to continue the Correspondence which Mr. Custis carried with you.

Yours of the 16th of March Mr. Custis rec'd before his Death with his Account Current inclosed wch I believe is right; and he had put on board the Ship King of Prussia Capt. Necks 28Hnds of Tobacco and wrote to you for Insurance for it, I now inclose the bill of Lading for the Tobacco which I hope will get safe to your hands, and as have reason to believe it is extremely good, I hope you will sell it at a good Price, Mr. Custis's Estate will be kept together for some time and I think it will be proper to continue his Account in the same manner as if he was living. Please to send an Account Current when the Tobacco is sold I am gentlemen Your Very hbl Servt

Martha Custis

I smiled at the last few lines. I hoped this letter going to London— and the two others I would send to our other factors in Liverpool and Glasgow—would act as a subtle warning that just because Daniel was gone, they had better not cheat us. If they did, the Custis plantations would go elsewhere.

Perhaps. I realized my threat was limited, as we were dependent on these British factor companies to handle our crop, sell it for us, and return to us the proceeds (after taking their own compensation, of course). There was no way for us to know if we were being treated fairly, and actually, we all assumed we were not. But as mere colonies, five thousand miles from our mother country, we had little alternative. As the colonies were prohibited by law from selling to any nation but England, and from shipping our products on any but English ships, we were at their mercy. As we were also at the mercy of pirates, privateers, and inclement weather, which could cause shipwrecks. Putting our tobacco upon a ship and seeing it leave port always caused a stitch in the stomach and elicited many prayers for its safe delivery. And fair treatment.

Yet Daniel and I had discussed focusing on another crop. Tobacco was labor intensive, it depleted the land in a most horrible way, and we recognized it might be advantageous to grow something that was of more dire need within the colonies themselves. People did not *need* tobacco. It was a cheap pleasure.

But one does not easily detour from the path of many past successful generations. And so I proceeded in the course my forebears had so carefully constructed before me.

I set the letter aside with the other two, feeling quite proud of myself. I was certain James had never intended I act as my own steward in such matters. That it caused me to feel a bond with Daniel . . . that with so much beyond my power, I longed to assert this small margin of control . . .

I *was* willing to let others help. I left my various overseers in place, assuming they would continue as they had. I employed the services of my younger brother, Bartholomew, at twenty, an attorney. He sought the advice of two more sage counselors, who agreed with my intent to act upon my own behalf—with their kind and wise instruction.

Also, regarding income, Daniel had often loaned money, charging interest. I continued to do so and kept careful records. I signed various powers-of-attorney to expedite stock and money, paid our debts, and dealt with our taxes. And the inventory, needed to hasten the division of the estate into thirds for myself and the children, was being carried out through men appointed by the court. (In this, I was well relieved to be avoided of the burden.) In the three weeks that had passed since being drawn from my sickbed by the necessities of our estate, I had accomplished much.

And accomplished it well.

Daniel would be proud.

I put the key in the door and swung it wide. I hesitated but a moment, letting my eyes glance upon my father-in-law's Williamsburg home, Six Chimneys. Daniel and I had stayed here periodically when balls, concerts, and parties had drawn us to the city. In my mind's eye I remembered him coming down the stairs, dressed in a new satin coat and breeches he had instructed be made of blue—my favourite colour.

"Ma'am? Is something wrong?"

I had forgotten about Mr. Bowen, the solicitor I'd hired to come with me this day. Without answering him, I entered the house.

My house now.

He followed me inside and closed the door against the brisk autumn air. "A stately place," he said.

Indeed.

I stepped into the parlour and my eyes were immediately drawn to the portrait of my father-in-law above the mantel. His eyes looked down upon us—in every connotation of that phrase. "Take that for the sale," I instructed Mr. Bowen.

Mr. Bowen removed his tricorn hat and cloak, draped them on a settee, and sat at the desk by the window. He took a bound book of lined paper and quill from his leather pouch. He removed the top from the inkwell and scribbled a notation. Then he looked up at me. "You sure? Ain't that the owner?"

Not anymore. "I am the owner."

"Yes'm."

My eyes glanced over the furnishings of the room. Legally, two-thirds belonged to my children. They would have to trust me to do what was best. And what was best was . . .

"Auction the lot of it."

Mr. Bowen blinked twice. "Everything?"

"I will choose a few things here and there and mark those to stay. But the rest . . ." *I just want done with it.* I moved toward the door. "I am sorry to get you out on such a blustery day, Mr. Bowen. It appears I have miscalculated my need for an accounting. The shorter list will be what stays, and that will come on another day."

He packed his supplies and donned his outerwear. "Whatever you say, Mrs. Custis."

I saw him to the door, my mind reeling with the decision I had made. I had honestly intended to put a few items up for auction yet keep the majority. To have it be the other way round . . .

Without forethought, I ascended the stairs, realizing upon reaching the landing of my intention to start from the top and work my way down.

I opened the door of my father-in-law's bedchamber and found my insides quickening, tightening, rebelling at being in the very presence of anything that had been owned, touched, and chosen by John Custis.

I had never entered this room. As John had died before our marriage, I never witnessed his presence here, and yet even after his death I had never wished to enter, as if by doing so I would reawaken the animosity and yea, even the evil its previous owner had so freely doled upon us.

I did not wish to enter now, so assigned the room to the auction block.

I moved on to the bedchamber where Daniel and I had oft stayed, and found myself smiling. This one room, which had seemed ours alone, held no memories of John Custis. With as quick a determination as I had made in John's room, I made in this one: I would keep its contents in its entirety. I cared not that the dresser was not carved with the precision of the one in the master bedchamber. I cared not for quality at all, only for the sweet memories the space elicited. *Those* were of the highest quality indeed.

Leaving the sanctum of our room, I paused briefly in the room where our children had stayed. Yes, its contents could also be kept.

At the end of the hall, I opened the door to a small room. There was but one narrow window at its end, yet in the dimmer light I made out a mishmash of belongings, unneeded for the moment. And certainly unneeded by—

My eyes fell upon a cache of paintings, leaning against one wall. I flipped through the outer few, finding them to be portraits. Were these John's ancestors? Certainly there were not any from his detested wife's side of the family. Except for taking over his wife's Parke fortune, John Custis had wholly wiped them from his conscience.

Now it was my turn to return the favor.

I left the room, willing the contents to the auction. It seemed cold, giving away portraits of those who had come before. And yet . . . there were no familial ties between these people and my children. John Custis was never a grandfather to them. That he died before they were born would not have changed that fact. I could not imagine his ever being a true grandfather, ever bending down with open arms to have grandchildren run into his loving embrace.

With a softer heart I thought of my own father, who had been the ideal grandfather. All four of my children had cuddled in his arms, fallen asleep against his shoulder, and bounced upon his knees. That he was now gone . . . *that* was a tragedy.

One of many.

My children had known one grandfather and one grandmother, both bearing the Dandridge name. They had no bond to this side of the family at all. If it were not the penchant of the Parke-Custis family to embrace conflict, their father would have been a happier man.

In fact, if not for their inherent strain and stress (which they shared with great generosity), he might still have been alive.

Anger accompanied me as I descended the stairs to the public floor. I made quick work of the parlour's contents, finding no desire to sit where my father-in-law had sat, or prod a fire with a poker he had touched.

In the dining room, my eyes were immediately drawn to the window's ledge, where coloured wine bottles were displayed in a line. I remembered Daniel explaining that his father had collected hand-blown bottles and took great stock in them. He had even ordered some made for himself, having his seal set into the glass. They *did* sparkle nicely in the sunlight. . . .

I found myself admiring the floral china in the hutch, certainly brought at great expense from England. Its delicate painting must have come from his wife's side of the family. I could not imagine the stubby fingers of John Custis ever holding so fine a teacup.

Next to the china were a set of sixteen wineglasses. I held one to the light. They were not European made, but of fine quality nonetheless.

I set it back, realizing that, most likely, the glasses had never been used. We had never used them, so who . . . my father-in-law had no friends. Friendship was a phenomenon requiring affection and determination. It required a deftness of careful effort. It required giving, listening, and being emotionally and even spiritually intertwined, one with another. It involved caring. These were all attributes that had died in John Custis long before his death—if they had ever been present.

I closed the doors on the hutch and saw some delft tea bowls on a serving cart. I studied one and realized it was rare and exceedingly fine.

These have value. I shall keep them.

Cruel memories interrupted my thoughts: John Custis disparaging the Dandridge family in the streets of Williamsburg. Our family name was of the greatest value.

I thought of Daniel's life, taken too soon because of the browbeating and the unmerciful, vicious attacks by the owner of these rare bowls. Daniel's life was of the greatest value.

And these valuable bowls . . .

Suddenly I grabbed the bowls and set them on the cloth covering the dining table. I reopened the hutch and removed the sixteen wineglasses, adding them to the lot. And last, I emptied the windowsill of my father-in-law's wine bottles. They clinked and clanked against the porcelain and glasses, falling down upon each other in a most discourteous manner. My lifelong dictum to "be careful lest they break" was put to the test as I gathered the four corners of the tablecloth and slung the heavy load upon my shoulder.

I heard breakage.

I ignored it and moved toward my destination.

Awkwardly I opened the back door but had to drop my load upon its step, my shoulder rebelling at the weight.

More breakage. Fueled by the sound, I lifted and dropped the bundle again and again from higher heights, then lower, shaking it in between. The pitch of the breakage rose as the pieces grew smaller.

My heart pounded, my breath was labored. And yet I smiled.

I carried the burden through my father-in-law's beloved garden to the well nearby. I let it drop to the ground beside it, the tablecloth opening to reveal the inner destruction. One bowl had escaped. This would not do.

I plucked it from its victory, leaned o'er the well, and tossed it against the stone side. I welcomed the breakage as it fell into the water far below.

I spotted a bottle where my father-in-law's seal accosted me. These bottles had been created and filled at his commission, and he had been vain enough to have them apply a seal sporting the Custis coat of arms.

It mocked me. He mocked me. He cared more about wine and gardens than his own family. . . .

I found a sharp pebble at the foot of the well and scraped it across the seal till it was unintelligible.

You are being childish.

With fresh ferocity I tossed the bottle into the well and relished the *pluop* sound when it met the water below.

Looking upon the rest of my handiwork, convinced by inspection that not a single piece was whole, I lifted the tablecloth to the edge of the well, held the outer corners, and let the pieces fall away. I shook the cloth, making sure the water would get its full offering.

As a final gesture, I let the cloth follow its booty, watching it flutter and float to its death in the dark depths below.

I stood at the well a moment, leaning over its cavern, my breathing constrictive within my corset. I thought of saying something vile and biting into the well—one last adieu to a man who had never done good for anyone.

But I held my tongue.

For I knew the well would echo my words back at me. I could not risk it.

Instead I plucked a pink rose from a bush, drew in its heady fragrance, and left the premises, locking the door behind me.

⁂

"I think that is a grand idea," I told my brother Bartholomew.

He looked surprised. "I really do not need so elegant a house, Martha. I only wished to let one that was better than the flat where I currently live but—"

"I am very glad to have you rent Six Chimneys," I said.

Very happy indeed.

My father-in-law's public condemnation of our family returned to my ears: *"I would rather throw all my possessions into the street than have the daughter of John Dandridge have them."*

He never said anything about the *son* of John Dandridge.

━ Two ━

I waited until the door to Daniel's study—now my study—clicked shut. Then I said the words I had been aching to say: "Good riddance!"

Elias Finch, the overseer at White House, had just left my presence. If I were a man, I might have kicked him out. Perhaps I should have done so even amid my petticoats. Such a sight might have grabbed his attention, forcing him to take notice, to take me as seriously as he ought.

I had heard rumours of his cruelty toward the slaves. His drunkenness. The fervor needed to accomplish the work of a large plantation could be misguided. I had often overheard Daniel chastising the overseers, trying to get them to recognize that pushing too hard, or exacting too harsh a punishment, would only lead to runaways, or even worse, a revolt. Productivity could not be won at the cost of common sense and safety.

Did I reach Mr. Finch through my attempts? As a woman I had so little recourse. I had no masculine physical presence with which to threaten—and at but five feet in height, I had little physical presence of any means. I could only cajole and urge strongly through words.

Was I successful?

Time would tell.

Time . . . I had too little of it. Between my household duties, the children, and the added duties which had been Daniel's, I had nary a moment to eat, let alone have a thought that was not linked to some ought-to or must-do.

What I ought to do is sleep. Perhaps just a moment . . .

I leaned on the desk and rested my head upon my arms.

"Ma'am? Mistress Custis?"

I opened my eyes and sat erect in a single movement. Cully, our butler, stood on the other side of the desk. I pressed a hand against my hair. "Yes. What is it?"

"Mr. Carter is here to see you."

Charles Carter. I had known him most of my life. He was from a wealthy Virginia family and was an esteemed member of the governing body, the House of Burgesses. His father (Robert "King" Carter— who earned that derisive title through aggressive action) owned three hundred thousand acres and over a thousand slaves.

Charles was . . . interested in me.

As a woman.

As a wife.

He had sent word he would be visiting, but in my busyness, I had forgotten. I wondered how many days he would stay. Distances were too great not to linger.

Especially when one had good motive to delay.

I pushed back from the desk and stood. "Send him in." I pressed my hands against the folds of my dress to ease them into place and pushed my corset downward so I could breathe. Presently, Charles appeared, the sage brocade of his coat a pleasing complement to the deep green of his waistcoat and breeches. He looked the essence of the upcoming spring.

I ached for spring. Renewal. Hope. New beginnings.

He bowed and I offered a curtsy. "Nice to see you, Mr. Carter."

"I have stayed away too long. Let me just say . . . I do not mean to begin our conversation on such a sad note, but I do feel it incumbent . . ." He studied his fingernails. "I was sorry to hear of the death of your sister Frances. She was but fourteen?"

"Thirteen," I said. "Too young." First my baby Frances, and more recently my sister of that name . . . "Will you please sit down?" I rang the bell and asked Mirella for tea and scones. I was not certain of the hour. How long had I slept? I looked at my watch and saw it was nearly one in the afternoon.

Charles pointed at my timepiece. "How unusual."

"Daniel had it made for me. A well-run house runs on time." I rose to show it to him. "See how the numbers are absent, and in their place the letters of my name."

"Martha Custis. Just enough," he said.

"Just."

" 'Tis always advantageous to know how time passes."

I was not convinced he was correct. For when one grieved too much, time passed too quickly. Could I ever win such a race?

He squirmed upon his chair. I knew why he was sitting before me. He had made it clear in other meetings and through correspondence since. And though I had not answered him plainly before this time, *at* this time I was ready to—

"You know why I have come?" he asked.

I was shocked by his directness. Yet perhaps it was best. He *had* proposed at least twice before in his life. He had experience. Two wives now dead and buried.

"I do know," I said.

"Would you do me the honour of being my wife, Martha?"

I was glad he had not knelt before me, for 'twas far easier to reject him with space between us. Perhaps he feared his elderly knees would not make the gesture gracefully. He was twenty-four years older than I.

"I am sorry, Mr. Carter, but I cannot."

He looked genuinely surprised. "Whyever not?"

Because you are an old man, because you have twelve children—nine girls and three boys. The eldest daughter is nearly my age, already married with a child of her own . . . you are a grandfather. And your father is at least as tyrannical as was John Custis. I will not willingly enter in with tyrants.

To his face I was more diplomatic. "I am not yet ready to love a second time."

He opened his mouth to speak, and I stared at him, daring him to say love was of no import to him—as in truth, I believed it was not. The man required a mother for his vast family. Although I adored children, I had no wish to voluntarily take on a dozen. All at once. I wished to have my own. With a man nearer my own age who at least had a fighting chance of being there, of helping me bring them into adulthood.

I stood. "How long will you be staying with us at White House, Mr. Carter?"

He blinked, clearly flustered. But then he rose to his feet and said, "Why, I . . . I have business in Williamsburg. It is best I press on."

"I understand," I said. I held out my hand. He kissed it, nodded his good-bye, and left.

I looked at the door and waited for regret to reach me.

It did not.

Good.

One down. Many to go.

Being the wealthiest widow in Virginia was not an easy occupation. Mr. Carter was not the first to show his intentions, nor would he be the last. In many ways my position was one to be envied. There was only one richest anything, and among Virginia widows, that title was mine.

Yet attached to the position were obstacles. With women still in the minority in the colonies—with many succumbing to death through childbirth—our gender was in high demand. It was the norm to marry two or three times within a lifetime. As far as being a woman with a fortune? I was expected to remarry in a timely manner.

Although my friends and family had introduced me to dozens of eligibles who, in theory, might have been perfect for me, I had no interest in any of them. I owed it to Daniel to marry prudently, to someone who would appreciate, not decimate, his family fortune. And I owed it to myself to marry someone my own age, someone I could love and adore, someone I could partner with in every way. Someone who could give me my own new babies to love.

I sat at the desk once again, the papers of the estate before me. Yes, I was weary of handling everything alone. Yes, I longed for the companionship and mere conversation of a man I could love. It was lonely here at White House. I was surrounded by my children and servants, but with Daniel gone there was no adult to talk with, to confide in, to advise me.

Yes, I was ready to marry. But not to just anyone. The right one. I prayed God—I trusted God—would bring him to me.

Soon.

———

I was more than happy to attend the afternoon social at the Chamberlaynes' home. The Chamberlaynes were dear friends. Richard and his wife, Mary, lived at Poplar Grove, just west of White House. Richard's brother Edward and his wife, Rebecca, also lived on the property, as did their sister Elizabeth, who, though twenty-three, was still unmarried. I had gone to school with Elizabeth and her sister Anne. Alas, Anne had died in childbirth two years previous. In an irony of our little community, a year later my dearest sister, Anna Maria (whom I called Nancy) married Anne's widower. I had not been able to attend their wedding, as I had just given birth to my Patsy, but their marriage further bound our two families. And because of this bond, I was much eager for both me and the children to be in the presence of such lifelong acquaintances and their guests.

The family home at Poplar Grove (and a large warehouse on the property) were faced with a brick that always impressed me with its permanence and stability. It was so different from the white clapboard used on my childhood home at Chestnut Grove and our current home at White House. The brick laughed at our Virginia's variable weather. Even though it was a more expensive prospect, due to the labor-intensive work of the brickmaking, there were obviously advantages, to say nothing of the status of owning a brick home. Six Chimneys in Williamsburg was made of brick. . . .

My thoughts soon left issues of architecture and genealogy behind as we were enveloped in the hospitality of our neighbours. In the warm springtime, all the children ran off to play as we adults enjoyed some refreshing lemonade and animated conversation. For a while I was able to forget the dictates and responsibilities of White House and just be a young woman. It was a joy I thoroughly embraced.

But then an unexpected visitor came to call. I had met the dapper Colonel Washington at various soirées in Williamsburg and, of course, had heard tales of his heroism fighting the French and Indians out west. Those western borders were held precariously. I had heard Daniel speak of horrendous violations endured by many of the brave settlers. I had also read portions of a journal Colonel Washington had written about his exploits. Apparently it had been published on both continents.

We gathered in the foyer to receive this new guest. I had not remembered him to be quite so striking. He stood well over six feet, towering over me and the other ladies—and even most of the men. His torso was sturdy, his hands and feet enormous. His hair held a reddish cast and was pulled into a ribbon. His nose was large, his eyes a pale blue. The only weakness about him was his face, which was a bit gaunt and pale as though he may have been ill of late, and scarred, most likely from a bout of the smallpox.

"I am so sorry to intrude, Richard," he said to our host. "But when Bishop and I found ourselves at William's Ferry, I thought of you and . . ."

Richard patted him on the back. "You came to visit, as you should have."

A servant took the colonel's hat. Richard turned to the rest of the party and made introductions. Most had met under previous circumstances, and sincere greetings were made amongst the circle. We moved back into the parlour, and Richard relinquished his chair to Washington, taking another for himself.

"So, George. Tell us, what news of the war?" Richard asked.

Richard's wife, Mary, had other concerns. "Enough, my dear. Let George get a breath in first. You do not look well, George."

The colonel's blush was a welcome addition to his pallid complexion. "I have suffered for months from . . . a delicate complaint."

By his hesitation I made my own conclusions. It was most likely dysentery, the bloody flux that was often the bane of soldiers forced to eat and drink in the wild.

"I was in Williamsburg seeking the aid of a physician there, for I can brook no more of it." He scanned our faces. "I detest being of no use."

"Never!" said Edward, our other host.

A servant appeared at the edge of the room. "Dinner is ready, mistress."

Mary rose. "Shall we?"

—⚬⚬⚬—

"You did not partake freely," I told the colonel as he and I returned to the parlour after our afternoon dinner.

"Not for want of its deliciousness," he said. He waited until I sat before taking a chair nearby. "I am careful to eat prudently until I am completely cured."

"May that be soon."

"Thank you, Mrs. Custis."

Our heads turned toward the entrance to the room as we heard the double doors being pulled shut. I caught a glimpse of a grinning Mary before the doors closed.

"It appears we are being manipulated," I said. "Please forgive Mary. She—"

"Truly, I do not mind," he said. Then he hesitated. "Do you?"

It was time for me to blush. "No, I do not." I did not say so to flatter him but because I did appreciate his company. He was a fine conversationalist, and as dinner had progressed, I'd found myself drawn to him in a way that was most . . . intriguing.

"I am sorry for your loss," he said. "Your husband was a fine man."

"Thank you. The eight months since have been arduous. Busy and arduous."

"A great plantation is not meant to be run by one, alone."

"You speak from experience, Colonel?"

"Certainly not to your extent. I rent a small plantation called Mount Vernon from my brother's widow. It is on the banks of the Potomac."

"How far?"

"One hundred twenty miles, to the north and some west," he said.

"A goodly distance. Add another twenty-five miles to Williamsburg and—"

"The distance is gladly traveled, especially in the direction of home. Although business with the militia and the army often takes me to see the governor in Williamsburg, I find the distance far shorter in the return direction."

I smiled. "The place draws you back?"

"Draws me home." He moved to the outer portion of his chair, his eyes bright. "It is as though the land and I share the same blood and sinew, and neither one is complete in absence of the other."

"Does the land share this opinion?"

"I can only assume it does, because under my care it thrives."

"You both thrive, one with the other."

"Indeed."

He looked toward the fire, which had been stoked for our benefit against the cool spring evening. "I have many plans for Mount Vernon. The war has taken me away, and it has suffered in the absence of . . . of . . ."

"Someone who loves it?"

"I have lost livestock, outbuildings have crumbled, and the crops were not brought in to prime amount. And the house . . . I am having the roof raised and a second story built."

"The roof raised? How does one accomplish such a feat?"

"With difficulty. Especially when I am not there to oversee. I have ordered supplies from England, windowpanes, mahogany furniture and such. And they have come but have not all been implemented because of my sickness. For six months I have lain abed with plans brimming in my head but no strength to see them carried out." He looked at the floor. "Six years ago my dearest brother, Lawrence, died of a lung disease, and I thought I had that problem in addition to the . . . the other." He looked directly at me. "I feared I was dying."

"Oh my."

"While at the war front, I was bled many times, but the doctors did not know what to do with me. It seemed the treatment for one problem only begat another. They kept telling me to rest. But six months of it and still I was no better."

"Did the doctors in Williamsburg offer true help?"

George gave me a shy smile. "Dr. Amson assured me I was not dying."

"A good prognosis, all in all."

He took a deep breath. "If ease of mind affects strength of body, I am determined to find total relief in the near future."

"I will offer prayers for that very outcome, and that you and your beloved Mount Vernon can be reunited in a happy, flourishing state of shared health and prosperity."

"I never refuse an offer of providential intercession."

"A wise man."

He sat back in his chair again. "Your children are charming."

"And very dear to me. I lost two others."

"I am very sorry."

"As am I."

"I hope for the blessing of children someday." He blinked, then quickly added, "Upon marriage, of course."

"That is the way it is properly done."

He blushed. "You enjoy teasing me, Mrs. Custis."

"Immensely." I smoothed the lace that lined the edge of my over-skirt. "I will stop, if you prefer."

"No need."

"Then I will continue as the moment warrants."

"I look forward to it."

He was so delightful I wished our conversation to continue for a lengthy time, and so I did something to ensure it: I asked him about himself. "Tell me some war stories, Colonel. I have not traveled beyond the wilderness of New Kent, though I am quick to enjoy the safety your efforts impart on behalf of our king."

"Are you certain you wish to hear? The stories are more frustrating than glorious."

"I long for true stories, Colonel. If they portray frustration, then so be it. Such is life."

"I have learned much."

"From hard experience?"

He nodded and fidgeted in his chair. I had heard about his humiliation at Fort Necessity. But that was years ago. Would he mention it? Or would his pride keep the hard facts hidden from me?

"The French and their Indian compatriots do not fight in the European fashion."

"Meaning?"

"We colonials, fighting with the British, are trained to march in columns, to shoot upon command while standing."

"In very regal uniforms. It is quite impressive."

"Not if the enemy hides in the brush, wears subtle colours, and cannot be seen. "

"Ah."

"There is a fort at the conflux of three mighty rivers in Pennsylvania—the Ohio, the Allegheny, and the Monongahela. It is a strategic position for transportation, trade, and expansion. The French built Fort Du Quesne there and claimed all the lands for their king Louis. Since we colonized this land for King George, we believe it is ours. I was sent to take it back. To claim the fort for England."

"A mighty cause."

"A heady goal, but one not easily achieved. The French have many Indian allies. We British, but a few. Yet the chief of the Senecas, Half King, agreed to ally with us. His motives were not as honourable as I would have hoped, and when a party of French soldiers approached, I allowed myself to be pulled into battle when they were only warning us off. One of their officers was shot. As I was finding an interpreter to speak to him, Half King . . ." George looked away. "He murdered the French soldier. All in the French party were killed but one, who ran back to the fort—with reports of the incident."

"Half King incited the incident."

"With my misguided participation. After the battle I knew the French would come find us, wanting revenge. Half King and his scouts reported there were over six hundred on the march toward us—before he and his men handily disappeared. With this knowledge I returned to our encampment at Fort Necessity, in Great Meadows, and prepared for battle. I did not want to fight the enemy in the woods, so I had my men build a stockade. I hoped for reinforcements from the south. I believed I was prepared as best as I . . ." His voice trailed off. "My actions . . . my confidence was misplaced and ill appropriate. I allowed myself to become cocky. I thought our position in a valley was an advantage; I believed the marshy terrain would keep the enemy out."

"It was not so?"

He shook his head in a mournful manner. "The hidden enemy shot from the precipices. We were targets in the open. Then the rain came and made our marsh a prison of mud. We were forced to surrender. In our negotiations . . ." He pulled in a fresh breath. "I had only two men who spoke French, and the best of those was wounded. So I sent a Dutchman to negotiate our surrender, but they took advantage of him. The French inserted some wording where, by my signature, I admitted to assassinating their envoy. The entire affair ended in failure. My failure."

I did not know what to say. For a man who had been deemed a hero to admit defeat . . . "I am so sor—"

"I do not know why I tell you this. I never speak of it. Frankly, I do not speak much at all. People think me quiet. I have been called stoic and—"

"You are hardly stoic, Colonel."

"Not around you, Mrs. Custis."

"I take that as a high compliment."

He nodded once, sealing it as so. And with his nod, I found I wanted to hear more. Much more. I wanted to hear everything he would tell me. "Please continue, Colonel. What else did you learn in the wilderness and in battle?"

"I learned that past ways of warfare do not apply here. And I told General Braddock as much, but he—"

The doors to the parlour opened and Richard entered. "Excuse me, George, Martha, but I wanted to tell George I have instructed

Bishop to put your horse to stable. Apparently you had given him the impression you would not be staying long?" His eyes passed between us, sparkling with mischief.

The colonel stood. "Oh dear. I *had* implied as much."

Richard raised a hand, stopping his movement. "It has been taken care of. Besides, you cannot leave."

"I *cannot* leave?"

Richard flashed a full smile now. "It is family policy—I will not let my guests leave after sunset."

"Sunset?" We both looked out the windows. The red glow of the parting sun offered the only light.

Before we could respond, Richard took the handles of the double doors and backed out of the room. "Your children are nearly ready for bed, Martha. I will send them in. Until then . . . carry on."

As his wife had earlier offered a grin, he left us with a wink.

I felt guilty for leaving my children in the care of others for so long. Ready for bed? "Richard is nothing if not obvious," I said.

"We have given him reason, have we not?"

I did not answer but rose to poke at the fire. George took over the task, and the fire sprang to new life.

"Richard spoke of Bishop. I heard he used to be General Braddock's manservant?"

"He was. In fact, he came over with the general twenty years ago. He was fifty years old, e'en then. At first he fought with us, then became the general's servant. When the general was killed . . ." He paused and returned to his chair. "I have skipped too far in the story."

"You left off saying you told General Braddock about the Indian style of warfare?"

"After my humbling defeat, I quit the military, but when the French increased their attacks in the Ohio Valley, I volunteered to be of service to General Braddock. He accepted my offer because of my knowledge of the wilderness. As a surveyor I had learned many ways of the wild."

"You are an attentive student—in all things."

He smiled slightly. "If only the hard way were not *my* way."

"Life rarely offers easy lessons."

He nodded, then continued. "At first I found the general challenging. He looked upon the colonies as void of both honour and honesty. He was a difficult man to argue with, as he would never give up any point he asserted, no matter how unreasonable."

"He does not seem a man to respect."

"On the contrary. He had forty-five years of military experience, where I had but a few months. And yet . . ." George sighed. "He did not fully understand our predicament. Even our respected postmaster, Benjamin Franklin, tried to warn him about the new way of doing battle, but the general insisted that though the colonial militia may have had trouble, the British army would not."

"Oh dear."

George nodded. "When I accompanied the general back to Fort Necessity, with the power of hundreds of troops alongside, I hinted at the mistakes I had made, warning him and the other officers of the new way the French and the Indians took to battle. But the British officers were so in favor of regularity and discipline, and in such absolute contempt of the enemy, that the admonition was suggested in vain."

"Why would they not listen to you? You who had experience?"

"I was not a British soldier, only a colonial volunteer. The British do not respect us. In their eyes, their formal training holds stock over our hard experience."

I shook my head. It seemed logical that the gift of practical wisdom would be recognized and put to use.

The colonel stood and meandered to the mantel, where he straightened a candle. "The general was so confident in the traditional ways of warfare, we proceeded north to Fort Du Quesne, certain we would never be attacked."

"But you were."

"We were slaughtered."

At these horrific words, I let out an inconsequential, "Oh."

"The enemy stormed upon us with a barrage of fire, chasing us into the woods. Our shocked soldiers were ordered back into line like rows of deer, waiting to be shot. From our rear came another band of the enemy, and another, and another. For over three hours we fought as best we could. I had four bullet holes in my coat, and had two horses shot out from under me. I was the only aide of General Braddock not killed or injured. Our soldiers ran out of ammunition and fled, some across the river to safety. The Indians did not follow them. They were too busy scalping and—" He stopped his discourse, his jaw tight. "Forgive me. 'Tis not for a lady's ears."

Too late. The image was already vivid in my mind.

"The cries of help from the wounded and dying were enough to pierce a heart of stone."

"You are a man of deep feeling, Colonel. You are not a man of bravado."

"I can be."

"As you should be, and have earned the right to be. Yet I see inside of you a softer side where true empathy reigns."

"One must be empathetic to the needs and suffering of others."

"No, actually," I said, "one does not. But you do. 'Tis a strong mark in your favor."

He smiled. "So you are making marks for and against me?"

"The list grows quite lengthy. Now . . . back to your story. I do need to hear the end, sensitive or not."

He nodded and added another log to the fire. He did not speak until he was through. "General Braddock was wounded during the battle. We lost nearly one thousand out of the fifteen hundred who fought.

We lost twenty-six of the eighty-six officers, with seventeen more wounded. The French lost a handful. The Indians a few more."

"But you were a hero."

He turned toward me, his face stern. "I was deemed a hero, not for winning a battle but for leading the defeated survivors to safety."

"You led them."

"Yes."

"And they followed."

"Yes."

"That is one aspect of heroism. Getting others to follow."

He looked pensive. Then he said, "If I did any good there, it was to bury the general properly, wisely. After four days he died, and I had him buried in the road, at the front of our column. Then we proceeded east, walking over his grave, making it look like a common road so no Indians would find him and desecrate—" He stepped upon a piece of ash that had escaped the fire. "Bishop, Thomas Bishop, the man who accompanies me here . . . with the general gone, I asked if he would work for me. He agreed. And the general had bequeathed me his horse and a sash. Also a pistol. I cherish them all." He looked at the door. "Poor Bishop. He has probably stood ready to leave for hours."

"Richard informed him of your intent to stay. Surely he is well off to a good night's rest."

The colonel nodded once. "I do not mean to detain *you* from rest, Mrs. Custis. When your children come in, if you feel the need to retire, I would understand. I would regret your parting, but I would understand."

"I feel no need to retire, Colonel. In fact, I feel quite invigorated."

The parlour doors flew open and the children rushed into the room, as though bidden by his mention of them. Three-year-old Jacky and nearly two-year-old Patsy looked adorable in their nightshirts, with their bare feet padding upon the wooden floor. There was something delightful about a child's bare feet.

Jacky virtually jumped into my lap, with Patsy climbing up behind. "Oomph!" was all I could manage amid their oblivious elbows and knees.

Once settled, Jacky looked at the colonel as though seeing him for the first time. "Who are you?"

I should have admonished his forthrightness but instead chose to answer him. "This is Colonel Washington. He has been fighting out west."

Jacky used his finger as a gun and shot the colonel with a *pyoo-pyoo* sound.

To his credit, the colonel put his hands on his heart and groaned. "I am hit!"

Patsy mimicked her brother with her own gun and *pyoo-pyoo*. The colonel suffered again for her benefit.

Mary Chamberlayne stood at the doorway, missing nothing. Her sisters-in-law, Elizabeth and Rebecca, stood close by. "Come, children," Mary said. "Kiss Mamma good-night."

The very fact these three women had brought the children and had not sent them by a servant, spoke of their curiosity as to what exactly George and I were doing behind closed doors. If I would have told them we were discussing battles, they would have been disappointed.

I, however, was not. As the children were led away I realized I was willing to talk about most anything as long as it kept me in the presence of Colonel Washington.

⤜⧫⤛

The fire had died, its embers a flicker. My companion looked at the clock, then back at me. "It has moved from late night to nearly morning."

I had not noticed. "So it has."

George stood (for during our all-night conversation, we had

progressed from Colonel Washington and Mrs. Custis to George and Martha—at least in private). "I have kept you awake. I have prevented you from—"

"You have not *kept* me awake, nor prevented me from doing anything other than that which I desired to do." I extended my hand to him. He hesitated, then took a step closer to take it. "I can honestly say I have never enjoyed myself more than I have conversing with you, George. The very fact that time had no meaning, that we did not notice the coming dawn, nor the dying of the fire, holds great significance."

He raised an eyebrow. "Perhaps we are each other's dawn, each other's fire?"

I would not have been so bold—nor so eloquent—but was pleased he had chosen to be. "Very well said. As expected."

He offered a bow.

I rose and glanced at the door. "Perhaps we should retire, e'en for a bit."

"We shall speak again in the full morning, yes?"

"Of course." I offered him a flirty smile. "I am not done with you yet, Colonel Washington."

He blushed—a response that put him even more in my favour.

We did have more chance to speak. After breakfast the next morning, we were conveniently left alone—again. There was no more talk of battlefields, nor of any incidents of our past. We spoke of the future, of our hopes and desires. And we spoke of the one thing which I found made George come alive: we spoke of Mount Vernon.

I had never witnessed so much passion for land. I had often observed men coveting land, and heard them talking with zeal about obtaining more, but the passion that fueled George's talk sprang from a deeper place, as though he found true connection with the soil and the agricultural roots he planted, as though they were intertwined with his own.

Although my Daniel had been very interested in our land and in the success of it . . . although he had offered many plans, in retrospect I realized they were more the plans of defense, to sustain what his family had started. On the other hand, George planned on the offensive, dreaming about what he would change to make things better. Where Daniel had exhibited ambition of the mind, George was consumed with an ambition of the soul.

"I wish to make Mount Vernon the greatest plantation in all Virginia."

"You do not think small, George."

"Nothing is accomplished in small dreams." He cleared his throat, then offered more details. "The grass that breaches the hill toward the house has died. It needs to be completely reseeded. I wish for the first prospect of Mount Vernon to take one's breath away with its beauty, with trees lining the road, and flowers accompanying the guest's journey closer."

I had to smile.

He noticed. "Have I said something humourous?"

"On the contrary. I smile because I am deeply impressed."

"By flowers?"

"By men who surprise me. By men who can speak of battles *and* beauty. You seem to be a man complete in all things, Colonel Washington."

"Not all things." He looked away.

The time for his departure was nearing. I did not want him to go. And though he had not spoken directly, by all means indirect, by all methods of female intuition I possessed, I knew our minds and our hearts had connected. And with this connection . . .

We would see.

— T H R E E —

I entered the parlour and spied Jacky at a window, his knees perched upon a chair.

"What are you doing, son?"

"Is he coming soon, Mamma?"

"Yes. Soon. But I am not certain of the time. You should come away from the window and go about your day. I am sure Patsy would love to have you play with—"

"No! I am waiting here. I want to be the first to see him."

As long as I am the second.

I looked about the parlour, making certain everything was just so. This would be George's second visit to White House in less than a month, and if my intuition was correct, this visit would result in a proposal. If it did not, I would be sorely disappointed, for during the two occasions we had spent time together, I had come to revere him as a man, respect him as a soldier, relish him as good company, and react to him as a woman. When in his presence, I wished to be nowhere else. And when apart, I longed to be with him.

Was I in love?

If so, it was a different love than what I had felt for Daniel. Perhaps it was Daniel's age that had made my love for him rooted in comfort and security. With Daniel I was the woman I had spent my entire life training to be: I was the wife of a plantation owner and the mother of many. We complemented each other, he and I. But—may Daniel forgive me—there was never any true passion between us. There was an amiable regard, a fondness, a mutual respect and acceptance, but I do not remember feeling pulled beyond myself, lured into a place where the known Martha became a different Martha, someone more than I had ever been before.

When I was with George . . . he made me feel as though I was incomplete as I was now. There was more to Martha, more depth, more complexities, more excitement that was yet to be harvested. In his presence the world was vast and wide and held secrets I longed to explore. My role by his side would expand beyond the normal framework of a plantation wife. I did not know how, but the possibilities were enticing.

And frightening.

I had never traveled beyond the twenty-five miles to Williamsburg. When I married Daniel, the move from Chestnut Grove to White House encompassed but a short distance.

But George . . . George had been to Barbados with his ailing brother. He had surveyed wilderness lands never surveyed before. He had fought Indians and the French in the far-off Ohio Valley. He knew rivers with odd names like the Monongahela and Youghiogheny.

In our last visit he had confided he had not been raised to be a gentleman. His family was considered (by his own words) second tier. His father, Gus, had sired two sons by his first wife—George's older stepbrothers, Lawrence and Austin—before marrying George's mother, Mary. They had six children in seven years, George being the eldest. With each passing pregnancy, Mary grew more bitter and angry. It was not a pleasant household and was devoid of happy memories. Then Gus died young—at age forty. George, only eleven, was forced into the role of man of the house, forced to deal with a sour and resentful mother who was incapable of showing love toward her children or joy of any kind.

When he told me the story, I grieved for him, for one of my largest goals was to create a happy home for my Jacky and Patsy. Children were a blessing that deserved the full dedication of their parents. Nothing less.

Yet George did attain happiness through the intervention of his stepbrother Lawrence. Lawrence had been a soldier, fighting with Britain against Spain. George was enthralled with his brother's military bearing *and* his uniform. (When a boy is used to homespun and rough linen, the fine fabrics of a vivid costume are sure to impress.)

Lawrence had inherited some land on the Potomac that he named Mount Vernon after his commander, Vice Admiral Edward Vernon. He married the daughter of an extremely wealthy landowner who lived in Belvoir, just four miles away. The family of Ann Fairfax held nearly five million acres of land. When Lawrence lost three children in four years, he began to think of his little brother as a son, and he and Ann groomed George to be a gentleman, teaching him how to dance, speak, fence, dress, ride a horse, and otherwise giving him his first real education. Colonel William Fairfax, the master of Belvoir, gave George free rein to his vast library and taught him about art and the finer things of a cultured life. The life he experienced with his brother and with the Fairfaxes was a stunning contrast to the silence and oppression of his mother's house at Ferry Farm, where the library consisted of a Bible and a book of sermons.

When Colonel Fairfax's son, George William, came home from attending school in England, he and George became fast friends, even though George William was seven years his elder.

George confided to me that his goal, even at that young age, was to appear honourable and virtuous. Toward that end he even hand-copied a Jesuit guidebook on manners in order to instill them in his mind. He had always been self-conscious about his looks, especially his height. He was six feet three inches, and his teeth were bad. Regarding the latter, he rarely laughed full voice, and when I caught him once and saw his teeth, I knew why he kept his reactions restrained. They were gray and at least one was missing. I, for one, had been blessed with lovely teeth. If ever the time seemed right, I planned to share my homemade tooth powder with him.

That George had had to fight for his honour and position, work hard for it . . . these things raised him in my eyes. Obtaining position and distinction through inheritance was one thing, but to obtain them through determination and merit was far another. Through his confidences, I was endeared to him even more. Not all men would admit lowly beginnings.

Nor failures.

I adjusted the books that sat upon a table and found myself smiling at the memory of another of George's shared confidences. He had sat in this very chair and fingered the edges of these books as he told me the story.

He had just returned from the horrible defeat under the command of the late general Braddock. George had thought it his duty to explain why they had lost—as a means to prevent such a slaughter again. Colonel Fairfax had listened to his impassioned report and had spread the word to those higher up in the military.

In response to George's wisdom, he was made colonel of the Virginia Regiment and commander in chief of all the colonial forces. Quite an accomplishment for a twenty-three-year-old man with no formal education.

George could have left his rendition of the story to me there—with his triumph—but he did not. He proceeded to tell me that feeling proud in his new position, he decided to visit the Virginia Regiment at a parade ground in Alexandria. He forecast his coming and yet . . . only ten officers and twenty recruits showed up. "It was evident I was commander in chief of nothing and almost no one."

I believed all he said, but none of his assessment. For from what I knew of Colonel George Washington, he was a true commander, and would eventually have a myriad of troops at his beck and call. I could see it in him, in his eyes, in his stance, in his heart. He was a born leader.

And I was ready to be led.

"He's coming! I see him!" Jacky jumped from the chair and ran to the door.

I discreetly looked out the window and watched as our groom Eustis took the horse's reins. They exchanged some words, and Eustis stayed as George took a cloth from his pack and carefully wiped the dust from his boots. The simple act touched me . . . always a gentleman. Then he procured something else from his saddle, a small pouch.

Moments later, our butler, Cully, opened the door, and Jacky was right there, taking George's hand. "Come in, come in! I have been waiting ever so long."

To his credit, George allowed himself to be pulled inside. Cully took his hat. As soon as George saw me, he brought forth the pouch and carefully opened it against his palm. Inside were lovely dogwood blossoms. "The trees are in full flower, dotting the hillside amidst the other trees which have not yet leafed out. I stopped to bring you a few blossoms." He offered them to me, a gentle transfer of petals from his hands to mine.

"They are lovely, George. Exquisite."

"They are flowers," Jacky said with disdain. "Did you bring me anything?"

"Jacky!"

"As a matter of fact, I did." George pulled a hand-carved wooden pistol from the pocket of his coat. "I believe you will find it much more effective than a finger."

Jacky took it, aimed, made the appropriate noises, and ran upstairs—to show Patsy, no doubt.

"I carved a little doll for Patsy," George said.

"You are too kind."

I led him into the parlour, then hesitated. "Would you like a respite from your journey?"

"No, I am fine, thank you. Actually . . ." He twisted his hands together. "I would feel best if I could . . . if I could say . . . ask . . ."

My nerves fluttered and I sought the support of the settee. "Do you have something on your mind, George?"

He began to sit in the chair nearby, then detoured to his knee. He took my hand. "Dearest Martha. Would you, could you, consider being my wife?"

To have this hulk of a man kneel at my feet, his large hand engulfing mine, his blue-gray eyes peering up at me . . . imploring me with their sincerity.

"I would, could, and will," I said. "Yes, I say yes," I added, just to make sure he understood my affirmation.

He brought my hand to his lips, then after a slight hesitation, stood tentatively and leaned forward to kiss my mouth.

I allowed it.

Welcomed it.

Longed for it.

Martha Washington.

It rang quite pleasant to the ear.

⌘

As soon as George left from his visit, I made my own visit to see my mother in my childhood home at Chestnut Grove. I wanted to be the first to tell her the news.

Jacky and Patsy went off to play with my little sisters, Betsy, age nine, and Mary, who was the same age as Patsy—just two. For Mother to have a daughter and a granddaughter the same age . . . such was life. My brother William, though still unmarried at twenty-five, was a sometimes resident, being in the military, which often took him away.

Mother linked her arm through mine. "Shall we walk?"

It was Mother's way of telling me she had something important to speak about. As Chestnut Grove was a small home, populated by too many impressionable ears, I easily agreed, for my news was also best told during a walk.

We eased away from the house, and I noted the loveliness of the bee balm and coreopsis dotting the lane. Once a safe distance from all possibility of prying ears, Mother said, "When is the wedding?"

I stopped our walk and faced her. "How did you know?"

She shrugged. "Servants talk; errands bring them together. . . ."

She had stolen my surprise. I felt cheated. Then I realized she had not offered her congratulations. Not even an embrace or a kiss.

"Undoubtedly you approve?" I asked.

She began to shrug a second time, but I stopped the movement by putting my hand upon her shoulder. "I will not accept that response. Tell me how you could object. Surely, I cannot imagine why."

Mother lowered her chin and stared at me. "Surely, you can."

"I do not find any pleasure in these sorts of games, Mother. If you have something to say, say it plain."

She took up our walk but did not take my arm. Although I would have rather spoken face-to-face, I followed her lead. "You desire my reason; here it is: you are the richest widow in Virginia. Colonel Washington is . . . much beneath you."

"He is a war hero. He has the ear of the governor—of many men in power."

"As an underling. As a strappy, eager soldier wanting to be noticed. And as a colonial officer willing to be called to duty at their beck and call. He is *not* of the British command."

I felt my colour rise. "I beg anyone—man or woman—to tell me how his manners, his appearance, his actions, are anything less than those of a gentleman."

"People can learn manners and proper dressing."

I could not say more, for I knew George *had* procured the attributes through those very means.

"His plantation is struggling. I have heard he needs a substantial influx of capital to keep it going. By marrying you . . ."

"I will be happy to use a portion of my wealth to assist him in achieving his dreams."

"His dreams?"

"My dreams."

"So you will live in Mount Vernon?"

We had not talked about that detail. That large detail. "We will live wherever it is best we live."

"What do the children think of him?"

"They love him. You should see how Jacky waited at the window for his arrival. They need a father."

"He knows nothing of fathering."

"I know enough for both of us."

"But if he is away fighting the French, he will not be around to be a father. Or a husband. Or the master of any plantation—large or small."

"He has chosen to go on one last campaign. The new prime minister, William Pitt, has seen the potential in the militia and talks of them with the respect they deserve. Many more are joining. Finally, George has a goodly contingent to lead."

"So much for his loyalty to you and the children."

"So much for his loyalty to our colony. To our king. George heard Brigadier General Forbes is going to take fifteen hundred British regulars and even more than that number of Virginians to fight the French at Fort Du Quesne."

"Have we not suffered enough at that horrible place?"

I bridled on George's behalf. "George has a personal stake in such action." I did not want to mention his first humiliation at the nearby Fort Necessity, lest Mother not know of it, but since she had implied knowledge of the fort, I could mention the common news of

Braddock's defeat. "Certainly you know of our defeat when General Braddock was killed?"

"That was years ago. Two, maybe three years."

I stopped walking, forcing her to face me once again. "So old news is best forgotten? We should suffer a defeat and move on? I think not. The French are still persisting in their quest for land—land they do not deserve. If we are ever going to have the space to expand westward, we need to stop—"

"Since when do you care about the expansion of our colonies? Or politics? Or war?"

Since George. I resumed our walk and this time it was Mother who was led. "I see nothing wrong with having knowledge and interest beyond the Tidewater. There is a large world beyond our simple borders."

"One you need not worry yourself about."

I understood her desire for ignorance. Until George I too had been content to know little beyond the boundaries of my small world. But now . . . George had made me see a larger picture. "It is a world that may thrust itself upon us whether we like it or not, Mother. Braddock's defeat effectively started a world war. Prussia and England allied against France and Austria, fighting each other there as we fight here . . . 'tis quite a mess."

"You were raised to be the wife of a plantation owner, not a soldier."

"George's greatest desire is to quit the military and concentrate on Mount Vernon. In fact, he has promised me once this campaign is over, he will do just that. In spite of all that should be fair, there is no future for a Virginia regimental—however honoured—to rise in the ranks of the British army and have true power. The British hierarchy think of him as a mere colonial and lesser than themselves. No matter how hard he fights or how brilliant his strategies might be, they will not allow him into their fraternity as an equal. That being a truth, once his duty is fulfilled, he will come home and be a planter again. Be my husband."

She sighed. "When do you plan to marry?"

"Perhaps December. We both must order our wedding clothes with the sailing of the spring ships. We will not receive them until late autumn. . . ." It was my turn to shrug. Such things took time.

"So. You are determined."

"I am determined."

"Even though . . ." She took a second breath. "Even though he is in love with another woman?"

My feet halted. Mother had to come round to face me.

"You did not know?" she asked.

"You had best not make such an accusation unless—"

"I only have gossip, but gossip is oft based on some modicum of fact."

I wished I had stayed home. Why had I come thinking I would get my mother's congratulations and support? I did not wish to know more, yet . . . I needed to know more. I swallowed with difficulty and asked the question that begged to be asked. "What is her name?"

"Sally Fairfax. She is married to his best friend, George William Fairfax. They are neighbors at Belvoir, just a few miles from Mount Vernon—within sight of each other, I have heard."

Belvoir.

At the mention of this place, my memories returned to George's first visit at White House. *The happiest moments of my life were spent at Belvoir. I cannot trace a room in the house that does not bring to mind the recollection of pleasing scenes.*

"Apparently, Sally is very beautiful. Tall and quite sophisticated."

And I am short and simple.

After a moment, reason interrupted my fears and I shook my head vehemently. "George would never do anything untoward with a married woman, especially someone married to his best friend. He is too honourable a man."

"He is a *man*." Mother looked toward the house. "Your father was a man of honour too, and you know how his urges . . ."

I nodded quickly so she would not have to linger amid the pain of my father's illegitimate son and daughter—one of slave blood, one white.

Mother continued. "The British gentry take no contention of fidelity. Perhaps this George William has his own dalliances and allows his wife—"

"Stop!"

Mother took a step away. "I know it is not a pleasant thought, Martha, but it is always wise to know the facts before entering into such a life-changing union."

"The fact is, I . . ." I was going to say I loved him, and yet I feared she would discount such romance as a trifling. "I respect George and admire him for all the right reasons. We complement each other and will make good partners. We are not British in this regard. We are Virginians, and colonists, and our tolerance for such sins is of much smaller measure."

"Perhaps," Mother said, though clearly unconvinced. "We tolerate what we cannot change. Perhaps we do so as an act of defense."

"Perhaps as people entrusted with a new land we should not do so at all. Is this not a chance to hold ourselves to a higher standard? Display higher morals? We would all be better off if we chose to obey God's commands with all our might."

Mother shook her head and turned back toward the house. "Men are still men, my dear, with high intentions, weak bodies, and flawed wills."

I caught up with her, pulling her to a stop once more before we returned to the house. "You will not speak of this again, to anyone."

"I did not start the gossip, Martha."

"But you can stop it. Stop it right here."

"And if someone brings it up in my presence?"

"Tell them you believe it cannot be so and they must be mistaken. Defend the honour of my future husband, and as such, my honour as well."

She looked at me, her eyes busy with consideration. "As you wish. I only want you to be happy, Martha. I know you are weary of the responsibilities of widowhood, but wisdom and common sense must still prevail in such decisions."

"I feel I am being very wise and sensible," I said. "Now . . . would you like to help me design my wedding attire, or not?"

*

I was back at White House, the children in bed, the daylight waning. I combed through my hair, making ready to retire.

To her credit, Mother did not revisit the subject of Sally Fairfax after our walk. I knew nothing of the woman, but for the *beautiful, tall,* and *sophisticated* attributes which Mother relayed via the gossip grapevine.

But even so, I hated her.

As if in response to my ungracious thought, my comb found resistance in a snarl. I segregated the lock of offending hair and attacked. I found victory, but not without many casualties within the teeth of my comb.

Such was the unexpected consequence of hatred. At other times I had witnessed its other casualties, far more serious than a few strands of hair. My father-in-law had wallowed in such a state, causing a bevy of repercussions both private and social, mental and physical. My Daniel had died as a result of his father's bitter hatred.

I lowered the comb to my lap and stared at my reflection in the mirror of my dressing table. I rearranged the long locks of my hair about my shoulders. In the proper light its brown hue held the richness of chestnut. I leaned closer to peer into my eyes. They were hazel with golden flecks when one was very close.

George will be this close. Closer.

We were an interesting pair, the two of us. My hazel eyes were a happy complement to his blue ones, my short stature a foil to his considerable presence. My ease in talking with anyone about most anything offered a cover for his tendency to say little, unless among close friends. And my determination to move forward from the state of sorrow and pain would serve both of us well.

Who needed beauty? Or height? Or sophistication like Sally Fairfax?

That the first two were decreed by God and thus beyond my control was a consolation. As for the latter? I could hold my own with any icon of society. I may not have had a vastness of experience, but I was not one to shirk a challenge, nor give up without a fight.

If my George still held the thought of Sally close to his breast, it was up to me to pry any memory of her away and replace his thoughts and desires of her with thoughts and desires of me.

My George.

This is what it came to. Whether he held any feelings for Sally or not, the fact was, he had proposed to me. He had chosen me.

And I had chosen him.

That, in itself, was a momentous victory.

I encountered no more tangles—in thought *or* grooming.

His letter had been cryptic: *I am coming to White House on June the fifth. I will not be able to stay, yet I must see you.*

I sat at the desk in my bedchamber and reread the note again. And again. I tried not to interpret anything within his words, nor the fact he would not be staying over. Was he having second thoughts? We had not seen each other since April, and though we had exchanged many letters, I was wise enough to know that they were a meager surrogate to an actual embrace or a gentle touch.

I had set aside all worries about Sally Fairfax—or at least pretended I had done as much—yet I knew I would not feel totally at ease until we were legally wed. After all, he had known Sally for years, and me but a few months. We had only been in each other's presence three times before today. That Sally lived but four miles from Mount Vernon . . .

I shook my head against the jealous thoughts. My chiding comments to my mother stating that George was too honourable a man to succumb to anything untoward seemed weak and ineffectual as the weeks, and yea, even months, passed without seeing him. Absence may make the heart grow fonder, but the truth was, fondness grew stronger when one body was in close proximity to another.

He would be in that close proximity soon. It was wrong of me to worry. Would worry add one day to my life? He was coming. To see me.

But why so short a visit? Did he not feel the same needs that my heart had developed during our time apart? The need to grab hold and never, ever let go?

I looked toward the door of my bedchamber. I had vowed *not* to wait downstairs, fearful I would pace and make the children and servants nervous with my actions. From the vantage point of my desk, I could still see the entry road, allowing me to suffer my anxiety in private.

Suddenly, the door to my room burst open and Jacky and Patsy ran in. They were the only ones who were not required to knock.

"Is he here yet?" Jacky asked.

I gave him a look. "You know very well he is not here."

Patsy shook her head. "Nah here."

I pulled one child into each arm. "But he will be soon. I am certain of it."

"I wonder what he will bring me," Jacky said.

"He does not need to bring you a present," I said.

"But I want him to."

"Me too!" Patsy said.

"You are spoiled children." Yet I said it with no condemnation in my voice. For I did spoil them. Horribly, I suppose. I could not help myself. They were all I had and, as such, would want for nothing.

Jacky and I both heard the sound of a horse at the same moment, and both turned toward the window.

"He *is* here!"

The children ran out of the room. I paused at the mirror and was about to pinch my cheeks when I found they had flushed on their own accord.

I headed downstairs with a prayer upon my lips. *Please, God . . .*

George accosted the children—and gave them gifts.

"You do not have to do that," I said.

"I do so because I want to." He looked from them to me. "But since our time is so short . . . if I may have a word with you? In private?"

"Of course." As I called Amanda to come take my darlings away, I found my heart beating in twice its time.

"Would you please close the doors, Amanda?" George asked.

With a glance to me, she replied, "Yes, sir," and did just that.

Of course he would like privacy. If he is to tell you it is over, that your marriage is not to be . . .

I began to sit in my usual chair, but he took my hand and led me to the settee. "Please," he said, indicating the seat.

I sat, and he, beside me. He angled his knees toward mine, the cloth of my dress making contact. "I am so sorry," he said.

My heart stopped. My worst fears were to be realized.

"Sorry that we have not been able to be together. Sorry that I must come only to leave so quickly."

He pulled my hands to his lips.

He smiled.

And with those two gestures I knew he had not changed his mind. I took a deep breath, releasing the frustrations and insecurities that had held me captive. I tried to speak but found my throat dry. "I have missed you."

"And I you." He leaned forward and kissed my cheek.

As he pulled away I nearly cried with relief.

"Are you unwell?"

I attempted to laugh it away. "No, no, I am very well. Very glad to see you and know . . . and have you here beside me. Close. Finally close."

He nodded and I knew he felt it too.

He left my hands free and reached inside his coat. "I have a gift for you. It is the reason I had to come."

George removed a burgundy pouch. He fumbled the pull-strings open and poured into his palm the object of his intent: a ring. He held it for me to see. "Upon your accepting my proposal, I had it made in Philadelphia. It is a pearl—your birthstone, yes?" He smiled. "I have heard an engagement ring containing the bride's birthstone is said to bring good luck." He looked up to gauge my reaction.

"It is beautiful."

He took my hand and slipped it upon my finger.

"It fits!" I said.

"It fits," he said.

We both looked, one to the other, as if this simple fact was a sign that *we* would fit, one with the other.

"Thank you, George." I kissed his cheek.

Before I could withdraw, he held my face close. We sat, forehead to forehead. "I must be off now," he whispered, his breath hot upon my skin. "The war beckons. The French have become cocky and lead raids upon our settlers, basing their violence at Fort Du Quesne. The fort must be taken."

"When will you return?"

He sat aright. "I do not know. As soon as possible, I assure you."

"Just . . . return. Return to me, safely."

"I will do my best."

We had only a few minutes together before he left me. I stood at the porch and waved after him until he offered one last wave before the fork in the road took him from my sight.

My gaze moved from his departure to the ring he had left behind. A ring, binding us together.

Why had I worried? Those moments wasted could never be returned.

I vowed to do less of it.

May God help me.

———※———

How could I not worry? Although I had dispensed of my worries regarding George's sincere affection and intention to marry me, with him away to the west, fighting the French, and the Indians that fought at their sides . . .

What if he did not return?

His stories of previous defeats and slaughters offered no comfort. Had he not already done his duty regarding Fort Du Quesne? Must he be on the forefront again?

The answer was . . . yes.

When George had heard that General Forbes had plans to advance against the French fort, he volunteered with vigor—and pluck. He wrote to those in charge and asked for a command that was distinguished in some measure from the common run of provincial officers. As he owned the most experience regarding fighting the French in that area of the wilderness, his offer was accepted and he received command of a brigade.

Upon stopping in Winchester to gather troops, George discovered that he was just in time for an election for the Virginia House of Burgesses. Even though he was going to be gone before the election commenced, he convinced some fellow officers who were to stay behind to campaign for him. They did, in rousing colonial tradition, with casks of rum, wine, and beer. And my George was victorious. How he managed to gain a seat in the House as an afterthought, while heading to war . . .

I fear he did it to impress me. Did he not know that I needed no more impressing?

And yet . . .

I also sensed the flame of ambition in his breast. And anxiety and passion. For some reason my George felt compelled to achieve. To overcome a meager childhood?

I knew better than to hold him back by comment or suggestion. For a person to feel complete, he had to believe he had attained all he was meant to attain. I had no full notion of where George's aspirations would take him. As for my own? I wished to be by his side and in our home during each victory or defeat. I wished for us to be a family. And I wished for more family. Two, perhaps three more children? I relished the notion of a house brimming with this precious blessing.

As spring turned into summer, life carried on.

Until the day I was reminded of death.

It was a beautiful summer day, though hot to the point of weariness.

And tempers.

It was a day when working inside, which offered shade but limited movement of air, was of marginal advantage over working in the sunny tobacco fields with benefit of full breeze.

Even the children chose outside over in, flitting from the porch to the shade of the trees out front. I watched them from the window and took comfort in the sounds of their voices and laughter when they slipped out of sight. Amanda was supposed to be watching them while she weeded the day lilies.

I was making new breeches and shirts for the workers. They wore them through so quickly, it often was a struggle to keep up. I prided myself in small stitches, knowing the better I sewed them this first time, the better chance I had of not repairing a rent seam tomorrow. I had tried to teach servants this art, but they took little pride in fine work—or speed. I paused a moment to watch one such servant, Hildy, to see what made her production so tedious.

She took an inordinate amount of time threading the needle, squinting, and holding it far, then near.

"Are you having trouble seeing the needle hole?" I asked.

She blinked, as though clearing her eyes. "Didn't use to."

"How old are you now?"

"Forty, best as I know."

"You need spectacles."

She looked shocked. "No one has those."

She was right. None of our slaves had spectacles. And yet . . . "They are not needed for large work, but this . . . I need you to help with fine work. I will see you get some on our next visit to Williamsburg."

Hildy grinned. "That would be fine, mistress. Real fine."

I went back to my sewing, glad for the busyness, yet wishing it were a chore that used my mind more than it did. Perhaps I should have worked on the correspondence today, the ordering of supplies. That would have been a better choice for this eighth day of July.

This anniversary of death.

There I went again, thinking about it, marking the date with this horrible memory of Daniel's end. I had no one with which to share my misery. Some of the house servants were aware—I could tell by Amanda's and Cully's kind eyes that morning that they had remembered—but the children had no concept of time and date. And I did not want them to know. It did no good to commemorate tragedy. It only served to keep it alive.

And yet . . . I knew. I remembered. And I suffered.

Alone.

It was not too late to do the correspondence. I could leave Hildy to the sewing. I was just about to do so when I heard the sound of horses and a wagon driving up the road out front. My first concern was the children. With a glance I saw Jacky and Patsy were safe, digging in the dirt by a tree. My second concern was whether we were gaining visitors. Had the windows in the guest room been opened this morning? If not, that room would surely be as hot as Hades.

But just as I made to go check the windows, I saw that it was not a carriage. It was a delivery wagon. I relaxed and left it to Cully to disperse the goods. But then I found renewed interest . . . could it be my wedding clothes? I had not expected them until the autumn, but such schedules were varied and unreliable.

I heard Cully talking with the driver, heard their voices but not their words. I watched as both men moved to the back of the wagon and peered inside. Then suddenly, Cully shook his head violently. He pointed back down the road.

"Back? I ain't goin' to take it away." The man lowered the back gate of the wagon, readying to remove the cargo.

Cully pointed again, more vehemently. "Go! We cannot have that here. Not today."

They exchanged more words, their voices rising. Whatever were they arguing about?

I walked onto the porch and proceeded down the front steps. When the men saw me, they halted their argument and Cully hurried forward, as if to intercept me.

"Sorry, mistress. I got it handled. It ain't nothing you have to—"

I sidestepped his concern and spoke to the driver. "What are you delivering today?"

His face turned red and he suddenly acquiesced, as if upon seeing me, he conceded to Cully's side of the argument. "It is a mistake, ma'am. Sorry to bother—"

My curiosity would not be appeased but through full knowledge. I walked around the man to the lowered gate. There, half covered with a length of burlap, was the source of the argument.

Cully was by my side. "I am sorry, mistress. I told 'im to take it back to Williamsburg. It don't go here on any account. And specially not to—"

Today. On the anniversary of Daniel's death.

I looked at the man. "Pull it forward so I can fully see it."

The man grabbed hold of a hunk of burlap and pulled the cargo on top of the lowered gate.

"A fine tombstone, this," he said, patting its corner. "Come all the way from England. Marble, they tells me it is."

It was a fine tombstone. Just as I had ordered. *One handsome Tombstone of the best durable Marble to cost about £100. . . .*

Cully was looking at me, not the tombstone. "I told 'im to take it back. Take it to the cemetery at Queen's Creek, where he . . . where it belongs."

I nodded. Cully was right, of course. The tombstone did not belong here. Daniel was not here.

"Didn't mean to upset you, ma'am," the driver said. "Just doin' what they told me to do."

I nodded. "You will be paid for your trouble," I said. "And fed." I turned to Cully. "Take this gentleman to the kitchen and see what you can do for him."

"Thank you, ma'am. My apologies for the muddle of it, but—"

I waved him away.

Cully looked at the wagon. "He should move it, yes, mistress?"

"No," I said. "Leave it here for now."

Cully raised an eyebrow. I did not need to give him an explanation. "Go."

I waited until the two of them had rounded the side of the house, then—

Seeing me alone, the children came running. "What came?" Jacky asked. "Something for me?"

I sought Amanda and found her watching the scene from the flower bed by the porch. "Amanda? Take the children inside for a cake, or some nuts."

"See, Mamma! Patsy see!"

I drew the children to my side and kissed their heads. "Not now. It is not for you. Go with Amanda and she will get you something to eat."

The promise of food appeased them, and I was left alone with the unhappy cargo. I read the inscription to see if it was as I had ordered: *Here Lies the Body of Daniel Parke Custis Esquire who was born the 15th Day of Oct. of 1711 & departed this Life the 8th Day of July 1757. Aged 45 Years.*

It was correct. I ran my fingers across the chiseled letters that honoured the life of my husband. Yet seeing it now, I realized it said too little. A name. A date of birth and death. An age. Perhaps I should have added something sentimental: *Beloved husband and father.* Yet at the time I had written the order, I had not felt sentimental. Only overwhelmed.

"I am sorry, Daniel," I told the stone.

Yet with the apology, I gained a thought that might make some amends. I would order a mason to create a brick foundation upon which to set this stone. It would be a strong statement, a small representation of Daniel's place in this world.

I nodded to myself, the decision made.

I kissed my fingers and touched his name. I stood there a moment, my hand upon the cold stone, remembering the warm man who had brought me joy. The feel of his arms as they enfolded me, the smell of his clothes after a hard day at work, the sparkle in his eyes that revealed the affection he felt for me.

I pulled my hand away from the stone. My memories were what sustained me, not some slab that only commemorated dates and a resting place. The place Daniel truly rested was in my mind. And in my heart.

I headed back to the house. It was good the stone had mistakenly come here. It was good it had come on this day. Providence did not deal with coincidence. This was God's way of giving me a note of finality to this day of remembrance, as well as a note of finality to my past.

The past was not a place I had chosen to live. Its lure continued, but with God's help, and with the presence of my two children, I had managed to be victorious over its snare.

And George . . . the addition of George in my life had been instrumental in turning my eyes away from what was and letting me gaze toward what was yet to be.

With one final glance at the wagon I said good-bye to the man I had known all my life, and looked forward to once again seeing the man I was to marry.

A man I barely knew.

My stomach tightened, but I pushed the condition away. Marrying George was the right thing to do. A good thing. Yet good or not, his absence was difficult. How I wished he were here beside me, making me revel in happy thoughts and warm feelings.

Soon, George. Please come home soon.

It was something.

Although I longed for George to be with me in person, his latest letter—a lovely letter—was some consolation. With the children safely to bed I sat in my room, near the window, making full use of the last rays of the sun to read it yet again:

> We have begun our march for the Ohio. A courier is starting for
> Williamsburg, and I embrace the opportunity to send a few words

to one whose life is now inseparable from mine. Since that happy hour when we made our pledges to each other, my thoughts have been continually going to you as another self. That an all-powerful Providence may keep us both in safety is the prayer of your ever faithful and affectionate friend.

"Another self." Such a lovely phrase. One that would do much to sustain me as I waited for our two to become one.

— FOUR —

"Y ou may kiss the bride."

Upon Reverend Mossom's suggestion, George did just that. Our wedding guests clapped as we reluctantly turned away from each other, toward them. Our first moments of married life were met with genuine pleasure—on everyone's part.

Including my own.

I proudly took the arm of my new husband and stepped toward the center of the parlour at White House, letting the well-wishes of family and friends envelop us. Hugs and kisses to the cheek for me, and handshakes and slaps on the back for my George.

My George. Such a luscious phrase.

My sister Nancy pushed past others to offer her pleasure. "You look exquisite, sister." She leaned closer. "And your husband . . ." Her appreciative smile finished the sentence.

On this special day, I knew both statements to be true. My dress—delivered from England—was lovelier than I had hoped. It was deep yellow, of rich brocade, the skirt open at the front to reveal a white silk underskirt with a weave of silver through and through. Silver lace edged the neck and sleeve. As a pleasant contrast, I wore purple silk slippers with a silver buckle and embroidery, and had a string of pearls running through my hair. I felt much like a queen.

And George . . . George had ordered his own wedding clothes: a cotton velvet suit the colour of a bluebird, with an ivory waistcoat and gold buckles on his shoes and breeches. His clothes were a bit tight, for even though he had given his exact measurements and specified in his order the suit was needed for a tall man, that definition was subjective, as few men were as tall as George. The tailors must have been disbelieving of the measurements, and they merely made the clothes the way they preferred. And yet tight or not, his blue and my gold complemented each other—a condition I prayed would continue toward more important matters beyond fashion.

It being my second wedding, a small affair would have been understandable. But from the beginning I had decided on a full-fledged event. It was important for all our friends and family to see how committed we were to our new life as man and wife. A minor ceremony with a handful in attendance could have signified the practicality of many second marriages. The inevitability. I, however, wished to signify there was nothing inevitable about our union but the grace of Providence working to achieve it. The wealthy widow Custis and the heroic Colonel Washington were two individuals to be reckoned with, as a pair united by God. . . .

The new governor of Virginia, William Fauquier, was next to congratulate us, looking quite regal in red robes, flowing wig, and intricate sword. "Congratulations, Colonel. Mrs. Washington." He looked at his wife standing beside him. "We extend best wishes to you both."

"It is not 'colonel' anymore," George said. He looked down at me and smiled, for he had resigned from the military and looked forward to our civilian life—together. The seven months we had been apart was far too long and I vowed it would never happen again. "My soldiering days are over, Governor."

"We will see about that," the governor said. "Though hopefully, with God's mercy, we will have no more trouble with the French."

The quest to take Fort Du Quesne had been successful just that November, and the fort had been renamed Fort Pitt after our prime minister. Apparently overwhelmed by the incoming presence of nearly four thousand colonial and British troops, the French had retreated, exploding gunpowder and burning the fort in their wake.

But at the moment *that* victory had little to do with us. The past was past, the future was—

The children broke through the crowd and crushed us with their exuberant embraces. They were also dressed in new attire, looking very much like miniature adults. I picked up Patsy, and George scooped Jacky into his arms.

"Are we married yet?" Jacky asked.

"We are," George said.

"Then can we eat?"

He laughed. "We most certainly can."

I looked at the guests who had thronged around us. "Jacky is right. It is time to celebrate our wedding. On this January 6, 1759, on this Twelfth Night, we say good-bye to the reverence of the Christmas season and invite you to revel in our happy day. Please enjoy the reception in the dining room. If you want for anything, please let me know."

As we let the children down, George leaned close, with words for my ears alone. "I want only you."

I kissed his cheek, wanting the same. But that would come later. Right now we had a celebration to attend.

The dancing went on for hours, the chairs of the parlour moved aside to make room. The cold of the January night was not felt inside, and there were more than a few faces flushed with the heat of the dance.

All joined in, even the children. The more reserved minuets made way for our favorite reels. There was something about the rhythm of a reel that made it impossible to sit by, uninvolved.

George was an excellent dancer, but upon dancing our first dance as man and wife, a memory from a Williamsburg dance many years previous came to mind. "I do believe we have danced before, husband."

"Surely not, for I would have remembered it."

"Surely we have, for I never forget true grace."

"You flatter me."

"Of course. And I intend to add to my list of flatteries as the night wears on."

His blush was delightful.

As one of the guests of honour, I was not forced to handle the hostess duties alone. Mother was there, as were my little sisters, Elizabeth and Mary. And Nancy came with her husband, Burwell Bassett, along with my brothers, William and Bartholomew. The siblings of George who were able to attend traveled a distance to be with us: his half brother Austin and his wife, John Augustine and Hannah, and his dear sister Betty and her husband, Fielding Lewis.

Beyond family, friends from both parts of Virginia were in attendance, making the day merry. Days, most likely, for everyone was invited to stay over and continue the festivities. Every corner of White House was taken, as well as places in the outbuildings for the men. No one would be turned away from our hospitality.

Yet being the center of attention was exhausting. I took a moment in the foyer to lean against the wall. I closed my eyes and let the sounds of music, laughter, and conversation swell and parry.

One voice broke through from the other side of the wall. "Washington got the better deal of it. All this land and money. I hear he is ambitious. Taking over what Daniel started will set him for life."

"Taking over everything that was Daniel's."

They snickered.

If I had not been so weary, I would have created a pointed comeback, but as it was, I left the wit behind and rounded the corner, placing myself directly in front of the two men—acquaintances from Williamsburg.

"In your discussion regarding what my husband *takes*, I believe you need to remember what he has given to these colonies in which we live. Did you know while fighting the French and Indians he was so courageous and heroic the Indians stopped firing upon him because they believed he *could* not fall? They feared him and thought he was protected by spirits and could not be killed by mere humans."

One man swallowed with obvious difficulty. "I did not know that."

The other gentleman shook his head.

"I thought not." I sighed. "So . . . I think it would be wise to note that an extraordinary gentleman such as my husband, a man impervious to bullet and death, whose life is obviously blessed by Providence, will surely not be broken by the opinions of ignorant men who have most likely never faced anything more dangerous than saddle sores or the threat of a stray ember from their evening fire." I smiled sweetly. "May I get you more cake, sirs?"

They wisely declined.

"I am sorry your mother was not here."

George did not answer. Was he asleep?

I rose up enough to see his face. "Did you not hear? I am sorry your mother was not with us."

"I heard you."

Ah.

I settled in against his shoulder and changed the subject. "I think we should move to Mount Vernon."

It was his turn to move in order to see *my* face. "But you were not sure. You love your home here. Your family is close. The soil is of better quality, you are nearer a port for trade, your estate is far more vast than mine, you—"

"I wish to move to your home."

"When did you make this decision?"

I was not certain. In fact, I had not wholly made the decision until I heard myself say the words. Yet . . . I remembered the rude comments of the two men at the reception regarding how George was marrying me for my wealth. That he would benefit—for now legally, everything I owned was his—was inconsequential. Any man who would marry me would benefit. It was a fact I could not change. But that did not mean others should think he offered me nothing. Beyond the man he was, he had a plantation where we could live. Yet beyond even that, he offered me a dream. His dream would become my dream. As I had helped Daniel fulfill his hopes of a vast plantation, I would help George fulfill his. I could not ask him to merely manage the fruits of another man's purpose. He had his own. And my purpose . . . was to be by his side as a helpmate and partner.

In every way.

Although we did not know each other well, I sensed one of the traits George admired in me was my gumption and work ethic. He did not choose me above all other women hoping I would sit in the corner and look beautiful (neither the idle sitting nor being beautiful was possible); he chose me to be an integral part of his life.

"Dearest?" he said.

"I make the decision now. The plantation here is well established and can run without us. But Mount Vernon . . ."

He laughed. "Needs us. Yes indeed, she needs us very badly."

"And we need her."

Our eyes held until he leaned over and kissed me. "This is but one reason I married you."

I showed him another.

⁓⁓⁓

In but a few days we will celebrate our third month as man and wife. It was time we left White House and headed north to Mount Vernon.

We would have left sooner but had to spend several weeks in Williamsburg while George was sworn into his post in the House of Burgesses. That this ceremony was accomplished on February 22, his twenty-seventh birthday, made it doubly special. I was utterly proud of him and had the distinct feeling there would be few times, few actions, that would not elicit that emotion. We met wonderful people there, and George was impressed by Patrick Henry and a neighbor, George Mason. He observed everything, soaking in all details regarding how our government was run.

I had already said my good-byes to my family. Mother and Nancy were tearful, yet understood my desire—my need—to leave. They helped me determine what goods to take: my mahogany desk; six beds with all their curtains, spreads, and linens; ninety-nine napkins; some tables and chests; two cases of knives and forks; over sixty glasses; two sets of china; a tea set . . . things a bachelor like George may not own. It was my responsibility to assure we could entertain properly.

Many of our possessions went north on a barge, for the rough roads would wreak havoc on my fine breakables. For our own portage the carriage was made ready, with another wagon following behind full of clothing and household items. Also coming with us were a number of house servants: my maid, a seamstress, a laundress, a cook, a waiter, four carpenters, and the children's maid.

Two children, Tiggy and Susan, were also coming, to wait on and play with Jacky and Patsy. George did not enjoy the cramped quarters of a carriage, so he planned to ride his horse alongside. He definitely was a man who enjoyed the fresh air and felt few places as natural as astride a horse.

Finally ready, the carriage pulled away. Jacky was immediately on his knees upon the seat, peering out the window. " 'Bye, house."

Little Patsy—always one to mimic her big brother—climbed off my lap to the seat beside me and repeated, " 'Bye, house."

The carriage hit a rut and jogged when it should have jigged, sending Patsy off the seat. She cried and was upon my lap once more.

"There, there," I said. "Everything will be all right."

Or so I hoped.

Although I mourned her pain, in a way 'twas a blessing, for it offered a distraction from my own good-byes. By the time she was settled and happy again, the house was out of sight.

Just as well. Sometimes it was best not to think *too* much until the peak moment of sentiment was past.

───

I so enjoyed watching George ride beside us. He was incredibly striking upon his horse—very regal. If this country would but have its own king, he would suit the bill. In many ways.

Suddenly, he looked ahead, his face on full alert. Then he shouted, "Halt! Halt right here!"

With much commotion from driver and horses, the carriage came to a stop. Had we come upon something in our way? The spring rains had washed many roads useless, replacing the dirt with rocks and branches that had already hindered our progress.

"What is wrong, George?" I asked out the window.

He rode up to me—close. "This is the place," he said for my ears alone.

I looked around. We were in deep woods. It did not look like any *place* I would wish to linger. "I do not under—"

"We are twenty-five miles from White House."

Ah. Yes.

"I must see. I must get out," I said.

George got off his horse and opened the carriage door, pulling down the steps. He offered me his hand.

"Are we here?" Jacky asked.

"Not at Mount Vernon, no," I explained as I descended the steps to the ground. "But we are at a special place."

Jacky jumped down, and George took Patsy into his arms. I stepped away from the carriage enough to turn full circle. "Are you sure of the distance?" I asked George.

"As near as I can determine."

I nodded and turned my back on where we *had* been, and faced the direction in which we were going. To my eye there was nothing unusual or different about the road and woods facing me from those behind, and yet . . .

George strode toward me. "Now it is all a new world, my dear."

It was. "Twenty-five miles from home . . . I have never been farther."

"Until now. With me."

I leaned my head against his arm. "I would not venture so far for anyone else."

He whispered to me, "And I promise Mount Vernon will not be the extent of our world. There is much to see in this great land, Martha. There is Philadelphia and New York City and—"

I laughed, stopping his listing. "For now I will be content with our home in northern Virginia."

"Our home."

Our home.

We got back in the carriage and proceeded on our way.

Forward.

Never looking back.

It would take us five days to traverse the one hundred twenty miles from White House to Mount Vernon—normally four days, except for two visits with family along the way.

The first was with George's sister, Betty, and her husband, Fielding Lewis, in Fredericksburg. I had met them at the wedding and had been struck by the resemblance between Betty and her brother. She was very tall, and they shared the same nose and mouth. I was told if she donned a hat and cloak, the siblings were nearly indistinguishable. It was amusing to imagine such a scene—which had obviously taken place on more than one occasion with much laughter.

Although Betty was a year younger than George, she and Fielding had already been married nine years and had four children—though only two sons had survived: Fielding junior, aged eight, and little George Augustine, but two. Betty was about to give birth to number five.

"Any time," she told me as we settled into the parlour with our four children playing noisily around us.

"I envy you."

"Children will come, on their own terms, in their own time."

"It has already been three months."

Her laugh also reminded me of her brother. "Young Fielding was born just nine months from the wedding night. What of your first?"

"My first husband's namesake was not born until we were married eighteen months."

"There. That is your way. Some time must pass."

Perhaps.

She set a hand upon her expanded belly. "You have also lost two?"

The grief returned with new teeth. "Does one ever get over it?"

She shook her head. "Never over it. Past it, perhaps." She sighed. "Life goes on. Blessedly."

"Do you . . ." This was awkward. "Do you find yourself fearful for the two you have?"

She blinked, as though she had never thought of such a thing. "I am careful, to be sure, but not fearful. Children will be children. Life will wield its worst—and best—upon us. I do not dwell on could-be's. I pray for the best and do my part to create a happy life." She looked upon me warily. "Is your worry cumbersome?"

"Sometimes. I do not wish it to be, but I often catch myself hovering too near, watching at the window if they play outdoors, pulling them to my skirts when a horse comes riding close, holding them in crowded rooms for fear of a tipped candle or bumped elbow."

Betty shook her head, incredulous. "My, my. A bumped elbow."

Upon her lips it did sound like a frivolous fear.

Her smile turned mischievous. "You wish for something to fear?"

"Not particularly."

"I hear you are visiting our mother tomorrow."

"George thought it best. Since she could not come to our wedding—"

"*Would* not come."

Really.

"If you wish to fear anything, fear her," Betty said.

Apparently my face showed confusion, for she expanded her explanation. "Surely George has told you about her, warned you?"

"He has said she can be difficult."

There was that laugh again. "Since God has determined by George's lack of details his intent to honour our mother, I will only add that prayers regarding your visit will not be wasted."

Oh dear.

⁂

"Martha, do not grip so hard!"

I let go of George's hand, unmindful I had been clutching it with desperation.

The carriage pulled up to the Washington family home at Ferry Farm, and for this shorter ride, George shared the space with us. He patted my knee and bumped shoulder against shoulder. " 'Twill be all right. She does not bite."

"I never thought—"

"At least she did not do so the last time I visited her."

I shoved his hand away. "You may make fun of me, husband, but I can only gauge my nerves upon the scant information you and your sister have given me. And by that evidence I feel fully justified to owning a goodly amount of trepidation."

Jacky bounced in his seat. "We are here! We are here!"

"Shh!" George was suddenly serious. "As we go into the house, you must both use your polite voices."

The carriage drew to a halt and I watched George steady his shoulders, raise his chin, and take a deep breath—as though preparing to go into battle.

It appeared my trepidation was catching.

⁂

Much can be measured by the way two people embrace.

Whenever I greeted my own mother we drew each other close as though taking strength from the physical contact, as well as giving measure of our love and devotion. Give and take. An enrichment and celebration of the bond we shared.

When George embraced his mother there was no such exchange. His hands barely touched her upper arms and she stood stiff, with her own arms by her sides. Her only concession to his presence seemed to be a slight turning of her cheek to accept the flutter of his lips against it. Once this awkward prelude was complete, George took a large step back as though seeking safe distance.

Although I had not thought twice about embracing his sister Betty upon our visit, to make such overtures to my mother-in-law seemed wrong.

And unappealing.

When her pale eyes turned toward me, I bowed my head and offered my best curtsy. "Mother Washington." When I looked upon her again, her right eyebrow had risen. Had I not executed the curtsy correctly? Surely she was not affronted because I had not approached her with an embrace.

At that moment Jacky and Patsy ran through the front door. "I cannot wait outside anymore," Jacky said. "I want to come in. We want to come in."

George reddened. He had asked the children to wait on the porch. Although I wished to object—for I always presented the children and myself as one—in this case, on his family's home ground, I allowed it, and George and I entered the Washington home alone.

The children rushed to their usual place by my side, and I put a protective hand about them. I waited for George to make the introductions, but upon a glance, he seemed tongue-tied.

"Mother Washington, I would like to introduce my children, Jacky and Patsy."

"I dislike shortened names. My Betty would do well to call herself Elizabeth as intended."

I corrected myself for her benefit. "This is John Parke and Martha Parke."

"Parke? What kind of name is that?"

Why had I mentioned their middle name? To explain we had been forced to include the Parke surname in order to remain in my father-in-law's will would not impress. Besides, this meeting was not about *my* past, it was about *our* future.

" 'Tis a family name," I said.

Mary peered upon Jacky. "You one of those ruffian boys who shout and run and cause chaos wherever you be?"

Jacky pushed himself between the folds of my skirt.

"He is a good child, Mother," George said. "And little Patsy is a delightful child. Your grandchildren."

She made a face, then said, "Not my blood, nor yours neither," before turning toward the parlour.

And though we would have preferred to retreat to the carriage, we followed. The room was small, the furnishings simple, and what little adornment existed was ordered, as though everything had but one place that had been determined the *right* place and there could be no deviation.

Mary sat in a rocker by the fire, and George allowed me the chair across the room. He stood behind me. The children climbed upon my lap. The gap between her and us was as cavernous as we could make it. Yet it was not a pointed decision to create the yawning space but a decision of instinct.

A foreign decision. I, who was at ease with all people, stranger and acquaintance, did not understand this desire to be apart and away.

Yet I embraced it as the best course.

Mary retrieved a long pipe and, taking a reed from the fire, used it to light the tobacco within. The four of us watched as smoke puffed and swelled about her, veiling her as though she existed in another world not quite clear to us.

She tossed the reed into the fire. Her eyes turned upon me, and with effort, I did not turn away. "So. You are a widow. How long? Details. Tell me details."

Although I had no wish to rehash this grief—especially with the children present—I was relieved to have conversation. "My husband was named Daniel Parke Custis. His family owns many acres near Williamsburg. Our home, White House, is—"

"Seventeen thousand acres, Mother. Daniel was very successful."

"So you are rich, are you?"

I felt the heat upon my face. "I was well provided for."

"Humph."

She made it sound like a deficit toward character. I tried to explain. "My family and friends have been very supportive and—"

"Why are you not staying there 'stead of coming up here to Mount Vernon? It will not suit you, you know. Not when you are used to fancy ways and fancy clothes." Her eyes skimmed my dress. "Some people have no time for such frivolities. Some people must depend on others for their very sustenance."

She glanced at her son and he did not contradict her, even though I knew he had recently sent her a generous amount. Somehow I sensed "enough" was not a condition Mary Ball Washington ascribed to.

From my lap, Jacky looked into my face. "Can we go now?" he whispered.

"Go . . ." Patsy said plaintively, cuddling deeper.

George answered. "Yes, perhaps we should. I am eager to reach Mount Vernon. I have made many improvements, Mother. You should come and visit, to see—"

"I have no wish to see that place. Your father left it to a son born through his other marriage. Gave them the best of things, leaving you and me to make do and struggle and—"

George stepped to the front of me and took Patsy into his arms. "You are welcome to visit anytime, Mother."

"You know I hate to travel."

"I would send someone to fetch you. I—"

"Too busy to fetch me yourself?"

"No, I . . ." He extended his hand for Jacky, who climbed from my lap and eagerly took it. With a short bow to his mother, he said, "Good-bye, Mother. Let me know if there is any way we can be of service."

"Oh, there will be little to none of that. Not now that you have a new family to care for."

Relieved of the children, I stood, offered a quick curtsy, and left, pulling the door shut behind me.

The driver and servants who had accompanied us scrambled to the carriage and wagon, clearly surprised by our quick exit.

"Go!" George commanded as soon as we were settled. "Come now. Away!"

Faster. Take us faster . . .

Away.

⸻

As the miles from Ferry Farm increased, our pace settled into one that ceased the violent jarring across road and rut. The children lay asleep upon the seats, each one's head in a lap as George and I faced each other.

His jaw remained clenched, but his shoulders had lowered to a more serene state. "We made it," I said, offering him a smile.

"Made what?"

"Made our visit and made our escape."

A smile softened his jaw. "Now you see why . . ."

"I wish to understand why," I said. "I will only ask this once, and then you need never tell me again, but I do wish to know your mother's history. I wish to understand this bitterness that emanates from her like heat from a fire."

The horse took twenty strides before he answered me. But then, finally, the story began.

"As you know, my two older brothers were born from a different mother. Father doted on them and took them to England for an education. When he returned to Virginia, he found his wife had died."

"How horrible."

"It was a blow. Soon after, he met my mother, Mary Ball, who was twenty-three at the time." He looked at me, then away. "She had never been married."

This one fact was telling. In a land short on women, women who were unmarried, even at the age of twenty, made questions arise as to their . . . suitability.

"My father had heard she was headstrong, but he thought he was up to the match."

"What did her parents think of it?"

"Her parents were dead. And there is some shadow regarding *their* marriage. There is a rumour her mother was an indentured servant."

"Oh."

"We colonials value hard work, but you know as well as I that the level of servant who traveled to the Americas to work off their passage waned as England began emptying its gaols on our shores."

"Your grandmother was not—?"

"No, no. Not a convict, as far as I know. But her lowly beginnings . . . When Grandfather Ball died, his wife remarried multiple times. All this when my mother was a mere child. When my grandmother died, Mother was only thirteen. Though she had some inheritance, she was shuffled between relatives. I have always understood it was not an amiable situation."

"She was not loved, did not feel secure."

George rode on, his profile stern. "Upon her marriage to my father . . . that deficit in her life did not improve. Father had many grand plans but was not very adept at making them succeed. And he chose to be gone more than he was home. My childhood was tense. Mother was left with six children—though my baby sister, Mildred, lived but a year. Mother did the best she could, but there was no room in her heart for survival *and* affection."

I nodded, my own heart finding empathy for this bitter woman.

"When Father died . . . I was the eldest, yet only eleven. Unlike your situation upon Daniel's death, Father left most of the good lands to the sons of his first marriage. He left Ferry Farm to me, under my mother's tutelage until it was mine at age twenty-one, but the other children . . . it was as though they did not exist to him."

"That is not fair."

"No. It is not."

"Without an estate, with six children, and with her reputation of character, my mother was not a widow who was sought after."

"She was—she is—lonely."

"I suppose she is."

"Yet if she desires companionship, why does she not make it easier for her children to visit, to draw close and offer her the comfort she desires?"

"I do not know." George's face was drawn with an inner pain. "I wish to love her, Martha. Truly I do. Yet even though I know the reason for her bitter ways, I find that to be in her presence . . . I find it draining upon my soul."

I extended my hand across the gap and he took it. I squeezed, offering my commiseration, compassion, and encouragement. "You are a good son, George."

"I am not."

"You are. For you continue to attempt to bridge the gap between you. You send her aid. You write to her."

"But I do not love her."

"Perhaps honour must do when love is impossible."

We let go of each other's hands. We continued to Mount Vernon in worlds and thoughts that were parallel rather than intersecting.

⌘

We were getting close.

I could tell by the speed with which we traveled, and the many times George looked from left to right out the windows. He was like a little boy with something to show.

But this was not a new toy or rabbit. It was our home. It was the object that was rooted at the core of his dreams.

Suddenly, he took my hand and placed it upon his knee. "We are nearly there."

He was breathless.

We approached from the west and I caught glimpses of gardens with inviting pathways to the side. We ascended the hill and—

"There it is!" George shouted, pointing out the window.

I only caught a glimpse before the carriage pulled up the drive. The house was a whitewashed two-and-a-half-story with a red roof. It was not as grand as White House but basked nicely in the afternoon sun.

"I added sand to the paint to make it appear as stone. I also added the new story." As we approached, we could not fully see the house, and George seemed ready to burst at this deficiency. "When I stayed here with my brother Lawrence, there were but four rooms and a single hall. Considering the extent of my renovations, some say I was foolish for not tearing down and starting fresh, but I could not do that to all Lawrence had accomplished. I do not ever wish to wipe away the past but to build upon it and make it better."

I was not sure which held my interest more: the upcoming view of our new home or the rapt look upon my husband's face as he shared his thoughts.

"I am sure it is lovely," I said.

These words brought him out of his reverie, for he looked at me and said, "It makes an attempt but still has far to go. But now I have even more reason to make it shine." He looked upon the children, then at me.

The carriage turned round a circle drive. It stopped. George did not wait for the coachman to open the door but pushed it open and exited. He lifted the children out, and then me, placing me gently upon the drive.

A welcoming door stood before us.

But nice as it was, grand as it tried to be, the welcoming glee on my husband's face was far more poignant.

—⊷—

It had been a long day. A long trip in distance, emotion, and symbolism—for the children and I had left behind one life and were now ensconced in the next.

The children were safely tucked into bed, and my body longed for its own soft mattress and pillow. I would sleep well tonight and arise in the morning eager to start afresh.

I closed the door to the children's room with a soft click and turned round to see George waiting for me.

"Come walk with me," he said.

I did not feel like walking, yet I could not turn him down. Not on our first evening here.

He led me down the newly created walnut stairway into the foyer, which was a respectable thirteen feet wide. Wood paneling had been installed, topped with intricate cornices painted in a lovely ocher.

We made a sharp turn beside the stairs and he led me out the back door of the house. We had not been there yet, too consumed had we been to get our baggage unpacked and the children settled after a meal.

Once outside, he swept his arm across the vista before me. "Voilà!"

My hand flew to my breast. "Oh, George!"

I knew my reaction pleased him, because he drew me under his arm. I was just the right height to fit. . . .

"That is the Potomac River," he said.

"It is far wider than the Pamunkey."

"Far wider."

"And the woods and hills . . . the area around White House is so flat by comparison."

He pointed to a section of trees. "Those are cherry and apple trees, and the tall ones are poplars."

"The blossoms are beyond lovely."

"They have bloomed just for you. They wanted to show off."

I laughed. "We have come at the right time of year. A happy coincidence."

He shook his head sternly. "There is no such thing." I felt him take a deep breath. "I belong here, Martha. We belong here. Our marriage, our life together . . . it was Providence who brought us together, who brought us here."

I did not, could not, argue with him.

— FIVE —

I stood outside the door of the small room George used as a study, not wishing to startle him. He was busy at work and did not look up. The light of the candle was still needed as it was not yet dawn.

I did not mind his inattention but enjoyed watching him in this clandestine way. His red hair was pulled back, though slightly tousled from sleep. He had put on breeches and shirt, but the latter remained untucked, its sleeves rolled. His feet were bare, and I resisted the urge to admonish him about staying warm because *I* was chilled. I had already learned our tolerance for hot and cold were not the same. Where I took great pains to adjust to variances in temperature, George seemed immune to them. Perhaps his extensive time spent in the wild had toughened him.

He sighed deeply and stretched his arms above his head. It was then he saw me. "Martha? What are you doing out of bed?"

"Seeing where my warm blanket had gone to."

He smiled and held out his hand to me. I went to him and he pulled me close.

"What are you working on?" I asked.

"I am working on you, on your New Kent holdings. I wish to do right by you, and by what the Custis family amassed over so many years."

"Believe me, I am relieved to be free of the burden."

He pointed to a letter. "I have written your factor—"

"Our factor."

"Our factor in England, Robert Cary and Company, and have informed them it would behoove them to treat us fairly, as the Custis and Washington fortunes are not without influence, and if they do not treat us well, we will take our business elsewhere."

"Bravo, husband!"

Spurred on by my support, he read a portion aloud: " 'Regarding prices, you must take some pains to inform yourself exactly, because should the prices differ from those of the estate, I might possibly think myself deceived and be disgusted.' "

I laughed softly. "You are most certainly direct."

"A necessity when there are thousands of miles between us. But in truth, beyond the sales of tobacco—of which I never know how much I am going to be paid or how much will be lost en route or stolen—I am fed up with how many of the material goods we order are inferior. Machinery comes with parts missing, certain goods are absent or used by the crew along the trip, and I have heard rumours that merchants in London add ten percent to any order they know is coming to the colonies. Goods from London are mean in quality, but not in price, for in that they excel. And to not know the price until we receive the goods . . . 'tis a situation ripe for disenchantment."

I agreed. "I have learned one must be very specific, though even that does not fend off deviations. I have oft instructed my representatives not to shop the most expensive stores but to seek better prices. I have ordered a dress stipulating the highest cost to be paid and have been disappointed in the quality, or have been baited with a dress of higher cost. I refuse to fall victim to such nonsense."

"As much as we have the power."

I pulled his arm around me once more. "They do not think very well of us, do they?"

He shook his head. "We will always be a stepchild to them—an annoying, bothersome stepchild. My brother Lawrence told me even when he went to school in England, he was looked down upon as a mere colonial. How much land or status we have here has little bearing in England."

"And we have little recourse to change their minds," I said.

"None. Our mother country has us under her thumb, yet never embraces us or pulls us close, giving comfort within the folds of her skirts."

"Aptly said, husband." And though I did not say it aloud, I was struck by the similarity in the treatment Mother England assessed us and the treatment George's mother availed *her* children: demanding compensation, but not willing to give much of anything—at least not without a high price.

I kissed the top of his head. "Come back to bed, dearest. You have done fair work and 'tis not e'en day yet."

George nodded and followed me to a place where comfort, appreciation, and reason prevailed.

I was torn.

On the one hand I ached to see George's beloved Belvoir and meet George William and Sally Fairfax. But on the other . . .

I was afraid.

Would she be as beautiful and charming as I had heard? Would I feel like a wild flower compared to her carefully pruned rose?

When the invitation came for us to dine at Belvoir, my initial reaction was a petulant no. I saw no reason to stray past the safe and lovely halls of Mount Vernon. Yet I knew that was not possible. Neighbours were of high import in the colonies, where towns of any size were few and far between. Neighbours were important and hospitality was held in highest esteem. No visitor was ever turned away, and invitations were given and accepted with great frequency. It was a duty.

And a joy—which this time, I did not feel.

As we rode the four miles to this first meeting I tried to console myself with the hopes that all praise of Belvoir *and* Sally had been exaggerated. It was a fact that the grapevine tended to elevate the best and amplify the worst. The truth generally lived in the middle. This time, above all times, I wished that to be true.

George slipped his hand through my arm. "I do hope you will like Belvoir and the Fairfaxes as much as I do. Both are very dear to me."

My throat went dry. Dear indeed.

⁂

"Welcome, welcome," Sally said.

She drew me into a close embrace before I had a good look at her. Once I was released I had the unfortunate chance to see that, for once, the grapevine had not exaggerated. She was truly beautiful. She was quite a bit taller than I, and slim—though shapely in all the right places. Her face was long, her hair dark, her jaw wide. Her eyebrows were arched in just such a way to enhance lively eyes. Within moments I witnessed how she used them to complement her expressions.

"So this is the widow Custis I have heard so much about," she said.

"Widow no more," I said. I looked to George, but he was conversing with Sally's husband, George William. "George and I are thoroughly enjoying the delights of marriage."

She hesitated a moment, as if making a judgment. I did not waver but held her gaze. I was determined to be the victor of this initial foray, to claim that which was mine.

Finally she said, "You are very lucky indeed, for George is most certainly a man of many talents."

Her innuendo was palpable, but before I could react, the men joined us and we were taken on a tour of Belvoir.

I declared the first battle . . . a draw.

Three stories containing nine rooms, including a library. There were scores of fine paintings, intricate accessories, delectable fabrics, and paper on the walls—all imported from England. Although determined to remain unimpressed, I could not feign indifference. "The house is exceptional," I said. "Exquisite."

"Why, thank you." Sally ran a hand along a golden candelabrum. "My father-in-law had fine taste, and as the agent to his cousin Lord Fairfax, he did his best to make this home one to be remembered by all who saw it."

George moved beside me. "You can see why I was so enamored with this place as a boy."

"You were a part of the family," George William said. "After all, your brother married my sister."

"You were our pet," Sally cooed. "A Fairfax protégé."

It held the implication of insult, yet I saw George took no offense.

She moved to the window of the parlour. "See how we can e'en see each other from our house to yours? I find that quite invigorating, don't you, George?"

He blushed, then said, "I always find it a comfort to see neighbours."

George William slapped him on the back. "Said by a man who has seen his share of wilderness. When the two of us used to go out to survey my family's land, we would travel days without seeing another soul."

"You were company enough for me," George said. "Repeatedly beating me at cards around the campfire . . . though I had much rather lose my money to you than to spend it on some flea-infested inn."

Sally shuddered. "I am spoiled. I admit it. No campfires, dirty inns, or fleas for me, if you please." She turned to find my opinion. "Right, Martha?"

"Of course I prefer the luxuries of life, and yet . . ." I pointedly looked at George. "If a time came when I was given a choice of that or hard conditions and being with my husband, I would be willing to suffer. A bit."

Sally clapped. "Bravo, Martha! All the right words said quite rightly. You have a keeper here, George."

I was relieved when he looked only upon me—and smiled. "Indeed I do."

In this foray I declared myself victorious.

This time.

George pulled back the covers and got in bed. He waited for me to do the same, yet I lingered at my dressing table, brushing my hair.

"You are pensive. Did you not have a good time at Belvoir?"

"Your friends were very gracious."

"They wish to be your friends too, my dear."

"Mmm."

"Why do you say it so? 'Mmm'?"

I twisted upon the stool to face him. "She is still in love with you."

" 'Tis not love, Martha."

At least he did not insult me by feigning ignorance. "Then what is it?"

He rose to sitting, adjusting the pillow behind him. "Sally and I have suffered a flirtation. As she said, I was the Fairfax pet. I was their protégé and they enjoyed teaching me the finer points of society."

I shook my head. "It is more than that."

He was silent, confirming my instinct.

"Perhaps . . . perhaps it was more, at one time. When I was in the army, away from home for an extensive time, she wrote to me. I wrote back. I wrote to other female friends too—'twas not just Sally."

Though intended to make me feel better, it did not.

"I have always enjoyed the company and friendship of the fairer sex. Although I am not witty or particularly good at the banter many desire, I do enjoy their outlook. 'Tis so different from that of men."

I would not be distracted into another discussion. "When you wrote to her . . . was she married to George William?"

George smoothed the sheet across his chest. "She was. Has always been as long as I have known her."

"Did you not think that . . . improper?"

"Though others may have thought so, we . . . and George William . . ." He sighed. "You must understand it is just Sally's way. Where *you* are a nurturer, she is a seeker of pleasure. She is flirtatious. And though I took flattery in her attention at first, I soon saw she extends it to all men. Coyness and wit and hints of flirtation . . . 'Tis hard to ignore, to not be drawn in."

I believed him. I had witnessed Sally's talent at repartee firsthand. Just the way she walked across a room or offered a teacup . . . she knew how to fully utilize the sway of her body, the linger of a hand, the pull of a pointed gaze.

"She is a flirt, but that is all she is, dearest. Neither she, nor I, ever entered into any kind of untoward . . . We would not do that. My friendship and loyalty to George William, and e'en toward the old gentleman, Lord Fairfax, is too important to me. I would not abuse the vast kindnesses they have bestowed through the years. I would not, did not, and will not do it."

His face had grown red with emotion. I set the brush aside and climbed into the space beside him. I cupped his face in my hands. "I believe you, husband. And I will not speak of it again."

"There is no need," he said.

"I know. The subject is hereby closed."

"I chose you, Martha. Where Sally may intrigue, you challenge me, you make me believe anything is possible. With you, I am a better man."

There was no higher compliment.

We did not speak of Sally again, though to my own shame, I did not completely forget the spark that lingered between them. For I knew the sin of temptation does not rest easily. Nor die.

To our credit—and George's—the children and I settled nicely into Mount Vernon. He became busy with the duties of a farmer, and I with the duties of a farmer's wife. I was well versed in these, as the household of White House had been mine to handle for seven years while married to Daniel, and another eighteen months after his death.

I enjoyed being a plantation wife. The gardens were my responsibility, as was the household. I had many men and women to help me inside, and spent much of my time overseeing the work in the outbuildings: the kitchen, the smokehouse, the dairy, and the spinning house, where I trained spinners to make cloth and clothing for the family and the slaves. And the list of goods that were needed was constantly amended. There were many mouths to feed, bodies to clothe, and ailments to heal. And it was my responsibility to do it all.

I enjoyed my challenges. And George his.

Or so I thought.

One summer evening, I could not find him. He was not sitting behind the house—a favourite place when work was done, because the view of the Potomac was so restful. Nor was he in his study. "Have you seen Mr. Washington?" I asked Cully.

" 'Tis upstairs, I believe. In your chamber."

It was odd for George to be upstairs at that time of day, especially with the weather so warm. Although all the windows and doors were kept open to capture the breeze, we usually did not venture to the hotter second floor until the sun had set.

I paused in the hall outside our bedchamber. The door to our room was nearly closed, and I heard movement inside. Without a sound I pushed it open enough to see. George stood before the mirror, adjusting the line of his militia uniform.

My heart leapt to my throat. I forgot my quest for silence and rushed into the room. "You have not been called away again, have you?"

It took George a few moments to grasp my meaning. "No, no. I am not going anywhere."

I released the breath I had been holding. "Then why the . . . ?"

He retrieved a letter from the dresser. "I know I should not take stock in such things as much as I do, but I received a letter from my Virginia Regiment, congratulating me on my retirement."

"How nice of them."

He cleared his throat. "In it, they call me the soul of the corps." He swallowed and his forehead furrowed. "It touched me greatly."

"As it should, dearest. They obviously respect you very much."

"And I them. No one can appreciate the pangs I felt upon leaving such a regiment, one that shared my toils and experienced every hardship and danger by my side. I hold them with true affection for the honour of being called to lead them. If I acquired any reputation, I derived it from them. I humbly accept the love and regard they show me. It is my reward. And my glory."

"You are a true leader, George. Men follow you. That is not a condition many men can claim."

"I only wish I had served them well *all* the time."

The way he said it implied a specific event.

"There was a time . . . ?"

He seemed to blink away a memory, then looked at me. "I cannot speak of it. I will not."

His face looked so pained. "George, I am sure you were the best of leaders. You can be no other. The letter from your troops reveals as much."

He shook his head. "If only it were so." He took a fresh breath and removed the blue coat. " 'Tis silly to try this on. If not for the letter, I would not have done it. In fact, I do not know why I have e'en kept it." He held it up for his own viewing. "I designed it myself and had it made especially."

"I did not know that."

He let the coat drape over his arm. "You and I are both aware of the effect clothing has on one's bearing, as well as upon one's status. A wrongly worn coat or dress can alter a reputation. Clothing speaks and people listen. "

"Well said *and* well worn, my love." I sat in the chair nearby. "Do you miss the military? Is this plantation enough for you?" *Am I?*

He stroked the coat that draped his arm. "I do not miss the frustrations of it, never having ample supplies or weaponry. Just getting the men to stay and fight was a battle. And as far as trying to train them? The attitude of a colonial is one of independence. A positive attribute on most occasions, the trait is a detriment when uniformity and following orders are required. Plus, the home responsibilities of each man were a constant lure that kept them from any true commitment to a fight."

"Yet they still followed you."

He shrugged. "E'en that was marginal, for as mere militia I had no true power. Though I achieved the highest rank in all of Virginia, though I was *the* ranking officer, any British officer—of any rank— could contradict my orders."

"That is hardly fair."

"It is a travesty. It is the true reason why I can leave the military behind. No matter how hard we fight or how brilliant our strategies might be, they still consider us inferior."

"Then you belong here, where you are truly the master of your domain."

He smiled. "Flattery will get you most anything, my dear."

"As intended, my love."

I sat outside upon a rocker overlooking the Potomac. I watched Jacky and Patsy playing tag upon the grass. Jacky was relentless in teasing his sister. He could always outrun her.

"Let her catch you, Jacky!" I yelled.

He ignored me and ran faster, seeming to slow down but pulling away as soon as she drew close. Only when Patsy began to whimper did he truly stop so she could tag him.

Jacky pulled his sister to the ground, and they tumbled upon the grass. I stood, ready to intervene against injury, but their laughter allowed me to return to my seat.

The scene was idyllic: high upon this hill, with cool breezes coming off the water. It was far different from the flat and damp land surrounding White House.

George appeared around the corner and, upon seeing me, came to join me. He sat. "You enjoy the view, my dear?" he asked.

"In a manner twofold." I extended a hand toward the children *and* toward the majestic view.

George began to rock. "I have always taken high comfort that Mount Vernon is most pleasantly situated in such a high, healthy country. Its latitude lies between the extremes of heat and cold. And the river . . . it is one of the finest in the world, stocked with abundance of all kinds. We are edged with ten miles of clean tidewater."

Three of his words returned for further scrutiny: *high, healthy country.* "It does seem a healthy place. By now in the season 'twould be muggy and hot at White House. In many ways, 'twas not a healthy place for the children. The diseases born in marshy water were a constant worry."

"You need fear little of that here." George took a deep breath. "Smell that wonderful air. Such freshness bears only the best of health."

I gazed at the children, who were hunched down, heads nearly touching as they looked upon some sprig of clover or ladybug nestled in the grass. Perhaps here I *could* learn to let the worry subside.

Perhaps.

"John Parke Washington!"

I heard George's bellow coming from his study. I rushed downstairs in time to see Jacky scurry behind a chair in the dining room. I left him be and moved to find what my husband was angry about.

I entered the study. George stood at the wall behind his desk. "Where is Jacky?"

I did not tell him. "What did he do?"

"Look! Look at this!"

He pointed to the wall, which had been drawn upon. Grand pictures of horses and soldiers and guns and trees.

"He is improving," I said.

George's mouth dropped. "Surely you do not approve of such disregard, such wanton disrespect for our home?"

"He's not even five, George."

"Five or fifteen, he has no business being in my private study, desecrating a wall—"

"It is hardly desecration. It can be cleaned. Or painted over."

He stepped toward the door. "Which is exactly what I am going to make him do, after punishing—"

I stepped in front of him, stopping his movement. "You will not punish him."

"I will not what?"

An attempt to stand to my full height had little impact in front of George's mass. "I am his mother. I will talk to him and explain—"

"This is not the first naughty act he has accomplished, Martha. That boy runs wild. Just last week when you thought he had run away, you wanted us to search by the river, certain he had drowned."

" 'Twas a valid fear."

"Not for most mothers, because most boys of nearly five know their boundaries and are considerate enough to abide by them. The children need rules, Martha. E'en at three, Patsy can take responsibility for her actions. She cries like a baby when she does not get her way. 'Tis not right. A child needs to be taught they do not know best, taught that sometimes their parents must induce limits, for their own good."

My breathing had grown pronounced. "How dare you tell me how to raise children! You, who have had none, against me, who has borne four—and lost two." I felt my chin quiver. "Until you have held a child in your arms and seen the life fade from his eyes . . . My children are everything to me, and if I wish to indulge them in order to assure their happiness, I will do so, and no one—not e'en you—can stop me!"

We stared at each other . . . a standoff.

When George spoke, his voice was composed. "Happiness stems from leading a life of control, knowing the margins of society, and making wise choices. Letting the children run amok, out of control, will ultimately lead to their future unhappiness. And ours." He touched my shoulder. "And for your information, the children—and you—mean everything to *me*."

I was chastened by his words. "I did not mean to imply you do not mean anything to—"

"I know you did not. But if we are going to live together in a loving, peaceful household, then we need to work together to attain and maintain that peace." He pointed at Jacky's drawing. "*This* must never happen again." He dropped his arm and sidestepped me, entering the hallway. "Now, where is he? Jacky?"

I hurried after him. Although in essence I knew everything he said was correct, I did not want poor Jacky to be distressed or afraid.

"Jacky? Oh. There you are. Come out from behind the table, young man."

Jacky stood, his eyes clearly fearful.

"Oh, George . . ." I said. Jacky ran into my arms and I comforted him. "There, there."

I heard George sigh. "There is no 'there, there' to the situation. Did you draw upon my wall, young man?"

Jacky did not answer and held me tighter.

"Let go of your mother, Jacky. Stand up like a man and accept responsibility for your actions."

With difficulty I let go of him and was relieved when he did indeed stand alone.

"Did you write upon my wall?"

He did not answer.

"Did you?"

I could not suffer the moment any longer. "He did. We all know he did." I tried to apply a sterner voice. "You should not do that, Jacky dear. If you need writing paper, I will make sure you have—"

"He has plenty of paper at his disposal. This has nothing to do with a lack of paper. It has to do with a lack of respect for the property of others."

Jacky was back, clinging to my side.

"He will not do it again, George. I am sure he will not." I lifted Jacky's chin to look at me. "You will not, my dear boy?"

Jacky smiled and shook his head.

George tossed his hands in the air. "Dear boy? You coddle him. He is not a dear anything when he acts this way."

"He is always dear to me, and he has said he will not do it again."

"He has not *said* anything. He has not said what I am waiting to hear."

Ah. I stroked the top of Jacky's head. "Tell your poppa you are sorry."

"I am . . . I am sorry."

"There," I said. "He is sorry and all is well. Now go off to play, dearest, and I will be with you—"

George shook his head. "It is not all well. There is something that needs to be done to rectify your naughtiness." He looked pointedly at Jacky. "You know what needs to be done, my boy. You know what needs to be done in order to make it right. I expect you to make the appropriate reparations."

"He does not know what *reparations* means, George."

"He knows. He knows exactly what I mean. Don't you, Jacky?"

Jacky did not move, shake his head, or nod.

George strode to the foyer and donned his hat. "I must go check on the north fields. When I get back I expect all will be as it should."

"Why not take Jacky with you?" I asked. "He so enjoys riding—"

His look made me stop. He went outside.

Jacky let go. "I hate when he is angry at me."

"He is not really angry. But you need to try harder to be a good boy, and—"

Jacky ran for the front door. "I'm going outside."

"But, Jacky, you need—"

And he was gone.

I looked back to the study. I had hoped he would do what his stepfather had asked. I too wished for peace in the household. If only we agreed upon how to achieve it.

Three hours passed in which I was consumed with overseeing the curing of meat in the smokehouse. My legs were tired and I longed for a moment to rest them. I entered the main house from the back, and upon passing by George's study, I remembered his implication that Jacky should clean the wall.

I prayed my son had done so.

I entered the room and was confronted with the drawings, untouched. George would be returning from the fields soon. . . .

There was only one thing to do.

I went outside to the pump and filled a pail with water. I gathered a cloth and soap and returned to the study.

I got upon my knees and began the work.

Later that evening, I overheard George telling Jacky, "I am proud of you, son. Don't you feel the better for making amends and cleaning the wall?"

Without a moment's hesitation, Jacky said, "Yes, sir."

I felt a twinge of resentment, and another of an odd emotion: fear. It was disconcerting that Jacky had taken credit for work he had not done. And the ease with which he had accepted praise for it . . .

I let the twinge pass. If it would bring peace to the house, I was willing to let it slide.

It came. It finally came.

Before we moved to Mount Vernon, we had spent much time in Williamsburg while George attended the meetings at the House of Burgesses. During my free time I had come up with an idea of a gift for my new husband. One afternoon, with the children in tow, I had sought a notable jeweler and made my order. I had hoped to receive it before the session of the government was concluded, but George became suddenly concerned about the spring sowing, and we had left early to make our way to Mount Vernon.

Although I had wished to delay, I could not very well say, *But, dearest, I need to stay because I have ordered you a gift.* 'Twould have ruined the surprise, and as a plantation wife, I knew the green earth and crops waited for no man.

Or woman.

But now, the gift was created and the delivery made. But how to best give it? 'Twas not George's birthday till February, and even Christmas was too distant. And our anniversary was in the January in between. . . . There was no special occasion looming.

Except that I loved him and wanted him to have it.

Perhaps 'twas reason enough.

And so, I waited for a day in which we were not too busy and he was not too exhausted over his hard work. I waited for a day when things went well, when he had no pressing worries upon his mind. I waited for a time when we were alone. And on that day, in that time . . .

George set his boots outside the door to our bedchamber for his servant to make clean from the day's dust and dirt. He shut the door and stretched. Then, with a groan, he pulled upon his shoulder.

An idea surfaced.

"Come," I said, moving behind the bench of my dressing table. "Sit and let me rub your shoulders."

"Gladly. You have the mightiest, tiniest hands in the county, my dear. My shoulders thank you in advance."

He sat upon the bench and I began kneading his sore muscles. "They are tight as knots," I said.

"They do not always agree with what I ask them to do." He hung his head forward and moaned slightly. I did my best to make good work of my goal, knowing tomorrow my hands would ache for the effort.

George was not greedy. After but a few minutes, he lifted his head, reached a hand back toward mine and said, "Thank you, my dear."

It was time. Quickly, I said, "Just a moment more." I reached back to the place behind my jewelry box where I had hid the present. I quickly unclasped the silver chain and reached it round his neck.

"What? What is this?" he asked, putting a hand upon the pendant that hung low against his chest.

I connected the clasp and moved to see the result. " 'Tis a locket I had made for you while we were in Williamsburg. Open it."

His large fingers made trouble of it, but he managed to release its catch. " 'Tis a picture of you."

"I had it painted one afternoon while you were at a session. I had the locket made to fit."

He gazed upon the miniature, a bit beyond an inch in length. "Though it does not do the subject justice, 'tis a nice likeness."

"I think he made my eyes too close together, but the nose and mouth are right."

"It is lovely," he said, pulling me onto his lap. "I will wear it always. This way, whether near or far away, we will always be together."

"Near or far? You are not planning to go—"

"No, no. I am here for good. Of that you can be certain. There is nowhere else in the world I wish to go, nor anything else I wish to be but your husband." He took my hand and placed it upon the locket, which lay against his heart.

I had made a good choice.

In so many things, in so many ways.

～ Six ～

I felt his lips upon my cheek. "Mmm" was all the response he
required each morning when he arose at four, leaving me to sleep.
He shaved, dressed in the clothes Ned had laid out for him the
night before, and descended to his study to put in many hours of work
before breakfast.

Of late he was worried about tobacco. The soil at Mount Vernon
was not of good quality because tobacco was a crop hard on the soil,
and the demand for and price of tobacco were both undergoing a
decline. Tobacco was now bringing half the price it had a year ago, and
by the time all took their cut, we only received twenty-five percent of
what it was sold for—and from that we had to pay production costs.
George had ordered many books from England written about new
agricultural methods. He had studied them intently, knowing changes
had to be made if our plantation would prosper. He had mentioned
both wheat and corn because there had been bad wheat harvests in
Europe, creating a need. George was much interested in trying out
new seeds, and kept meticulous records. He also had the affairs of
my White House plantation to attend to—land, crops, slaves, and
overseers spread over many counties. As I was relieved of this burden,

his burden was increased manyfold. Plus, there were the numerous London factors to attend to. . . .

He was still much in debt. While he had been in the military, Mount Vernon had sustained itself but not prospered. Although unfortunate, it was expected. Without the landlord present, work was accomplished in its own time and to a lesser degree.

I knew George had overextended himself to make the main house nice for us. Its mahogany furnishings, Wilton carpets, Chinese porcelain, silver cutlery with the Washington coat of arms, and other accoutrements were all very fine. *Fine* was a word George used often to describe the quality he longed to possess. We even ordered a four-poster bed with fluted mahogany pillars for feet posts. It had blue-on-white chintz for the bed curtains, quilt, festoons adorning the cornices, and chair covers. And though I appreciated his efforts (as well as his good taste and his bow to my favourite colour), I regretted I was partially the cause of his current predicament.

And yet, what would I have thought if I had come to a home of only four rooms, with pewter plates, odd pieces of furniture, and natty bed linens? I had grown up with nice things and upon marrying Daniel had been exposed to goods of an even higher degree. That George had surpassed the quality of what I owned at White House was to his credit, but . . . but did I *need* it? Did I long for that quality to such an extent that I expressed a level of disappointment at its lack—albeit unintentionally?

If I was honest with myself, I would have to say yes. If liking fine things was a sin, I was guilty. If preferring a lovely teacup to a spun mug of pottery was against the will of the Lord, then I had apologies to offer.

However . . . when you take any woman off the road and offer her china or tin, silk or homespun, she will choose the better product. 'Tis human nature. It would not take even the poorest of men long to become used to such niceties and to suffer disappointment if they were suddenly taken away. No indeed, the sin did not lie in the enjoyment, but in the worship of luxury at the expense of the worship of God.

Of this sin, I strived to remain innocent. All things—fine or not—belonged to the Lord, and if He should choose to take them all away from us, I would grieve (and ponder why) but finally accept His will as superior to our own. George and I both believed the Almighty had His reasons for all things. We relished the occasion when He let us in on the secret.

Though at other times, I still did not understand why I lost two sweet babies . . . and Daniel.

And yet if I had not lost Daniel, I would not have married George. Not that one man was better than the other, but there was something about George that hinted of a destiny beyond the norm. I had no proof and had received no signs. But my intuition as a woman, as a wife, as a human being with an intellect and sense that had its own level of merit . . .

Mark my words, there was a reason beyond our knowing that caused me to marry George Washington. There was some upcoming fate that would lead both of us—as a pair—to some great challenge.

But as for now . . .

Although I tried to go back to sleep, I could not.

So go the annoying meanderings of a morning mind.

⸺⸺

Dawn was usually my alarm clock, but today, mind racing, I arose before its rays reached the windows.

So be it. There were guests in the house who would want breakfast at seven.

After dressing I went downstairs and unlocked the food stores. I removed enough for the day's needs at the mansion, as well as the food for the workers at the Mansion House Farm and the four other Washington farms nearby: the Dogue Run Farm (named after the

Dogue Creek that edged it), Union Farm, Muddy Hole Farm, and River Farm. Each had separate overseers and workers, and all had to be fed. And clothed.

With wealth came great responsibility. My father and mother oft cited the verse *"For unto whomsoever much is given, of him shall be much required: and to whom men have committed much, of him they will ask the more."* My days were full of requirements and those asking for more.

Addie, the cook, must have seen my light, for she appeared, her cap askew, still tying her apron. "Mistress? Has there been a change in plans?"

"Breakfast should still be at seven. Four guests, the children, Mr. Washington, and I."

I saw her relief that I had not added to her burden. "I will get you some tea."

"That would be much appreciated."

———

No one left one of my breakfasts hungry.

Except, perhaps, my husband.

Mr. Tanner was the first to notice George's Spartan tastes—while his own plate was heaped with ham, chicken, eggs, spoon bread, biscuits, and hominy doused with molasses. "Are you not hungry this morning, Mr. Washington?"

George poured honey over his cornmeal Indian cakes. "I have many hours on horseback ahead of me. My steed appreciates my partaking of lighter fare."

"Tea and Indian cakes," I said. "That is all I can ever get him to eat no matter what delicacies I produce."

Mrs. Tanner licked her fingers noisily. "I simply must have the recipe for this sweet bread. 'Tis lusciously delicious."

I nodded. Visitors were often asking for recipes. Many were my

mother's. And her mother's. I often wished I shared George's preference for light fare because my family's penchant for plumpness was not
aided by my fondness for the breads. Yet if the host *and* the hostess
did not partake of the foods offered, the guests might feel the need to
restrain themselves. The duty of any hostess was to ensure her guests
ate unto their limit.

"Would you like some more coffee, Mr. Tanner?"

"Yes, please. 'Tis very rich and flavorful."

"We had it sent from Jamaica."

"It is excellent." He turned to my husband. "I would love to hear
about your exploits in the Ohio Valley, Colonel."

I saw a familiar look pull across George's face. He put his fork
down, took a final sip of his tea, and stood. "I would love to discuss it
with you, Mr. Tanner, but I am afraid my duties will not wait."

He kissed me on the cheek and, with a bow, left the room.

"Well, then," Mrs. Tanner said. She looked appalled, as if George's
departure had offended her.

I had little tolerance for such opinions. I was more than willing
to open my house to visitors, however weak the thread that bound
us—the Tanners were cousins of George's sister Betty's husband—but
I would not, could not, let them undermine the to-dos of the day.

In fact, I had my own departure planned. During my first year as
a wife, married to Daniel, I had discovered that guests had a tendency
to monopolize my time—if allowed. And so, I did not allow it.

One particular time we had guests for a week. My preference
was to have an hour's worth of quiet time after breakfast, alone in my
room, reading the Bible or some sermons, and praying. No one was
to disturb me at this one time that was my own. And God's.

But during the second day of the guests' week-long visit, upon
missing my quiet time twice due to their unending ability to chat
about absolutely everything and nothing, I created myself a new policy:
an hour after breakfast commenced, I retired to my room, leaving
the guests with suggestions of good reading material in books and

newspapers, a walk in the garden, or a play upon our harpsichord. I made a point of saying I was retiring for a biblical communion with our Lord. I found that no one then—nor since—had the gumption to argue with me.

I glanced at the clock on the mantel. Twenty minutes to go . . .

"Have some more ham, Mr. Tanner."

I was a worrier. 'Twas not a good trait to own. In fact . . .

I sat in our room during my quiet time, the words of the Bible open before me: *Therefore I say unto you, Take no thought for your life, what ye shall eat, or what ye shall drink; nor yet for your body, what ye shall put on. Is not the life more than meat, and the body than raiment? Behold the fowls of the air: for they sow not, neither do they reap, nor gather into barns; yet your heavenly Father feedeth them. Are ye not much better than they? Which of you by taking thought can add one cubit unto his stature?*

But alas, I took only partial comfort in the words. For I did not worry about food or clothing. In those needs, my life was heartily complete.

I read the verses again, searching for contentment regarding the concern that haunted my thoughts. Only the last verse offered any hope of peace. I knew I should not worry because it did no good to worry, and yet . . .

Why was I not with child? It was not as though . . . George and I were close, as a husband and wife should be. And I was obviously capable, having given birth to four children in six short years. Was something wrong with me? Or . . . I could not imagine George was to blame—although he *had* suffered smallpox while traveling with his brother in Barbados. . . . Yet what more virile, healthy sort could there be than my George?

Women bore children. It was a fact that was oft complained about for its frequency. Never had I heard anyone complain about a lack of pregnancy. There was no other who would understand. My mother had given birth to nine children, the last, Mary—born the same year as my Patsy. Mother had been forty-six at the time of Mary's birth. My sister Nancy, married not even three years, had already borne one child and was expecting another. George's sister, Betty, already had five children and could expect many more. Large families were the bastion of our lives. Not having children was unheard of.

Nearly.

There was one neighbour who might give me insight or comfort or . . . I was not certain what I sought, nay, what I truly needed. Only that I needed to speak to some other woman about my condition—or lack thereof.

And that someone was—had to be—childless Sally Fairfax.

I called upon her alone. 'Twas not my habit to do such a thing with any of our neighbours, and yet this was not a visit where I wished George to be present. Nor the children. Nor even a driver. My plan was to travel the four miles to Belvoir, talk with Sally, and return before George or her George William ever knew of the exchange. 'Twas not that either husband would object to our friendly discourse—we had exchanged visits many times over the past year—but if asked the reason for the visit . . . I did not wish to lie, and though I did not know with certainty Sally would suffer the same compunction, I did not wish to force a lie upon her.

And so I went. Alone. To seek satisfaction of any sort. The entire four miles was spent in prayer, seeking wisdom. Seeking solace. Seeking answers and divine help.

Sally greeted me at the door of the grand parlour. "My dear Martha," she said, kissing my cheek. "What a wonderful surprise. Do come in." She turned to the butler and ordered tea and scones, then settled into the blue damask chair near the settee upon which I had settled. "So then. What has brought you out on this beautiful autumn day?" Although on other occasions I had taken pleasure in bantering with

Sally, on this day I had neither the inclination nor the ability. "The subject of children brings me here."

Her forehead furrowed. "Are Jacky and Patsy all right?"

"They are fine," I said. "My subject lies in the . . . the lack . . ." Oh dear. I had thought I would feel free with someone as outspoken and bold as Sally to just say it. Just state my concern and be—

"You have been married . . . ?"

"Two years in January," I said.

" 'Tis not *that* long a time, Martha. I have been married near eleven years and we have no . . ."

I nodded. "Which is why I come to you, to try to understand, to learn what to do, to find solace, to . . ." I took a new breath. "Honestly, I do not know exactly why I have come, except I knew that you, of all people, might understand my anxiety."

Sally's eyes grew blank, as though she had left the room and had entered a place of her own thoughts. "Many times I have asked God why. Why has He not blessed us with children?" She blinked once, returning her eyes to this time and this place. "Especially since the entire Fairfax inheritance—which as you know is extensive—rides upon an heir. Old Sir Thomas never married, hates women, and has no direct heirs."

"Why does he hate women?"

"He was spurned at the altar in quite a dramatic fashion and as such, will take no brook of the female sex."

"But surely as a cousin, your George William will—"

"For now we have his favor, but 'tis tenuous. The next generation must be secured, and . . ." She fingered the lace upon her sleeve, looked at me beneath her lashes, then away. "There are other issues—totally unfair and unfounded, but nonetheless embraced by Lord Fairfax and his associates back in England."

My George had told me the smallest bit of the rumours, assuring me they were not at all true. But it was not my place to reveal this knowledge. If Sally chose to tell me, then I would offer comment. If not . . .

Sally placed her hands into her lap, letting them find company, one with the other. "There is rumour of mixed blood in the Fairfax line. George William's father wed a woman in the West Indies. It is intimated she may have been of . . . of mixed heritage."

She waited for me to comment. "Oh" was all I dared say.

She stood and began to pace between the chairs and the fireplace. "People in England do not understand, do not have any tolerance for even a hint of . . . If it *were* true, by now the association would be so diluted it makes no difference to me, nor should it to anyone, but those people in England . . ." She stopped her movement and faced me, her lip curled in distaste. "They flaunt themselves as superior and above our lives here, and hold the treasures we need at arm's distance, as though only those without taint might dare step across the ocean and touch—" Her face had grown red, her words fierce. She returned to her chair. "Forgive me. I have no tolerance for such things. Did you know a few years ago, after my father-in-law died, George William took more than one trip to England with the purpose of showing all those cretins he is not a Negro's son? He had some aunts who were positive he would turn dark upon puberty."

"I had no idea."

"And then there is the issue . . ." She shook her head. "Lord Thomas does not like me. Not one bit. On my honour I know of nothing I have done to offend him except by achieving guilt through the unpardonable offense of being female."

"Has Lord Thomas indicated you and George William will *not* be his heirs?"

"Of course not. He dangles his title and treasure for his pleasure. At the moment, we serve a purpose here, managing his riches. We are the only heir who resides in the colonies. The others are willing to take the spoils, but have no wish to leave their soft English beds."

I did not know what to say. Although I longed for more

children—for George's children—I had not the pressure nor consequence of barrenness Sally endured.

She seemed to remember the core of our discussion and put a hand upon my knee. "Forgive me. I rant and rail upon things you did not need to hear. You are worried about future children. I feel for you, Martha. I truly do. For George is a gentleman through and through, a man of not only physical but emotional, spiritual, and intellectual stature. As such I cannot imagine God would not want his—and your—progeny to cover the earth."

Suddenly, I realized the immensity of her concession. The support it extended in spite of their . . . history. With one more look at her sincere eyes, her flushed cheeks, her determined jaw, I fully relinquished any residual jealousy to the past. Sally and I were both safely and irrevocably married to our respective Georges. We were neighbours living in a land where every neighbour counted. And most of all, we were women with common aspirations and dreams.

Sally looked toward the door. "Ah. Tea. Very good."

And it was.

On the way home from Sally's, I determined, through no proof or sign from above but through my own desire for a logical explanation, that God had not blessed us with children because I was not a good enough mother.

I vowed to remedy that deficit in every way possible.

I would be an exceptional mother.

Our future depended upon it.

Although I enjoyed teaching the children, with George's doubling the size of Mount Vernon (he purchased over eighteen hundred acres and was on the lookout for more), with his doubling the number of tenant farmers in his Ohio Valley land to eighteen, with his becoming obsessed with three dozen new fruit trees and a desire to create hardy strains of cherry, peach, and apricot . . .

I was exhausted, for each increase in our worth added to the work. Mount Vernon was becoming the essence of a small town, and its administration fell upon our shoulders. I was glad for the help I had within the house—I had grown up in a household where workers were needed in the fields and could not be spared in the house—but even so, the children suffered the attention to education they needed.

And so we hired a tutor.

Walter McGowan was an amiable Scotsman with a zest for learning and teaching. The children adored him, and I respected his ability to make them keep to their lessons. Jacky was always one to put play before work, yet under Mr. McGowan's tutelage kept to the books and thrived. Besides the basics in reading, writing, and numbers, Mr. McGowan requested we purchase books on Greek grammar, history, geography, and bookkeeping. It afforded me great joy to pass the parlour and see the children bent over paper or book, or hear them heartily singing their alphabet or answering Mr. McGowan's questions. The tutor's accent was delightful, though I did worry just a bit when it began to rub off on the children. When Patsy said, "Nay, I canna go to bed yet, Mamma," and Jacky said, "I dinnae know where my shoes maeght be," I nearly said something to Mr. McGowan, but ended up not. He was a good influence, though if the children asked me to cook haggis and neeps and tatties, I would have had to decline.

Yet as a member of Virginia society, I knew that book learning was only part of the knowledge required. Music held a vast place in every family's life, and ours was no different. Although George could not carry a tune and had never learned to play an instrument, he was adamant the children received a proper musical upbringing.

This was accomplished in many ways. Firstly, we employed the services of a traveling musician, Mr. Christian, who visited Mount Vernon and the homes of our neighbours three or four days a month.

He taught our children to dance, and Mr. Stedlar (a German who lauded himself as a "musick professor") joined in to teach the children to sing and play instruments. So successful were these sessions that neighbour children were added to the group, culminating in evening dances where the adults joined in. I always enjoyed these times. They were the highlight of every month. Although dance was not my passion, it *was* George's, and he took full advantage of each occasion. He was much appreciated by all the ladies.

George supported these efforts and even ordered Patsy a flute and a spinet from London. For Jacky he ordered a violin, but knowing the instrument maker would send their worst violin once they knew it was coming to the Americas, George wisely asked our factor, Mr. Cary, to imply it was an instrument for him. There were ways to work within the system, flawed though it was.

I was very involved in the vocal aspect of their education, having received a wonderful book of English songs called *The Bull Finch*. The first time George ever wrote my married name was when he inscribed it to me the first year we were married. Mr. Stedlar has been of assistance helping us determine which melodies went with the words. Oh, if only the books would supply more than the lyrics!

One evening I sang a new song I had learned called "Gifts." I sang it for George because it imbued his philosophy of life—and more. I stood by the spinet and cast my eyes right upon him. Then I sang . . .

"Give a man a horse he can ride,
Give a man a boat he can sail;
And his rank and wealth, his strength and health,
On sea nor shore shall fail.

"Give a man a pipe he can smoke,
Give a man a book he can read:
And his home is bright with a calm delight,
Though the room be poor indeed.

"Give a man a girl he can love,
As I, O my love, love thee;
And his heart is great with the pulse of Fate,
At home, on land, on sea."

I received applause, and capped the moment by moving to my husband's side and kissing his cheek. I whispered, " 'As I, O my love, love thee . . .' "

He blushed.

I so enjoyed the power of music.

———

The years passed.

'Tis such a relentless statement, yet true. Our life at Mount Vernon became a journey upon a familiar road. We grew to know the ruts and curves, yet were occasionally surprised—but still managed—the detours, delays, and trees fallen in our way.

Having barely known each other before marriage, George and I came to close acquaintance. One might think this was a given after years of marriage, as inevitable as fire creating ash, or an apple tree apples, but I knew from speaking with other women friends that it was not necessarily so. Two souls must desire close bonding for them to be bound. We had the desire. The procurement of the end result . . . ?

As expected, there were adjustments to be made—some willingly, and others with more reluctance.

I heard one of George's friends state that George was a master of himself. This was true.

Too true.

George had a temper. Only rarely did I witness its fury. The time in question came after a worker had been caught stealing—not from us, but from another worker. To worsen his situation the man lied about it. I watched from a distance, but I could still hear my husband's shouts of anger. And then, when the man had the audacity to shrug,

George jumped from his horse and took him by a wad of his shirt and nearly lifted him off the ground.

I could not hear the words said with face nearly touching face, but when George let go, the man stumbled and ran away. Obviously, enough had been said to eradicate any chance of another shrug—or act of theft and deceit.

At the time, I had not realized Jacky was in close proximity, but upon seeing the man run away, he came close to me and said, "Poppa will not get that angry at *us*, will he?"

I could honestly say, "Never" but did use the moment to say, "Lying and indifference are as unconscionable as stealing, young man. You must strive to be a man of honour, to do your poppa and me proud at all times."

Jacky nodded fervently.

My husband's anger did not bother me. Nor did his penchant for wanting things done in *his* time, in *his* way. He seemed to know what everyone was doing. One time he became convinced his workers could get more lumber each day from the trees they felled. They had the audacity to disagree. So George spent an entire day observing their work (with watch in hand) and found they could produce five more feet of lumber a day. A four percent increase. That they did so in the imposing presence of the master of the plantation did not surprise me.

Although he was the master to others, it did not take George long to realize I did not react well to barked orders. Only once did I have to remind him, "I am not one of your soldiers, George." His apology had been profuse and the offense had not been repeated.

No, I was not bothered by his strong nature; in fact, I was heartened by the depth of emotion it represented. My husband was a man of distinct virtues and expected the same virtues from others. If he had a tendency to be relentless in the pursuit of the goals he set for himself (and for others), if he oft showed a critical nature, I knew it was due to the high standards to which he held everyone—of the foremost himself. Most plantation wives complained of their husbands not helping enough. With George, he oft helped too much—he needed to have a hand in everything.

Yet if I had any real complaint regarding his nature it would be the distance which seemed ever present. Although I knew life touched him deeply—both the good and the bad—it could not oft be witnessed through his bearing and countenance. I knew that many thought him cold and aloof. Impassive. At first even I thought he owned those traits. But as the years passed, I grew to see that this barrier to emotion was one that was carefully placed and maintained, partly to benefit the witness and partly to benefit George himself. 'Twas as though a fire burned within him that he dared not fuel through any cleft or fissure in character lest it consume himself and all others in his path.

I respected this control, and yet . . .

One evening, when I knew he had experienced a foul day, he sat by the fire, staring into it. He could have been a statue for the lack of movement in his bearing. Only by the twitching of the small muscles that lined his neck and jaw could I see the battle he fought within.

After watching him as long as I could bear, I knelt beside his chair and put my hand upon his. "Tell me what happened today. I heard there was a fire at the Muddy Hole Farm."

Fires were never welcomed, of course, but I had heard all was under control. The damage to the outbuildings was not too great.

"Is it something else?" I asked. "Was there something else that disturbed your work today?"

He did not even look at me but continued to grace the fire with his attention.

"Please, George. Tell me what bothers you so."

He swallowed, but with difficulty. He was holding something back.

I tried another tack. If imploring words would not incite him to share his concerns . . . I stood and said, "I am your wife. I work as hard as any man on this plantation to make it what we want it to be.

If you do not share with me the situations and conditions that affect us all, then—"

"My brother has died."

"Who? Which . . . ?"

"Austin. He died of tuberculosis." For the first time, he looked directly at me. "He was only forty-two. My other brother Lawrence died of the same disease at thirty-four. My father, at only forty-nine."

And George had just turned thirty. . . .

"I oft have coughs and breathing ailments," he said. "They dog me. Are they my destiny? Will they be the death . . . ?"

He did not finish the sentence. I knelt beside him again. "There is nothing to say you will die as they have. You take great pains to keep yourself healthy. And you are not alone. I am here to watch over you, and I will not let anything happen to you. By God I will not."

The faintest of smiles came—and went, as despair and fear returned. I watched his face struggle to contain them.

I put a hand on the back of his head. "George. You do not need to hold your worries inside."

"I do."

"No, you do not. Not with me."

With his nod of reluctant agreement, he allowed me to take him into my arms, where I made every attempt to make all things right.

— S E V E N —

A visit to my family back in Chestnut Grove was a special treat. My brothers William and Bartholomew came to visit with their families, and I took great pleasure in spending time with my sisters Elizabeth, Nancy, and her dear husband, Burwell, and my littlest sister, Mary.

George could not take time to accompany me, but as a treat for Mary, I brought Patsy along as a playmate. The two little girls, both nearly eight, gave us many joyful moments.

I left Jacky behind at Mount Vernon. George had suggested it be so, had actually suggested I might enjoy my family visit more without the burden of my children. I could not do such a thing in good conscience and was going to bring them both, until Jacky was so naughty that the very thought of having him with me brought with it a measure of exhaustion that seemed beyond my ken.

Mother asked me about his absence. "He must have done something extremely bad," she said at dinner the first evening of my visit.

"He is a good boy. Generally," I hedged.

"He is a boy," Nancy said. "And as such needs a firm hand. I imagine George provides just what he needs."

He would like to. I could not tell them of my inability to let my husband father the children in full. It was an unexplainable compunction on my part, and one that did not make me proud. "I try to keep the children close by. There is so much upon a plantation which can harm, and . . ." I took the moment to turn around to find little Pat.

"She is fine. She is with Mary and the nanny," Mother said. She gave me an admonishing look. "You must relax, my dear. The children will be fine."

"The children may not be fine. You have not lost—" I stopped the words I had oft used against George. In the present case they did not suit, for my mother had also lost two children. And a husband.

"My children were lost when they had grown past the early years of childhood. John was seventeen and Fanny but thirteen," she said.

"This is supposed to comfort me?"

"This is supposed to remind you that death is not prejudiced against the very young. It comes when it chooses."

"That is why—"

She held up a finger. "That is why you cannot spend time worrying beyond a normal degree. Too much worry skews happiness, Martha. You must be happy when it is time to be happy, and leave sadness and fear for the time of sadness and fear."

Elizabeth closed her eyes and quoted a verse: " 'To every thing there is a season, and a time to every purpose under the heaven: A time to be born, and a time to die; a time to plant, and a time to pluck up that which is planted . . . A time to weep, and a time to laugh; a time to mourn, and a time to dance.' "

I nodded. I knew how things should be, yet seemed unable to do what I should do.

"Enough admonition—for the moment," Mother said. "Tell us what Jacky did that has kept him at Mount Vernon without his dear mamma."

I was more than willing to set my own indiscretions aside toward the naming of my son's. "George has purchased a fishing schooner to sail the Potomac and into the Chesapeake. If good catches continue, he says we shall take one million fish from the tidewater this year."

Nancy shook her head, incredulous. "Surely not one *million*?"

"Surely it is so," I said. "The very number boggles my mind e'en as it pleases me. For one million fish means fish that need to be cleaned and salted and sealed in barrels to be sold in the colonies and West Indies. George says there is great profit in it, and I believe him. And this is not accounting the profit of serving fish to the people at Mount Vernon with great regularity."

"Your George is very industrious," Elizabeth said.

"Beyond measure," I said.

"So," Mother continued. "What did our little Jacky do?"

"He was down at the dock with George and the overseer, watching the crew bring in a good portion of the catch."

"He did not fall in, did he?" Nancy asked.

"No, no. But he did dive into the river. To swim."

There was a moment of silence. "Had he not swum there before? I seem to remember you saying—"

"Yes, yes, he swims in the Potomac all the time, with the children of the slaves, and his neighbour friends."

"Then what was the problem?" Mother asked.

I could not attest to *my* problem and focused on my son's. "He and the boys were being exuberant and . . . and he nearly drowned."

Nancy put a hand to her chest. "Oh, Martha, no! Not like—"

Perhaps they *would* understand. "Our brother John, yes. If John drowned in the lowly Pamunkey River when he was seventeen, with the strength and constitution of a man, then how can I not worry about a nine-year-old, with a reckless manner and no thought to danger or common sense or—"

"I am surprised you are here, then," Mother said. "If Jacky nearly drowned . . ."

Oh dear. I had taken the story in a direction that was not completely forthcoming.

Elizabeth stood. "You must go home, Martha. As much as I relish our time together, if poor Jacky—"

I felt Mother watching me, and she was the one to halt Elizabeth's discourse with a hand. "Jacky did not nearly drown, did he?"

She knew me too well, read me like the page of a book. "Well, no. Though I do hate the rough play, he is quite a strong swimmer and George says I worry too much and that boys need to be allowed to be boys and—"

"He did something naughty." Mother said it as a statement. For beyond knowing me, she also knew her grandson.

I could avoid it no longer. "After swimming, he ended up falling into . . . a crate of flopping fish."

The ladies round me were silent. I was not sure if it was for shock or—

Nancy began to laugh. Then Mother. Then Elizabeth.

" 'Twas not funny," I said. "The more he wiggled to get out, the deeper he went, until he was thoroughly covered with the smell and slime."

Mother covered her mouth with her hand. "He did not make good company for quite the time, I suspect."

"George had brought him down on horseback, but made him walk beside all the way to the house. Poor little—"

"Poor nothing. I am certain he was warned time and again to stay back."

Although I did not nod, I knew it was true.

"So he has been left behind as punishment," Nancy said.

"Well . . . actually . . ."

"You did punish him, Martha, didn't you?" Mother asked.

I did not. "George made him get cleaned up all by himself and wanted to make him wash his own clothes. I put a stop to that, as I thought the walk back home was punishment en—"

She shook her head. "You are too lenient. A boy of Jacky's age needs a firm hand or he will become a wild boy."

"My hand is plenty firm," I said.

"I do not see it," Mother said. She quoted me, " 'Poor little Jacky' indeed."

"So if you did not leave him behind as punishment, why is he not here?" Nancy asked.

The truth would not help my cause. "He wished to stay behind. With George."

"With the one who punished him." Mother nodded with far too much pleasure. " 'Tis interesting."

To my luck Patsy wailed from the next room. "If you will excuse me."

Dogs barking.

I snapped awake and sat erect in bed. It took me but a moment to remember I was at Chestnut Grove.

Away from home.

Away from George and Jacky.

It was still dark, but the dog . . . was a visitor coming with a message announcing horrible news that Jacky was ill or hurt in some accident?

The dog persisted. Old Joe did not bark for no reason.

I hurried to the window and peered into the darkness, looking for a horseman.

Out of the corner of my eye I spotted a deer running through the clearing toward the woods. The hound ran after it and both disappeared amid the trees.

The yard was silent but for the swish of the breeze through the branches.

Jacky is fine. There is no need to worry.

Need or no need, the worry remained.

To appease it, since I could not check upon my son, who was a four-days' ride away, I tiptoed to the hall and into my sister Mary's room, where my little Patsy had begged to sleep.

The two little girls lay together in bed. Mary had taken more covers than her share, so I gently pulled them away in order for my daughter to stay warm. Patsy murmured a sound of cozy warmth. I kissed her cheek, pushed a stray hair from her forehead, and left the room.

I returned to bed and adjusted my own covers against the coolness of the night.

Patsy was fine. Jacky was fine. I could sleep appeased by that knowledge.

I could sleep.

But I didn't.

I regularly thanked God for caps.

"Pin it up and tuck it under, Amanda," I told my maid. We were back at home and I had much to do to catch up. "I have neither time nor patience for the whims of my hair today."

Although I did not often despair at my hair, on some occasions it did not cooperate, or I did not have the time or inclination to have Amanda fiddle over it. Enter my thanks for the fashion of the cap. Although most ladies chose those that did not venture too high from the head, I preferred a cap that owned a bit of puff to it, one that gave the illusion of a height I do not own. When I am around the Dandridge side of our family, I do not feel out of place, for they are the source of my height. But when visited by George's side, or Sally and George William, I feel puny—in height at least.

My other complaint (since I felt petty) was that because of my small height and family propensity, I was plumper than I would like. Give me three or four more inches to stretch out my weight and I surely would have been stunning. Although some of my neighbours had ceased wearing corsets while at home, my vanity suggested I could not follow the comforts of their fashion. I wished to know who invented corsets. Most likely a man, attempting to torture us and keep us from true relaxation. My only concession was to order stays easy made, and in the summer months, very thin, for when the heat made any clothing unbearable. How comfortable we would be if not for the shame instigated in the Garden of Eden.

My, my, I was in a mood. And over such inconsequentials too. Such disrespect for priorities did not become me.

The children rushed into the room. They were dressed and ready for breakfast and their studies.

"Mamma!" Patsy ran to my side and climbed upon my lap. She was beginning to be too big, but I would never dare say as much. And blessedly, my dearest girl did not care whether my hair cooperated, or the height of my cap.

Jacky ignored me and began to jump upon the bed. I saw Amanda flash him a look, but she waited for me to chastise him.

"Come give your mamma a kiss, young man."

He jumped from the bed, nearly on top of Patsy, and did his duty. For this near-miss he did receive my ire. "You be careful of your sister. You nearly—"

Suddenly, I felt Patsy begin to tremble. My first inclination was that she was chilled, and I thought of getting her changed into a warmer dress or procuring a blanket. But that thought was gone in a blink as her entire body shook its way out of my arms, sliding onto the floor. I attempted to cushion her decline and focused on keeping her head from hitting too hard.

She continued to shake—with violent jerking—and her eyes rolled back in her head.

"Mamma!" Jacky yelled.

Amanda backed away.

I pointed at her. "Go send for my husband! Quickly!"

Amanda hesitated a moment, her face pulled with fear, but then she bolted from the room and I heard her calling out to the household. "Get the master! Get the master! Quickly!"

I realized her trumpeting would bring the curiosity of other servants. "Jacky, close the door!" My eyes returned to Patsy.

She was choking!

I tried lifting her head to a better position, but she flung out of my arms, hitting the floor with a thud.

"Hold her, Mamma!" Jacky said.

I tried, but she had the strength of a man and would not be contained. I moved the bench of my dressing table away so she would not flail against it. "The coverlet!" I yelled at Jacky.

He tossed me the coverlet that sat at the end of our bed. I attempted to wrap it around my daughter to cushion her limbs against the hardness of the wooden floor.

There was a knock on the door and Amanda reentered. "Is he coming?" I asked.

Her eyes scanned Patsy, then met mine. "He is at the River Farm, but I sent Linus to fetch him." She did not venture closer. "Can I . . . can I help?"

As suddenly as the seizure had taken her, Patsy was still. No one moved. I held my breath.

She opened her eyes and I moved into her sight line. "Sweet child! I am here. Mamma is here."

Patsy blinked slowly, as if returning from another place.

Jacky poked her shoulder. "What were you doing? You were shaking and—"

"Shh, son. Help me get her to bed."

We half carried, half walked Patsy to the mattress. She stared straight ahead and seemed groggy, in a daze. "Get her a glass of water, Amanda. And a damp cloth."

I tucked her limbs beneath the bedclothes and stroked her hair. "There, there, sweet girl. Mamma has you safe."

But did I?

An hour later I heard heavy footfalls on the stairs. George burst into the room. Seeing Patsy upon the bed, he raced to her side. "Dear girl. Are you all right?"

"I am fine, Poppa."

He looked to me. "Is she?"

I motioned him out of the room, leaving Patsy to play with Jacky. They were drawing pictures of horses.

I closed the door behind us. I told him all I had witnessed, and in addition told him she had no memory of the incident, and apparently felt no pain—though her right elbow was sore.

"It sounds like epilepsy," George said.

Oddly, I was glad it had a name. "You have heard of it?"

"Seen it. One of my soldiers fell into a fit once. Thrashed about wildly, knocking things over, hurting those who were trying to contain him. Some Indians saw it and said some word that meant *demon*."

"Demon!"

He took my hands, shaking his head. "No, no, dear. Please. I must learn what to share and what not. Apparently those without education have no other explanation but to say demons are involved. I have heard those in medieval times thought the same. But science has given it a name. Epilepsy."

"So there is a cure."

He let a breath go in, then out. "I do not think so." He brought my hands to his lips and kissed them. "But we will find one, my dear. I will send for Dr. Laurei immediately, and if he cannot help, then I will send for Dr. Rumney, and another doctor and another. I promise we will find the answers we need."

My husband always kept his promises.

—⋙⋘—

Dr. Laurei and I stepped out of Patsy's bedroom. His face was grave.

"Will she be better?" I asked.

"Has she suffered such a fit before?"

"No," George said.

"Any other oddness or loss of contact with the here and now?"

I could speak to *that* symptom. "She is known to fall asleep at odd times."

His eyebrows lifted. "How so?"

"Once she was playing with a doll, then suddenly seemed to stare into nothing. When I looked away, then back at her, she had fallen asleep. And she was not tired. I know she was not."

George nodded. "I have seen her so at supper. And one time seated by the fire. She has always been a quiet, pensive child, so I did not think anything wrong. Too wrong."

He had suspected something? Why had he not said anything to me?

Dr. Laurei continued. "I have no experience with this condition, but I will return to Alexandria and consult my books and others in my field. Then I will bring you medicines."

"So there are medicines that will cure her?"

He seemed confused. "I am sorry, Mrs. Washington. I am not aware of any cure."

I could not speak. But George asked, "What can we do when such a violent episode occurs?"

"You can move things out of her way, put a cushion beneath her head."

"But she choked," I said. "I feared—"

"I have heard of various iron rings to bite upon. I will look into it." He put one hand on each of ours. "I am sorry 'tis not better news. I will do my best to help her. I promise I will."

Another promise to be fulfilled.

———∞———

Dr. Laurei came again and brought with him various bromides and methods to rid Patsy's system of the poisons. He bled her. As another seizure was not forthcoming, we believed her better.

She was not. After a time the seizures returned. We requested the presence of other doctors, but none offered anything but conjecture and experiments. One even had the audacity to try to attempt comfort by saying Julius Caesar, Alexander the Great, and Joan of Arc were epileptic. I cared not a whit for this fact. My daughter was afflicted. Only she mattered.

I had been accused of being a hovering mother before, and now . . . my state of anxiety increased. How could it not? But then came the day when my worries were amplified beyond measure.

I was seated at Patsy's bedside after one of her fits. She slept and I kept watch—over what, I was uncertain.

George slipped into the dimly lit room. "How is she?"

"Other than the fact she is sleeping, I cannot answer your question. What are we going to do?"

He lowered his head as he shook it, and I noticed a piece of paper in his hand.

"What is that?" I asked.

He raised it up, lowered it, then raised it up again. " 'Tis a letter," he said.

"I can see that. Who is it from?"

His sigh was deep. "Your mother."

By the look on his face I knew the news was not good. "Please, George, just tell me. I am in no mood for foul news."

"Mood or not . . ." He did not raise the letter to read it, but did tell me its contents. "Your little sister, Mary, has died. A fever is all that is said, but you know how that symptom covers many afflictions and—"

I moved from my bedside vigil and nudged him into the hall. I shut the door. "Let me see."

George had not withheld any information. *Your dear little sister has died. A fever overtook her last Saturday and after three days, she succumbed.*

"No, no," I said. "This cannot be. She was the same age as our Patsy. She cannot be—" I did not allow myself to finish the sentence, for I knew too well death could do as it wished.

"I am so sorry, Martha," George said as he pulled me into his arms.

I pushed away from him. "Mary cannot die! If she dies, then our Patsy . . ." I knew it did not make sense to claim one with the other, but I did not care.

"What can I do to comfort you?" George asked.

I put my hand upon the doorknob. "There is no comfort for a child's death. I *know*."

"I know you do."

I opened the door a crack, then stopped the movement. I looked into his eyes. "You wish to know what you can do? Cure my daughter."

"Our daugh—"

I shut the door on him and went back to Patsy's bedside. There would be no more dying in this family. I would not allow it.

George did what he could. My insistence that he cure Patsy's affliction softened as I witnessed his efforts and expense to do just that. Our prayers became repetitive and I sometimes wondered if the Almighty might get weary of them. Yet until God gave me a healthy child . . . He would just have to endure our supplications.

Unfortunately, there were other issues that forced our attention and worries, the main one being finances.

I will admit to having exquisite taste. 'Twas a condition shared by both of us. And I must also admit to compensating for what we could not do to heal Patsy by buying her gifts. To see her squeal with joy when tiny kid gloves were delivered, or a silk dress to match mine, or pretties for her hair. We bought her a tea set and silver-plated spoons. And for Jacky . . . there was a miniature coach and six horses with a toy stable. We also endowed him with a gold-plated toy whip.

Anything purchased for the children came out of their portion of the Custis money. This was my idea, as George *was* a generous man and offered otherwise. And, of course, I had offered my money toward the betterment of Mount Vernon. No one was more pleased than I that our lands had increased from seventeen hundred to ninety-eight hundred acres. And George had done well with Jacky's holdings, doubling their value. In all honesty, we were taken by surprise when told all my cash was used. Yet, although our tastes *were* extravagant, there were other determining factors.

Although the tobacco crop taken from Jacky's Custis lands brought in twice the price as the Mount Vernon tobacco, one ship carrying our tobacco went down in the Bay of Biscay, and privateers took the goods from another. And the factors continued to tweak and twitter our money away as *they* saw fit. As we could only trade with England and no other country—by law—frustration became a close acquaintance. Plus, most of the goods we ordered were delivered to White House first because that is where the Custis factors were used to sending it. We then had to pay for transport to Mount Vernon. Oh, the letters we sent trying to rectify this change of address! Deaf ears. Deaf, or arrogant, or apathetic ears.

And even if we found a market for our goods within this land, each colony held their own currency for trade. Pounds sterling were used in common, but they were rare to find. George and his friends contended this was so arranged to keep us from trading with each other. Our England was adept at handling colonies and keeping them in line.

Personally, we were land rich and cash poor. 'Twas not an unusual trait for gentry, but it did add to the stress of our lives. Many a time I found George at his desk with papers and bills spread around him, trying to manipulate the numbers for our livelihood. The last time . . .

He let out a sigh and leaned back in his chair with a *humph*. " 'Tis not their fault," he said.

I stopped dusting the books on the shelf nearby. "Whose fault?"

"Our factors. The merchants back in England. Their prices have been raised because they are being taxed to pay the country's debt for the Seven Years War."

"Which war?"

"The Seven Years War. That is what they have named the fighting within Europe while here we fought the French and the Indians. Apparently, Britain is in debt to the tune of one hundred million pounds and partially blames us."

"So Englishmen are taxed?"

"They are. It is said the unfairness of the taxation has forced forty thousand Englishmen into debt—forced them into debtor's prison."

"Hardly what the government wished."

"And as such, and with the rebellion among the populace there, they have withdrawn many of those taxes."

"That is good," I said as I dusted a copy of Plato's *Republic*.

"That is bad," George said. "For the crown still needs money to pay off the war. And so they have decided to tax us."

"Us?"

"The colonies. They say it is because we need to pay for the troops stationed here to defend us. Personally, I would like them to leave. We have proven—with the bravery of our volunteer troops—that we can defend ourselves. We no longer wish to be under their control."

"I am sure they would beg to differ."

He shrugged. "We all know any tax has more to do with past debts than new ones. It is the first time in fifty years Britain is not at war. I accuse them of having too much time on their hands."

I left the books alone and took a seat before his desk. "What kind of tax are they inflicting upon us?" I asked.

"The proclamation that called it into place is called the Stamp Act. All papers here in the colonies are taxed and a purchased stamp is placed upon them: newspapers, documents, every printed piece of paper, and even playing cards."

"That is absurd."

"Indeed. Although I have never admired taxation, I accepted it when it seemed a natural part of trade, but when it seems extraneous and is being used to pay for debts England has incurred . . . They have already taxed molasses, food, and wine."

I assessed the full impact of his words. "There can only be disadvantage if we refuse to pay."

George shrugged. " 'Tis not just our disadvantage. Taxes which cause us to buy fewer items from England will hurt those who manufacture those items. Who is to suffer most in this event—the English merchant or the Virginia planter?"

"I care most about the latter."

"We pay either way," he said. "And if we do not pay . . . the Stamp Act declares we will be punished in court, without a trial by jury."

I thought of the poor quality of goods we often received and the prices that continued to rise. "I am weary of paying, constantly paying . . ."

"As are we all."

"But what can be done about it?"

"I am not certain, but when the House meets in May, I am sure we will hear talk of it."

"You do not embrace dissension, do you, George?"

"These colonies have existed for one hundred fifty years. We have prospered, created our own representative governments, have built towns and farms and societies rooted in virtue and personal liberties. British cities reel with murder, poverty, crime, and societal inequities. We have done it better. Why can they not see that and leave us to handle ourselves?"

I smiled at his passion and leaned closer, offering a whisper. "Treasonous thoughts, husband."

He looked shocked. "Not at all. I do not wish for trouble, just to be left alone to deal with things as we know best."

"Kings are not keen on letting go."

He looked back to the papers littering his desk. "I cannot think of that now. I must handle today, today."

"But Jacky. We were going to discuss Jacky's future."

"I cannot deal with Jacky's incorrigibility, Patsy's illness, unfair taxes, overdue bills, *and* this plantation, my dear. Not today."

Today, tomorrow . . . I knew from hard experience troubles were tenacious. More tenacious than I?

We would see.

⸘

Two months passed. In May George traveled to Williamsburg for the session of the House of Burgesses without us. I feared for Patsy and did not feel it would be wise for the children and me to travel. I *would* miss the balls and social events, but sacrifices had to be made. My duty was here. At home.

George was gone a month and when he returned I was more than willing to hand the running of the plantation back to him. Although, during this absence things *did* run in a smoother manner because, late of last year, George had hired a distant cousin, Lund Washington, to manage Mount Vernon. He had worked previously for a neighbour and came with high regard—which he deserved. Five years older than we, I found Lund to be an amiable bachelor, a fine asset to the estate.

Usually when George returned from a governmental session, he was weary of mind. But this time he fairly jumped from his horse as he rushed into the house.

I met him at the door. "What is wrong?"

He shook his head, handing me his hat and gloves. "Action has been taken against the Act!"

The only *act* of recent mind was the Stamp Act. "The session voted on it?"

"Of a sort." He noticed the dust on his boots and legs. "Outside. Come out. I am fouling the house with the dirt of the road."

We withdrew to the stoop, where he proceeded to brush off his clothing with a handkerchief as he gave his discourse. "For three weeks the House discussed nothing of more consequence than ferry permits and wolf bounties. Most members left and were on their way home—as was I. Only thirty-nine of the one hundred sixteen remained."

"When . . . ?"

"When a new member—nine days new—stood before those still present and offered some resolutions. If only I could have been there to hear . . . I received word Henry's zeal holds a power to mesmerize."

"Henry what—what is his last name?" I asked.

"His last *is* Henry. Patrick Henry."

"By your reaction I take his zeal to be of a positive nature?"

He stopped brushing to consider. "I am not certain as yet. But perhaps he is just what we need in this time. He offered forward five Stamp Act Resolves, which"—George smiled and shook his head—"which were nothing less than bold and courageous." His eyes sparkled as he faced me. "They stated as colonists we have the same rights as the English, in particular the right to be taxed only by our own representatives. Since we have no representation in England's Parliament, they should not tax us. We should not have to pay any taxes except those which our Virginia House decrees."

I stood in awe. "These resolves were passed?"

"They were, although a fifth one—stating that anyone who supported the right of Parliament to hold sway over us should be considered the enemy—was rescinded the next day, by an even smaller contingent still present."

I put a hand to my chest. "These . . . these sound nearly treasonous."

"The last one was indeed, which is why cooler heads . . . but the rest of them spoke with enough force they upset Governor Fauquier and he—" George shook his head in disbelief—"he dissolved the House of Burgesses. We are dissolved, Martha."

"I am not sure what that means."

"Alas, neither do we. But the resolutions, Martha. 'Tis the start of something."

"What exactly?"

"I am not sure, but change is in the air. I feel it."

———

News of the actions by Virginia's House sped north, and though there was general approval of the resolutions, as well as general disapproval of the Stamp Act, no other body of colonial government took action—until after the riots.

News came to us in various ways, in the form of letters from friends, from visitors who lived in other colonies, and through newspapers, which were often tardy with the news we had heard elsewhere.

One day Patsy came running into the dining room, where I was choosing the setting for a dinner party. She was crying hysterically. I immediately stopped what I was doing. "What is wrong? Shh, shh. Calm now. Calm." I imagined all sorts of injury but saw nothing of an obvious nature. And yet I knew strife often brought about one of her fits. She needed to be appeased, quickly.

She pressed her face into my shoulder. "He hung Marabel."

"Your doll?"

She nodded and pulled away enough to make her full accusation. She pointed toward the bedrooms upstairs. "Jacky. He hung her to death!"

At the first mention of *hung* I had imagined the doll being hung by a string, perhaps wrapped round her body. But at the dead comment . . . I imagined the worst.

I stood and Patsy was quick to take my hand and pull me toward the stairs. Although Jacky was often her ablest protector, he was also her keenest tormentor.

I found Jacky in his sister's bedroom, the doll duly hung—by the neck—from the back of a chair. Jacky stood guard over her with his toy sword. "Here you die on the Liberty Tree, you tax-collecting scum! Liberty and property forever!"

"John Parke Custis!"

With a look in my direction, he sheathed his sword, clicked his heels together, and offered me a bow. "Mother, I have saved us from English tyranny!"

If not for Patsy's distress, I might have smiled at his playacting. My little protector.

"He killed her!" Patsy said.

Although at age nine Patsy was old enough to let such play slide, I knew Marabel to be her favorite.

And who knew what declarations of rebellion she had heard before Jacky's latest.

By the strident look upon Patsy's face, I knew I had to take action. "Move aside, rebel!" I told Jacky. "Quick, mayhaps we can save her yet!" I unknotted the end of Marabel's noose and laid her on the bed. "Water and a handkerchief," I told Pasty. "We must dress her wounds."

"She will not get a proper burial," Jacky said. "Her kind deserve to be fed to the dogs."

"Jacky!"

He seemed to realize he had gone too far, for he moved to the window, where he poked his sword through the opening, offending only the September air.

I wrapped the handkerchief around Marabel's neck and declared, "There. She will recover."

Patsy tenderly took the doll into her arms, rocking her toward comfort. "Tell him not to do it again," she whispered.

I would. But I also needed to find out what had compelled Jacky to his violent play. Although I did have fair notion . . .

"Jacky? Come please."

He followed me into the hall, and though he pretended no worry, I could tell by his furtive glances he realized in *this* his Mamma was not pleased.

I closed the door to Patsy's room and took him down the hall for some privacy. "Tell me where you have learned of such awful things as hanging and—"

"This morning I heard Poppa talk about it with Cousin Lund. I heard him. In Boston, mobs of drunken men hung tax collectors and the lieutenant governor on a tree—the Liberty Tree near the Common."

I had not heard this. "Killed them?"

"No, not them, Mamma. Stuffed people. Like Marabel is stuffed."

I breathed again. They hung effigies of those they thought guilty.

But Jacky had more for me. "Then they went to the men's houses and ripped them apart. They slashed paintings and stole money, and burned furniture in a big bonfire. They did not stop until the men said they would not take no more taxes from us."

"Would not take *any* more taxes."

He ignored my grammar lesson. "Poppa said there are no more tax collectors in all the colonies. Every one of them has quit." He brandished his sword again. "We won! They are beaten!" He blinked away his playacting and looked at me. "I am hungry, Mamma. When is supper?"

My mind swam with implications far beyond my son's violent play. The colonies had taken a stand that would have far repercussions. As George had said, change was in the air. Thickly, in the air.

I did not like change.

Eight

"But, Mr. McGowan, you cannot leave the children."

The tutor stood before me, shaking his head. "I 'ave done the best I ken."

"Patsy so loves her lessons—when she is well enough. And Jacky . . ." I did not finish without offering a lie, for we both knew Jacky avoided learning and books like most people avoided snakes and spiders. "You have been with us over six years."

"Time enough for trying," he said. "Perhaps a school of boarding would be best for the young man. He is thirteen now. Nearly a . . . he is thirteen."

"Nearly a man" was a phrase I knew could not be stated. Would Jacky ever embrace responsibility and honour the way a boy his age should?

"I know of a good school run by a reverend Boucher in Caroline County, Maryland. He is highly respected and—"

"If it is a question of more money . . ." I offered.

"Ye's paid me fine enough. It is merely time. I travel to England with hopes of being ordained. I leave tomorrow."

He bowed and left me to the news.

I caught a glimpse of a shadow in the hall, then scruffing feet running upstairs. Had Jacky overheard the news? As much as I loved the boy, I knew he would rejoice.

A moment later, Molly appeared in the doorway to the parlour. "Mistress? Miss Patsy is feeling poorly."

I was on my feet. I had one child who sorely needed me and another who thought he needed no one.

What was I going to do?

———

George handed me a letter and sat on a wing chair as I read it. *The chief failings of his character are that he is constitutionally somewhat too warm—indolent and voluptuous. As yet, these propensities are but in embryo. 'Ere long, however, they will discover themselves and if not duly and carefully regulated, it is easy to see to what they will lead . . . a young person sunk in unmanly sloth.*

"See?" I asked George. "He does not excel at school there either."

"That should not bring you satisfaction, my dear." George lit a candle against the autumn dusk. "For five months after McGowan left, Jacky did no work. He did not e'en look at a book."

" 'Twas springtime. A hard time to ask any child—"

"The surveying equipment I bought especially for him? So he could be in the outdoors he enjoys so much and learn a skill that served me well? It too remained untouched."

I had no dispute. At his tutor's departure, Jacky held no pretense to learning and ran across the farms like an animal checking for a breach in a fence. He grew uncontainable. The boarding school Mr. McGowan had suggested—run by Reverend Jonathan Boucher, the writer of the letter—had been willing to take him.

May God help him.

How dare I have such thoughts! And yet, as I settled in my chair by the fire and watched the embers glow, I found I could think no other way. Although I loved my dear son, he had grown too much for me, especially since his sister required so much of my attention. Although last fall she had seemed better—well enough for George and me to travel without the children to partake of the waters at Warm Springs with George William and Sally Fairfax on a little holiday, during the summer Patsy had suffered a fit while on a horse and had fallen. The scare . . . people whisper that it is bad Custis blood. How can I refute it? So many of the Custis clan have died from sickness.

Although Dr. Rumney did his best for Patsy with his frequent visits, purges, vomits, light diets, and valerian medicine, 1768 was not a good year. George called in other doctors, and one suggested she wear on her finger an iron ring especially made for her condition— with the additional benefit of being of use to bite upon during her fits. George called in Joshua Evans, a blacksmith, who knew of this secret technique from the fourteenth century. George was skeptical but deferred to my desperation.

The iron ring was secret to the disease, that is for certain, for she became no better. As the spring progressed, I . . . I resigned myself to believing my hopes must turn to Jacky. He must become a fine young man. He must because he was my . . .

I hesitated to say it, yet it was a truth.

Jacky was . . . my only hope.

"Martha?"

George was looking at me. How long had I been silent and pensive?

"We must continue to put our hopes in Reverend Boucher's expertise. It is Jacky's best hope."

Agreed.

Things got worse. Jacky got worse. The letters from Boucher regarding my son made me cringe. I read the newest for the second time—this time aloud to George and Patsy. Although it was steeped in eloquent civility, it still stung: " 'Jack's love of ease and love of pleasure, pleasure of the kind exceedingly uncommon in his years. I never did in my life know a youth so exceedingly indolent . . . one would suppose nature had intended him for some Asiatic prince. And I have never seen any student more attracted to the social life than Jack. Unfortunately, he has been badly influenced by a wild boy, the son of Samuel Galloway. This boy has done your ward more harm than he or his family can easily make amends for. And then there are the girls . . . young Galloway's sister is . . .' " I stopped my reading and cringed.

"Is Jacky in trouble?" Patsy asked.

"It is this other boy," I said, folding the letter closed to lock away the words of condemnation. "This Galloway is the tempter. He is the one who is harming our Jacky."

"Jacky has always sought amusement," Patsy said. "He makes me laugh."

At her remark, I wished I had not read the letter aloud in her company. I wanted her to look up to her brother, not be privy to his weaknesses and errors. "Patsy, why don't you go practice the harpsichord. That Bach piece you have played of late is quite delightful."

She shook her head. "I want to hear what is to be done with my brother. If he is in trouble I wish to help."

George strolled behind her chair and kissed the top of her head. "I fear the helping must come of Jacky's own accord. He has had a myriad of people wanting to help. 'Tis only by his own determination any progress toward maturity will be made. He must learn that life is not only dogs, horses, guns, dress, and equipage."

"I wish I were the one at school. I enjoy books and learning."

"Mr. McGowan always praised your industrious work," George

said. "But there is no more for you to learn away from us. Your mamma is the best teacher."

I accepted his compliment. As the probable wife of a plantation owner, Patsy had no need for Greek or Latin or mathematical complexities. I knew of no woman who had ventured to learning beyond lessons provided by family or tutors.

George fingered the books on a shelf. "I was forced to end my schooling when my father died. Since then I have learned by reading and studying of my own accord. I wanted Jack to have all the advantages I did not have, but if he continues to squander them . . ." He looked at me. "Speaking of advantages, I did not tell you this, my dear, but I sent Jack to Baltimore for a stay of a few weeks to be inoculated for smallpox."

"Smallpox! Why did you not consult—?"

"I have had the smallpox, Martha." He motioned toward his face. "The entire world can see the evidence of my suffering."

"The pockmarks have faded."

"You miss the point. There are inoculations newly available. With Jacky out in the world where he will be exposed to many illnesses . . . I wanted him to have the full advantage of modern medicine. You do wish for him to be safe?"

'Twas a silly question. "You should have told me."

George shrugged. "I did not wish for you to worry. I only tell you of the inoculation now in order to reveal to you further evidence of Jack's disregard for responsibility. While recuperating in Baltimore, Jack manipulated the doctor as to his suffering, and had him send a letter to Reverend Boucher stating he would need another week for recovery."

I stood. "So the inoculation made him ill! We must bring him home and—"

George stopped my words with a hand. "Jack was completely recovered and was seen frolicking and drinking at a wedding party."

Patsy shook her head. "Oh, Jacky . . ."

"Oh Jacky, indeed," George said. "His infrequent letters home are so full of spelling errors one would think they were written by a street sweeper. I know he probably scribbles them quickly, but—"

"I am not a good speller either, dearest."

"You have no need to be. But Jack must groom himself to be fit for more useful purposes than . . . than a horse racer."

"I know you wish to have him take over Mount Vernon someday and—"

I watched as the muscles in my husband's neck tightened. I then watched as he found the control he so extolled. When he spoke again his voice was soft. "Since we have no children of our own . . . he is my only hope."

There it was again. The shared sorrow over a lack of children, and our common desire Jacky would somehow, someway, achieve his potential.

<hr />

I stood in the storehouse for the kitchen and made inventory. It was a difficult task to think ahead to future needs. Although there were a few shops in Alexandria, it was a full day's outing, and they did not carry the quantity of foodstuffs needed for a plantation the size of Mount Vernon. We depended on sugar from the West Indies, and on England for most everything else.

The government back in England was intent on submerging the colonies in "acts." The Sugar Act taxed sugar from the West Indies, foreign cloth, indigo, and coffee; the Currency Act stated we could no longer issue our own money; the Quartering Act made it mandatory to house and feed any British troops at any time; and the Townshend Act taxed paper, tea, glass, lead, and paints. Add to those a proclamation that prohibited us from settling west of the Appalachians . . . Did George not fight a war to better open that land for safe settling? After the violence up north that was instigated by a clandestine group called the Sons of Liberty, Britain wisely repealed the Stamp Act, but in the same breath passed the Declaratory Act stating they had the right to bind the colonies in whatever way they deemed necessary, and then suspended the New York Assembly for not complying with the Quartering Act. They took, gave back, slapped our hands, and then took some more.

"We really need more sugar, mistress," our cook Addie said as she counted the bags.

"I know. But the price . . . and many are urging us to boycott British luxury items."

Her eyes grew larger. "Is sugar a luxury?"

Not to me. "I am not certain."

"But if we do not buy the goods, what will we do? The children so enjoy their sweets. And so many of your guests comment on your Great Cake—which alone takes four pounds."

And forty eggs, and five pounds of flour and fruit, and four pounds of butter. I sighed. "Until George instructs us to join the boycott, let us cut back the amount in the recipes where we can."

She nodded, though by the crease between her eyes I knew she was not happy.

It could not be helped. These were difficult times, which I feared would only grow more difficult. If only Britain realized by tightening its reins it was igniting our independent natures, those traits which served Britain well for one hundred fifty years. A governing body could not be lax with rules for decades and then suddenly become the stern taskmaster and add *more* rules. Not without pushing its subjects toward a rebellious end.

I finished the inventory and headed to the main house. We were to leave for Williamsburg before the end of the week for the spring session of the House of Burgesses. I looked forward to the society and balls. Both would be a welcome respite amid the politics and positioning.

I saw George in his office. I did not stop to chat, as we both had much to do before our journey.

But he saw me and called out, "Martha, come here. There is a letter from Ann Mason."

George and Ann Mason were Fairfax County neighbors. George Mason had previously served in the House of Burgesses and had been instrumental in protesting the Stamp Act. They too would be in Williamsburg for the season's events.

I took the letter and sat in a corner chair to read it. After some pleasantries it said, *We ladies have decided to go to the ball the Burgesses are giving for the governor in dresses made of homespun. If Britain insists on taxing our silks and satins, then we have no use for them. Will you join us in our small act of rebellion, Martha? 'Twill be a challenge to make such fabric presentable, but one we are willing to take for the Cause.*

"Something she says distresses you?" George asked.

I thought of telling him . . . yet I did not want to feel guilty if I chose not to go along with the women. Although George and I had simplified our tastes since the Stamp Act a few years earlier, I was not ready for homespun. If only Ann hadn't sent the letter. If only I could feign ignorance. Dressing up for the events in Williamsburg brought me such joy.

"You are distressed?" George asked again.

I forced a smile. "Ann sends her greetings."

He nodded once, then looked back upon his papers. As I moved to leave he said, "I forgot to tell you. I have heard of a Williamsburg doctor who may be able to help Patsy. He is well respected. Dr. John de Sequeyra. He is a Sephardic Jew."

"Which means?"

"He is from Spain. Or Portugal perhaps."

If he could help Patsy, I did not care if he was from the moon.

"I have contacted him and he has agreed to see her," George said.

All thoughts of homespun or sugar stores evaporated.

All thoughts, as always, returned to Patsy.

My George was not one to press a point. He always prided himself on his good relations with those British who were in power within Virginia. And yet, it was my George (with the help of George Mason) who caused quite a commotion in Williamsburg.

Jacky was still in school at Reverend Boucher's, so after settling into the old Custis mansion of Six Chimneys, it was only Patsy and I who perused the shops. In the ten years of our marriage, such excursions always brought me great pleasure. I admit to being a gregarious sort and enjoyed chatting with the shopkeepers and getting their views on the latest fashions. But this visit . . .

Each time I entered a shop all talk was of boycotts and "taxation without representation." And I, as the wife of George Washington, a respected member of the House of Burgesses, was called upon to be an authority.

"What plans are hatching at the House?" a milliner asked me.

I adjusted a yellow-feathered bonnet upon my hair. "We must all await news." I turned to Patsy. "Does this flatter or does it make my face look too wide?"

Patsy studied the effect. "I am afraid the latter."

I removed the hat. I respected my daughter's taste. For at thirteen she had developed an eye for fashion. "May I try on that one?" I asked the milliner.

She removed a flattened straw hat with a violet spray upon the ear. I set it on my head. "It looks the essence of spring, does it not?" I asked.

Before Patsy or the milliner could answer, a man burst through the door. "Governor Botetourt has dissolved the House of Burgesses for claiming exclusive right to levy its own taxes!"

"Dissolved?" I asked.

But he was gone, gone on to the next shop, and the next.

Patsy pressed a hand upon my arm. "What does it mean, Mamma?"

I did not answer but removed the hat.

We had to get home.

———❧———

I paced. And paced. But still no George. Were the members of the House of Burgesses arguing with the governor about his decision to dissolve their body? If so, I could imagine much shouting. There were many who did not own a cool head in such situations, Patrick Henry among them. If he so wanted, Mr. Henry was quite capable of arousing the populace to violence. That was my biggest fear, that George had been hurt.

"Mamma, please sit. You make me nervous," Patsy said.

For her sake, I forced myself to sit and took up some embroidery.

Blessedly, George arrived in time to save my fingers from abusive pricking. I met him at the door. "What happened? Was there fighting?"

"No, my dear. No fighting. Lord Botetourt told us to disband and had soldiers interrupt our meeting, so we complied." He smiled. "We reconvened in Raleigh Tavern and discussed a unified boycott of British goods. If they are going to tax us unfairly, then we will do without those items they deem taxable. We must become more self-reliant. Parliament has no more right to put their hands in my pocket without my consent than I have to put my hands into the pockets of my neighbours. Personally, I was thinking we need to expand our flax, hemp, and wool production so we can weave more of our own clothing. And since British iron will be unavailable, we need to create more of our own tools in our smithy. We can sell salted herring to the West Indies, and increase our mill to create a higher yield with our wheat." He paused to take a much-needed breath. "There is much to do."

"I had hoped it would not come to this," I said.

"They are forcing it to come to this," he said. "We must take a stand, Martha. *I* must take a stand, e'en though it grieves me greatly. I am presenting a position on nonimportation tomorrow."

This was not like George. He was interested and responsible when it came to the governing issues in the colonies, but he was not one to make bold proclamations or declarations. He had worked *with* the British for too many years to willingly provoke them.

I hung his hat upon a hook in the foyer and led him into the parlour. "Hello, Patsy," he said. "Did you have a nice time shopping with your mamma today?"

"Yes, Poppa, but now . . . if we stop receiving goods from England, how will we shop at all?"

She had overheard—and mirrored my thoughts.

"We will have to make do. It is far from the ideal. I too enjoy nice things, but the time has come to put the common good above our own desires. It is only prudent to reduce our debt to England and encourage colonial production of the taxed goods." He sat in his favourite chair and sighed. "Some say I have been too long to get involved. I try to explain I am one who needs to think things through before making a decision, but assure them that once made, such decisions are immovable."

"There are plenty who act first and think later. I would imagine they appreciate your steady contemplation, logic, and common sense."

"I am not a radical. I can never be a radical no matter what fun they make of me."

"Who makes fun of you?"

"Henry, Mason, Jefferson." He shook his head. "It does not matter. I have had good reason to hesitate—reasons common to many. I am a farmer. Our livelihood depends on trade with England and the good graces of our factors there. If we anger them we will pay in many ways. If angered enough there is the possibility the British government could seize our land."

"They would not dare."

"They rule us, Martha. Not well and not wisely, but they still rule. And unless we choose to change that fact . . ."

"How would we do that?" Patsy asked. Her face was fearful.

George offered her a smile he reserved for her alone. "I should not have mentioned such an outlandish suggestion." He slapped a hand upon his thigh and stood. "Giving up a few material pleasures will make us stronger in character. The necessities of life are mostly to be had within ourselves. Do you not agree, ladies?"

Reluctantly.

The next day George did more than present the nonimportation position; he proceeded to take it upon himself to travel the expanse of Virginia to elicit support from the populace. The boycott would not be effective unless it was adhered to by a majority. When he finally returned to Mount Vernon, he reported he had personally spoken to over one thousand of his fellow Virginians. By his own efforts the boycott was embraced.

As was he.

"They listened to me, Martha," he told me on the first evening after his return.

We sat on the back approach to Mount Vernon and watched the fireflies of summer. "Of course they did, dearest. You are a man who demands—"

"I did not demand," he said. "I spoke with them. I enjoyed their company. I am proud to be one of them."

"This is a far cry from the ambitious colonel, demanding his British commanders pay him due attention."

To his honour, he blushed. "In my youth I worked toward my own gain. But now . . . the Cause is beyond any one man. The Cause is for unity. The Cause is noble."

As was he.

"Boston, Boston." George looked up from the *Virginia Gazette* and sighed. "What are we to do with those people?"

George read the paper as I darned stockings. Jacky wore holes in his stockings faster than we could weave new ones. "Is there more dissension there?"

"More than dissension. This time, violence."

I set my darning upon my lap to hear more.

George lowered the paper and told me the latest news from that bastion of rebellion. "Some citizens, angry about taxes, accosted a group of British soldiers—whose presence is now commonplace and quite unwelcome. The Bostonians began throwing snowballs at the soldiers—and insults, I am sure. One of the soldiers fell, his gun went off, and then there was gunfire all round. Five of our men were killed."

"Innocent citizens? Unarmed?"

"No mob is unarmed. And as for their innocence . . ." He turned the paper toward me and showed me a print of an engraving signed by a Bostonian named Paul Revere. It portrayed a group of colonists, fallen and bloodied by a line of British troops firing into the crowd.

"I do not see any snowballs," I said. "Nor snow at all."

George looked back at the paper. "Hmm. And there is an officer behind the soldiers, ordering them to fire. The troops are there to keep the peace, not to incite a war."

"So you think the print inaccurate?"

"I think . . ." George rubbed his chin. "I think the men of Boston—Samuel Adams, his cousin John, John Hancock, and the volatile Sons of Liberty—have strong motivation to incite action."

"You think they caused this?"

"I think they live under conditions far different than we are experiencing here in Virginia. While we feel the inequities of taxation from afar, they see it up close as the ships enter the harbour. There are too many men whose livelihood depends on trade to have them remain unaffected—or neutral." He set the newspaper in his lap and placed a hand upon it. "I fear the time of neutrality has slipped away."

"Meaning?"

"The time is coming when the civilized exchange of letters and the creation of proclamations may not bring the desired results."

Without intent, my breathing grew pronounced. "But we cannot fight them! England is the most powerful nation in the world. And we are their subjects. Their king is our king. England is our mother country and we are her children."

George glanced back at the newspaper. "Disobedient children?"

It could not be denied.

George continued. "A parent will chastise her children, and if England is not satisfied in our contrition—or if we show no contrition but continue to push for our way above hers . . . we will be punished."

I shivered. "But perhaps if we continue to discuss our differences and—"

"I fear the chance for discussion has passed. Once blood has been spilt . . ."

He suddenly stood. "If you will excuse me, my dear. I have some letters I must write."

"About Boston?"

"About our future."

———

George and I stood beside Patsy's bed—again. Eight days previous, she had suffered a fit of such power it had sent her to the floor and then to bed with horrible ague. The chills and sweating took turns, her body burning with fever. We had called for Dr. Rumney and he had once again traveled to Mount Vernon to apply his knowledge. He bled Patsy, but the fits returned.

"I have one more remedy to try," he told us.

I dabbed a cool cloth on my daughter's forehead. "Anything."

He nodded and pointed to the candle on the bedside table. "That must be moved as far away as possible. What I will use—ether—is very flammable. A flame need not even touch it to have it flare."

I did not understand. "Is it safe?" I asked. "If it is so flammable, how can it do a patient any good?"

"You must accept my confidence that notwithstanding the extreme subtlety of the ether, it is perfectly innocent and safe to take."

I glanced at George, who had his hand on his chin, his usual stance when listening to anything with intensity. "How is it administered?"

Dr. Rumney took a deep breath. "There are two ways." He pulled from his satchel a corked phial containing a clear liquid. He held it for us to examine. "Ether is colourless, its smell sulphurous. If I were to wet my finger with it or drop a little upon the hand, it would vanish instantly and leave no moisture behind."

"I still do not understand," George said. "If it evaporates so quickly, how is it dispensed?"

"I would first attempt an external application. You may procure a bit of linen rag to cover the palm of the hand, moisten it with a little of the ether, and instantly apply it to her forehead, or hold it beneath her nostrils." He looked at Patsy, then continued. "If that does not give her ease, the general dose for a grown person is a common teaspoonful, and the best vehicle to take it in is a draught of cold water. If Miss Patsy has any objection to water, she may take it in any agreeable cold liquid."

"How often?" I asked.

"Twice a day. It . . . it may make her lethargic."

It was to be expected. "I have rare found a medicinal that does not cause some effect." I looked at Patsy. She looked back at me, listless from the fever and the exhaustion of the fits. "Does this seem all right with you?"

Her eyes turned sad. "What choice do I have?"

The doctor suggested we wait until evening for our first dispensation. At George's insistence, he was the one to do it. The sight of him, cradling dear Patsy in his arms as he held the foul-smelling tincture to her face . . .

'Twill never leave me.

Although George and I had been married twelve years, my mother-in-law remained . . . difficult. Yet George followed God's laws and honoured her with loyal duty, visiting her when he was close to Ferry Farm and giving aid whenever asked. But now, at age sixty-three, she was no longer comfortable staying in such isolation.

He offered her a home at Mount Vernon, but to our relief, she declined. Instead he purchased a home for her in Fredericksburg, just a few miles northwest. He left to administer the move and was due home—

I heard a horse out front and met him at the door. "You return," I said simply. I knew better than to ask many questions regarding his maternal visits. The information was best obtained on George's own terms and time.

He kissed my cheek, then walked through the house and out the back door, overlooking the river. There, he sat. And sighed. And rubbed his face.

"It is done. She is moved."

"Is it a nice home?"

"Not nice enough. She says she is abandoned by all of her children."

"But Betty and Fielding are close by."

"And ten grandchildren who should bring her joy." He shook his head. "She does not understand joy."

Or appreciation.

"She insists she is going to die any day now, and will be buried in an unmarked grave."

It was a common strain of her whining. That, and her constant desire for more money. George had been more than generous. To no avail.

I tried to think of something to cheer him. "The looms! I should tell you about the looms. We have spun the greatest multitude of thread and have woven enough fabric to clothe all the slaves and servants—at no cost."

"That is wonderful, Martha. Your industry—"

"We have used our creativity well. We have woven cotton broadcloth, checkered dimity, and wool in stripes and plaid."

He smiled. "No matter where I go or what I encounter, I can always count on you. What would I do without you?"

I leaned over his chair to kiss his lips. "Suffer. Suffer most cruelly."

———

Patsy pinned her hair back and looked in the mirror. "I am so glad you are having our portraits done again, Mamma. The last one of me was when I was only two, and it is odd looking. The face . . ." She looked at her best friend, Milly Posey, who was helping with her hair.

Milly finished the sentence. "You look just like your brother." She turned to me. "Why is that, Mrs. Washington?"

"Looking back, I believe our portraits—odd though they are— were the extent of Mr. Wollaston's ability. He knew how to paint *that* face."

The girls laughed and Milly said, "How lucky you are you bear it little resemblance." She stepped back. "You are beautiful, Patsy. The pearls in your hair are a crown."

Patsy turned at her dressing table to look at me. "They were Mamma's. They are the Custis pearls she wore in *her* hair upon her wedding day to Poppa."

I blew her a kiss. "You do them great justice. And I like that both of us wear them in our portraits—as well as the same pearl necklace. It binds us, two as one."

With one last glance to the mirror, Patsy stood. "I think I am ready for Mr. Peale now."

The girls exited the bedroom, their giggling and banter continuing down the stairs. I was glad for the joy Milly brought into the house. To see Patsy behaving like a normal sixteen-year-old girl was a pleasure. And a relief. George was also pleased with the girls' friendship—for their sake, yet was not pleased Milly was the daughter of John Posey. John was a shiftless man who did little and owed George much. That Milly might find evidence of a finer life and good work practices in her many visits to Mount Vernon was a benefit which made him acquiesce to Milly's presence.

I straightened Patsy's dressing table and followed the girls downstairs. There was much commotion in the parlour as Jacky finished his seating and Mr. Peale positioned Patsy in hers. Mr. Peale had already finished my miniature—a work created at Jacky's insistence—and a grand portrait of George would be accomplished soon. I was firm about his being portrayed in his Virginia militia uniform. He agreed to letting me have my way, though he was moody during the posing. He had just had some teeth removed and was in great pain. His teeth always caused him distress. I was glad Mr. Peale would only be with us two days.

Jacky sprawled on a settee, one leg over its arm. "Try to be pretty for the man, Pat." He turned his mischievous smile upon the painter. "How old are you, Mr. Peale?"

"I am thirty."

"A little old, but . . . are you married? For you see, my sister is not and—"

"Jacky!"

Mr. Peale arranged the black ribbon of Patsy's necklace. "I am honoured you think me worthy of your sister, Master Washington, but I am happily married."

"What is your wife's name?" Milly asked.

"Rachel."

"Do you have children?"

"Yes, we do. In fact we have—"

I felt the need to save the poor man. "Enough, children. Let Mr. Peale do his work in peace. Jacky, come with me."

With great reluctance Jacky followed me into the hall. "You must not tease your sister so. Did you not see how she blushed?"

"She should blush," Jacky said. "She needs a beau, yet by her own words tells me she has none, not even a stray lad or two come to call. You are not holding her captive here, are you, Mamma? For she is a handsome girl. Her eyes are quite mesmerizing and her lush eyebrows are quite coveted."

I had to smile. "Since when did you become expert on feminine beauty?"

It was Jacky's turn to blush. "I *am* eighteen, Mamma."

Enough said. I changed the subject. "When are you going back to Reverend Boucher's?" I moved toward the dining room to check on the setting for supper.

Jacky took my arm. "Why *are* there no men calling on Patsy? Besides her good looks, she is wealthy. Surely that is a draw to many a young man."

I found it hard to have discussions with Jacky since he had grown to manly size. Although I would admit to never having authority over him, now, having to look *up* at him . . .

"We have decided it is best *not* to encourage beaus. Your sister's health is precarious. And you know how embarrassed she would be if she would have a fit while being visited by an eligible young—"

"So you prevent all possibility? That is not protection but restriction, and constriction. It makes her a hostage to her condition."

I had no defense he would understand. For I knew, in a place where mothers knew, that my daughter would not live long into adulthood. So rather than have her inflict the pain of widowhood upon a husband, I chose to keep her a happy girl, free of complicated commitment. Besides, I was not certain she was capable of safely being a wife, in . . . fulfilling a wife's duties.

"You are not going to answer me, are you?"

I lifted my chin, trying to portray a confidence I did not feel. "I am not."

"You are wrong, Mamma. When are you going to learn you cannot keep us children forever?"

He walked away before I had to answer *that* unanswerable question.

⁂

After three long years, Jacky—Jack to everyone but me—was graduating from Reverend Boucher's school. I had never been completely certain Reverend Boucher was the proper man to have control over my son—such as control was possible. For I was not blind to Jacky's faults, and in times of reflection, I even admitted that perhaps his untamed ways were because I had been too lax with discipline. The Bible said, *He that spareth his rod hateth his son.* I did not hate Jacky, but I could admit that I may not have helped him. At the time I thought I was loving him. I *was* loving him, in the best way I knew. Perhaps I was too aware of the pain my Daniel had borne under the unloving punishment of *his* father. That I had opted for love and little punishment—which now caused its own pain . . . I grew weary of the implications.

"Does any parent ever get it right?"

George looked up from his desk. "What, my dear?"

I had not meant to speak aloud. I held the latest letter from Boucher. "I was reading another missive from the reverend."

"What has Jack done now?"

I wished to admonish George for his quick words, but could not. For 'twas too true. Jacky was always in trouble. I consulted the letter. "He writes that Jacky 'appears illiterate amongst men of letters and he seldom goes out without learning something I could have wished him not to have learned.' " I sighed and looked to George for his response.

"It is time we got him to a college, to a place where a true atmosphere of learning amongst young men eager to learn will affect him in a positive manner."

To my horror, a laugh escaped. "Forgive me."

"I agree Jack's escapades 'twould play well as a comic farce, and the possibility that he will suddenly transform into a scholar . . ."

I regained composure. "We must try."

"That, we must. And we shall." He leaned back in his chair. "The College of William and Mary in Williamsburg is the closest but—"

"Which makes it preferable."

"But not the best for Jack."

"Whyever not?"

"Its students are well known to be rowdy, and with the proximity of the taverns, directly across the street . . ."

Oh. I moved to other alternatives. "Reverend Boucher has previously implored us *not* to let Jacky go to the College of New Jersey. He deems it a nest of radical patriots."

"Boucher supports the crown, even during these despicable tax acts, so any group that sees differently than he . . . I was leaning toward King's College."

"Where is it located?"

"New York City."

"New York? So far," I said. "And a big city. I am not sure—"

"But by being a big city it is populated by young men from many locations and backgrounds. It might be good for Jack to be exposed to a wider range of people."

"It could also lead him to discover new ways to misbehave."

With a shrug George sat forward again, going through the mail that had accumulated while we had been gone for the spring session of the House. I knew the discussion regarding Jacky's schooling was not concluded.

Then suddenly George said, "Speak of the . . . Look at this, in the pile—a letter from Jack."

"How did we miss it?"

George opened it, scanning the page. "I see his penmanship has not improved . . . but . . . oh no. No!"

"George? What does he say?"

"He is engaged! To Eleanor Calvert, aged fifteen."

I reached across the desk, needing to see the words myself: *You will like her. Eleanor is a beauty and is from a good family. Her father is a son of Lord Baltimore. We are very much in love and hope that you will rejoice with us upon this happy announcement.*

"Happy? He is but eighteen!"

"He is not of age. This only proves he is undisciplined, inconsiderate, unconscionable—"

"He must come home. We must speak to him in person."

George took out a piece of paper and quill.

~

We were rather surprised Jacky agreed to come home to speak to us. My biggest fear was that he and Eleanor would run away and marry before we had the chance to make them see reason.

Patsy was the first to hear his approach. We expected him on horseback, but instead she informed us, "He is not alone. He has come in a carriage—a fine carriage."

My stomach turned. Surely he would not have the audacity to bring Eleanor with him. I removed my apron and moved to greet . . . them?

"It is two men with him," whispered Patsy from the front window. "Older men."

Reverend Boucher? But no. Patsy had met the reverend. She would have said if it were he.

The mystery was solved soon enough. Jacky entered, his face flushed with excitement. He removed his hat with a sweep of a hand, hugged me, and kissed my cheek. "Mamma! I am so glad to see you."

And I you. However . . . "Who are your guests, Jacky?"

"Please call me Jack, Mamma." He moved to present them. "This is my future father-in-law, Benedict Calvert."

I believe I smiled. Somehow.

He kissed my hand. "So pleased to meet you, Mrs. Washington."

"And this—" Jack moved to the older gentleman—"is Sir Robert Eden, the governor of Maryland."

I did not smile. I could not smile, as the shock was too great. I must have curtsied because Sir Eden bowed and offered a greeting—though I could not have repeated it.

While Patsy was introduced, my mind wandered to our next obstacle: George.

I spotted George coming toward the house from his daily rounds. I stood, said, "If you will excuse me, gentlemen," and exited the parlour. I made my way out the front of the house and intercepted my husband.

"George!" I said in hushed tones, motioning him toward me.

"Eustis said Jack has arrived? In a carriage?"

I pressed my hands upon his chest, forcing him to stop his stride. "He has. And he has brought two visitors."

"Not..." he said. "Certainly not Eleanor."

"Not Eleanor." I took a fresh breath and told him the names.

"That little conniver!"

"They are the most charming of men, dearest. And Jack is on his best behav—"

"We order him home in order to stop his marriage, and he has the audacity to bring reinforcements? Without our knowledge? I knew Jack to be immature, but I did not think him a coward." He sidestepped me and strode toward the front door.

I ran after him. "What are you going to do?"

"I am going to greet our guests."

Just the way he said it . . . this would not be pleasant.

———

Jacky was oblivious—or if not so truly, became well rehearsed at assuming such a state. And though George was gracious to our guests—actually enjoying a discussion with the governor about George's proposal for a Potomac River navigation project—I could tell by the tautness of his neck he was seething inside. There was no mention made as to the engagement.

Our guests claimed they were on their way to Williamsburg on business and were traveling together because they were good friends, but we all knew they came at Jacky's suggestion, as his buffer against our anger.

He wished for me to call him Jack? No. I would call him Jacky, for he acted like a child and deserved a child's name. That I was to some measure to blame for this . . . this master of manipulation, grieved me greatly. As to his poppa's condition? Jacky remained oblivious—

Until Calvert and Lord Eden moved on. At that time George ordered Jacky into his office, closed the door, and told him what was what. I was not invited to the foray, but stood at the door and listened. I did not have to strain. George was adamant and did not allow Jacky to speak—for we both knew how adept the boy was at bending his words toward attaining his own will.

I admired my husband for his determined resolve against the marriage, even as I remembered the disdain and pain inflicted by my own reluctant father-in-law, John Custis. I was only sixteen and Daniel thirty-eight when we became betrothed. And yet, as diverse as our ages were, 'twas a better situation than this, in that Daniel was a mature man past the imprudence of a passionate youth. My Jacky's character was enthroned with recklessness. Yet the pain John Custis had caused by disputing the match; were we causing Jacky such pain?

"We do not disapprove of Eleanor, per se," George was saying, "as her family has station . . ."

There was the difference. Daniel's father had disparaged the Dandridge name quite loudly, for anyone to hear. We respected the Calverts. Although Benedict was the illegitimate son of Lord Baltimore, we did not hold that against him. Not many colonists could delve into their upbringing without exposing some modicum of impropriety. But the advantage gained by Eleanor was far greater than the other way round. Jacky was a rich young man and would be even richer at the time of his majority. I was not against marriage. Only to their immaturity and age, *and*—most stringently—the manner in which the engagement was made. Respect was an essential ingredient to adulthood, one both Jacky and Eleanor had to learn.

George's voice caught my attention again. "Your mamma and I have decided to enroll you in King's College. We will go there, you and I, next month."

Jacky was allowed a response. "But that is more than two hundred miles—"

George continued. "It is decided. In the meantime, I will write a letter to Mr. Calvert, that you will deliver to him, hand to hand. And then you will await his reply and bring it back to *my* hand. Do you understand?"

There was a hesitation, but then—blessedly and to my great relief—Jacky replied, "Yes, sir."

I moved away from the door to give them the image of privacy. The door opened and Jacky came out. Our eyes met. With great restraint I did not open my arms to him, nor even make a step in his direction. With a nod, he brushed past and out the door.

George appeared in the doorway. "You heard?"

I nodded. "I am sorry you had to be so harsh. Jacky—"

"It was time someone was harsh, my dear. Past time." He put a hand on the door. "If you will excuse me, I have a letter to write, to Mr. Calvert."

"What will you say?"

"Enough, and perhaps a bit more."

He shut the door between us.

─────

George read me his letter aloud.

". . . I should think myself wanting in candour was I not to acknowledge that Miss Eleanor's amiable qualifications stand confessed at all hands, and that an alliance with your family will be pleasing to his. This acknowledgment being made, you must permit me to add, sir, that his youth, inexperience, and unripened education are, and will be, insuperable obstacles in my eye, to the completion of the marriage. To postpone the marriage is all I have in view. Not that I have any doubt of the warmth of his affections, nor, I hope I may add, any change in them; but at present I do not conceive that he is capable of bestowing that due attention to the important consequences of a marriage state and am unwilling he should do it till he is. If the affection which they have avowed for each other is fixed upon a solid basis, it will receive no diminution in the course of two or three years. If, unfortunately (as they are both young) there should be an abatement of affection on either side, or both, it had better precede, rather than follow after, the marriage."

He stopped reading to look for my approval. "I mention more about Jacky's eventual wealth, and I invite the Calverts to visit, but this is the gist of it. Do you approve?"

"I am very proud of the letter, and grateful to you for taking the time to word it so carefully."

He rubbed his hands across his face. "It exhausted me more than a day's riding round the plantation."

"With results just as valid and profitable." I saw a bit of dust on his desk and stood, rubbing the edge of my apron across it. "Jacky will take the letter to Mr. Calvert tomorrow, then?"

"Tomorrow."

"You expect no problem?"

"None. I also expect no dowry. As the second of ten daughters, no matter what wealth exists, Mr. Calvert must be modest in his promises."

"Our boy. Married," I said.

"*After* he has gained a proper education," George said.

Yes, yes. Only then.

⸻

Visitors were a pleasure. Although it meant extra work, I was attuned to the job. I felt at my best when surrounded by the delights of friends, neighbours, and family. And though George and I had expressed our doubts about Jacky's engagement to Eleanor Calvert, as spring progressed into summer, Eleanor became a regular visitor to Mount Vernon—a delightful one. She often came with her mother and a variance of sisters. I welcomed her as Jacky's fiancée but also as a friend to Patsy. On one occasion the three of us had a glorious time unpacking a shipment of goods George had ordered for Patsy from England the previous summer—before the embargo had caused such orders to halt: dresses of silk, amber beads, a lovely velvet collar with a pearl bow from India, garnet shoe buckles, leather shoes with her name in them, a new prayer book with clasps of silver, two pairs of silk slippers—one gold and one silver—a powder puff and box, a copy of *Lady's Magazine,* and an assortment of more mundane items like hairpins and thread. To her credit, Patsy was very generous with her sister-in-law-to-be, giving her many items as gifts. As George was generous with our Patsy, so she passed the attribute on to others. I was very proud of her.

On the latest visit, in June, Eleanor had brought along a Calvert family servant named Miss Reed, Eleanor's governess. Then George's dear brother John Augustine came to visit from Bushfield, along with his wife, Hannah, and two of their children. The one hundred miles that usually separated us were soon forgotten amid lively talk, delicious food, and fine weather.

Even more than the pleasure of the visit was seeing Patsy in good health. Her cheeks were pink and her laughter merry. After attending Pohick Church in the morning, we settled into a fine supper midafternoon.

"So, Miss Calvert," said John Augustine. "When can we expect you to become a full-fledged member of our family?"

With a glance toward George and then me, the wise Eleanor said, "As soon as his parents deem it time—the right time."

John laughed. "Well put, my dear. I see you have learned the art of wise flattery."

At the table beside her, Patsy put a hand on top of her friend's. " 'Tis not flattery, Uncle John. Eleanor is true and does not say anything that is not in her heart. She—"

Suddenly, Patsy's eyes grew large. She froze for but a second, then began to shake in such an extreme manner that she fell to the floor.

"Patsy!"

I ran to her side, took the iron ring from her finger, and tried to put it between her teeth. She was flashing too wildly. George came to my aid and we managed to put it where it should be.

"What can we do?" Hannah asked.

"Nothing," George said as he tried to contain her arms from harm against the floor. "It will pass."

"She has been so much better of late," I said, trying to calm the ill ease of my guests. I had to raise my voice above the pounding of Patsy's legs and feet as they gyrated against the floor.

"She has not had a single episode during our visit," Eleanor said.

"And now, on such a fine day," Hannah said.

I was not certain her comment had any meaning other than to be words said in order to say words, but I did not contest them. Yes, indeed, on this fine sunny June day, after being so well . . . I knew Patsy would be appalled that a fit of such a degree was suffered in front of guests. At such times, she was always rife with embarrassment and apologies. I had grown harder against feeling shame. All I felt at that moment was concern for—

As quickly as the fit had come, Patsy stopped all movement.

"There, there, sweet girl. George, carry her to bed."

I patted her hand and waited for her eyes to open, for them to change from distant to present in the here and now.

But they did not open.

I patted her hand harder. "Patsy? Patsy, wake up."

George pulled her into his arms, cradling her, trying to rouse her. "Come now, dear girl. All is well. After a short rest you can rejoin the party."

"She is not moving," Hannah said.

"The fits wear her out," I said.

"Shall I send for a doctor?" Eleanor asked.

I leaned over her and gently spanked her cheeks. "Patsy? Patsy, dearest."

"Let me." John Augustine knelt beside her and put his head to her chest. We all held our breaths and were silent. He sat upright. "I do not hear . . ."

I pushed him away and put my own ear to her chest. Pressed against the lovely yellow chintz of her gown, willing my ear to hear—

What was not present.

I sat aright and stared at George. "George?"

George moved Patsy to the floor so he too could listen for her heart.

I held my breath.

He sat up. He shook his head.

"No, no," I said. "It cannot be. I will not let it be!"

He looked down at Patsy and lifted her to where she had been before, cradled against his shoulder. He stroked her cheek and ran a hand across her hair. "Oh, dear, my dear, dear, girl."

I shook my head with utter incredulity. "No. I tell you, no! She was fine. She was better." I looked to George. His eyes had filled with tears. My husband did not cry unless . . .

Unless confronted with true tragedy.

My body froze. I did not breathe. I did not think. Time stood still.

Then, as thought and breath forced their way upon my being, all sorrow sped loose. Sobs attacked with greedy vengeance and I flung myself upon my daughter's limp frame. I clung to her, willing her to stay with me.

George's strong arms encircled us both.

But to no avail.

No avail.

PART II

· OUR GLORIOUS CAUSE ·

— NINE —

How can God be good?

How can God be right?

For what is right and good about the death of my Patsy?

"Martha?"

I did not respond to our neighbour Sally, but allowed her to enter Patsy's bedroom of her own accord. She closed the door with a gentle click and sat upon the bed beside me. She put a hand upon the yellow chintz dress I held in my lap.

"I have no words," Sally said.

Good. Because there were none adequate.

"The funeral was . . ."

As with the death of a child, there were no words for the funeral either. Although we had just returned from the family vault which lay just a hundred yards south of the house, I had little recollection of the words offered by Reverend Massey. I had the vague notion that many of the slaves had come to pay their respects, and knew John Augustine's family had been present, along with Eleanor, Miss Reed, and Sally and George William, but they were only dim shadows on the edge of my world. In truth, my world did not exist anymore. My world had died with my daughter.

Logically I knew I had a son, but Jacky was away at King's College. A man. Removed from the realm of my existence.

I pulled the dress to my face, closed my eyes, and inhaled. *Ah! There she is!* My dear Patsy, who never caused me a moment's trouble. A moment's worry, yes, but the illness was not her fault, and if I could have bought it as *my* illness, I would have done so. If I could have died in her place, I would have gladly succumbed.

Suddenly, a thought . . . "I should have offered!"

"Offered what, Martha?"

I looked at Sally, having forgotten she was there. "Offered to die for her."

Her forehead creased in confusion. "I am sorry, I do not understand."

The thought took firmer hold. How could I have been so blind? "If only I had offered my life for hers! If only I had prayed to God that He take *me* if someone needed to be taken." I grabbed Sally's hand. "I did not offer!"

She clasped my hand between hers. "Martha, dear lady, you cannot think in such a way. God does not take one life in return for another. Even if you would have offered, He would have declined. Patsy's fate is her own, and though incomprehensible, unchangeable."

I pulled my hand away.

"You and George did everything possible to cure her, to give her comfort and peace. You could not have done more. Do not ever think such a thing."

The tears intruded yet again. "I will always think I could have done more."

Sally did not argue with me but put an arm around my shoulder and touched her head to mine.

I heard their voices in the foyer. "Are you certain you would not like us to stay?"

George answered his brother. "I am certain. You take the others to Belvoir and have a nice dinner and evening there. Martha and I will be best here."

I heard the door close and the sound of horses and carriage upon the drive.

We were alone.

For the first time since . . .

He entered the parlour, took a breath, and attempted a smile. "So."

Why was it so hard for me to respond? George was taking great measures to comfort me. Friends, neighbours, and family also tried. They rallied round me with true love and compassion. The house was abustle with guests coming to offer condolences. Eleanor's father and eldest sister had come to visit. They would take Eleanor and Miss Reed home in a few days. I did not relish their absence.

I feared the silence, and if I had owned the strength, I would have argued with George about his decision to send the others to Sally's for the evening. *Do not leave me! Do not allow the quiet to encase me like a shroud.* Because in the quiet was solitude, and in the solitude, loneliness, and in the loneliness the void. The void that would never be filled.

George strolled beside my chair, brushing his hand against my cheek as he passed. I knew he did not know what to say. I knew his pain was severe, and I grieved I could be of no comfort to *him.* Should we not comfort each other?

I was incapable. A selfish grief enveloped me, held me captive, and would not let me free. Yet I felt it was my duty to offer the first words to bridge our privacy. "Has Jacky been notified?"

The relief at my utterance—of any words—was evident on my husband's face. "I wrote to him."

"Why has he not written back?"

George sat in the chair across from me. "There is reason. I have heard from the president of the college, Dr. Cooper, and he informed me that when my letter arrived—with its thick black seal—Jack had feared something was seriously wrong, and took the letter to Mr. Cooper to read *for* him. Dr. Cooper wrote that Jack's response to us may be delayed because the shock was so severe."

I put a hand to my face. "So I must worry about Jacky too." It was not a question.

George came to me, kneeling at my feet. He took my hands in his and peered into my eyes. "If there is worry, we will do it together. Please let us do it together. I know there is no answer to the pain. And I know you have suffered more than your share of loss, but—"

I sat aright at his mention of something I had been considering. "Years ago I lost two children, then a husband, and yet the pain of Patsy's passing cuts the deepest. Not that I did not grieve the others, but back then . . ." What I was to say might hurt him, and yet I needed to say it. "Back then I had prospects of a long life ahead of me. I thought there could be other children with another husband and—" I stopped myself from saying more.

He stood. "And there have been no more children."

"No. There have not." It was my turn to stand and take his hands. "I do not understand why God has not blessed us with our own off-spring. But it seems clear it is not His will to do so. A few days ago I was forty-two years old. I have long since realized it is not to be." I put a hand upon his cheek. "So that is why I grieve so heartily for Patsy. She was, and is to be, my only living daughter. I wished to see her married with children of her own. I wished to grow old with those grandchildren around me. I . . . it is only proper I died before she."

George took me into his arms, pressing my head against his chest.

His heart beat upon my ear, constant, strong.

And alive.

———∞———

Since grief knew me well, it settled in like it was visiting an old acquaintance.

Aggravating me. Pestering me. Punishing me.

I knew all the facets of its face intimately. The anger, the feeling of betrayal, the frustration, the hopelessness, the wistfulness, and the utter despondency.

Others tried to help. I could honestly say all that could be done to comfort me *was* done. George ordered mourning clothes and a ring for me that I could not imagine ever removing. Eleanor visited often, bringing along various members of her family. I found her to be a balm, a true blessing. That she was near the same age as my Patsy . . . though I believed I also filled a need within her. As one of ten children, I gave her attention she could not receive at home.

George even invited my mother to come live with us at Mount Vernon, and I knew it was not an empty invitation. He truly would have enjoyed having her with us. But Mother was happily ensconced in New Kent. And her health was not the best—she had never even visited us here—so I accepted her decision as best.

Jacky suggested we move to New York City and get away from this place which suffered so many memories. Surely being around people and the excitement of a city would offer plentiful diversions.

Crowds, noise, narrow streets, and filth. I could think of no place I would like least.

I thanked God I was not an idle woman, for while doing my work—the work that could not be deferred by time nor delegated to another—I found moments of release when I would not think on Patsy. But then the chore would end and the knowledge of her absence would flood over me and I would drown.

George was as wonderful as any husband could be. For three weeks George remained at home with me until the work demanded his attention. Then he invited me to join him on his daily rounds. At first I rejected the notion, but by his persistence, I often went with him. Some days it was a help. Some days . . .

George sat astride his horse, and I sat sidesaddle on my much smaller mare. We were far from the main house, riding from field to field, farm to farm, making certain all was going as planned. All were working. All was growing. I usually enjoyed George's commentary on the progress of our plantation.

Usually.

George swept an arm from left to right. "We are rotating four crops to keep the soil fresh. Those who follow this practice usually do three, but I am experimenting with four, and may even try up to seven in seven years." He put his arm down and rested it upon the horse's withers. "The land must be nourished if it is to sustain itself. I am considering the use of manure to fertilize the crops. I have noticed its benefit in the areas where the animals—"

I could take no more. "I am sorry, George. I must . . ." I kicked a heel into the side of Arrow, and she sped away.

"Martha!"

I called over my shoulder. "I am fine!" I kissed my gloved fingers and lifted them into the air as my adieu.

Then I rode. And rode.

I had no destination but to be away. For everywhere I looked, every sound I heard, every aroma that reached my nostrils—good or foul—reminded me of Patsy. Since a tiny child, Mount Vernon had been her home. She had grown up there, and had delighted in its lush wonders that *I* could still experience, and she, could not. I had tried to create a haven for her, a safe place where she would thrive. That she had not . . . that she had not . . .

I pushed Arrow ever faster, the black of my mourning dress a stark contrast to her white coat. Although George and I often went riding, and though I found speed invigorating, I had not ridden like this since . . .

My mind returned to a time as a young girl when I had ridden a horse into my uncle's house—and up the stairs. How I had laughed. And how I had earned the wrath of my family. I had been young and carefree—it had been before my marriage to Daniel when I was sixteen.

Sixteen. Patsy had been sixteen. Only sixteen. Never beyond sixteen.

Tears assailed me and I rode even faster in hopes the wind would blow them from my cheeks. I rode past the slaves in the fields, past the overseer—who belatedly, in seeing it was me, tipped his hat—past fences, past . . . everything that could ever have been seen by Patsy. I needed to find some place she had never been, some place free of *her*.

I spotted a small path leading into the woods, pulled back on the reins to slow Arrow, and took it. Branches, untrimmed by our labours, accosted me rudely, forcing me to raise an arm in my own defense. The afternoon was darkened by a roof of limbs and leaves. A deer, frightened by my intrusion, pranced deeper into the forest. I slowed even more, realizing I was indeed the intruder and must show respect to the intrinsic serenity.

I spotted a clearing ahead and walked Arrow toward it, needing sky, needing light. The trees opened up and I dismounted—awkwardly, as I was used to George's steady hands to set me to the ground. Arrow immediately took advantage and began eating the tall grasses and bountiful leaves. I took a deep breath and raised my face to the sky. It was vivid blue with clouds moving fast, as if on parade.

On impulse, I descended to the ground and stretched onto my back. I removed an offending stone from behind my ribs and cradled my head with my hands. Thus settled, the world appeared different. The sky was framed with green, as a portrait on a wall. The walls of trees surrounding me and the green of my bed below formed a continuous mass, an encasement holding me, folding round me like a baby's bunting, making me feel secure and safe.

Here in the woods was a land untouched by man. This place belonged to its Creator and was therefore perfect and right. And I, lying in its midst . . .

I was a creation too. His creation.

Then I felt something—from the inside rather than out. An assurance. A hand upon my heart saying, *You belong to me and I to you.*

New tears came, but from a different source than before. These tears sprang not from despair but from a poignant release. A tender relief. I was not alone. God was with me. And though I would never—ever—understand His ways, with the soft touch of His hand upon my heart I felt I could accept them as something beyond . . . everything.

And it was good. Somehow, it was good.

I lay there, purposefully embracing each new breath and letting it out, purposefully letting the feeling embrace me and comfort me and do its work upon me. I removed one hand from behind my head and raised it skyward, extending it toward the heavens, where God lived. And Patsy.

And though I knew it was not so, I seemed to feel the slightest pressure upon my fingers, as though my gesture was reciprocated, that contact had been made.

Suddenly . . . a raindrop. Then three. Eight. A fine rain began to fall from the clouded sky that held only patches of blue. And though I had never been one to allow a rain access, in this time, in this place, I remained lying in the grass and let it fall upon me. It was as though God were sending heavenly tears to keep my own company.

I closed my eyes and let us cry together.

And be cleansed.

George strode from the house, his face heavy with worry. "Martha! Where did you go? I knew you needed time alone, but you were gone so long, and then the rain . . ."

Eustis held Arrow's reins and George helped me dismount. As he put his hands upon my waist, my feeling of ease continued. God was with me and so was George.

He set me gently to the ground and looked down at my face. "You seem . . . different."

"I am."

"What happened upon your ride?"

"I found a way."

He looked confused.

"A way to go on."

I had no idea if the feeling would last, and feared the panic and pain would return often, and with intensity. At the present all I could do was live with *now*.

It would have to do.

Sally embraced me, then kissed both cheeks. "I will miss you," she said.

"And I you. England is so very far away."

"Too far," George William said. He pointed to some trunks on the Belvoir wharf that were being loaded onto the ship that would take them to the mother country. He looked incredibly weary. "Since Lord Fairfax has replaced me as his agent here in America, all is lost." He wrinkled his nose in distaste. "This Robert Martin, this spendthrift, rake, and man of questionable constitution . . ." George William sighed. "Hopefully the Towlston estate in Yorkshire can be obtained as my true inheritance. We must have *some* income." He looked to my husband. "You will try to rent Belvoir for a goodly sum, yes?"

"Of course," George said. "You can trust me to do my best for it. And for you."

George William embraced his best friend. "You are the best of men and the best of friends. If only this horrible nonsense in the colonies would end here and bring some loyalty back to our king. I simply cannot tolerate such treasonous goings on."

Sally patted him on the back. " 'Twill be better for us to be in England until all this annoying dissension has blown over."

As we finished our good-byes and waved from the dock, George said to me, "I fear there will be no 'blowing over.' "

"Then perhaps it is best they go to England. They will be safe there."

"But away from us . . ." With a final wave he put his arm around me. "Let us go home."

Another loss. Would they never end?

<hr />

Summer burned itself out and autumn slipped into its place, with me unawares. One day I woke up and noticed the trees had turned orange and red. *When did this happen?*

It was a sobering moment, realizing time continued whether I cared to notice or not.

What truly made me notice autumn—and made me attempt to enjoy it—was when Jacky came home from King's College.

His embrace was full and sincere. "Mamma, I am so glad to be home to see you and Poppa." He let go to shake George's hand. Then he pulled a letter from his pocket and handed it to his father. "Read it. It is from Dr. Cooper, the president of the university."

My heart dropped. Had Jacky been expelled? Surely not, for he was all smiles.

George opened the letter and read aloud, " 'I am very pleased to inform you that young Jack Custis has commended himself in his studies and has shown an admirable purity of his morals. You should take great pride in him, as we do, at King's College.'" George lowered the letter, his face incredulous.

Jacky laughed. "I deserve that look—my past deserves that look."

I wrapped an arm around his waist and hugged him. "We are indeed proud. Such a letter! We knew you could do great things."

George appeared to be reading the letter again, as though he could not believe its contents. Then he folded it and placed it in the pocket of his coat with a pat. "Yes, Jack. This is great news. When you go back to school—"

"I am not going back."

His words hung in midair. We did not know how to catch them.

He looked from me to George, then back again. "Eleanor and I want to get married. Soon."

George was the first to speak. "We have grown to love Eleanor. She is a fine girl, good in action, thought, and heart, but she is still too young. And you . . ."

"I have proven myself."

"One semester is not proof. The proof would come in completing something, in attaining a degree."

Jacky plopped himself upon the white settee in the front parlour, crossed a leg, and draped an arm across its back as though totally at ease. That the portrait of his poppa in his militia uniform hung behind his shoulder was notable, surrounding him front and back by his father's presence.

He bit the tip of his thumbnail, then said, "It is not as though I have to impress someone to gain employment. I have a position waiting for me, running the Custis estates. I have my birthright."

George opened his mouth, drew in a breath, then closed it.

Oddly, although I had settled on the children waiting a few years, the suggestion the marriage might occur sooner rather than later appealed to me. Greatly. Since Patsy's death I had gained a new disdain for wasted years.

But I knew I would need to approach this new opinion gingerly. "Perhaps it *is* time for a wedding," I said.

I had anticipated George's reaction, and received as much. "Martha! Surely you cannot—"

I stood and motioned to Jacky. "Please leave us."

The grin that pronounced across his face was so certain I would be on his side that I nearly called him back to seating and agreed with George.

But alas, I did not. I let him go.

Which he did.

Closing the door behind him, leaving me alone with . . . our opposition.

George came close and lowered his voice, obviously sharing the certainty of Jacky's ears just outside the room. "How could you give him hope like that?"

With great resolve I did not make a space between us. George's towering frame could overwhelm—I had seen him strike fear into the constitution of a slacking worker by standing just so—but I stood my ground.

"Did you and Jacky conspire for this moment?" he asked.

"No, we did not. Up until he made the announcement, I was resigned to having his marriage be years away—as we had discussed."

"Exactly, Martha. As we had discussed. And settled. E'en Eleanor's father agreed to a delay."

At this point I returned to my chair. I turned Patsy's mourning ring around my finger—a recent habit I had no intention of breaking. "I assure you, I had no premeditation for considering a change of plans. But the fact Jacky has done so well at college—receiving a written commendation from its president—tells us his time there bore fruit."

"New fruit. Unripened fruit. Untested fruit."

I acquiesced with a shrug. "He has proven he *can* apply himself. Marriage will mature him e'en more."

"But he is not ready for marriage! Do you think his wild ways have been contained in a few months? Who knows what mischief he visited outside the eyes of Dr. Cooper. King's College is a large establishment, not the small school of Reverend Boucher, where the reverend could keep close tabs on Jack's exploits." He thought of something else. "Since Jack managed to behave wildly under the close scrutiny of Reverend Boucher, it only follows he would have perfected his methods, enabling him to do quite whatever he wanted in New York, beyond the eyes and ears of those in authority."

His logic made sense, and at first I felt beaten, but then I saw a way. . . . "I agree with you."

"You do?"

"I agree Jacky's untamed ways have probably not been reined in—more likely covered over with deft practice."

"Then you agree he could still find himself in dire trouble. He has not matured enough to—"

"Then I agree he could still find himself in dire trouble that may ruin his life." I leaned over and patted the arm of the chair beside me, wishing George to sit so we could talk more intimately. Once George was nearby I continued. "I know how it is with headstrong, lusty boys like Jacky, boys with wit and charm, and yes, those used to getting their way. They attract those of the opposite sex with great alacrity. And there, my dearest George, is my main argument toward marriage."

It took him but a moment to join the direction of my thoughts. "Another girl."

"Yes. One far less suitable in character and family than our dear Eleanor."

He looked across the room as though considering. Then he looked back to me. "But if his ways are thus . . . marriage may not stop his . . ."

"Philandering?"

"Exactly."

"Yet being away from the temptations of New York City, being back in the limited confines of White House, out in the country, busy with running a plantation . . . the opportunity for misbehaviour will be limited, and so, Jacky's chance at having a successful marriage will be increased. We will be saving him from himself."

"But he is still only eighteen—almost nineteen—and Eleanor seventeen. His youth, inexperience, and unripened education are and will be insuperable obstacles to the completion of an early marriage. If Jack gets married before he has ever bestowed a serious thought of the consequences, all will suffer. I feel quite adamant about this, Martha."

"As do I. Now, if you will excuse me, I have supper arrangements to complete."

I was not running from the confrontation. I was merely—wisely—leaving in order to regroup, in order to win the battle.

Surely Colonel Washington would appreciate my strategy.

***

Reinforcements often determine the victory. And so, in the matter of Jacky and Eleanor's marriage, I enlisted as many as possible. But, as is the essence of a good tactic, I did so under cover, surreptitiously writing to family—Custis, Dandridge, and Washington—as well as to neighbours, friends, and even to Reverend Boucher. In the pursuit of success one must not keep any stone unturned. To reinforce the power of their loyalty to my cause, I had them address their volleys directly to George. There would be no letter written to me that I would have to read aloud to my husband. No indeed. For that would be like sending a spray of bullets through a hedge of thick brush. I wished for George to receive their hail of support directly.

He was not amused.

One day he sought me out as I oversaw the washing in the washhouse.

"Mrs. Washington? If I may speak to you, please?"

I saw he held more than one letter in his hand. My stomach wrenched. Was this the moment when the outcome of the battle was at hand? I turned to Trudy and pointed at a shirt. "Make certain you embroider our guest's initials in their garments so they do not get mixed." Then I donned my cape and followed him outside. We walked away from the house and entered the snow-covered lower garden. We walked slowly. He wished to have this discussion out-of-doors?

So be it.

The December air was cold but not bitter. The snow under our feet was packed hard from the comings and goings of many feet. I slipped, and his hand immediately steadied me, placing my hand in the crook of his arm. Although my slippage was sincere, I recognized the act of his gallantry and our physical connection to my advantage.

"You wished to talk to me?" I said as the rhythm of our gait was settled. Within these few steps, my feet were cold. His boots offered protection, but my cloth slippers, with their slim soles, allowed the cold to permeate into my toes. Yet I did not complain. The happiness of my Jacky—and his Eleanor—was at stake.

He held the letters before me. "I have received these."

I recognized my mother's handwriting, and that of his sister, Betty. "How nice. Is the family well?"

"They do not speak of their own condition, but focus completely on the condition of Jack. They talk exclusively of the advantages of a timely marriage." He looked down at me. "They use familiar arguments."

I did not dare look at him but concentrated on the path before me. "Perhaps the arguments are familiar because they are true and hold logic."

He stopped our progress and faced me. For the first time I wavered in my resolve. Perhaps I should complain of cold feet. . . . I glanced at him, then away. I pulled my cloak closer and offered a shiver that was timely but not forged.

He put a finger under my chin and raised it as he often did when he had something he sorely wanted me to hear. "Are you certain you never studied military tactics and methods of war?"

I tried to contain a smile but was only partially successful. "I do not know what you mean, Colonel Washington. Surely you, as the commander of many men—"

"Surely I, as your husband, know when I have met my match."

I let a smile fully escape. "So you will agree to their marriage?"

He lifted the letters between us. "What choice do I have against Jacky, who has his own inclination; the desires of his mother; and the acquiescence of almost all of his relatives. As he is the last of the family, I dare not push my opposition too far. And so I yield—contrary to my judgment."

Although I wished to leap into his arms and kiss him, I knew his defeat was keen and was best accepted with dignity. I raised his hand to my lips and kissed it instead. "He *is* the last of the line, George. The future of the Custis land—and Mount Vernon—depends upon his settling down and taking responsibility."

"And having children."

I blinked at his words.

"Do not dare say this was not a factor in your strategy, Martha, perhaps e'en the true spoils of your victory. With Patsy's passing . . ."

"I do long for there to be children in my life. The joyful product of a good match made with the approval of two great families—three great families: Custis, Washington, and Calvert."

He laughed. "No more flattery is needed, my dear. I have surrendered. Victory is yours."

Ours. For in my heart I felt this marriage would bless us all.

"You *could* put aside your mourning clothes, dearest. No one would fault you," George said.

I stood at the armoire in our bedchamber, peering at the clothing inside. Jacky and Eleanor were to be married on February 3, and I was trying to decide which dress to wear—or whether to have a new one made. George had already given Jacky money for his wedding clothes.

I ran a hand along the lovely satins and brocades. I so enjoyed lovely dresses, and George had said I could have my heart's desire in a new one made especially for the occasion.

I let my hand stray to the bodice of the black mourning dress I was wearing. The trim on the front was frayed. Although I had ordered many black dresses made after Patsy's death, their constant use over these many months . . .

My eyes returned to the happy colours of my other dresses before falling back upon the black. Happy. Sad. The vivid dresses seemed to dare me to choose. *You have had enough mourning. Choose us! We will make you happy.*

I shook my head at their temptation. They would *not* make me happy. I was not sure anything would. Not completely.

Have a new dress, Mamma.

The memory of Patsy's voice accosted me often. Things she would have said came to me unannounced. Sometimes when I heard someone in the hall outside a room, I would look up and think, "Patsy is here!" But then I would remember she could not be there, and when someone else came in, I suffered disappointment and pain as grief sliced open a fresh wound.

Dresses. I was thinking about dresses.

Patsy had loved clothes as much as I. But how could I ever wear a pretty gown when my Patsy was not able to join me?

I took comfort in the knowledge my girl was in heaven with

our Lord, and yet I still fought with the Almighty over the arrangement.

Everyone said Patsy was better off now; her sufferings were over. Even Jacky had written me . . .

I moved to the drawer of my dressing table, where I kept his letter. *Her case is more to be envied than pitied, for if we mortals can distinguish between those who are deserving of grace and who are not, I am confident she enjoys that bliss prepared only for the good and virtuous. . . . Comfort yourself with reflecting that she now enjoys in substance what we in this world enjoy in imagination.*

The page easily folded upon itself from much perusal. My Jacky was not an eloquent boy, and yet in this letter, he had proven himself far capable of that trait. Perhaps God had enabled him a temporary gift because the Almighty knew how much the son's words would comfort the mother.

I would never know, of course, but took pleasure in imagining it so.

I gave the letter the kiss it deserved and then set it back in its place—ready for the next time.

Then I left the room to find George and tell him I would indeed have a dress made for my son's wedding.

The horses were restless, the carriage ready and waiting.

For me.

George stood in the foyer, readying the clasp of his cloak. Then he held my cape open.

For me.

I did not move to put it on.

"Come now, Martha. A storm looms. We must get on the road. Mount Airy is sixty miles away."

I stepped away from the cloak—from him. "I cannot go, George."

He did not respond at first. Then, "Whyever not?"

"I cannot sap the joy from the occasion by attending in my mourning clothes. It would not be fair to Jacky and Eleanor."

His eyes skimmed my black travel clothes. "Then wear something festive. You had a new dress made, no?"

It was my turn to hesitate a response. "No."

"No?"

"I could not do it. Not yet. It has only been eight months."

"But it is your son's wedding—your only son's wedding."

I began to cry. I knew he was right. I knew I should go, and yet I could not.

He moved to comfort me. "Martha, come. You will regret it if you stay."

"Jacky will understand. He grieves for Patsy as much as I."

"We all grieve for Patsy. That is not in question. Do you think people will think badly of you if you celebrate the wedding of your son?"

"No, no, I do not do this to appease others."

"Then whom do you appease?"

An appropriate question. Finally, I answered: "Myself."

George looked down at me, his disapproval evident. "Your *self* is definitely at play, my darling. And though I understand your grief, I must say this appears an act of selfishness. Think of Jacky. Think of Eleanor. Think of me."

Although I wanted to sob and have him take me in his arms, I knew if I did so, he might stay behind with me. And that, I did not want. So instead, I lifted my chin and said, "I do not need nor appreciate your insults. If I am being selfish by staying behind and showing honour to the memory of my daughter, then so be it. It is something I am intent on doing—alone." I moved to the door and opened it wide. "Go. Give everyone my best."

With one last look that spoke of his frustration and

incredulity, George kissed my forehead and went outside to the waiting carriage.

I stood with my back against the door that separated us until the sound of the horses and wheels had dissipated into silence.

The silence was suddenly heavy and I yanked the door open, running out on the stoop. The servants stood apart from each other and looked up from their chatting. "Mrs. Washington?"

With a shake of my head I withdrew indoors. Sobs I had held in check threatened. Amanda stood upon the stairs. "Mistress?"

With another shake to my head I hurried past her, up the stairs to our room. There I shut the door.

And wondered what I had done.

⁂

"Your brother should be married by now, Patsy."

I put my hand on the wooden door of the family crypt. As the day—February 3, 1774—dragged on, I found myself useless. Although I tried to distract with chores and busyness, each tick of the clock's hands, each chime at the quarter hour, brought my mind to Mount Airy and thoughts of the happenings occurring there. On this day.

Without me.

Eleanor and her nine siblings, her parents, her grandparents, George's sister and brother and their families. Dozens and dozens of friends and neighbours, all drawn together on this happy day.

All but me.

By my own choice.

That was the rub. There was no reason I could not be there. No one had dictated it was too soon to doff the mourning clothes that had shrouded me these past months. No one had scolded and said that wearing the mourning clothes would ruin the event. I could blame no one but myself for my choice.

Reckless choice?

I stroked the door. "I did it for you, Patsy."

I could almost hear her voice saying, *I never asked you to do that, Mamma. I would never want you to do that. Do not do it again.*

I nodded, agreeing. I had made a mistake—one large in magnitude, for my son would not get married a second time. I had missed one happy milestone because I had been too enmeshed in a tragic one. A way to overcome the tragic was to focus on the happy. I had forgotten that and caused others—and myself—sorrow and regret.

Yet . . . though I may not have chosen rightly, I had chosen from the heart. And was that ever truly wrong?

I kissed my fingers and pressed them against the door. "I am sorry, Patsy, for using you as an excuse. I will make it up to you—and to Jacky. I promise."

<hr />

Mistakes are inevitable. Yet the only way they are tolerable is when we learn from them and become better for them.

So it was with my mistake regarding Jacky's wedding. The spring of 1774 was better for me. I was better. On the day of the wedding, at the tomb of my daughter, I gained more strength to move forward.

Reason and rationalization entered my consciousness. Looking back upon my intense distress at Patsy's death, the lingering of the pain, made me weigh that grief against all others. The difference was necessity. When my other children, when little Daniel and Frances died, and even when my husband Daniel passed, I had not had time to mourn in solitude. The logistics of living each day had demanded my attention. I had not had time to wallow and allow the sorrow to spin a smothering cocoon around me. Although I now had many of the same duties, I had more help. And perhaps as a consequence of age I allowed myself the luxury of grief. Perhaps the death of Patsy— so sudden and unexpected after we had been so encouraged by her improvement—had added to the deaths of my Daniels and Frances until it had simply become too much.

Whatever the reason, as Jacky and Eleanor came to visit us often, as I could see the extremity of their happiness, I was able to embrace *that* emotion as my own. It was a good thing, this happiness. This pursuit of happiness. I knew Patsy would approve.

That I could find happiness even as we dealt with severe financial setbacks confirmed my relief was God-inspired. . . .

Our London factors decided to cut off our credit line. George and I admitted we did not take as much notice of our debts as we should, and when crops did not perform as hoped, all was made worse. But without the support of Robert Cary and Company, we would be isolated and have nowhere to sell our goods. The answer—ironically—came from Patsy.

Upon her death her portion of the Custis fortune was divided equally between Jacky and me. And as a married woman, my portion went to George. Most of her holdings were in cash and Bank of England stock. At first, George was averse to use it, but I insisted. The crisis was diverted as the factors were paid. If she had been alive, Patsy would have been eager to offer the funds, but George would never have done it.

On a lighter note, when George went to Williamsburg in May for the House of Burgesses meetings, I went with him. Surprisingly, I was eager to go and my eagerness added to my joy. And his. For he too had suffered with his own grief, and as witness to mine. He was a good husband. I could not imagine better.

There was much going on in Williamsburg. The governor of Virginia—Lord Dunmore—celebrated the arrival of his wife and daughter from England. We were friends and dined with them multiple times. The governor was quite solicitous regarding Patsy's death, sending the kindest of letters: *I do condole with you for your loss, though as the poor young lady was so often afflicted with these fits, I dare say she thinks it a happy exchange.*

Although focusing on Patsy's freedom from all pain and tears in heaven was hard fought, I did agree with such offerings of comfort. Reluctantly.

But then, in the midst of the session of the Burgesses and the festivities for the coming of Lady Dunmore, news arrived that changed everything.

After a day at the Burgesses, George came home, much distressed.

"Sit, dearest," I implored as he made his way up and back in front of the mantel—for the tenth time.

"Why do they force our hand? Why can we not work out our differences without this constant tit for tat?"

He often came home this way from his meetings. It was best to let him fume. He would tell me the details as he was ready.

Suddenly, he stopped pacing and faced me. "The king has closed Boston Harbour."

"Why?"

"Because of the tea incident last December."

"When the colonists dressed up like Indians and dumped it into the harbour?"

George nodded. "It was a nonviolent protest against the taxation of the tea. That Parliament would remove other taxes yet leave the one . . . such an act was mocking. I supported the action by the Bostonians—which was mirrored in other ports."

"But if the harbour is closed, then how can Massachusetts survive?"

"It cannot. Which, I am sure, is the point. Britain has also strengthened the law that we quarter their troops, and makes it possible for a British officer in need of discipline to be tried back in safe territory—in England—as if his trial would be anything but a sham in that venue. These acts are intolerable and are testimony to the most despotic system of tyranny that has ever been practiced in a free government!"

"Those are fighting words, Colonel Washington."

He paused long enough to let two breaths in and out. "Perhaps they are. We are being forced into such a position, Martha. If need be, I will raise one thousand men, subsist them at my own expense, and march myself at their head for the relief of Boston."

That was the last thing I wished to see him do. "What did the Burgesses do about all this?"

"We voted to have a day of prayer and fasting to showcase our solidarity with Boston's sufferings."

"That is a laudable idea," I said. "Was it yours?"

"Not mine. But that of Thomas Jefferson, Richard Henry Lee, and Patrick Henry."

At the mention of Henry, I shook my head. "I do not like the latter. I find him crude and prone to speaking too often and too loudly with too much emotion." I leaned closer and lowered my voice. "I have also heard talk that he keeps his wife locked in the basement of his house."

I could tell George wished to refute my words but could not. "She is not well. Mentally. He has little choice."

I shook my head. "To love and honour, in sickness and in health . . ."

"I am certain he cares for her as well as he is able."

I was not so sure. I did not trust the man.

George rubbed the space between his eyes. "Martha, this is not about Patrick Henry, nor about any one man. This is about the rights of all men being assaulted."

I chastised myself for being petty. George did not like gossip and I knew it was not a godly act. "When is this day of prayer and fasting supposed to—"

"You have not heard the last," he said. "Lord Dunmore—my friend, with whom we have dined often—has dissolved the assembly and called for new elections to fill the seats!"

"But he is our friend."

"Though not a friend to our Cause."

"But the ball in honour of Lady Dunmore is tomorrow."

"I know, I know. And once we were disbanded we met in the Raleigh Tavern and discussed that among many other issues. Most were sure their wives would not wish to attend, but most—"

"Disagreement or no, it would not be right to snub Lady Dunmore."

He held up a finger. "You did not let me finish. Most men thought their wives would agree with *you*. And so, I think we should go."

I was relieved. "It is difficult to keep friendships, civility, and politics separate."

"Indeed. I have heard people in England think we are a race of convicts, rascals, robbers, and pirates. I prefer to have them think of us as thinking men who only react when provoked, who only wish to be treated fairly and with respect."

He looked so worried, so downtrodden, that I went to him and wrapped my arms about his waist. "I support you, George. In all you do, I support you—and our Cause."

He pulled my head against his chest. "May God help us all."

⋙———⋘

We did not eat all day.

We prayed.

We entered the Bruton Parish Church in Williamsburg on June 1, 1774, a Wednesday, at ten o'clock in the morning, just as instructed in the resolution drafted by Thomas Jefferson calling for fasting, humiliation, and prayer. This church was familiar to us, as our place of worship when in town.

The white pew boxes were full with the members of the House of Burgesses, their wives, family, and others who wished to partake of this important day. I nodded to our friends as we passed to our box near the cross aisle and slid in, with George coming after. The mood was dignified. There was no shaking of hands or talking. Only a nod here and there in passing.

I had heard Reverend Mr. Gwatkin had been chosen to give the sermon with Reverend Mr. Price to offer the prayers, but the former declined due to a disorder in his breast—but he did write the sermon for Reverend Price to offer us in his stead. I did not question his ailment—especially since it would be his words we were to hear—and yet, seeing as how Reverend Gwatkin was the tutor for Lord Dunmore's oldest son . . . I was certain a portion of his ailing breast might have been due to torn feelings regarding the direction of common sentiments toward the mother country.

I imagined torn feelings were rampant in the minds and hearts of most colonists, and would continue to be so.

Once all were settled, Reverend Price stepped to the pulpit, opened the Bible, and began: "Today I speak from Genesis. Abraham stands before God asking about the Almighty's plan to destroy the wicked towns of Sodom and Gomorrah. 'Wilt thou also destroy the righteous with the wicked?' Abraham asked the Almighty. God said, 'I will not destroy it for ten's sake.' "

Reverend Price closed the Bible and swept a hand across the room. "We are more than ten gathered here. More than ten righteous people who wish to uphold the attributes and blessings that have made America prosper for one hundred and fifty years. Now, when our hard work is being threatened, we must stand firm. We must not let evil conduct quash all that has been accomplished with God's help. Our brothers in Boston have been forced to action against an oppressive tyranny. Miles away, we empathize with their fight, support them with provisions and capital, and pray for them with our whole hearts. With humble supplication we pray that the will of the Almighty will prevail, the oppression of our present will be subdued, and the peace and prosperity of our past will be reinstated with His blessing."

Amen.

— TEN —

S old! To Mr. Washington."

From the seat beside him, I shook my head.

"I know, I know. But you and I have seen Sally use that serving cart a hundred times."

"But we do not need a serving cart," I whispered.

Or a mahogany shaving desk, wash desk or tallboy, a set of dining room chairs, a gilt mirror or . . .

Our dear friends the Fairfaxes were not returning from England. The uneasiness of the colonies held no appeal, and since they were no longer the agent to Lord Fairfax, they were not comfortable in America. So . . . the Fairfaxes had left Fairfax County for good, leaving George to auction off their property.

That he had bid on many pieces of Sally's personal furniture was of interest.

Not that I had failed to recover from any jealousy I felt regarding the bond they shared in their youth—before he met me. Yes, I had seen the ember of a spark even after we were wed, but I was also certain it had never been fanned into a flame. A person cannot help feeling an attraction toward another, but they can implement self-control and honour to never act upon that attraction. I believed, with my whole heart, George never acted in any way untoward. As friends have said, he was the master of himself.

George leaned toward me, discreetly pointing to the front of the room. "Would you like that cloisonné vase? Sally often had it on the mantel."

Actually . . . "Certainly," I said. For Sally and George William did have exquisite taste. And Sally was my friend also.

A friend I missed.

As the disagreements between England and her colonies grew, how many other friends would I lose to political loyalty?

"Sold!" said the auctioneer, holding up the vase. "Again, to Mr. Washington."

And his wife.

Our guests were to bed and we were on our way toward that same location. As George washed his face and arms at the washstand—Sally's washstand—I took the coat he had worn at dinner and hung it upon its hook.

A letter fell from the pocket.

My first reaction was not worthy of me—or George. But first reactions seldom are. My first reaction was to think he had kept a letter from Sally, and because she had been on our mind of late . . .

As penance for my unwarranted thought, I picked up the letter and took it to my husband. "Here," I said, holding it toward him. "This fell from your pocket."

He gave it but a glance, then said, "Open it. It is from Jack."

"I have not read it?"

"No," George said while drying his face. "It was sent directly to me." He nodded toward the letter. "Please."

I opened it and read, *I am at a great loss of words to tell you the level of esteem I hold for you. You have been my father in every way. I have nothing but affection and regard, both of which did not I possess in the highest degree for you. I shall strenuously endeavour by my future conduct to merit a continuance of your regard and esteem.*

I heard George's laughter. "You are surprised?"

"I am stunned. The boy . . . to have him express his feelings so eloquently." I folded the letter and handed it back to him. "It makes me proud."

"Why do you think I carry it with me?" He crossed to the armoire and placed the letter in the pocket of the coat he would wear tomorrow. That done, he faced me. "Although I did not agree to their marriage at first, I must admit it might be the best thing that could have happened to our Jack."

I put a hand to my chest, feigning this additional shock.

"Do not make fun of me, Martha."

"I *will* make fun of you. But note I am pleased by your acquiescence. I have but one question."

"What is that?"

"Since, in your frustration at having to give in to the arguments put forth by myself and my family regarding the children's marriage—"

"Pressure. Steady, relentless pressure."

I shrugged. "Since you allowed your frustration to be played out in a new project of adding additional wings to our house here at Mount Vernon, I was wondering . . . since you now agree with us in all entirety, since your frustration at not getting your way is abated . . . are you going to tear down the new wings? For they are no longer needed for their original purpose."

He slipped under the bed's coverlet. "I did not build the wings because I did not get my way. I would not—"

"You would. And you often do." I got into bed beside him. "There is merit in directing such feelings into new projects. I do not fault you. I was just wondering if your zeal to build would continue without its source."

He blew out the candle.

As spring progressed into summer and then into fall, we all came to terms with one fact: times were changing and there was little we could do to stop it. It was not a matter of fighting or not fighting, as Britain continued to change the rules and show themselves increasingly intolerant and aggressive. They sent more soldiers to Boston, tried to make us accept taxation by making comparisons between how much we were taxed versus their citizens at home (they *did* suffer worse than we) and then refused to let soldiers who fought in the war against France claim the land in western Virginia, as promised. Our mother country showed itself to be a bully and dishonourable to her word, forcing us to action—or to fall down in surrender.

If she thought we would do the latter, she did not know her children well. Although we began by offering action as individual colonies, we soon came to see the only way to beat a bully was to band together. And so, when our compatriots in Massachusetts called a meeting of all the colonies—a Continental Congress—George became a delegate for Virginia along with six others, including Patrick Henry and our neighbor Edmund Pendleton. Before heading off to the meeting in Philadelphia, these men came for a visit at Mount Vernon.

I was happy to do my part in providing them a safe haven to discuss the issues that plagued us. The pressure upon their shoulders to act, and act wisely and prudently, was enormous. If I could offer them solace with good meals, warm beds, and a homey environment, then I was wont to do so. If only I could do more.

When it came time for them to leave the next morning, I stood outside to see them off. I felt tears threaten as these men—with so much to lose—were heading off with a willingness to sacrifice everything for the sake of a better life for us all.

And George . . . sitting tall in his saddle, his chin set with a deep-rooted determination to do his best. I trusted him above all men. If anyone could help us weave our way through this horrid gauntlet, it was he.

"Thank you, Mrs. Washington," said Patrick Henry.

"Yes, thank you," added Edmund. "Your hospitality and graciousness are a balm to our troubled souls."

"I am happy to do it," I said. "I hope you will stand firm. I know George will." I stepped back to let them begin their journey. "God be with you gentlemen."

I watched until I could see them no more, then said a silent prayer for their journey and their objective.

It would be but one of many.

I sat at the dining table with George's cousin, Lund, going over issues of the plantation.

Lund read through some meticulous notes he had kept for George's benefit until he returned from the Continental Congress. "George had said he would like the bricklayer's house moved several hundred yards to the east. He believes it will be more efficient at that location. So I have moved it two hundred fifty yards and . . ." His voice trailed off. "Your mind is not on bricks, Martha, nor much else other than George, I would guess."

I nodded. "It has been difficult to know that serious issues are being attended to in Philadelphia and only learn about them second-hand from newspapers and letters from George." I reached over the table and put a hand on Lund's. "You have been invaluable to us both—as usual."

"I am glad to help."

I sighed and rubbed my eyes. "Although the running of Mount Vernon has kept me busy in hand these six weeks, it has not done as much for my mind." I looked toward the window.

"He will be home soon."

"None too soon."

The winds of November blew hard and cold.

I did not care.

George was home again.

Yet after our initial greeting on the morning he arrived, his time had been diverted to the must-do's of the plantation. Lund had his ear most of the day, and though I resented their companionship, I understood the need of it. I would have my time alone with him. Eventually.

It was dark evening before I had my chance. George found me sitting before the fire in the parlour. He entered and closed the door behind him.

If it could have been bolted, I would have done so just to ensure his continued presence. He moved behind my chair and kissed my head. I raised my hand to gain his and we remained there a moment like two connected subjects sitting for a portrait.

When I heard him sigh, I said, "So? Tell me."

"We have made an effort."

"A valiant one, no doubt."

He moved to the fire and poked it to new flame. "We *all* have borne so much. We have long and ardently sought for reconciliation upon honourable terms. Yet it has been denied us. All our attempts after peace have not only proved abortive but have been grossly misrepresented. We have done everything that could be expected from the best of subjects, but the spirit of freedom beats too high for us to submit to slavery."

I took a deep breath. "There is no choice but rebellion."

He shook his head. "None of the colonies will ever submit to the loss of the valuable rights and privileges that are essential to happiness. Without them, life, liberty, and property are rendered totally insecure." He looked from the fire to my eyes. "More blood will be spilt on this occasion than has ever yet been recorded in the annals of North America."

I found my hand resting upon my bodice. "There will be war?"

"We are halting all imports from England December 1, and if Britain does not repel the Intolerable Acts, we will cease all exports next year."

"We are cutting ourselves off."

"We are taking a stand against their tyranny. And yet . . . we went to the Congress with no sense of unity—feeling wary, timid, and skittish of each other. We went believing the rebels of Massachusetts were hotheads."

"But now?"

"We have made every attempt to think and act as one." He sat in the chair next to mine. "We are warning the people to prepare for a fight. We must not be caught unawares. We must support Massachusetts as one unit."

"It is a new concept."

He nodded. "And one that is still confused in its intent. Ironically, before parting we gathered for one last dinner and toasted our England." He raised an arm in a mock toast. " 'To His Majesty, King George. May the sword of the parent never be stained by the blood of its children.' "

"Thirteen brothers rising up against their parent."

"We do not wish it so. But we must receive some consolation. We have asked the crown to remove its military presence from Boston. If they will agree, then . . ."

"They will not agree."

His shoulders dropped. "It is doubtful."

The thought of fighting. I shuddered and turned conversation to the personal. "How did *you* fare at the Congress?"

"I listened more than I spoke."

"As you do."

He smiled. "Patrick Henry told me if one wanted eloquence,

Mr. Rutledge of South Carolina was the greatest orator, but if one wanted solid information and sound judgment, I was the greatest man on that floor."

"Bravo, my dear."

"Of course he also said my thinking was slow in operation." He cleared his throat and changed his voice to match Henry's. " 'Being little aided by invention or imagination, but sure in conclusion.' "

"How dare he!"

George shrugged. "I took no offense. Henry may be brusque in manner, but he is right in content. Where he attends the Congress to impress and raise people to action, I feel no need to impress. I attended to learn. You know I do best debating issues one on one. I do not feel at ease before large groups."

"You manage well enough."

"It helps if I know my audience personally. I made great effort to get to know every delegate. A fine group of men they are, though disparate in opinion. Most delegates from Pennsylvania and New York came with instructions to find resolution with England, while the other colonies are less loyal to the mother country, but in varying degrees. 'Tis like getting a yard full of chickens to agree on which seed to pluck from the ground—and when." He nodded once. "By the by, our own Virginian Peyton Randolph was elected president of the entire Congress."

"A good choice?"

"Absolutely, though they are all able men. Men of great interest and bearing."

"Any man in particular?"

"Actually, yes. John Adams. An attorney and planter from Pennsylvania. Where I listen, he is happy to speak—more than he should at times."

I wondered more about this man. "Is he married?"

"Very much so. His wife is Abigail and seems very much involved in the Cause. They have five children. He talked much about them."

I felt a twinge of jealousy—for the prodigious children and for Abigail's involvement. For the one I had no cure, and as to the other . . . I was as involved as I could be considering the distance involved.

George sat back in the chair and I watched his shoulders relax. "John and I make quite the pair. He is—by his own words—short, thick, and fat with a voice wont to boom where mine tends to softness. Our friends laughed at our disparity, and feared we would suffer great arguments between us."

"This did not happen, I assume?"

"It did not. I enjoyed him immensely, as I believe he enjoyed me. For one thing, he impressed me, for he has the education I lack. He went to Harvard."

After our experience with Jacky's aborted education, I knew the tenaciousness and strength of character required to earn a degree.

"John countered my admiration with his own appreciation of my soldiering abilities. Apparently he feels guilty for not fighting against the French. He also is quite in awe of our land. Our forty-thousand acres compared to his forty . . ."

"There is much to be in awe about. You are an expert at running our farms."

George shrugged. "John also enjoys hunting and horses as much as I, along with appreciation of a fine Madeira. And he agrees with me on the need to keep keen financial records." He paused a moment and pushed his right foot toward the fire, then back. "I attended Presbyterian services with him while in Philadelphia, and then, led by curiosity and good company, together we tried a Romish one. Actually, there was much churchgoing. Late in September, I attended two services for the delegates in one day: one at a Quaker meetinghouse and another at St. Peter's Episcopal."

I laughed. "I am pleased to see the delegates seeking His wisdom with such alacrity. That there are so many ways to seek it . . ."

George's face drew serious. "We *are* seeking it, Martha. Every day's congressional session began with prayer. And personally, I enjoyed experiencing the different congregations, as I enjoy the recent trend to find a more personal God within our own faith. If He is not with us, we will not prevail."

"I have been praying also."

"I know you have. And please continue."

The need for prayer made me think of sacrifice. "George . . . if all proceeds in the direction it is going . . . we may lose everything."

"There is the chance. The sacrifices will potentially affect every aspect of our lives."

I could accept the material sacrifices, and the cultural, and even the social. What I feared most was losing . . .

George must have sensed my thoughts, for he leaned forward from his chair, his hand seeking mine. "If there is fighting, dearest . . . you know I feel no need to be a hero."

"Be a hero all you wish. A live one."

"I will do my best."

I believed him. But would Jacky and my nephews follow such prudence? For surely they would be called to fight. To believe in a cause yet fear the cost . . .

I knew it would not be the last time I would ponder such thoughts.

<hr />

I heard the sound of a horse coming toward the house at high speed. I looked up from my mending to see our neighbor George Mason hurl himself off his steed. He strode toward the house. The door was open to catch the spring breezes. I moved to greet him, but George intercepted him, running up from the four acres he had set aside for fruit trees. George was determined to create hardy varieties and had hired a full-time gardener to graft the trees.

"Is there news?" my George asked.

"Too much," Mason said.

"Come in and sit, gentlemen," I said, luring them into the back parlour. I ordered cool drinks for them both before returning to hear their discourse.

". . . one thousand troops to Boston."

I had to play catch-up. "British troops?"

"Yes," Mason said. "Their General Gage had apparently heard we were stockpiling arms and ammunition. It is no surprise Parliament did not take it well. They accuse our Continental Congress of illegitimate plotting."

"Plotting in our defense, I say. We would be fools to sit by."

Mason raised a hand, stopping George's comments. "I agree. We all agree. The British continue to show little respect for any of us. Of our militia . . . they call us a disorganized mob and do not believe we can offer much resistance."

"I too have my doubts," George said.

"Doubts or no, there is no turning back."

"Gage was successful in capturing our arms?"

"Not completely. Paul Revere and William Dawes rode across the countryside warning people the British were coming so by the time their troops arrived in Lexington, a few dozen minutemen were assembled and much of our ammunition stored there and in Concord was hidden away."

I had to interrupt. "Minutemen?"

"Colonial militia ready to fight in a minute."

I nodded and Mason continued. "We were sorely outnumbered, and our commander, a man named Parker, told our men to disperse, but in the dispersing, shots were fired—by whom we do not know—and many were killed. What was started as a political argument between members of the same family had become a blood feud."

I put my hand on the back of George's rocker. "Gage and his men?"

"They retreated into Boston with our militia dogging them the entire way, fighting from bushes and barns. Even women took up guns and nearly three hundred British soldiers were killed, as were nearly one hundred of our own. I heard it said Gage is frustrated. It is one thing to have an army fight against an army, but to have an army fight against an entire populace . . ."

"I would take up a weapon to defend Mount Vernon," I said.

George pointed at me. "No you would not, my dear. You will not put yourself in danger."

"I may not have a choice."

George turned back to Mason. "Does fighting continue?"

"The British moved to Concord to find our stores of ammunition, but found little, though they did destroy what was left behind. Boston is amass with red coats, and the countryside has reacted en masse. It is said twenty thousand colonials have camped across the river from Boston, all angry and ready to fight."

George let out a puff of air. "Twenty thousand?"

"Ready or not, it has begun."

"We may have twenty thousand men, but twenty thousand men who know how to be soldiers? I doubt it." George turned his head to gaze over the expanse of our dear plantation. The place was a hive of busyness with people going about their work, ignorant of the chaos happening up north. Would the fighting reach Virginia? Perhaps the proper question was *when* would it reach Virginia?

"Gage has ordered John Hancock—the richest man in America—arrested. As with Samuel Adams—a cousin of John."

"They have not—"

"Not yet," Mason said. "And if the good general thinks by arresting two he can arrest the fervor of America, he is sorely mistaken."

George nodded and I could tell by the furrow in his brow his mind raced. "The second Continental Congress is scheduled to commence in three weeks."

"A good thing," Mason said. "Though when the schedule was set, I am certain you had no thought as to the perfection of its timing."

"There were many things beyond our thoughts."

Things that now would *never* be beyond our thoughts.

———✦———

"I am not convinced of this, Martha."

George stood before me, trying on his striking red, white, and blue militia uniform. He looked as stunning in it now as he had twenty years before. At age forty-three he was still a handsome man, perhaps more handsome.

I brushed dust from his sleeve. I, too, was not convinced—of much of anything during these trying times. But I felt the need to be supportive. "The Congress is looking to appoint a commander over all the colonial forces, George. As much as I wish I could state otherwise, I know you are that man. Wearing your uniform, your hat, carrying your sword in its scabbard . . . riding in upon your horse . . . there will be no one who can look at another man and think *he* would be a more suitable commander."

"It is more than appearance, my dear. There are qualifications."

I shook my head, confused about his sudden reservations. How had our conversation veered from George convincing me of the possibility of his appointment, to my convincing him? "You have worked a lifetime for this, George. The British ignored your talents and never granted you equal status. Is it not time you made them regret their slight?"

"I am over it, Martha."

"Well, I am not!"

He looked surprised at my vehemence. I was surprised myself. I moved close and hooked my fingers in the coat as it met across his chest. "If I allowed myself to think only of myself, then I would tell you to remove the coat and lock the bedroom door so you would never leave me. But since I believe in our Cause and believe with my entire being you are *the* man to lead us toward victory, then I must . . ." My voice broke and I looked away from his eyes. "Then I must—however reluctantly—relinquish you to others, to the greater good."

He pulled me close. "*You* are good, dearest. There is no better woman, nor more supportive wife."

Guilt forbade me from raising my face to look at him. For beyond the essence of my support I was a realist. If others saw only the man George had become, I had known him when he was fresh from the French war—a defeated man with nary a victory to brag upon. I had seen him as an ambitious man who needed funds to further his dream of a great plantation. I knew he had risen above both disabilities by marrying me and gaining the Custis social standing along with my wealth. And thinking of the future instead of the past, I also knew we were sorely in debt. Though Lund was a good manager, there was a lesser chance of rising above our challenges under his tutelage rather than my husband's.

But . . . but . . . George did not need to be reminded of such issues. He was going to do this. He *had* to do this. And so, I had to support him.

I spoke into the wool of his coat. "You must know that e'en if I were not your wife, I would choose you to be the commander."

He held me closer still and we stood as such until our breaths in and out found rhythm. To send him away, knowing I was sending him into battle, into danger . . . for I knew by his stories he was not a general to sit in safety and watch. As he was a plantation owner who toiled in field and foundry, so I knew he would be a general who would fight *with* his men, and as such . . .

I pushed away from him to ask a question. "Who are the other men in contention?"

"John Hancock is under consideration. With his riches gained through shipping, added to his experience in the forefront of the issues that have plagued Massachusetts . . ."

"But?"

"But he is a politician and has no military background."

"A necessary qualification, I would think."

"There is one military man whose name has been mentioned. Charles Lee. He was a British soldier under Braddock and Gage against the French and also commended himself in Europe before coming back to the colonies a few years ago and joining our Cause. He has the most experience . . ."

"But?"

"These next may sound trifling, but I assure you they are not. He is careless in hygiene and dress, and is abrasive in manner. Plus, he is known to use the foulest of language with a thick British accent, both of which may rub the American-born militia wrongly. And, as he was once a British soldier . . ."

I understood the implication and had a new thought. "Perhaps it was Providence you were never offered a commission with the British army. Surely that position would taint your qualifications as it now taints Mr. Lee's."

George considered this a moment. "All things do happen for a reason."

Generally, I agreed with him, though I still saw no reason in the deaths of so many of my loved ones. I pushed such painful thoughts into the room of my memories that I kept locked but for private, pensive visits.

I smiled at my husband, who was very much with me in the here and now. "You, my dear George, a true gentleman from Virginia, are an amiable contrast to the officers who have already been involved in skirmishes in New England."

"My Virginia roots coupled with the support of other strong Virginia men like Henry, Jefferson, and the rest, *and* the abundant resources of Virginia . . ."

"*And* your qualifications as a businessman, a man who knows the necessity of details and economics and organization. *And* your knowledge of how a British soldier fights and ways to counter it. Not many men have such complete intelligence at their disposal."

George laughed softly. "My, my, I am quite the perfect candidate."

I pushed against his chest. "You are! Was it not Adams who stated that no one looks more the general than yourself?"

George glanced in the mirror. "Looks will not win a battle." He removed his coat. "How can I ever turn this band of citizens into real soldiers? The pockets of England are deep and the pockets of the colonies are empty. England can put hundreds of ships to sea and we have no navy. They can hire mercenary soldiers from other countries. We have no allies. We are alone, with few funds, no training and—"

"One glorious Cause."

He folded the coat and set it over the top of a chair. "But is that enough?"

Perhaps as a good wife, I should have said, *Of course it is*, but I could not alter the honesty that had held our union together for sixteen years. "Is it enough? We shall see."

"If another man comes forward as the leader, I will happily relinquish the chance," he said.

"There is no other man."

He bit his lower lip, staring at the blue uniform. "That is what I fear the most."

With George away, Jacky and Eleanor often came to visit me at Mount Vernon. There was nothing that made me happier, especially now that Eleanor was with child. She was five months along, and though happy with the state, did not feel well. I was more than willing to offer her encouragement and comfort as I could.

"Some tea, Eleanor?" I asked. "It might ease the inner churnings."

She lay stretched across the settee, one hand thrown upon her forehead and the other protecting her womb. "Anything," she said. "I am willing to try anything."

I sent for some tea and returned to my chair by the fireplace, though no fire was needed in the early summer warmth. Instead a breeze blew into the room off the Potomac. Occasionally I smelled honeysuckle or lilacs as the breeze filtered past plantings on its way through the window.

Jacky read a copy of the *Virginia Gazette*. Usually an avid reader of the news—since George was living in the heart of it—I had not had time to keep abreast. It had been three days since I had received a letter from George.

Suddenly Jacky exclaimed, "He got it! Poppa got it!"

"Got what?" Eleanor asked.

My chest tightened beneath my corset. "They made him commander?"

"They did!" Jacky lifted the paper and read aloud: " 'The representative from Virginia, Mr. Washington, stood before the Congress and outlined the traits he deemed necessary toward the position of commander of all the American army. Never once did he state *he* possessed these qualities, but it was by near unanimous acclaim he was appointed to the post himself. John Adams, a representative from Pennsylvania, stated, "There is something charming to me in the conduct of Washington. A gentleman of one of the first fortunes upon the continent, leaving his delicious retirement, his family and friends, sacrificing his ease and hazarding all in the Cause of his country." Upon accepting the position Washington said, "I this day declare with the utmost sincerity that I do not think myself equal to the command I am honoured with." As a native son, we applaud General Washington's appointment.' " Jacky put the paper down. "General Washington? From colonel to general?"

"A commander must be a general," I said, though the title also held me in awe.

"Is there more said?" Eleanor asked.

Jacky went back to the paper. "Let us see . . . yes, here . . . Oh my." He looked up at me. "Mother, it says Poppa will accept no pay, only expenses, no matter how long the war might last."

I nodded.

"You knew about this?"

"Your father and I discuss everything—as should you and Eleanor."

"But *no* pay? What if the war continues for an extensive length of time?"

"Surely it will not."

"But what if it does?"

I felt the slightest inner pull. "Then he will abide by those conditions. A man of honour does not renege on what he has promised. Besides, because we have much we have a responsibility to give much. 'For unto whomsoever much is given, of him shall be much required.' "

Jacky shook his head. "How am I ever going to be such a man as Poppa?"

"There is only one George Washington." I leaned toward my son and put a hand upon his knee. "You are not to be him, dear Jacky, but you. Be the best John Parke Custis you can be."

"You *are* a good man," Eleanor told him. "And the best of husbands."

"As you will be the best of fathers," I added.

Jacky's face was still troubled. "I was not the best of sons."

I could not buoy him with false accolades. "The past has offered many trials. But the future . . . from this day forward strive to do your best in all things. No one—not e'en your father or I—could ask for more than that."

He pulled my hand to his lips and kissed it.

The pact was sealed. I prayed my son would rise to the challenge.

I walked in the garden, choosing flowers to grace the rooms of our guests. For even though George was not home, visitors still arrived. I wondered if he had asked every acquaintance ever known if they would visit me, to keep me company.

Actually . . . I appreciated the diversion.

I stooped to cut some roses when—

"Mamma!"

Jacky ran down the path into the garden. He stopped before me, his face flushed, strands of hair pulled out of his tie. He reminded me of a twelve-year-old boy, not a man of twenty. Only the smile on his face prevented me from expecting news of an emergency. "My, my, son. What brings you here so flustered?"

He brushed the strands of hair back upon his head and took a much-needed breath. "I wish to join the army and fight with Poppa and the others."

A thorn pricked my finger. The pain told me this moment was real.

"You are not a soldier, Jacky."

"Most of the men aren't soldiers, Mamma. Poppa is making them into soldiers." He straightened and lifted his chin. "I wish to fight for the Cause."

I felt my head start to shake no, but stopped in time. This was not a request for another piece of cake or to go to Alexandria on a lark. This was my son asking permission to risk his life for a cause our family believed just and right. And yet . . . though Jacky used to play soldier, he had not the temperament of a good one—at least in my mind. But was my mind skewed because I did not wish him to fight, to risk, to leave?

"You have a child on the way, Jacky. Your wife is having a hard time of it. She needs you."

"She has you. She has her parents and many sisters."

This time I allowed my head to shake no. "She needs you here, not hundreds of miles away—in danger."

"Poppa is hundreds of miles away—in danger."

"Yes, but—"

"You need him, but you let him go."

I risked causing offense to make my point. "He is one man over many. No one else can do the job he does."

"And I would be a lowly soldier, one of the masses. I know that. I could accept that. I do not ask for special privilege but to do my duty as a citizen. Did not Patrick Henry say, 'I know not what course others may take; but as for me, give me liberty or give me death!'?"

Yes. He had.

All my life I had longed for my son to become a good man of honour, and now, here he was, standing before me, asking to act upon that honour. My thoughts raced with an answer that would satisfy both our needs and inclinations. "I admire your desire to help, Jacky. As would your father. However, considering the delicate situation with Eleanor . . . I would like to offer you the alternative of staying put until—if—the fighting comes closer. Certainly if Virginia herself is threatened, then you may, and should, consider joining the forces to defend her." I began to reach forward to touch his face, but pulled my hand back, not wanting to demean his brave offer with feminine touch. "Will you do that for me, Jacky? For Eleanor?"

He let out a puff of air. His shoulders slumped. "I suppose." He looked at me once more, his eyes sad. "I just want to help, Mamma. I just want to make Poppa proud of me."

Forgetting restraint I pulled him into a motherly embrace. "He is, dear one. He already is."

⁕

Letters. I had to be content with letters.

After the May meeting of the Second Continental Congress,

George did not have time to come home. His services as General Washington were needed immediately in Boston, where the British still held sway.

A myriad of letters from George were received by me as well as family members—most of which were shared with me in an attempt to stem the sorrow of our separation. My sister Nancy and brother-in-law Burwell Bassett came for a visit, and Burwell offered his letter from George:

> It is an honour I wished to avoid, as well from an unwillingness to quit the peaceful enjoyment of my family as from a thorough conviction of my own incapacity and want of experience.

And Jacky shared with me a letter in which George said,

> My great concern upon this occasion is the thought of leaving your mother under the uneasiness which I fear this affair will throw her into. I therefore hope, expect, and indeed have no doubt, of your using every means in your power to keep up her spirits, by doing everything in your power to promote her quiet. I have, I must confess, very uneasy feelings on her account, but as it has been a kind of unavoidable necessity which has led me into this appointment, I shall more readily hope that success will attend it.

George, George. Ever thoughtful of my condition when he was the one with whom worry belonged.

I sat at my desk and read the latest letter he had sent to me. Reread it as I would most likely do many times hence.

> You may believe me, my dearest, when I assure you, in the most solemn manner, that, so far from seeking this appointment I have used every endeavour in my power to avoid it, not only from my unwillingness to part with you and the Family, but from a consciousness of its being a trust too far great for my capacity and that I should enjoy more real happiness and felicity in one month

with you, at home, than I have the most distant prospect of reaping abroad, if my stay was to be seven times seven years. I shall rely therefore, confidently, on that Providence which has heretofore preserved, & been bountiful to me, not doubting but that I shall return safe to you in the fall—I shall feel no pain from the toil, or the danger of the campaign—my unhappiness will flow, from the uneasiness I know you will feel at being left alone—I therefore beg of you to summon your whole fortitude & resolution, and pass your time as agreeably as possible—nothing will give me so much sincere satisfaction as to hear this, and to hear it from your own pen.

I looked nearby at the page that was blank and ready for a reply. I then went back to his letter . . .

As life is always uncertain, and common prudence dictates to every man the necessity of settling his temporal concerns whilst it is in his power—and whilst the mind is calm and undisturbed, I have, since I came to this place (for I had not time to do it before I left home) got Colo. Pendleton to draft a will for me by the directions which I gave him, which will I now enclose. . . .

Per his word, he had included a will that left me everything and asked me to remember him to all if he were killed.

If he were killed.

I shuddered at the very real chance. . . .

No. I would not think on it. As the Indians believed George could not be killed, so I would think the same.

Or try.

I finished reading the letter.

As I am within a few minutes of leaving this city, I could not think of departing from it without dropping you a line; especially as I do not know whether it may be in my power to write again till I get to the camp at Boston—I go fully trusting in that Providence, which has been more bountiful to me than I deserve, & in full confidence of a happy meeting with you sometime in the fall.

In the fall. It was late June. If only I could withstand a few months more, I would see him. Surely he would come home victorious and our life could return to normal.

Or so I prayed.

⁂

A grandchild was coming!

I embraced this beam of hope during the long summer without George. As the month of Eleanor's confinement began, I traveled to Mount Airy to her parents' Maryland estate to be with her and Jacky.

I was thrilled to be awakened one morning by a knock on the door of my bedchamber. It was Jacky. "It has begun, Mamma."

I hurried to dress. I was glad I had a cap to cover my mussed hair. Who could think about dressing hair at such a joyous time?

I found a crowded hallway outside Eleanor's room. Her mother and three of her sisters. Her father and Jacky. All were bound closely together, heads down.

I approached quietly, touching Jacky's arm. "How can I help?" I asked.

Jacky's face revealed a horrid concern. "Pray," he said.

'Twas not the answer I had expected.

I looked to his mother, raising my eyebrows to ask a question between women.

"She is not doing well," she answered.

A scream pierced the hallway and all eyes turned to the door.

"I must go in!" Jacky placed his hands flat upon the door, resting his forehead against its panels. "Why can I not go in?"

I put my hands upon his shoulders, drawing him back. "The doctor

231

needs room." Suddenly, I wondered whether there was a doctor. Again I looked to Mrs. Calvert. "Yes?"

She nodded and clutched her husband's arm.

Another scream. The sisters held on to each other, and we clustered in such groups, awaiting news.

Keep Eleanor safe. Please keep her safe.

A baby cried!

We all gasped, looked up, then at each other. We broke into nervous laughter and tears. We embraced each other, offering hearty congratulations.

I kissed my son. "Congratulations, Poppa."

He kissed me back, then turned his attention to the door. He knocked loudly. "Now, now let me in! I wish to see them!"

I could hear commotion inside and our expectation at seeing the door open and the exhausted face of the doctor did not materialize.

Jacky began to shake his head. "Mother? Why will they not let me in?"

"They have work to do after a birth," I offered, but even I was worried. At the birth of my four children, Daniel was allowed inside immediately. That Jacky was not . . .

He put his ear to the door. "I hear movement. And Eleanor." He stood erect. "I hear Eleanor crying!" He pounded on the door all the harder. "Let me in! I demand it!"

Moments later, the door opened and we witnessed the haggard face of the doctor. He looked from eye to eye as if trying to find someone he could speak to, someone who would understand.

"I . . . I . . ."

Jacky pushed past him, running toward the bed where Eleanor lay. She raised her arms to him. "Oh, Jacky . . ."

No. No. No.

Eleanor's father took the doctor by the arm. "Tell us, man. Tell us."

"Mrs. Custis gave birth to a girl, but alas, she was not strong enough and—"

Mrs. Calvert screamed and collapsed upon herself.

I followed her to the floor. Her sisters followed, forming an undulating mass of female sorrow.

I saw Mr. Calvert's jaw clench as he fought for control. "And Eleanor?"

"She will recover," the doctor said. "I am sorry, truly sorry. There was nothing I could do."

I looked past him, through the opened door, where Jacky held Eleanor in his arms. They rocked each other.

Instead of a baby . . .

———

After a few days' stay at Mount Airy, I made for home. I let the jostling of the carriage take me this way and that, not having the energy to fight for stability—or to care. Our first grandchild, dead. A dear little girl, gone before she knew anything of the love that awaited her.

It was not fair.

I looked out the window thinking of George. Was he on such a road, coming home to me as he had promised in the fall?

I needed him so.

———

I arrived at a Mount Vernon void of my husband. And to make matters worse, I was greeted with a letter stating he did not envision a chance to come home in the near future. The fledgling colonial army needed him.

I threw the letter on the fire and watched it burn.

ELEVEN

e is what?"

Lund stood before me in the kitchen, where I had been cutting pumpkin for pudding. He was out of breath, but with a sweep of his furtive eyes over the servants assembled to help me, succeeded in moving our conversation out-of-doors. We walked toward the house.

"I repeat, Lord Dunmore is doing what?" I asked.

"He has ordered his British warships to sail up the Potomac and burn Mount Vernon and the Masons' Gunston Hall, and moreover, capture you!"

A laugh escaped. "Capture me? George and I dined with Lord and Lady Dunmore many times in their home in Williamsburg. Charlotte and six of their seven children. And I hear Charlotte recently gave birth to another. They are our friends."

Lund shook his head. "Not anymore. And he does not reside in Williamsburg. Not since he confiscated the ammunition stores there. He had to run for his life to take sanctuary aboard a warship in Norfolk Harbour."

"And now he threatens to sail those warships up our river?"

"He does. I know your sister's family and Jacky are here and your plan is for the lot of you to travel down country to their home at Eltham. With Jack and his wife so grieved over the baby, I know it is a much-needed trip, but—"

"But nothing," I said. "I will not let this arrogant Scotsman threaten our home, to say nothing of my person."

"But people in Alexandria are worried, Martha, and they have less to fret about because they are not mentioned by name." Lund looked to the right, then to the left, then back at me. "Mr. Mason, he takes it seriously. He is packing their valuables away."

I felt an eyebrow rise. Our neighbor George Mason was not a man prone to panic.

Nor was I. But I was also not a woman to ignore common sense.

I turned toward the house. "I will send Nancy and Burwell home without us. Then we shall gather a few things for safekeeping."

"I could do that, Martha. You could leave with your sister."

I stopped walking. "No. I will not leave. George has left Mount Vernon in our able hands and I will not abandon it. Let Dunmore come. I long to see him face-to-face and give him what for."

So there.

I urged Jacky and Eleanor to accompany my sister back to the safety of Eltham, but he would not hear of it. " 'Tis my home too, Mamma."

I could not deny him his stand, for it was mine.

The last trunk was nearly full with family heirlooms and George's papers. I looked upon the parlour with a new set of eyes, borne of this newest challenge. As it got down to what to keep and what was dispensable, I found that if tested, I could get by without most of it.

I let my eyes rest upon a blue porcelain tea set with its silver-spouted urn. What did it really matter? Or the silver-filigreed candlesticks upon the mantel? Although I had treasured every one upon its purchase, I now found their worth marginal. They were *things*. Even the house itself was just a house—a beloved home built with loving concern, yet I found that it too could be relinquished if need be.

People. People were not expendable.

And so I took care of that. With Jacky's help we determined an escape plan that would provide safety within ten minutes. I also instructed the servants and slaves if the British got this far, they were to step away and let them do their worst. There would be no deaths on account of property. I would not allow it.

That done, we went on. . . .

<hr/>

In a rare moment of idleness, I stood at the front window, allowing myself time to ponder the loveliness of the changing trees that lined the drive. Green was turning to red and gold. 'Twas my favourite time of year, when the breezes were cool and smelled of musk and spice.

The trees relinquished my attention as I noticed a wave of disquiet wash toward me. Slaves and servants alike had their heads together, discussing . . . something.

It took me only a moment to guess the bulk of their discourse. Lord Dunmore was threatening to offer slaves and indentured servants freedom if they fought for the British. I doubted he would ever go through with such a thing, as it would ruin the economy of Virginia— of patriot and loyalist landowner alike. But the thought of it spread like an infection. I knew not what to do about it. We treated our slaves well, providing them with home, food, clothing, and medical attention. We did not beat them as I had heard done by some. And yet I also knew that given a chance at freedom . . .

Once again, I wished George here, with me.

Then, in the distance, I spotted a rider, coming up the drive fast.

I walked out to the stoop and strained to see who it was. I recognized Johnny, one of George Mason's men.

He reined in with a scatter of dust. He did not dismount but accosted me from his horse. "Mrs. Washington!"

"Yes, Johnny. What is the matter?"

"Warships! Up the river! They are coming for you!"

On instinct I glanced over my shoulder toward the back of the house, toward the river. "Are you certain?"

He nodded vigorously and passed me a note. "Mr. Mason told me to give this to you, personal."

I opened the note: *Martha, the worst is happening. Run and hide. I am sending Ann and the children to safety and implore you to seek your own.*

Johnny waited for me to acknowledge it. "Thank Mr. Mason for the warning. We will be fine." With a dip of his hat, he rode away.

I stood a moment, watching the fallen leaves dance behind his horse's hooves. Leave Mount Vernon? Had it really come to this?

Lund came running from the stables. "Did you hear?"

I tucked the note in the pocket of my dress. "I heard."

"I have told Eustis to get the carriage ready for you, Eleanor, and Jack, to implement our plan to—"

I took another step forward, to the edge of the steps. "Take them to safety, but as for me . . . I will not desert my post."

Lund froze in place, his face unbelieving. "But you must."

"I must not run from such a deplorable bully as Dunmore."

"He may be a bully, and e'en deplorable, but the men under him will follow orders. Gunships, Martha. Soldiers with orders to burn Mount Vernon to the ground and take you captive."

"I would like to see them try."

He let out one breath and took a new one. "Lord Dunmore will not march up this hill so you can argue with him. He will send soldiers who do not know you, Martha. Soldiers who will only see the wife of General Washington as a great bargaining tool, and his possessions a great prize to pilfer and destroy." He took a step toward me, stopping directly below me as I stood on the top step. "I wrote your husband promising I would see you to safety if such an event transpired. I will not go back on my word. If you would be taken captive, do you realize the pain and sorrow it would cost him? The difficulty it would cause all who fight for the colonies?"

He was right. On all accounts. Now was not the time to be stubborn—even for the sake of taking a stand in courage. Now was the time for prudence.

I heard commotion behind me. Jacky appeared at the door to the house. "Mamma? Is it true? Are the ships coming?"

I turned to him slowly, playing the part I needed to play. "They are. Tell Eleanor we must leave immediately for safety."

Leave reluctantly.

———

There was an old planter's shed a few miles inland, a shed long abandoned to all but animals, insects, and damp. Yet it was ideal for our needs. When we had first heard rumour of Dunmore's plan, Lund equipped it with supplies.

We could not risk a carriage—for it would be difficult to hide—yet riding on horseback so soon after childbirth was not an option for Eleanor. And so we only rode in the carriage along the bumpy back roads as far as we could before walking through a field and into the woods to the cabin. Inside, there was barely room for two cots for Eleanor and me, with one more bedroll on the floor for my maid Amanda. Lund and Jacky stood guard outside.

I sat inside, upon a bed, my back to the wall, holding Eleanor, who beyond her fear, was not feeling well and was sorrowful over the death of her daughter. She had cried much during these past weeks and all I could do was hold her close. Words were of no use. I knew this from bitter experience. Amanda sat upon her bedroll, her knees brought to her chin. A candle flickered in the breeze that permeated the logs of the crude cabin. The cold breeze. How long would we have to remain in this dismal place?

I pulled a blanket higher upon Eleanor's shoulder.

"Will the British come for us?" she asked.

In odd relief, I was glad she was not fretting about the lost baby. "We are far enough away that if the soldiers land at our wharf they will be occupied with their evil at the house. They will not seek us so far away."

"Will they destroy everything?" she asked.

"Steal or destroy." I added a brave statement I did not completely feel. "But they are just possessions, my dear. Possessions can be replaced."

I felt her move beneath the blanket. Then, she sat upright, her hand patting the bodice of her dress. "My baby's lock of hair!" She was off the bed, frantically pulling at the bedding.

Amanda and I knew what she was searching for. Ever since the death of her daughter, she had kept a tiny cutting of her hair in a locket around her neck. Her neck was now bare.

"I must have it! Where is it?"

Eleanor flew through the tiny room, crazed with her need. I barely rescued the candle as she bumped against its table.

"Are you sure you had it on?" Amanda asked.

Eleanor stopped her search long enough to glare at her. "I always have it on. I will always have it on. Forever."

Amanda looked properly chastened and continued to search. I did the same, but soon realized it was not there.

At our commotion Lund cracked open the door. "Shh! You must be quiet. We hear shots in the distance."

Eleanor called for her husband. "Jack!" Jacky came to the door, musket in hand. "I have lost the locket!"

Jacky looked at me.

"We have searched the room."

"I must have it, Jack! I must. It is the only thing I have of our daughter."

With the door open, I heard thunder. Was a storm threatening us as well?

Jacky's cheeks were flushed with the cold night air. "You probably dropped it on the way here. We will look for it tomor—"

"I must have it!" Eleanor cried.

My son looked to me, imploring me to do something. I handed two extra blankets to Jacky. "Here. Don't you dare catch your death. If it starts raining, come inside with us. In the meantime, close the door."

The door closed, allowing me to turn my attention to my daughter-in-law. "Lie down, Nelly. Amanda. It is time to sleep."

"But my locket . . ."

"We will search for your locket in the morning. I am sure some tuft of grass or pile of leaves is holding it safe until morning."

Thunder rumbled overhead.

Or was it cannon fire?

I prayed for God to hold *us* safe until morning.

The storm was fierce and the men spent the night inside the cabin. We never slept deeply, only dozed. And we never blew out the candle. Total darkness was not something any one of us was willing to endure on this night.

I awakened for the fifth time and moved my neck to ease a crick. I looked about the room at the sleeping figures. Eleanor slept upon her side, her hand clutched at her bare neck. Amanda was curled tight like a child. Lund sat against the far wall, his head drooped in sleep, and Jacky sat with his back and head against the door, his musket cradled in his arms.

It was odd to look at him so, to have the chance to study him. He had his father Daniel's tall forehead, and his hair held the chestnut colour so common to the Dandridge side. He was a handsome boy.

Man. He was not a boy anymore. He was a man. And with a start I realized that at that moment, in that obscure cabin in the woods, I was incredibly proud of him. The ornery boy who had driven Reverend Bouchard to write letters dripping with frustration was now a man, protecting his family from an enemy we had never imagined would be ours. If Daniel would happen upon us now, he would be shocked and appalled at the dissension that was ripping the colonies apart. And war? Daniel had never been a fighter. In fact . . . which side would he have chosen? Although his familial ties to the colonies extended back a hundred years, it would not be a certainty that he'd have felt compelled to cut his ties to the mother country. If I were still married to Daniel, would we be discussing with utter disdain the sedition of the ungrateful rebels?

And yet, who would have thought my George would choose the side of mutiny? He who respected and cherished all things British.

There was no knowing where Daniel would have stood in this conflict, only the certainty his son was protecting us from it, even now.

Jacky took a deep breath and opened his eyes. He saw me looking at him.

I smiled.

He smiled back.

I went back to sleep, safe within his watch.

⟨∞⟩

Jacky rode off early to see what had transpired during the night. The rain had stopped, allowing us a chance to walk outside and into the woods to take our relief. The underbrush was soggy, and we had to lift our skirts high lest they become sodden.

Eleanor also insisted we search for her locket. Although Lund would have rather we returned to the shed, I knew Eleanor would not be still or palatable to be around until we had made a good attempt at its recovery.

Amanda was the one who won the prize. "Here!" she yelled from the bottom of the hill leading to the cabin. "I found it!"

We women gathered to place it upon Eleanor's neck once more, our relief full. Lund's relief was in the fact we could now return to the interior of the cabin. "Please, ladies. Until Jack returns with news . . ."

We made up the beds and tried to organize the space as best we could. The one small window allowed minimal light but was appreciated just the same.

"Shall I read aloud?" I asked.

It was agreed, and so I took up the Bible I had brought with me and sat near the window. I read aloud the story of Naomi and Ruth, her daughter-in-law. It seemed appropriate at such a time. Ruth's husband had died, and Naomi urged her to go home to live with her own mother. . . . " 'And Ruth said, Intreat me not to leave thee, or to return from following after thee: for whither thou goest, I will go; and where thou lodgest, I will lodge: thy people shall be my people, and thy God my God.' " I paused a moment because I had a reason for this particular story yet was uncertain how to approach—

"That is beautiful," Eleanor said. "And appropriate, for like Ruth and Naomi, you and I have a close bond."

Yes, yes. "It is something I cherish."

Eleanor picked wax off the base of the candlestick. "I would follow you." She smiled. "I did follow you. Here to this lovely cabin."

"Only the best for you, my dear." It felt good to laugh. But I had more serious issues upon my mind. "There may be a time . . ." I had to say it plain. "George has asked that I come to Cambridge and stay with him, near the troops, for the winter. Although he desired to return home this fall, it is not to be. With the issue of slaves possibly joining British forces, and the upheaval Dunmore is causing . . ."

"I thought we were going to visit your sister in Eltham."

"We are. And as soon as it is safe, that is where I wish to go."

"But then you plan to go to Cambridge?"

"Where is that?" Amanda asked.

"Massachusetts," I said. "Near Boston."

"Hundreds of miles to the north," Eleanor said.

Amanda nodded, but I knew she had no mental claim to its true locale.

"I still am not certain," I said. "I do not like the idea of leaving Mount Vernon."

"Lund will take care—"

"Lund does well, but he only knows the man's part of it. Who would take care of my duties?"

The girls looked at me blankly. Alas, I had hoped Eleanor would offer to stay behind. . . .

"Well, then," I said. "It appears I cannot go to Cambridge. I must stay in Mount Vernon and look after it for both of us."

"But Poppa longs to see you."

Yes, he does. Are you listening to me, girl? "And I him . . ." Yet I knew there was more to George's request than that. He wished for me to make an example so other wives of officers would come. It was the British way and would be a show of confidence, to say nothing of the heightening of officer morale.

We heard a horse and tensed. But then Jacky's voice. "They have been turned back. It is safe!"

We went outside to hear more. Jacky flung himself off his horse and hugged his wife, then me. "They got as far as the mouth of Occoquan Creek, but there they encountered the Prince William militia, who were determined not to have them pass." He smiled. "And then the storm . . . between the two, Dunmore had enough and retreated!"

"God be praised!" Eleanor said.

"Indeed," I said. "For the storm was His doing and *did* save us."

"So is it safe to go home?" she asked.

"Ready the horses," I said.

Home. Home sweet home.

———⊶⊷———

I was true to my word and visited Nancy and Burwell and their family in Eltham. It was best for Eleanor if she kept occupied with family visits. As George had instructed family to give me solace from his absence, I did the same for dear Eleanor, to assuage the absence of her child. That her absence was permanent, and that mine might be . . .

I tried not to ponder the danger my husband faced daily. I could only take solace in knowing God was with him and would watch over him. I also embraced an inner knowing that God was not done with George Washington just yet. If someone were to question me as to what tangible fact would make me think such a thing, I would be unable to comply. There was nothing corporeal in this knowing, yet that did not mean it was without merit.

Soon after our arrival in Eltham, Lord Dunmore made good his threat by issuing a proclamation giving freedom to all slaves who would fight with the British. Virginia roiled with the news. Did we not have enough to worry about from loyalists who lived among us that we now had to worry that those who worked for us might turn against us? The *Virginia Gazette* tried to counter the offer by stating any slave caught would be executed and their families sold into the dreaded West Indies. It ran an article imploring the two hundred thousand slaves in Virginia to stand firm and not be taken in by this treasonous claim.

As I read the article, I thought it odd the *Gazette* would use this method to stop the insurgency, for slaves could not read. . . .

And they did not listen, on any account, for we heard news that eight hundred slaves joined up, and Dunmore created an Ethiopian

Regiment. They were given the bright red uniforms, were trained, and were awarded their own motto: "Liberty for Slaves."

The exodus did not just affect those willing to fight, for another twenty thousand men, women, and children left their owners and asked the British for protection. Just how the British army was going to accomplish this, I had no notion.

As for Mount Vernon . . . I received news from Lund that we lost a handful, including a favourite cook, Deborah Squash, and her husband, Harry.

Amid this development George sent urgent word for me to join him up north, in a city where there were no slaves to cause worry. I was still uncertain I should—or could—leave Mount Vernon unguarded.

But then . . .

I received the last straw that made any thought of staying away from my husband untenable.

One morning, Burwell brought to evening supper a newspaper clipping he had received from up north. "Here," he said. "You need to read this."

Mr. Washington, we hear, is married to a very amiable Lady, but it is said Mrs. Washington, being a warm Loyalist, has separated from her husband since the commencement of the present troubles, and lives, very much respected, in the city of New York.

I let my mouth drop open. "How dare they!"

"What does it say, Mamma?" Jacky asked.

I passed him the paper and he and Eleanor read it together.

I pushed away from the table, unable to sit still. "Was it not bad enough one of these loyalist papers insinuated my husband had an affair with a servant girl?" The only evidence had come through a letter from another delegate, Benjamin Harrison, mentioning a "Kate, the washerwoman's daughter" in the same sentence as George. Our side had claimed it a forgery, but it made me think twice about all correspondence. It was far too easy for it to fall into the wrong hands where it could be altered, misconstrued, or simply forged. I slapped my hands against my thighs. "The Kate scandal does not e'en deserve a rebuke, but this other? The rumour I am now a Tory? Must they now disparage my loyalty to not only George but to the Cause?"

Jacky threw the clipping on the table in disgust. "How can they print lies like this?"

"They can print what they like," Burwell said. "The newspapers compete against each other to further their own agenda and loyalty."

I took the clipping, crumpled it into as small a ball as I could, and tossed it in the middle of my dinner. "This forces my hand. I am going to Cambridge. Tomorrow." On impulse I looked to Jacky. "You and Eleanor are coming with me."

It was not what I had originally planned, but considering . . .

∽∾∽

I, who had never traveled north of Alexandria—just nine miles from Mount Vernon—was on my way through colonies as foreign to me as England or France. Maryland, Delaware, and soon Pennsylvania, New Jersey, Connecticut, and Massachusetts. I was quite impressed with the beautiful country and its variances. It made me proud and held me in awe.

We did not travel at leisure, but with the greatest haste to beat the coming winter and fend off enemy troops. I could never forget the country was at war—one never knew if the people living inside a farmstead or running a shop were patriots or loyalists. The British soldiers were easy enough to spot with their red coats, but those who supported them . . . my nerves never left me. Especially when we thought about an old law—from the time of Henry VIII—that had been reinstated, saying anyone accused of treason against the crown (the taking up of arms certainly qualified) could be sent back to England to be tried, and if found guilty could be hanged, then drawn and quartered. I could not allow myself to think of any of that, yet knowing George was in constant danger from the war and from such a law . . .

Beyond that horrible death was the risk Mount Vernon and all our assets could be confiscated. The only escape to such a situation would be to run west, into the wilderness of untamed lands. Although I knew I *could* survive in such a place, I really had no wish to start over from nothing.

But I would. If I had to. Anything to save George. To be with George.

As many loyalists held on to the trappings of the pomp and circumstance of their position, I deemed we would travel with as little of those properties as possible. Eleanor and I wore homespun dresses, and I refrained from powdering my hair. Although our carriage was grand—we traveled in our lovely white coach pulled by four horses— that could not be helped. Because of her tenuous health and the time of year, we could not travel in an open carriage, and there was no time—nor logic—in buying something else just for this occasion. I made certain Eleanor was safely tucked with blankets. She would not suffer for this trip, not if I could help it.

But then, in spite of our desire for anonymity and speed (the latter well granted by our coachman, who seemed to enjoy going as fast as possible, making Eleanor squeal on more than one occasion), when we retired for the night at various inns, we were taken by a great surprise.

It happened from the very first. Jacky had gone inside to check on the arrangement made by George, and I helped Eleanor from the carriage. Suddenly, a man and woman burst from the inn and were at our sides, saying, "Lady Washington! You do us much honour! Please, please come in."

"It is Mrs. Washington, thank you."

But no matter how many times I protested and corrected, no matter what town we were in, I was called Lady Washington.

How odd. How disturbing.

Jacky thought it amusing and began calling me "your grace." I assured him, though I never punished him as I should have in his youth, it was not too late to begin. "We should have worn our best clothing, dripping in jewels instead of these simple nothings," he said.

"We should have done no such thing. In spite of their knowledge of us, we are not royalty."

"*Au contraire*, dear Mamma. To them, you are American royalty."

"I most certainly am not."

"Oh, Mamma," Jacky said. "Give them what they want."

"I will do no such thing. I will give them what I am."

And so, as we settled in at one inn followed by another, we were invariably greeted by well-wishers, lauding my husband—and me for being a wise and lucky woman to be married to him. Even the papers knew of our coming, and announced it to all.

But this was nothing compared to the welcome I received in Philadelphia. We were not even in the city when we were met by a group of handsome horsemen. Their leader introduced himself. "I am Joseph Reed, a good friend of your husband. He has sent us to ensure your pleasant journey into the city."

I spoke to him through the carriage window. "I had hoped to travel with a bit more discretion, Mr. Reed. Perhaps, considering the times, anonymity would be prudent?"

"Not in Philadelphia, Mrs. Washington. Everyone knows of your arrival. The most prominent families have arranged a ball in your honour."

Well then.

As our carriage made its way into the city, with citizens cheering in the streets and church bells pealing, I said to the others, "This is embarrassing. They treat me as if I am a very great somebody."

"You are, Mamma," Jacky said, waving out the window at the crowds. "You are the wife of the man who is leading the fight."

"The wife. I am not him. I did not make him who he is."

Eleanor spoke up from her place next to Jacky. "I believe a great person becomes great only by the encouragement of those closest to them. Poppa would not be who he is if you were not who *you* are."

Jacky applauded. "Bravo, dear wife!" He nudged his shoulder into hers and took her hand captive. "I have become a better man for marrying you. . . ."

"I agree wholeheartedly," I said. "You are a much better man for—"

Jacky pretended to take offense. "Was I *so* bad, Mamma?"

I turned my attention to the people outside. "Wave, children. Wave."

⁂

Finally, we left Philadelphia and were off to Cambridge. And the ball—proposed to be held in my honour—never materialized. Although the ladies of the city had wanted to pay tribute to me in this way, it was not proper to allow such conspicuous consumption when so many were suffering or were anticipating the coming winter with apprehension. There was a rumble against it, and so, when the committee came to me with their awkward concerns, I was more than happy to oblige. "The desires of your committee are agreeable to my own sentiments," I told them. And so my "sacrifice" was reported in the papers, elevating me to a lauded maven of the Revolution.

Reluctant maven. For I did so love a ball.

Yet the ball was soon forgotten as we neared Cambridge. We had a military escort part of the way, and men on horseback the rest, and on December 11, 1775, we arrived, unannounced. We had traveled five hundred miles, on rough roads, with winter threatening through every cloud. We were all weary and would have been happy with a cot in a corner. Actually, we did not have certainty of anything more.

After all, George had written about the appalling conditions he had found when he entered Cambridge six months earlier. The tents and lean-tos of the soldiers were poorly put together, and garbage was everywhere. The men were unruly and undisciplined, relieving themselves in the streets—they had to be reprimanded not to drop their breeches to shock passersby on the public bridge with a show of their backsides. They were often drunk and George had to issue a general order: "The vile practice of swallowing the whole ration of liquor at a single draught is to be prevented by causing the sergeants to see it mixed with water. In which case, instead of being pernicious, it will become very refreshing and salutary."

With no women in camp to wash for them, and thinking the job demeaning, they let their clothing become foul and rotten. They were not attuned to getting along with each other—for some reason any soldier from Pennsylvania was disdained. Officers from one colony argued with officers from another, and bored sentries ambled over to the bored British sentries to chat. The number of troops was variable, as the term of duty was for one year, and men were constantly coming and going at will. George had told me if he had known the extent of the task, he would never have accepted the job.

But he, being George, had set upon the challenge like the true general he was. First, he instigated rules—and punishment for those who broke them. There were a great many floggings those initial weeks. He also instructed the men to dig latrines and fortifications, organize supplies, take turns cooking, repair the wagons, strive for a level of hygiene, and learn the drills and skills of soldiering—which included learning how to load a musket without shooting oneself in the foot. Although progress was made, George intimated it took our soldiers eight days to accomplish what should have taken an hour. He feared we were sitting in an exceedingly dangerous situation.

The good news was that our troops encircled Boston, where General Thomas Gage commanded sixty-five hundred British soldiers under siege. The British took shelter in warehouses or in tents pitched upon the Boston Commons.

Upon our arrival we were not relegated to a cot but pulled in front of the army headquarters, which was situated in a home that had formally belonged to a loyalist, John Vassal.

When we entered, there was much commotion as soldiers, hard at work on the dining room table to our right, blinked in unbelief at the sight of me.

"Are you . . . ?"

"I am," I said. "Pleasure to meet you . . . ?"

"Private Collins, ma'am."

"Is my husband about?"

His eyes started, as if it were only then he realized it was George I had come to see. "He is in the back, in the writing room. I will—"

George appeared in the doorway, engulfing it with his large frame. He paused and looked at me, as though unbelieving. "Martha."

I was unsure what greeting he would give me with soldiers present. But as I opened my mouth to speak, he crossed the room and swallowed me in a full embrace. I even received a kiss upon the lips. It was I who blushed. George seemed not to notice we had an audience.

"Hello, my dearest. I have missed you."

"And I you," I said. I looked upon his face. "You have lost weight."

"I miss your fine meals."

"We will see what we can do about that."

He looked past me to the front door as Eleanor entered, followed by Jacky. There were more embraces, and fervent greetings. "Come," he said, edging toward the stair. "Come see the rooms I have made for us upstairs. They are not large, but their proximity to my office here in the dining room . . ."

He led us to two rooms—one for us, and one for Jacky and Eleanor. They were far from luxurious—I am certain the Vassals moved their best possessions with them to Nova Scotia when they made their escape—but it was better than I had expected.

"Will it do?" George looked as though he truly needed my reassurance.

" 'Tis a fine room," I said as I slipped my hand round his arm. "If I am with you, 'tis a grand room indeed."

With the children settling into their own room across the hall, he kissed me properly. Six months is a long time to ache for a kiss.

It was well worth it.

⁂

We stood on Prospect Hill, northeast of Cambridge. From there we had a spectacular view of Boston, as well as the British fleet in the Charles River and Boston Harbour beyond. I shuddered at the sight of the ships. We had no ships.

George turned to point behind us. "We stand on the summit of what the British named Mount Pisgah—from whence Moses viewed the Promised Land. The land he was not permitted to enter. The British named it as a slight to us, teasing us with entry into Boston—a land we can see but cannot enter."

"They certainly own arrogance."

"They call us savages, fools, and cowards." He sighed and put a hand upon the back of my neck. "We are none of those things, Martha. By God I will make sure of it."

I believed him.

"There." George turned us to the east and pointed across the bay. "There is Bunker Hill. That is where the shelling originates that disturbs you so. There, and Boston." He swept his arm to the south.

I shuddered at the mere thought of it, though I endeavoured to keep my fears to myself as well as I could. "The rest of you act totally unsurprised when the cannons fire, but I fear I will never be used to it."

"I wish I were *not* used to it," George said.

I looked toward Bunker Hill. "What town is there—was there? I see so much destruction. There are but a few chimneys standing."

"That is Charlestown. The British destroyed it when they took Bunker Hill last June."

I looked to the south, to the city of Boston. There were many fine buildings still standing. Only God knew how long they *would* stand. I had heard they were pulling up the wharfs for firewood.

"Come, my dear. You have seen enough of war."

A truth said.

Yet I knew I would see more.

More than enough.

Although war—and preparations for war—raged around us, I saw no need to throw civility to the wind. As the wife of General Washington, it behooved me to wear a state of calm concern and serenity. It did no one good to panic or encourage worry. There was enough of that behind closed doors.

And so . . . I entertained as best I could. I put on dinners and socials for officers and their wives, and set up a rotation so none were slighted. If the war could be forgotten for but a few hours . . . it did everyone good. The wives of the officers were the only women close by, for the wives of the soldiers were plenty busy at home, taking care of business, farm, and family while their husbands were fighting. We wives were a rarity, we few.

Actually, I enjoyed the wives, especially Lucy Knox and Kitty Greene. Their husbands—Colonel Henry Knox (a rotund bookseller turned officer) and Brigadier General Nathanael Greene (even at age thirty-three and the youngest general in the army, George considered him worthy to take over in his stead)—had become close confidants of my husband and were invaluable to the Cause.

As Lucy and Kitty were invaluable to me. We often spent the day together in the parlour of our home or theirs. I initiated a sewing circle among us and the other officers' wives, making the soldiers much-needed shirts and mending the ones they already had. I felt it imperative we make ourselves useful.

Kitty, small and pretty, only twenty but married a year, was vivacious, though a bit without education. She got along swimmingly with Eleanor. And Lucy . . . Lucy, also a babe at nineteen and married a year, was as outspoken as I about most everything, though she had a tendency toward volume I did not share. Where I was short and stout, she was tall and so. And yet, diverse as we were, we became three peas in a cozy pod, with me the willing mother of them all.

"Ouch!" Kitty put a pricked finger to her mouth.

Lucy held up her hands for inspection. "Callouses, Kitty. The key is to develop hard callouses on the tips of the fingers."

"And how am I supposed to do that?"

"By pricking them and letting them heal strong," I said.

Our laughter was a balm that spread across the tense day. Even Eleanor laughed—which was a relief, as she still mourned her dead baby. Yet I knew it was not easy for her to see both Lucy and Kitty pregnant with their first. . . .

"Want to hear some gossip?" Kitty asked.

"Of course," Lucy said.

"There is talk about you, Martha."

I adjusted a sleeve in its armhole and pinned it, ready to sew. "If it is good, tell me in the greatest detail, but if it is bad, then I wish not to hear it."

" 'Tis good," Kitty said. "It is from Mercy Otis Warren, and you know she is full of opinion." She leaned close. "Her plays, though they are billed as written by a person anonymous, are quite biting in their satire against officials unwilling to take a stand for freedom. So any positive opinion from her lips . . ."

"I *did* meet her and admire her zeal," I said. "Her good opinion would be appreciated."

"Then you shall be pleased, for she said the complacency of your manners speaks at once of the benevolence of your heart, and your affability, candor, and gentleness qualify you to soften the hours of private life, sweeten the care of the hero, and smooth the rugged paths of war."

Eleanor let her sewing fall to her lap. "How laudable, Mamma."

"How true," Kitty said.

I felt myself blush. Although I relished compliments as much as the next, I found it difficult to accept them in company. "I suppose this means I can never say an unkind word or complain about anything whatsoever lest I lose my complacent and affable status."

Lucy sighed deeply. "Alas, 'tis so. It's difficult being an icon of womanhood, is it not?"

I paused a moment, then sighed for dramatic effect. "Not that difficult."

We added more laughter to our day.

I peered across the hall to the dining room, where George met with the other officers, planning a war. He did not look up and his forehead was drawn with the seriousness of his task. So many depended on him.

As did I.

If I could sweeten *my* hero's care . . .

I took up my needle and thread. "Sew, ladies. The soldiers need their shirts."

A new year. A time to reflect and think ahead.

I tried not to think of the past, for I knew the idyllic years at Mount Vernon were golden. Whether they could ever be regained was unknown. Whether George would survive, whether any of us . . . whether our Cause would survive . . .

If it did not, we would all be executed as traitors. And Mount Vernon? It would be easy pickings for a British officer with a yen to own a plantation in America.

We had to be victorious. We had to.

Toward that end, on this New Year's Day in 1776, George developed a strategy. Not for a battle, but to elicit hope in the hearts of all patriots. His forces were dwindling as their one-year enlistment came due. If he did not do something soon, there would be no force to lead.

And so . . . we, along with other officers and wives, drove up Prospect Hill with a great purpose.

Upon my husband's instructions, a seventy-foot schooner mast had been set in place. It loomed large at the crest of the hill, the battlements of the soldiers' fortification trenches cut into the hill nearby.

"Come, my dear," George said, helping me from the carriage. "Watch the snow."

Lucy and Kitty came close, whispering, "What are we here for?"

"You will see," I said. For George had confided in me. As the soldiers drew close, their collective breath formed a mist upon the air. Once gathered, I watched as their General Washington removed a cloth-covered parcel from the back of the carriage.

He approached the mast. "Gentlemen. Soldiers. We have come to greet you on this first day of the new year, to offer you a symbol of our sacrifice."

With that, he removed the cloth and pulled out a flag. He, and General Greene, held it taut. It fought the breeze but was held secure. Its red, white, and blue colours were striking against the white of the snow and the gray of the sky.

"I present to you the Great Union Flag, whose creation was approved by the Continental Congress last year. The red and white stripes signify the uniqueness and unity of our thirteen colonies, and the Union Jack in the canton corner of the flag represents our wishes to keep close ties with Great Britain e'en as we long to be independent." He nodded to two soldiers to come forward. "Raise it high upon the mast, men, so all can witness our unity of cause—the Cause of freedom."

There was silence as the soldiers attached the rope to the flag and lofted it up the pole. When it was in place, George stood at attention and saluted it. All the men followed suit, and after a moment of dignified silence, the men erupted in loud huzzahs and cheers, along with a volley from thirteen guns.

I looked at the men's faces. In spite of their ragged clothing and their cold hands and feet, their eyes had taken on a new fire. I prayed it would be a fire that would warm them in the months—and years?—to come.

— TWELVE —

I do not know why I cannot write my own letters," I told George. "Although I never claim to be eloquent, I do not enjoy feeling ignorant."

George glanced at his secretary, Private Masten, who had penned the letter in question. The soldier looked back, awaiting instructions.

When George did not reply, I read the letter responding to an invitation from Mercy Otis Warren to take safe haven in her home in Plymouth should the British attack Cambridge. " '. . . she cannot but esteem it a happiness to have so friendly an invitation as Mrs. Warren has given.' " I shook my head. "Those are not my words. Would not be my words."

"Much correspondence is being intercepted, my dear. You know yourself a packet of letters was stolen from headquarters and delivered to General Howe. Including a letter I intended for you."

"But he sent it back to you. He proved himself a gentleman."

"I give him that one occasion," George said. "But only that. We are at war. Acts of gallantry can never be counted upon."

"If I may?" Private Masten looked to his general for permission.

"Speak."

"My intent in your letter to Mrs. Warren was to give no indication the invitation was for reasons of safety against the enemy. If word got out the general's wife was fleeing . . ." He let out a breath. "It would not be advantageous."

George nodded. "Exactly."

"But if you would have told me, I could have written such a letter myself."

"I know, my dear," George responded, "but with all you are doing at the camp, increasing morale to such high degrees . . . Do you know people say you could charm King George himself through your talent and ease with conversation?"

"If I had a chance to speak to the king, I fear I would not be very charming."

George took the letter and returned it to Private Masten's desk. With a hand to my back he led me out of the writing room of the Vassal House. "I did not mean to offend," he said once we stepped away, "only to ease you of the occasional burden. If it is agreeable, others will write such letters and you can sign them."

I stopped in the hall, physically turning him about so his back blocked those who busied themselves around us, creating a bit of privacy amid the constant chaos. Then I peered up at him, hooked my finger in a buttonhole of his lapel, and pulled him down to my level. "And you call *me* a charmer?"

I kissed his cheek, then let him loose to run the war.

And run the war well, he did.

I awaited news regarding our army's latest feat. In secret (though I knew of it, for George regularly used me as a sounding board) Colonel Knox slipped up to Fort Ticonderoga in central New York, and somehow—with great difficulty, through snow and rain—transported fifty-nine cannon more than two hundred miles to Cambridge, on wagons made into sleds. Then, during the dark of this night, the fourth of March going into the fifth, George called twelve hundred soldiers to get the cannons set on the brink of Dorchester Heights, overlooking Boston. How to do so without tipping off the British was the problem at hand. I had heard George order bales of straw to be used as cover for the men along the road to the summit, as well as used to wrap the wheels for silent passage. If the British heard or saw or suspected . . .

In the parlour, I paced, Jacky paced, Lucy Knox paced, and Eleanor sat by the warm fire—for she was blessedly with child once again and wished to take no chance of overexertion. Vassal House was nearly empty of personnel, as most had been called to help. No legs had been pulled to gain volunteers, for all wished the siege over. Progress was never made in inaction. We had stayed awake all night listening for the sound of gunfire or cannons coming from Dorchester, but it had been blessedly silent. Eerily so.

"It is dawn," Jacky said, peering out the window. "Certainly they know something by now."

"Maybe they did not get the guns in place," I said.

"Oh, they got them set," Lucy said. "I know my Henry. He did not trudge two hundred miles to have them sit where they would do no good."

"He is coming!" Jacky said, dropping the curtain aside. "Poppa is coming."

We moved toward the door and within moments, George entered amid the company of soldiers. Upon seeing us, he and the others stopped short.

"Well?" I asked.

"Are they set?" Lucy asked.

George smiled. "Upon awaking this morning, upon glancing out their windows to see whether the day was cloudy or fair, the king's men in Boston were accosted by renewed fortifications and rows and rows of cannon pointed their way."

A cheer went up from the soldiers, who then entered the house and spread about to do their work.

"They did not see you as you worked?" I asked my husband.

He took my hands in his and drew them close. "They did not. Providence shielded us from their eyes."

I kissed his hands. "Thank God."

"Indeed I do."

"What now?" Jacky asked.

"We expect a great battle," George said, removing his coat, stiff from the cold. "But we are ready for them."

"And my husband?" Lucy asked.

"He is well and will stop home when he can."

"I must go, then," she said.

As Eleanor helped Lucy into her cloak, George said, "If you will excuse me, family, the day—and my work—is not finished. I must gather a few things, then return to encourage the men. For they are truly worth the effort. They manifest their joy and express a warm desire for the approach of the enemy; each man knows his place and is resolute to execute his duty."

I took George's coat and spread it before the fire, for I too knew my place and was resolute to execute my duty to help in any way I could.

<hr />

Jacky burst through the front door. "They are leaving! The British are leaving!"

After a moment of incredulousness, we embraced, for it had been twelve days since our enemy had awakened to see our cannons looming over them from Dorchester Heights. At noon on that day they had sent a barrage of cannon fire our way, but only two or three men were killed or wounded. Some of the British troops were seen gathering, as though they were preparing to attack our position, but a violent storm arose and General Howe abandoned his plan. I have no doubt God had seen fit to thwart a maneuver which would surely have resulted in widespread bloodshed.

"Come!" Jacky said. "You must come and see the sight of it!"

Eleanor and I made quick work of our cloaks and entered the carriage that had been made ready at Jacky's request. We drove to a promontory where we would be out of the way, yet able to see.

"Look!" Jacky said, pointing to the harbour. "The entire fleet is sailing away."

The sight of dozens of British vessels heading away from us, the Union Jack flapping upon each mast . . . it took my breath away.

"I have heard there are ten thousand, all told," Jacky said. "The troops are joined by a considerable number of loyalists—Tories—taking passage with their families on board the transports. They bid adieu to their native country, without knowing what part of the world is to be their destiny."

"Although I grieve for their loss of home, I am glad to see them go. We do not need them left behind to cause trouble."

Jacky's eyes were locked upon the departing fleet. "Why do we not fire upon them? Why do we let them go?"

Although I had no definitive answer, by knowing my husband, I had a probable one. "They are not retreating as in battle, son; they have surrendered. Last week General Howe sent a flag of truce to your poppa. He stated he would leave—and leave Boston standing—providing his army was permitted to set sail without being attacked."

Jacky nodded. "Lord Dunmore burnt Norfolk to the ground so we could not have it. . . ."

"Lord Dunmore is not a man of honour," I said. "We have hopes General Howe is."

We watched a few moments in silence. And it *was* silent, for it was as if all Boston were holding its breath as ten months of siege came to an end.

Jacky spoke first. "I heard a rumour, an exclamation said to be from General Howe upon seeing the cannons on the Heights. Howe said, 'I know not what I shall do: the rebels have done more in one night than my whole army would have done in weeks.' "

I felt a surge of pride. These men, my man . . . great men, one and all.

"Where are they going?" Eleanor asked, still mesmerized by the ships.

"George believes they head to New York. He heard General Clinton left days ago for that city. It is where he himself must go next."

"We are moving?" she asked. Her voice expressed alarm.

I was glad George and I had already spoken of this. "We think it would be best if you and Jacky retire to your parents' home in Mount Airy for the rest of your confinement. Poppa does not want you anywhere near the fighting."

"But what if I wish to fight?" Jacky asked. "I am as able-bodied as most of these men. I am not a soldier, but neither are most of them."

"No."

I realized I had spoken too quickly.

"Poppa would let me. He admires men willing to fight. I am . . . I am willing."

"Your poppa will abide by my wishes, and I do not wish that you . . ." I drew closer to him, to appease him, to will him to understand. "You are the last of my children, Jacky. You are coming into your inheritance and need to find a home of your own. I cannot let you risk yourself."

"And I," Eleanor said, taking his arm, "I need you with *me*. I have already lost one child. I need you to help me be strong for this other."

Jacky looked from her eyes to mine, then back again. I did not know whose held the greatest power, but in the end he acquiesced with a nod—and was there not also a look of relief?

Eleanor kissed his cheek and turned to me. "And you?" Eleanor asked. "Are you going back to Mount Vernon?"

"No," I said, although the decision had not been made until that moment. "As you follow your husband, I will follow mine."

I quickly left the room before Jacky could find further argument. I understood his desire to serve. I did. But right or wrong, my mother's instinct to protect overrode even the sharpest call of cause and country.

—∞—

I did follow George. Briefly. We settled into the house of a British paymaster, Abraham Motier. But then, in May, hearing of epidemics of smallpox in Quebec and other locales, I chose to leave George behind and travel to Philadelphia to be inoculated from the disease. I hoped to lead others by example—especially my husband. Although he had no fear of the disease—having had it as a young man in Barbados—I thought it a wise move to decree all troops have the procedure. I heard John Adams say pox was ten times more terrible than Britons, Canadians, and Indians together.

In Philadelphia, my arm was scratched and pus from a smallpox pustule was rubbed into it. To invite disease into one's body . . . and yet it proved successful. It was hoped the inoculated—I would say *victim* but withheld that title for the genuine kind—would develop a mild case, recover, and become immune. Blessedly, it worked as expected, and within a few weeks I was well enough to travel.

But George said I could not come to New York with him. It was far too dangerous. And then, though I wished to be in Mount Airy for the birth of our grandchild, I could not go there, for other dangers hung close. Jacky wrote of British raiding parties that scourged the Potomac area in Maryland. Added to that was the risk of marauding slaves, let loose by Dunmore. Yes indeed, he was their hero. I heard it said there were an alarming number of slave babies named Dunmore.

I was in limbo. I knew George needed me. Through letters and newspapers I heard of grave problems in New York. The British general Burgoyne was threatening the city from the north, while Generals Howe and Clinton did their dirty work close by.

Then a spy was discovered in my husband's house in the guise of a maid!

And then, he was nearly poisoned by the enemy! He assured me he was fine in both cases, but I wondered if the incidents would have occurred had I been there to care for him and mind the details he was too busy to mind.

Details such as uniforms for the men. Many of our troops looked like bedraggled beggars. George planned to ask Congress to properly clothe them, and sought my advice. After all, I regularly clothed hundreds of slaves. Bearing through the heat of summer in Philadelphia myself, I had trouble even imagining the heavy wool uniforms. So I thought . . . why uniforms? We had one advantage. The Indians had taught the French and the French had taught us that shooting a gun while hunkered behind a tree or bush wearing a hunting shirt and breeches was far wiser than standing in a formed line, being shot at while wearing a brightly coloured uniform—a uniform that was restrictive of easy movement.

So . . . why not provide hunting shirts which were cool in the heat, and could be made warm by adding clothing under them when needed? Plus, making such shirts and breeches would be economical and easy enough for most seamstresses. George pointed out another advantage. Since the British opinion of us had moved from total disdain to fear that the men, as woodsy hunters, could shoot the gnat off a wart, we needed to take advantage of such misconceptions. Although the legend of sharpshooters may have been true for those coming from rural areas, the truth was, our city-based soldiers had trouble hitting the side of a house.

And so, for the first time in the history of European war, the uniform of an entire army was to be nonceremonial yet functional. George and his officers would still wear their blue regalia—for we both knew decorum and sophistication were required for those in charge—but George requested funds from Congress for the new soldier gear.

I was also not there when George received a commendation from Congress for his great success in Boston. He made light of it in his letters to me, and was far more proud of an honorary degree Harvard College bestowed upon him. He valued education, and if there was a weakness in his confidence, it stemmed from his lack of it.

And more news . . . as of July 4, 1776, we were no longer the united colonies but the united states of America. Congress signed a document here in Philadelphia that boldly stated we wanted no part of allegiance to another nation. This Declaration of Independence was written by none other than our friend Thomas Jefferson, that young soft-spoken Virginian who served with George in the House of Burgesses. I read its content more than once when it was printed in the newspapers. Its simplicity and eloquence were impressive:

> We hold these truths to be self-evident, that all men are cre-ated equal, that they are endowed by their Creator with certain unalienable Rights, that among these are Life, Liberty and the pursuit of Happiness. That to secure these rights, Governments are instituted among Men, deriving their just powers from the consent of the governed, That whenever any Form of Government becomes destructive of these ends, it is the Right of the People to alter or to abolish it, and to institute new Government . . .

George had it read aloud to the troops in New York City, to great cheers.

I must admit it made my throat tighten and my heart beat a little faster. Yet in spite of its stirring words, it also elicited a somber reaction: there was no turning back. There would be no end to this conflict but victory or defeat, no taking it back and asking Britain to return to the world we had before.

That world was gone forever.

Yet supposing victory—praying for victory—what kind of country would we have? Who would be our new king? What laws would govern us? Would our new way be a better way? If we were victorious, there would be incredibly much to do. . . .

The future was daunting.

The war was daunting.

The loneliness was daunting.

I wanted to go home.

⸙

I missed the birth of our second grandchild.

A granddaughter: Elizabeth Parke Custis—to be called Betsy— was named after Eleanor's mother, and carried the Parke name to appease that ancient and pesky appendage of a will by the Parke family that insisted on the name in order to receive the inheritance. George and I were named godparents.

Each morning when I awakened in Philadelphia, alone in my bed, so far from my family, I reached for the letter from Jacky, needing to buoy myself with that lovely news:

Mount Airy August 21ˢᵗ 1776

My dearest Mamma,

I have the extreme Happiness at last to inform you, that Eleanor was safely delivered this Morning about five o'Clock of a fine Daughter. I wish you were present You would be much more pleased, if you were to see the strapping Huzze. Her Cloths are already too small for Her. She is in short a fine a Healthy fat Baby as ever was born.

Poor Eleanor had a very indifferent Time, her pains were two Hours long & very severe. She is now thank God as well as can be expected and the Pleasure her Daughter gives Her compensates for the Pain. I wrote to the General the last two Posts.

I cannot pretend to say who the child is like. It is as much like Doctor Rumney as any Body else. She has a double Chinn something like His, in point of Fatness with fine black Hair, & Eyes, upon the whole I think It is as pretty & fine a Baba as ever I saw. This I not my opinion alone, but the Opinion of all who have see Her—I hope she will be preserv'd as a Comfort, and Happiness to us all.

Happiness to us all . . . I took comfort in the obvious fact that Jacky and Eleanor were happy, and indeed made for each other. It was a good thing we allowed them to marry. That our doubts had proved false was a relief.

But then, in my joy, I brought to mind new family pain. My brother William had recently died, drowned in the Pamunkey River. That cursed river of my youth! To have taken two of my brothers, one at seventeen and one at forty-two. Add to that this cursed war which prevented me from attending his funeral.

To add further to my woe I heard Mother was not doing well, and two of my sister Nancy's three surviving children were ailing. . . .

And what of Mount Vernon? Lund was doing his best, and I knew he sent weekly reports to George, but with no master or mistress present, and by the cause of my taking the best servants north, I knew there was little incentive present for anyone to do much of anything. In what state would I find our beloved home when I did manage to return to its beloved halls?

My worries contained issues of a larger scale. Things were not going well for George. A bit at a time he had lost New York: first Long Island and then Manhattan, Harlem Heights, White Plains. . . . He had been slowly forced back through New Jersey. Morale was low. Confidence waned. He himself wanted to quit. *I do not know what plan of conduct to pursue,* he had said in one of his letters. *I never was in such an unhappy, divided state since I was born.*

I ached to be with him, to console him, to encourage him.

To do something for someone.

But there I sat. Alone in Philadelphia. Unable to help husband, grandchild, niece, nephew, mother, home—or country.

Helpless and of little worth.

❦

In spite of the danger, I returned to Mount Vernon, the threat that the coming winter could strand me in Philadelphia causing me to brave the journey.

Besides, Philadelphia was no longer considered safe, as the British had pushed George and his troops back across the Delaware River into Pennsylvania. Congress, panicked, moved its meeting place to Baltimore.

They doubted George's ability to lead.

George doubted himself. The troops he had remaining from the seventeen thousand in Cambridge were a small number—down to a bit beyond five thousand, with a full third of those too sick or needy to be of use. The men were tired and wanted to go home, for they had farms to run and family to see.

As did George. He longed to be home . . . *in peaceable enjoyment of my own vine and fig tree,* as he'd put it.

I longed to have him there. For he had been gone eighteen months, and I a year. Never, in our worst nightmare, did we imagine being absent so long. And when I returned to Mount Vernon—'twas to a different nightmare.

One of my worst fears.

The house was in disrepair. I walked from room to room, my head shaking in disgust. I ran a finger along the furniture, leaving behind a marked trail. On the table of the west parlour, I wrote my condemnation: *Dusty!* The portraits of family—including a young version of myself, peered down at me, accusing me of dire neglect.

The young Martha Custis would not have allowed her home to be in such a state.

I went upstairs and found the bedrooms stale and dismal, the bedding untouched and uninviting. Even the mirrors seemed veiled by the dust.

Lund accompanied me. "Sorry, Martha. I can see now things could have been done here, but with the house empty . . ."

I put a hand on the blue paint of the doorway leading to our bedroom—our new bedroom in the addition we had built two years before. George had only had a few months to enjoy it, as well as enjoy his study directly below before cause and country had taken him north. I looked at the brown-and-white-checkered wing chair by the fire and could remember him sitting there, removing his boots, leaning back with a sigh as he transformed from the public George to the man who was mine alone.

"Martha?"

I blinked the memory away and addressed George's cousin. "I know things were difficult in our absence, Lund. I do not blame you. You had the farm to run. The house was of least concern."

"A farm to run with fewer slaves. When Lord Dunmore made the offer of freedom for fighting, we lost enough to matter."

"Has Dunmore honoured his promise to them?" I asked.

"I doubt it. They will probably be left wandering, away from their families, without means to survive."

My mind rattled with a list of things to do. "We must up the production of the spinners. The soldiers need shirts and stockings." I looked to some silk cushion covers that seemed far frivolous at such a time. "If need be perhaps we could unravel these and rework them with the homespun. Can we do that?"

"We will do our best."

It was all any of us could do. I put my hand upon the leather key basket that daily accompanied me upon my domestic rounds. "The world is indeed turned upside down, Lund."

"For all of us," he said.

I set to work, reclaiming this house as our home.

—∞—

I shivered myself to wakefulness.

I drew the covers close, but realized my body was not reacting to cold, but to something else.

I shivered not for the good news recently received of American victory in Princeton—news that was eagerly heard—but for the stories of how George had spent his Christmas crossing the Delaware River, in the dead of night, in silence, moving his entire army to the Hessian stronghold at Trenton, New Jersey, for a surprise attack. Although most Americans relayed the story as one of heroic magnitude, I knew that beyond the heroism it was an act of desperation. Our soldiers suffered horribly in Pennsylvania and needed supplies and indoor lodging. George relied on the fact that waging battle in the winter was simply not done. Both sides holed up and waited for better weather.

George could not wait. And so he arranged for his entire army to cross the icy river at night, march the eight miles up the snow-packed road to Trenton, and surprise the Europeans, who were hung over from Christmas merriment. And as the Almighty had saved Mount Vernon and me from Dunmore's warships by creating a storm in the Potomac, so God once again used nature for our side's benefit, creating storm enough to send the Hessian guards inside to get warm. Leaving the coast clear for our victory.

I shivered to wakefulness at the thought of our poor men, traipsing through the snow—many shoeless, leaving trails of blood upon the icy white. I shivered at the thought of George crossing a dangerous river . . . with the drowning deaths of two brothers, I would never be at ease at the thought of crossing water.

I turned on my side and put a hand across the pillow that should have cradled my husband's head. Last I'd heard, he was in Morristown,

New Jersey, where there had been an outbreak of smallpox. As the men were not in tents, but were staying in homes and businesses, the townspeople were none too keen on the close proximity of such an illness—or the dysentery that was a constant cloud upon our soldiers.

The outbreak was so severe—with nearly a fourth of the town's residents dying from these diseases—that George overturned his previous order against inoculation. He intimated that my bravery at getting such a procedure for myself helped spur him toward his reversal. The trick was to inoculate without the British finding out and taking advantage during the period when the men were laid up in recovery.

I could have helped nurse them. I would have been happy to, if only George would have allowed me to join him. Too soon it would be spring and there would be battles aplenty.

And though I suffered my loneliness for him, he suffered even more for being away from me, his family, *and* his beloved Mount Vernon. He wrote to me, grieving that my letters to him arrived in an erratic manner: *No one suffers more by an absence from home than myself.*

I believed him.

I heard footfalls in our private back stairs. Probably Lindy come to make a fire in the now cold grate of our room.

I considered lying abed. People would understand. 'Twas no stretch of imagination to know that all at Mount Vernon would have preferred to stay in warm covers upon this crisp February morn.

There was a light tap upon the door.

"Come in, Lindy. I am awake." To make myself truthful, I turned my legs over the side of the mattress and reached for my dressing gown.

The door opened tentatively and Cully peeked in. "Excuse me? Ma'am?"

"Just a moment."

He nodded and withdrew to the hall. I wrapped my gown around me and tied its fastening before opening the door. "Yes, Cully. What is it?"

"Sorry to disturb you so early, but a rider came by. He had a letter and said it was most urgent." He handed it to me and left me alone.

I took a switch and gained a flame from the coals to light a candle to read by. I sat at my dressing table chair and noticed the handwriting did not belong to George.

My stomach turned.

It had no reason to lessen as the letter came from one of my husband's aides at Morristown:

Dear Lady Washington,

I am sorry to inform you that General Washington is in dire sickness. We had three foot of snow at camp and he himself, being the General he is, oversaw the cleaning of the roads and town. For days he stood in the cold. And so, he now suffers from quinsy. His sore throat is extreme and though I do not wish to alarm you, I must state there are many here who are in an extreme state of worry. Please know everything that can be done to accomplish his complete recovery is being attended to.

I stood. "Not everything is being done, for I am not there!"

I would remedy that. If there was no carriage to take me north, I would walk.

Let the British or the Hessians or even the weather try to stop me.

⸻

I did not have to walk to New Jersey, but rode in a carriage arranged by Jacky. He, Eleanor, and baby Elizabeth had moved to Mount Vernon of late, and upon hearing of his dear poppa's illness rallied all forces to gain me access to care for him.

Jacky gave me a strong embrace before I left. "Make him well, Mamma. Please."

I looked up into his dark eyes. "I promise I will not allow death to take him. Bullets have spared him. I will not let sickness do worse."

The trip of two hundred and forty miles was more arduous than my trip to Cambridge eighteen months earlier, as the weather was far colder and my inclination for speed intense. Although Jacky sent ahead evidence of my route, as I neared Philadelphia I had received no message as to my husband's state. No news seemed bad news indeed. One would think on a trip of such a length all sorts of thoughts could tarry upon the mind. It was not so, for I had only one thought, one mind, one heart. I adjusted the rhythm of my prayers with each mile, each crook of the carriage, and each bump in the road. *Make him well, make him well. Make him whole.*

I arrived at a friend's house that would be my lodging for a night. We had just settled in to an evening before the fire when some soldiers came to the door. I did not think anything of it, as soldiers often came to residences, searching for provisions.

But as soon as my host spoke with them, he came into the parlour to get me. "They wish to speak with you, Martha. Alone." His face showed ample concern.

I attempted to ward off panic and met them in the dining area across the foyer. Their faces were grave yet full of compassion.

"Sirs?" I asked. I could not manage more.

With a glance to the parlour nearby, the taller one said, "Your husband, the general . . . it is serious. You must come now. He has requested you."

I sucked in a breath.

The shorter soldier reached a calming hand toward me. "We have orders not to let others know of his condition. If word got out . . . it would cause harm to many men."

Yes, yes. Indeed it would. The British would love such news, and the tenuous morale of our troops, finally optimistic after their victories at Trenton and Princeton . . . they could not know their leader was ill.

"I will make excuses to my hosts."

"We are prepared to fit your carriage with runners to speed our way through the forest."

"Indeed," I said. "Do it."

The soldiers bowed and left me alone in the dining room. My back was to the parlour, but I knew all eyes were upon me. I had to become an actress. It was imperative. I closed my eyes and drew upon the strength God always granted me upon such occasions. Then I put on a smile and crossed the foyer.

"What is wrong?" my host asked.

"What did the soldiers want?" asked his wife.

"They have come to ease my way," I said. "At this very moment they are making my carriage into a sled." I rolled my eyes. "It appears George is so eager to see me that he has sent them to fetch me straightaway."

"But it is sixty miles to Morristown. And it is dark."

I laughed. "I fear George will not take dark as an excuse. I greatly appreciate your hospitality, but as soon as they are ready, I really must go." I leaned close in confidentiality. "In truth, I too am eager to see him at the earliest time possible."

With that, I retired to my room to gather my things. But with the door closed behind me, I fell to my knees and my forehead kissed the back of my hands upon the floor. "O dear Lord . . . please let me get there in time."

———

We left for Morristown before dawn. As the snow sprayed around me, as the dark enshrouded our way through the black forest, I prayed double-time, my *Make him well* minuet turning into a brisk march of *Save him, save him, make him whole!* My breath filled the carriage with vapour and, in rhythm with my prayers, I pounded my clenched hands upon the blankets in an attempt to keep warm.

The carriage slowed at a house. I called out to a soldier. "Are we here?"

"No, ma'am. We are still sixteen miles. This is Pluckemin. A messenger met us and said to stop here—at the house of a Mrs. Eliot."

My heart stopped. Were they going to take me inside to give me bad news?

A woman opened the front door, a shawl around her shoulders. She smiled.

It seemed an odd thing to do if bad news lay inside.

I could not stand the questions another moment, so exited the carriage even before a soldier could open the door for me.

The woman took a step outside. "Is Lady Washington inside?" she asked, looking past me to the carriage.

I had been mistaken for a maid before. Perhaps because my husband was so striking in stature and bearing people assumed his wife would be also. They did not expect a short, plump woman of forty-five who preferred to spend the long hours of travel dressed simply.

Yet before I could correct her misconception, a man appeared in the doorway, and with a better look I saw . . .

"George!"

We ran toward each other and he lifted me from the ground and round about, as though I were a young girl. "Hello, my dearest," he whispered in my ear. "I have missed you."

When he let me gently to the ground, I looked upon his face. "You are well?"

"I am better. Better enough to come meet you." He drew my hand to his lips. "I have missed you beyond bearing."

"Ten months," I said.

"A lifetime."

"Time," I said. The word had much implication, for my prayers had been answered with this gift.

I leaned against him and wallowed in the sound of his heart beating against my ear. Only then did I notice the cold.

"Inside," I said, pushing upon his chest. "You are still not well. Inside, old man."

He turned toward the door. "Your wish is my command."

⚬⚬⚬⚬

I stood in the unfinished second-floor room of the frame home where George lodged in Morristown—now lodged with me, just outside the ballroom where his aides bunked. Our room had rough wood eaten by worms for the floor, and cold air sped through gaps in the walls. George immediately gave me permission to have it made better and so I commandeered a few of the men for the work. They seemed quite willing, as the house was warm and the work filled their days and allowed them to use their talents. I knew of no better source of contentment than purpose.

I pointed to the far side where I wanted a cupboard. "Now, young men, I care for nothing but comfort here, and should like you to fit me up a beaufet on one side of the room, along with some shelves, and places for hanging clothes on the other."

One workman put his hand in front of a crevice in the wall. "You would be wanting these plugged too, eh?"

The other ran a toe across the plank floor. "And this? We could add a layer and make it better for you and the general."

I put a hand upon both their arms. "Gentlemen, that would be glorious." I took a step toward the door. "Now, if you will begin, I will come up at eleven each day and bring you refreshment. And in the afternoon, when the general and I are done with our dinner below, you may come down and sup there too."

Their faces glowed with appreciation. "That would be wonderful, Lady Washington."

"Mrs. Washington will dō, sirs. Now, I will let you get to work."

———

Within the week the work was complete and I extended my delight to the workers. They seemed genuinely humbled, and all was well.

I instructed George to encourage his officers to bring their wives to camp, as spousal closeness was always of benefit. Lucy Knox came, but Kitty Greene—about to give birth to her second child, could not. The Greenes had honoured us by naming their firstborn George Washington Greene, and had intimated if this child be a girl, she would be named after me.

I spent time trying to set up sewing circles with the officers' wives and women of the town as I had done in Cambridge. Some seemed shocked I expected them to remove themselves from idleness. But by sharing stories of the men's sufferings, by cajoling them to action, they agreed to come.

I greeted them at the door. "Come in, come in, ladies. I welcome your company and your industry."

Two wives entered, attired in fine gowns and dressed hair. I knew they wished to impress the general's wife. I understood their desire but needed to make it known I was not one who wished to be impressed. I myself wore a simple linen dress with a woolen stomacher and petticoat, and had a scarf wrapped about my neck, tucked into the bodice against the chill.

As I led them into the parlour, I saw them looking me over. I saw looks exchanged between them. And I waited for either an upturned lip showing their disdain at my simplicity or a downcast eye revealing shame at their own frivolity.

We settled in and I gave them each a task toward making attire for the soldiers. I asked about their families and their origins.

And I waited.

Finally, Mrs. Connally, a candlemaker's wife, put down her stitching and sighed. "Oh dear. Forgive me, Mrs. Washington, but I can hold my tongue no longer."

"What is wrong?" I asked. I hoped.

She ran a hand upon the blue satin of her gown, letting her fingers linger on the lace that ran upon its edge. "I feel utterly foolish for coming here as if for a ball, when you . . . when we . . ." She took another breath as if to gain complete courage. "I wished to impress you, kind lady, and in doing so find myself ashamed. For I see now, by your action and words, it is not a time to build oneself up with acts of vanity, but for putting oneself aside toward acts of selflessness. I, for one, am truly sorry."

"I am too," said Mrs. Miller, the wife of a local printer. "We did not know. We did not think . . . your wisdom, your kind heart, and your dictum of hard work impress me beyond measure. I only hope I can strive to match your goodness in the days ahead."

Although I had hoped for them to see the error of their frivolity in such perilous times, I had not expected such utter humility and contrition. "I am moved, ladies."

I extended my hands toward theirs and we completed our bond with a gentle touch of like minds and hearts.

George and I were at supper with two of George's favourite young aides: Alexander Hamilton and John Laurens. Both had recently entered our military family and were like sons to us. Alexander won our hearts by admitting he had been orphaned at twelve, yet had grown to be the able, intelligent, and dashing man who graced our table. That he had proven himself to be a hero at Princeton only added to his worth in my husband's eyes.

John Laurens was the son of Henry Laurens, the president of Congress. He had come to our attention through a letter in which he had humbly offered his services—gratis—in any way in which he could be used. An able man, schooled in the law in London and Geneva, he was a delightful addition to our home and to our Cause.

John was regaling us with one of his many stories of near-misses—the boy was quite reckless and took little heed to danger—when there was a knock on the door. A Frenchman, clad in a stunning uniform, entered. My first impression was to his height, which seemed even grander than that of my husband.

A servant asked his business. "I have come to meet the *général*." He nodded curtly. "I am Marie Joseph Paul Yves Roche Gilbert du Motier, Marquis de Lafayette, come to join the fight for *liberté*."

George rose at once and I saw him smile. "Come in, sir."

The marquis gazed upon my husband, his eyes turning from curiosity to awe. "Are you *he*?"

George came round the table to greet him. "I am."

Lafayette saluted quite smartly and said, "I have left home and family to join you here. I, as well as my father and grandfather before me, have served in the French army. Although now an orphan, I have basked in their legacy. My family knows well what causes are just and right. And so, I come to volunteer. I require nothing but the honour to serve."

I caught Alexander and John exchanging amused glances. I gave them a look to behave, which they rightly observed.

George addressed the marquis, who looked to be more boy than man. "I suppose we ought to be embarrassed to show ourselves to an officer who has just left the French forces."

Lafayette snapped to attention. "I have come here to learn, *mon général*, not to teach."

George's eyebrow rose. "Then come. Let us begin by dining together."

And so our military family gained another son.

— THIRTEEN —

News. Cursed, blessed news. Even as I longed for each letter, each newspaper, each traveler who might know something about anything, I dreaded them and met every occasion with a stitch in my stomach. Sometimes the stitch relaxed; other times, it tightened with renewed ferocity.

Such was the news that filtered into Mount Vernon during the autumn of 1777 after I returned home from Morristown. News, like falling leaves, was undependable and fell upon us in its own time.

We rejoiced at a victory in the north, led by General Benedict Arnold at Saratoga, New York. But grieved and worried when George and his troops fared far worse with a defeat at Brandywine Creek and Germantown near Philadelphia. To add to my personal pain was the news Lafayette had been wounded in the upper thigh. George extolled the surgeons to treat the dear boy as if he were his own son. With all the ups and downs, I oft remembered George's words: *"We can win this war so long as we don't outright lose it."*

Which we could.

At any time.

Although I knew George was doing his best, I suffered each humiliation and frustration with him.

And then there were stirrings from certain generals and congress-men who wished to have George removed as commander in chief. Major General Horatio Gates (who claimed credit for Saratoga, even though he did little toward the victory) nipped at my husband's heels, wanting to take command. He insulted George by sending letters directly to Congress, plying his claim.

I felt utterly helpless.

But then a ray of hope. George was instructed to take winter camp near the city of New York, to protect it from further attacks. Since the British had what they wanted in Philadelphia, and prob-ably did not wish to risk leaving the luxuries of that city in the dead of winter, I hoped George would come home. We needed him here on so many fronts. . . .

Firstly, we had suffered horrendous rains that had all but ruined our crops. I knew Lund was sorely worried and could have used George's hands-on wisdom.

Secondly, at George's instructions, we and Jacky had taken shares in a privateer vessel. Its goal was to prey on British ships and gain their cargo for profit or for use of the army. I was very proud of Jacky for his industry, and for the fact that he put himself forth to run as a representative for the House of Burgesses for New Kent County. His involvement spoke volumes to his burgeoning maturity.

Thirdly, but firstly in my heart, I needed George home due to personal reasons. For on the seventeenth of December, my dearest sister, Nancy, died. She was only thirty-eight and the greatest favourite I had in the world. She left behind dear Burwell and three children. I wished to think of it as a relief—as she had been sickly for years, but the loss was shocking just the same. Most sobering was acknowledging that the large Dandridge family of Father, Mother, and eight children had dwindled to five: Mother, Bartholomew, Betsy, Frances, and me. I clung to the promise I would see dearest Nancy in heaven one day. I would see all those who passed before.

Adding to my sorrow was the desire to travel to Eltham to offer comfort, yet knowing I could not because I prayed for a letter where George would call me north, and I could not risk being farther away. And, dear Eleanor was due with her third child at any day. I had missed one birth. I would not miss another.

And so I mourned with my family from afar, waited for a letter from George that did not come, and . . . was made a grandmother for the third time on December 31. Her name was Martha Parke Custis— Patty. With that little babe in my arms, I found the only true solace to death. I vowed once again to take no one for granted. Ever.

The year 1778 arrived steeped with this familial happiness, for both baby and her sister, Betsy (who had grown fat as a pig), were healthy. Although my largest wish was that happiness would endure, I feared it would not. Knew it could not.

I sat in the small dining room, eating a scone for breakfast, the children off to attend to little Patty, the house surprisingly guest-free.

It was quiet. Too quiet.

The walls of the dining room tried their best to distract me, their surfaces ablaze with rich verdigris green. It made me remember the moment George chose such a hue three years earlier. "I suggest green, Martha, for I find it to be a colour grateful to the eye."

Grateful. I needed to be grateful for what we had when so many had far less, and had endured far more.

My eyes strayed to the corner of the room where a mahogany case for twelve large stoppered bottles sat upon the floor. It was a fine set ordered from England, but one that brought back another memory, this one of George's ire at being vastly overcharged.

A common miscarriage of justice in those times.

Which had led to these times.

In search of times more equitable than both.

Enough lingering, malingering, muttering, and suffering. There was work to be done, *today*.

I have been duly called to what George described as a dreary kind of place, twenty miles northwest of Philadelphia. I had never heard its name before his letter asking me to join him—at Valley Forge.

'Twas a strategically located camp: it guarded the road to York, where Congress had moved, it blocked a supply route into Philadelphia, and it was close enough to watch British movements.

On the last leg of my journey there was a drastic snowstorm at Brandywine that commenced to do a good job of covering sober evidence of a past battle. My carriage was met on horseback by an aide-de-camp, Colonel Caleb Gibbs. "Welcome, Lady Washington. I bring greetings from all the men."

"Much appreciated, Colonel, and I am eager to greet them in return, but as for now . . . there is only one soldier I wish to greet."

He grinned and tipped his hat. "His eagerness is duly matched—if not amplified."

After exchanging my carriage for a farm sleigh that would traverse the snow-clogged road, he accompanied me the rest of the way. I entered a camp of over ten thousand and found bedraggled, stooped men dressed in a mishmash of worn clothing, some with rags tied about their feet, many with bare legs, their stockings long worn out. They looked like a beaten band. I was appalled by their appearance, as well as the condition of their lodging—if thus it could be called: lean-tos, tents, rough shanties from discarded wood. Garbage was everywhere, and I spotted a dead horse blanketed with the recent snow. Although the snow had stopped, I saw all this through a thick haze of smoke as the men attempted to keep warm by burning whatever they could. They were in dire need of . . . everything. My inclination was to stop the sleigh and comfort them, yet what good would words do? They needed sustenance beyond words.

Then, in spite of their solemn condition, upon seeing me in the sleigh, the men stopped their work—and cheered!

"Lady, you are here!"

"Huzzah for Lady Washington!"

"God bless Lady Washington!"

I was overcome by intense embarrassment. I was not someone to cheer. I had nothing to ease their pain. *Shh! Shh! Enough of that now. Go under cover. Warm yourselves!*

Colonel Gibbs rode up next to me, his face delighted. "They love you, milady. They have been eagerly awaiting your arrival."

"How did—?"

"Why, the general told them."

Feeling sheepish, I waved at the men as we passed. My heart ached with their generous offering amid their extreme need. Tall men, short men, young men, old men . . . each one became a son to me, a son I wanted to protect, console, and encourage.

Yet I was just one woman of no great talent and little consequence. What could I do? I had brought supplies from Mount Vernon—fabric, thread, wool, ham, salt herring, bandages—but they would aid far too few to have meaning.

For the first time I shared the intensity of my husband's frustration, a feeling he lived with daily. Hourly. To see the passion and hope of these countrymen, to realize their dreams of a better life were at stake—to realize my dreams were in their hands . . .

I wanted to warm those hands, hold those hands, shake those hands.

I was much relieved to arrive at the stone house that was used as our headquarters and lodging—the Potts house—and even more relieved when George came out of the house and rescued me.

"Come, my dearest. You must be frozen."

No, I was not frozen. My chill compared to the suffering of the men I had just seen was an inconvenience amid true misery.

Upon retiring inside, upon taking a good look at my husband in the firelight, I was appalled by his pallor. I leaned close for his ears alone. "You are spent. I can see it. You need rest."

His eyes did not betray our conversation. "I need solutions to many problems more urgent than a good night's sleep."

We would see about that. For I knew the fate of many men depended on the fate of this one. And this one I could help.

———◦∞◦———

George gave me a tour of his headquarters—it did not take long. If I had allowed myself complaints at Morristown, they were nothing to these conditions. The front door opened to a room that was no more than sixteen by sixteen, a room that slept men by night, their beds turned into desks by day. Maps and papers were strewn upon every surface. Beyond it was another room for George's office. Upstairs George slept in a room barely large enough for a bed and small table. He stooped as he entered it.

"You quite fill it up, old man."

"I fit well enough. But you . . ."

I moved close. "I am with you."

———◦∞◦———

George needed sleep. I hoped that by having me with him—hence curtailing his worry over me—he would achieve it. Ensconced in our tiny room, in a bed that ensured the closeness we preferred, I settled in, tucked beneath his arm, my head upon his chest. I straightened the locket I had given him our first year of marriage, setting it in the center of his chest just so. "Sleep now, old man."

I felt him nod, but the silence, the prequel to sleep, only lasted a few minutes. "I know that in so great a contest we must not expect to meet with nothing but sunshine. I have no doubt everything happens so for the best. We shall triumph over our misfortunes and in the end be ultimately happy . . ."

At his pause, I asked, "But?"

He sat up, taking me with him. "But the suffering of my men

grieves me beyond comprehension. If the British knew half our sufferings, they would take advantage and attack. And defeat us."

"Then we will pray they do not find out."

George leaned against the wall and opened his arm to me. I took my place within his embrace. "Did I tell you I held a contest for the most ingenious shelter and shoes made of bark?"

"*That* is ingenious."

He shrugged. "I had to do something to spur the men to thinking beyond the norm. I have found most men enjoy—they need—a chance to use their minds, especially when their bodies are sorely tested."

"I agree."

"But I can only do so much. I need more support. Do you know why I chose this place for our camp?"

"Because of its luxurious accommodations?"

"Because a committee in Pennsylvania said they would withdraw all the soldiers from their state if we camped farther than twenty-five miles from Philadelphia. I could not risk losing so many men."

"You are making do here."

"The men need supplies. Their clothing is so minimal that when one is called to sentry duty, the other men pool their garments so he does not freeze to death." He tapped on my shoulder. "Last December Congress had the audacity to order a day of thanksgiving."

"I know its timing might have been questionable, but we should always be reminded we are to give thanks."

"Agreed. But with the order, they gave the men hope of a great feast. And then they provided only a half a gill of rice and a tablespoon of vinegar."

I sat aright. "That is disgraceful."

"It was cruel."

"When I saw the disappointment—the betrayal—in the eyes of the men, not to mention the reaction of the women and children . . ."

I looked at him through the moonlight. "I did not see any women and children."

"They are here."

"But why?"

"Why are you here?"

I returned to my place against his shoulder. The thought of families existing under the horrible conditions I had seen . . .

"I beg for supplies. But the head quartermaster at Congress quit months ago and has not been replaced. I can only imagine the pile of requests languishing on some ignored desk." He sighed deeply. "My army is fading before my eyes. I am holding it together by sheer will, and God's grace—though sometimes I wonder if true mercy would be attained if I told the men to go home."

I found his hand and clasped it. "No, George. We have come too far. As a defeated people . . . the home the men would return to would be of no worth. There is no—"

"No turning back. I know. I know. But we need help. If only the French would commit to us. Yet why should they? My defeats in New York have not impressed them. France will not risk Britain's ire to back a loser."

I tried to think of some ray of hope. "But Saratoga. Our victory there . . ."

"I am hoping it will be enough. Lafayette has sent many letters home soliciting aid, and Benjamin Franklin hopes to meet with King Louis. If anyone can cajole a king, it would be him."

It gave little comfort to pin our hope on a country we had fought against just twenty years previous. "With all these trials . . . what keeps the men here?"

He considered this a moment. "Hope. Hope is its own army and carries its own weapons. Without it we will surely perish."

I remembered a verse that had sustained me on many occasions. " 'Be of good courage, and he shall strengthen your heart, all ye that hope in the Lord.' "

He kissed the top of my head. "We must sleep. Tomorrow will not wait for us."

—⊶⊷—

"You are an angel, ma'am."

I put a hand upon the hand of the wounded soldier—it appeared to be the only part of him not in distress. "You sleep now."

He turned his hand over and took mine. "Will you come back tomorrow?"

The number of wounded was daunting, and there was only one me. "I will try."

I moved on to the next soldier, asleep upon a few boards, his tattered blanket nowhere near large enough to cover him. I attempted to tuck it beneath his feet—which bore no shoes. The act exposed his arms.

I turned to the attendant who accompanied me. "Is there a piece of cloth left in the basket?"

Raymond shook his head. "You used the last one four soldiers back."

I looked upon the sleeping soldier, wondering whether cold arms or cold feet were the larger discomfort. His hair was matted with blood from a gash that looked too wide for proper healing. *Too soon it will not matter.*

I started at my own thought. That I had come to be so matter-of-fact with death horrified me.

And yet, walking amongst the wounded day after day . . . seeing them come—and go . . . Most were not being treated for the wounds of war. There was little fighting going on beyond the occasional skirmish of one of our foraging parties coming into contact with one of the British, but disease was rampant: dysentery, pneumonia, and all sorts of complaints brought about by unsanitary conditions and poor or nonexistent food.

"Lady Washington? Since the basket is empty, are we done for the day?"

It was tempting. Visiting the men exhausted me. And yet, how could I go back to the Potts house and sit before a fire when they were suffering so?

"Not yet," I said, moving on.

I spotted a man—or half a man, as he was so gaunt—smiling at me. I went to his side.

"Are you *her*?"

I continued to blush at such recognition. "I am Mrs. Washington, yes."

He extended a bandaged hand. "We wait for you each winter. Did you know that?"

I felt tears threaten but held them back. "I am very honoured. I wait to come to *you*."

"We know it is a great sacrifice for you to leave your home and visit us."

I put my hand upon his shoulder, shaking my head. "My sacrifice is nothing, dear boy, compared to all of yours. My honour is nothing. All should go to you."

"No, no, dear lady, you—"

I had had enough adulation. "What is your name, soldier?"

"William, ma'am."

"I had a brother named William. A fine man he was. Just like you. Where are you from, William?"

"Vermont."

"I have not had the pleasure. Is it beautiful there?" I pulled a stool beside him and asked about his family and the life he had left behind—the life he was fighting for.

It was the least I could do.

Sadly, the least.

<hr>

I disliked this duty more than any. I was annoyed that too many women put me in this position, and yet, as desperate as they were, I knew I might have done the same.

"Sit, Mrs. Drinker."

Although our upstairs room was tiny, I could not impose upon the other spaces during the day when George and his men needed room to deal with the war.

She sat, her face hopeful, her hands keeping each other company in her lap. "I appreciate your taking my side, Mrs. Washington, and sending me to see your husband."

I knew of her meeting—her very, very brief meeting, for George had no time for traitors' wives.

"Do you have good news for me?" she asked.

I took a chair nearby, the two of us close enough for our dresses to touch. "I am sorry, Mrs. Drinker, but I am afraid George cannot free your husband from our prison. No matter how extensive is your love for him, or my sympathy for you, it comes to this: Americans should not sell supplies to the enemy."

She opened her mouth to speak but wisely shut it. She rose. "Thank you for your time, Mrs. Washington."

"And yours, Mrs. Drinker."

I saw her to the door, once again incredulous. I knew times were desperate. I knew citizens were faced with difficult survival decisions every day, but the truth was, it was past time to take sides. Completely. Utterly. As God did not like lukewarm people—wishing them either hot or cold, lest He spew them out of his mouth—neither did I.

So there.

⊰⊱

I arranged a party for George's forty-sixth birthday on February 22, 1778, in the new log addition he had ordered built at the back of the Potts house for dining and the sewing circles I held regularly. I brewed coffee made with acorns—the standard fare in such hard times. There was little more I could offer. But to make things merry, I asked a few soldiers who were musicians to play us a concert.

When they finished, we applauded and George stood. "Bravo, gentlemen! Bravo."

I moved to their leader and discreetly pressed into his palm fifteen shillings for their effort, then made a request. "Would you continue to play some songs for singing?"

The fiddle player looked in his hand, his eyes grew wide, then he bowed. "Of course, Lady Washington. Anything for you."

George laughed. "If only *I* would elicit such loyalty."

The soldier reddened and said, "Anything for you too, General, sir."

George—quite delighted and at ease in the celebration—shooed his concern away. "My soldiers are ever faithful, ever loyal. I could ask for none better."

"Hear, hear!" General Knox said.

His wife, Lucy, was quick to join the toast. "To the men who battle for us!"

There was agreement throughout the room.

And much singing. Even George, who could not list singing among his many talents, joined in with an exuberance that gave me great pleasure.

'Twas a good night. A good birthday for my old man.

Rumour had it a woman named Mrs. Loring had as much to do with the inaction of the British during their stay in Philadelphia as any act or action of a military nature. She was General Howe's mistress—and the wife of one of his officers—and had apparently so enamored him with her pleasures that he was content to party and dine and leave the war for warmer weather. Luckily, his officers and soldiers were content to follow suit.

Our officers' wives who had come to Valley Forge to live with their patriot husbands had great fun with such rumours, and I, for one, hoped they were true. Time. We needed time for our troops to be further trained, and time to hear news of an essential alliance with the French. Let the British carouse and be distracted. The longer the better. Although I made great attempts to bring laughter and joy to our lives at camp, I was ever mindful of the responsibility we had to care for these men, to buoy them up, to mold them into fine soldiers. George did his part and I did mine.

And the Indians did theirs.

We did not expect this help. But during the winter, when our troops were at their neediest, some Oneida Indians walked hundreds of miles from the north, bringing with them six hundred bushels of corn. Our men were so starved they wanted to eat it raw, but the Indians intervened—knowing the raw corn would swell in their stomachs and kill them—and showed them how to cook it. And eat gradually. One Oneida woman, Polly Cooper, stayed behind to help the sick soldiers and teach them how to cook the corn.

I was so moved by their help that I gave Polly a bonnet and a shawl. A poor trade on her part, but I needed to do something. Women are not so very different, no matter what their background.

Another to do their part was France. In April, young Lafayette returned from France in time to hear good news: our two countries had signed an agreement to be allies. Lafayette—in his demonstrative and dramatic way—responded by taking George by the arms and kissing both cheeks. The men cheered and soon the entire camp was awash in celebration. I spotted George playing hoops with some of the camp children, smiling as I rarely saw him smile.

At the end of the day George made a speech from his heart. "It having pleased the Almighty Ruler of the Universe to defend the Cause of the United American States by raising us up a powerful friend among the princes of the earth to establish our liberty and independence upon lasting foundations, it becomes us to set apart a day for gratefully acknowledging the divine goodness and celebrating the important event which we owe to his benign interposition.

Tomorrow, I declare an official day of public celebration beginning with morning religious services, followed by parades, marching, and the glad firings of cannon and musketry. When all is done, I will host a grand banquet and we will toast our country and the good king of all France."

Hurrah for King Louis! Hurrah for our United States! And thank God for both.

A sentry burst into headquarters. "They are leaving!"

I was in the dining room mending shirts, and ran out to hear the rest of it. George and some of his officers came out of his office. "Explain yourself, Corporal."

The man saluted, then put a hand to his chest as he gained his breath. "The British are leaving Philadelphia and heading toward New York! I saw rows of soldiers, and wagons upon wagons of supplies and civilians going with them."

We all looked to George for his reaction. "It appears they do not appreciate our alliance with France. 'Tis certain news has come to them as it came to us."

" 'Tis a new general in charge, sir. News is Howe went back to England. 'Tis Clinton who is retreating."

"Not without us upon their backs," George said.

"We are going to chase them?"

"We have not sat here for nine months to let them go with our blessing."

The men returned to his office to make plans, their voices rising with excitement.

I left my sewing behind and went upstairs.

The waiting was over. The war would begin again.

It was time I went home.

It was midsummer, and I was home. Each return was a blessing and a burden. For after being gone for five months, 'twas like starting all over. Everything, from house to chores to manners, had to be created afresh.

Jacky, Eleanor, and my granddaughters were my chief joy. I always did best with children about me. But Eleanor was skittish and needed attending to nearly as much as the girls. I was not certain why until one day I caught her in the breezeway that connected the kitchen to the house. She was not on any errand but was holding on to a column, peering at the Potomac beyond.

"Is something bothering you, dear?"

After a moment's hesitation, she nodded toward the river. "They could come get us."

Ah. They. The British.

"They have before."

Yes, indeed. Years before, Lord Dunmore had sailed warships up the river to kidnap me. "A storm turned them away. The warships did not come."

"We cannot depend upon such a storm in July." She turned her back upon the river to face me. Her brow was wet with perspiration— from the heat or concern? "Jack said there were two failed kidnappings during your trips north."

"Failed, Eleanor. Failed. And I was never aware of them until after the fact."

"I do not know why you keep going back."

"I go where I am needed."

"We need you here."

"Needed most," I said. I put my arm around her and led her toward the house. "We cannot dwell on such things lest we spend our days locked in a closet."

"But they might—"

"They might. And if they do, we will conduct ourselves with calm, bravery, and common sense."

"You have those qualities. I am afraid I do not."

"You may surprise yourself, my dear."

But in truth, I prayed she would never be faced with such a prospect. I too was afraid she would not fare well.

Unwittingly, the war taught me geography. Monmouth, New Jersey, was the newest addition to my knowledge. I sat upon the lawn of Mount Vernon, on a blanket spread with dollies and blocks. My little darlings played nearby: Betsy was just two and full of the vim and vigour of her father as she ran and fell, laughed, and stood up only to do it again. And sweet Patty, at nine months, crawled from blanket to grass and back again to push herself up upon my lap.

"No, no," I said to Patty, "we do not eat leaves."

The child did not listen to me but made her own decision that leaves were not tasty and, making a disturbing face, spit them out. In this way, she too was like her father, who preferred to learn things the hard way.

With the girls content, I was allowed a moment to read a letter I had received from George—actually, read it again, for away from his presence, I loved to hear his voice through his words upon the page. Especially good news.

Monmouth turned out to be a glorious and happy day. Without exaggerating, the trip of the British through the Jerseys in killed, wounded, prisoners, and deserters, has cost them at least 2,000 men—and of their best troops. We have 60 men killed, 132 wounded, and about 130 missing, some of whom I supposed may yet come in. Our enemy lost near 500 to desertion—most of those Hessians who became overcome by the scalding heat and damp. 'Twas not an easy battle, more due to the disloyalty of my own officers. General Lee was given orders to attack their flank, but upon riding up to help him, I found his troops retreating and in great confusion. They had not e'en fired a shot—and they wished to fight, but had been told to retreat because Lee did not think they were up to battle against British regulars.

You know I do not swear, Martha, but with the sight of Lee's cowardice, I did more than my share. I sent Lee to the back and took command myself, riding up and back among them, encouraging them into battle. The men rallied at my instruction—and were eager to do so—and performed with great distinction.

You will share my joy in knowing that young Laurens, Hamilton, and Lafayette distinguished themselves in a frenzy of valor. The first two had their horses shot from beneath them, but carried on just the same.

I was never so proud of the men. It seems all the hardships of the long winter did not break their spirit, but made them all the more determined. And though the British denied us a final glorious battle by sneaking away to safety in the dead of night, I feel as though I am finally being the leader I should be. The world may not remember Monmouth, but I, for one, will ne'er forget it.

You will also be pleased to note that Congress has seen fit to reward me with powers beyond those I have held as yet. I am now to superintend and direct the military operations in all the departments in these states. With reluctance—for the words are too glowing—I will quote for you from Henry Laurens, John's father and the president of Congress: 'Love and respect for Your Excellency is impressed on the heart of every grateful American, and your name will be revered by posterity.' To be on the verge of removal and now receive such notations . . .

I carry no reward other than the new ability to get done that which needs to be done in—hopefully—a more expeditious manner. I pray you and our family are safe and in each other's happy company.

Yours always, my dearest,
George

Yours always, my dearest . . .

Reading such a letter, sitting upon the lawn with my grand-daughters nearby, amid the haven of our home at Mount Vernon, I was a woman greatly blessed.

With the British having retreated to New York . . . perhaps this would all be over soon and George could join in our blessings.

Perhaps.

"But, Mother, I do not want to own that land anymore. It contains an insufferable quantity of mosquitoes, and running it . . ." Jacky shrugged.

We sat in the west parlour waiting for Eleanor to bring the children down to say their good-nights. I was glad it was I alone who witnessed my son's shrug.

I hated to admit as much, but I knew Jacky was not keen on running *any* plantation. Although he had proven himself to be a loving husband and father—he was to be a father again in the spring—he had not completely lost his wild ways. It seemed being elected a Burgess had gone to his head and he preferred spending his free time in society, or playing cards and gambling.

I adjusted a stocking on the darning ball. "Your poppa bought you that plantation with your inheritance money, invested in it for its fine value, but also with hopes that one day you and Eleanor would live there."

"But I am not good at dealing with overseers and slaves like Poppa is. I am not keen on business and find the act of selling crops most demeaning."

I took offense. "You consider what your poppa does with the greatest skill demeaning?"

Thankfully, he reddened. "Demeaning to me, Mamma. Because

I am not good at it and do not know the price I should get, nor how to get it."

"Those are skills you can learn, that every landowner must learn."

To my dismay he shrugged again. Although my son—as the sole heir to my first husband's fortune—did not need to concern himself with money, I was distressed at his penchant for inaction and the pursuit of pleasure.

"I wish to sell the land, Mamma."

I shook my head with vehemence. "Now is not the time to sell anything for cash, Jacky. Land for land. Your poppa has given you such advice himself. In the course of the last two years, with our currency losing value at an alarming rate, a pound may not, in the space of two years more, be worth a shilling."

"Which means now is the time to gain the cash, before it is worthless."

"You are not thinking. If you gain cash, it will only have worth if you spend it immed—" I stopped myself. Oh dear. I knew too well Jacky would have no trouble spending an immense amount with great proclivity. Even the fact goods were in short supply would not stop him.

I spotted a twinkle in his eye. He rose from his chair. "I am going to see to the girls."

And make your escape.

I looked at the door after he left. To have regrets as a parent was near as painful as grief. Perhaps it was another kind of grief—grief for what could have been in the present if I had been a different sort of mother. Sterner. Less indulgent.

I turned back to the darning but was interrupted by the memory of George's oft-heard admonition: *Martha, you spoil the boy!*

I had. Unequivocally. And worse, had chosen to do so, in spite of all better advice.

To what end?

To this end. To the creation of a boy—a man—who had little

interest in hard work and industry. A man who preferred instant pleasures to lasting satisfactions.

I stared out the window but only saw my reflection in the glass dividing the candlelit room from the darkness.

My brow was furrowed.

As it should have been. Regret and self-admonishment were serious business.

—✺—

Jacky sold his land for cash, yet did buy a property for himself and his family. It was nine hundred acres of land near Alexandria. It was called Abingdon and was situated on the west bank of the Potomac. It was once owned by the Alexander family, for whom Alexandria was named. Its position equidistant between Mount Vernon and Mount Airy gave the satisfaction Jacky had at least used logic in the purchase.

And it *was* logical they moved to their own home. They had been married four and a half years and would soon have three children. Although I grieved their departure from Mount Vernon, I applauded this step of independence.

And prayed it would not end in disaster.

—✺—

If I were a jealous woman . . .

I watched as George bowed and parried with Kitty Greene as his partner. Kitty—friend though she was—was a terrible flirt.

And a dancer equal to my George.

Although I had not danced in public in years, George thrived on it, and it gave me great joy in seeing *him* so joyful.

Of course, on this night, joy was present all around. I had joined George in Middlebrook, New Jersey, and times were quiet as the British moved south with their efforts. Sadly, Savannah, Georgia, had been taken, but up in the north, things were relatively quiet. I was informed I now had my own regiment: the Lady Washington Dragoons, commanded by Lieutenant Colonel Baylor. I was honoured beyond words.

I was also relieved at the scarcity of danger, for its release allowed many more wives to come to winter camp—and bring their children. Before this year it was a hard decision for women to choose between supporting their husband in camp or taking care of their children back home. In this year, in this place, the decision could be inclusive.

Tonight we celebrated many blessings and came together to honour each other, and our Cause. It was February 18, 1779, and we observed the one-year anniversary of our alliance with France. General Knox and his artillery company were the hosts, and we were all dressed in our finest—or as fine as we could muster considering the times. Seventy women and three hundred men were present. Knox's wife, Lucy, had taken the honour of the first minuet with my husband. My, my, she had gotten stout indeed. I, who struggled with plumpness my entire life, found a bit of satisfaction in seeing someone more rotund than myself. By many degrees.

I should not have thought such things, but from the sidelines I had time to discern and discuss those who partook of the gaiety in full view.

There was Esther Reed, the wife of the new Pennsylvania governor. British born and bred, she was now a patriot through and through. I heard she had suffered many hardships during the war, once escaping the British with her three small children and ailing mother, driven in a wagon by a young boy of fourteen. The lot of them chose the danger of the western Indian wilderness to the brutality of the British soldiers, who, so far from the morals of home, often acted in a way most vile and horrid. I admired her greatly.

I waved at Mrs. Ford, whose husband had died at Morristown. That she would be here to celebrate with us . . . her perseverance and dedication pleased everyone who met her.

And then my eyes returned to my husband—and to Kitty, his affable partner in dance. Although she was four-and-twenty and the mother of three children, she could have been considered the belle of the ball.

The present dance ended and the partners bowed to each other. Kitty tugged at my husband's sleeve and said to the assemblage, "I make a wager I can dance longer than any man here, and that includes you, General."

With a wink to me and a bow to her, George said, "I will take that wager."

After quitting at but three hours, Kitty lost the wager—for she did not know my husband.

That was only *my* pleasure.

———

On March 21, 1779, Eleanor delivered another daughter, Eleanor Parke Custis—called Nelly. The child was born at Abingdon. I hoped she would cement the feeling of security and family I wished my son to embrace.

That Eleanor was not doing well in her recovery . . .

I was a torn woman, wishing to be with my husband in New Jersey, my son and grandchildren in Maryland, and home at Mount Vernon.

If only I could be two places at once.

Or three.

— FOURTEEN —

Although each winter camp was different in its own right, all shared bad weather, worry, and waiting. The second time I was in Morristown over the winter of 1779 to 1780 was worse than the first. The winter was frigid to the point that the water surrounding New York City was frozen for the first time in the colony's history. Chesapeake Bay suffered a similar fate, all the way south to the Potomac. The snow was relentless, with drifts higher than common memory. In hindsight, many looked fondly upon Valley Forge.

We lived in a nice house supplied to us by a widow, Mrs. Ford, who insisted on moving herself and her children into the parlour, leaving us the rest of the house for our lodging and army headquarters. Again, George took for himself one bedroom above and one office on the main floor. The Ford home was rare in that it had an attached kitchen along the back third of the house, but even that was oft full of aides using the tables for work.

Though we were amply housed, our thoughts were never allowed to wallow in the warmth. Not with our men suffering nearby. They sometimes went five or six days without bread or meat, and sometimes two or three days without either. They ate every kind of horse food but hay. Townspeople were fed up with us, wanting more, more,

more from them. And some soldiers had taken to sneaking out at night and stealing what they could. George, of course, frowned on this, but did little to stop it. 'Twas not for material gain these men stole but to survive. The army was not supplying their needs. The entire nation was paralyzed by the freeze. In January drifts were ten feet high. Few supplies could get anywhere. If there were supplies to be had. Or money to pay for them. It did not help that the British counterfeited our colonial script.

The United States were bankrupt.

And waiting for it all to end.

It seemed General Clinton, sitting with his British troops in New York City, was in no hurry to press the matter. Yet we heard of battles in North and South Carolina. And Savannah, Georgia, lost in '78, was still in British hands. George could not leave to pursue such battles. George could not leave at all, for six of his eleven generals were unavailable, being ill or having returned to their homes on furlough.

When was my husband's furlough? When did he have time to be sick? To be well? When did he have time to spend the day in recreation or relaxation or (dare I say it?) idleness?

Although he could not go home, George and I spoke of Mount Vernon often, and I know his letters to Lund were replete with suggestions for horses, lambs, crops, and repairs. Our hearts were always there. . . . Although George had begun his time away at war by supplying Lund with weekly letters full of instructions, as the war progressed, his time to write the letters, and the ability to get the letters delivered, lessened. Lund was being forced to fend for himself. Last we heard, due to the fact the largest buyer of our grain crops—England—was obviously not available for our commerce, and our currency was now worth one fortieth its previous worth, Lund had let many fields lie fallow. He produced only what was needed to sustain Mount Vernon itself. George and I grieved we were forced to neglect our private concerns which were declining every day and would possibly end in capital losses, if not absolute ruin, before we were at liberty to look after them.

In actuality, I worried about George. This second stay at Morristown nearly broke him. He became morose and despondent, and in the middle of the night, in each other's arms, he confided his greatest fears. "The entire nation seems to rest upon my shoulders, Martha. It is as though we wait only for the end."

"I know, my dear. But things have looked glum before."

I felt him shake his head. "Our prospects are infinitely worse than they have been at any period of the war. Unless some expedient can be instantly adopted, a dissolution of the army for want of subsistence is unavoidable. And with the army, so goes the hopes of a nation."

I had no words to comfort him. No one did. He was indeed alone against the world, and all I could do was hold him close and let him know I was there. I would always be there.

As would the Almighty. We prayed with great fervency that winter. I sometimes imagined the prayers of the men and women at Morristown, rising from their huddled sources through the frigid gray air toward heaven like tendrils of smoke drifting upon the wind. My largest prayer was that these tendrils reached the ears of our God, and that He would be merciful and release us from our suffering.

And yet, forcing ourselves to look toward something positive beyond ourselves, our soldiers were gaining new respect. I heard a quote from a Hessian soldier who had fought against us: "I now see what 'enthusiasm'—what these ragged fellows call 'liberty'—can do. Out of this rabble rises a people who defy kings."

Defy logic. Defy common sense.

But we would not give up. The bridges of our country were burned. There was only one way—forward.

To victory?

We could not allow any other result.

I was awakened by the sounds of the alarm bell and the shouts of men. In a single motion George threw off the covers and pulled on his breeches and boots.

Sounds of men's footfalls upon the stairs broke through the night.

Not again.

George was just putting on his coat when the men rushed into our bedroom.

"Pardon us, General. Mrs. Washington."

Their apology was not needed. I snuggled into the bed and pulled the covers high in modesty *and* against the cold, which would—

Two soldiers whipped open the windows in our bedroom and aimed their muskets out into the dark, protecting us from the enemy.

I heard commotion in the other rooms as all windows were covered by these elite Life Guards, whose entire order was to protect headquarters. Each of the men, handpicked for the duty, stood over six feet in height.

These guards were necessary because the Ford house was situated a few miles from the main camp, with British outposts separating us. Mrs. Ford and I often agreed we did not mind the late night intrusions for safety's sake.

"There! By the tree!"

Shots rang out. I made myself as small as possible and comforted myself with the thought all this *would* be over.

Someday.

Although the capriciousness of weather caused me fits, and though I was discouraged at the impossibility of predicting its nature, I took solace in knowing God provided four seasons, and we could depend on them to eventually pass one to the next in line. Winter was always followed by spring. Eventually. Finally.

After suffering through twenty-six storms, many of them true blizzards, spring arrived, as it always did—praise God! The temperatures rose, the rivers thawed, and fish could be caught and served. Plants began to grow with the promise of berries, fruit, and other produce.

Yet with the thaw came the mud. Oozing mud that made one remember with fickle affection the pure facade of the snow.

But enough of that, for nothing could muddy the joy we received on the tenth of May, 1780. For upon that day, our dear boy, the Marquis de Lafayette, once again returned to us from France. He had heralded his coming with a letter, promising good news.

He did not disappoint.

The entire camp anticipated his arrival, for he had spent the past months in his homeland, lobbying for expedient support—for though France had agreed to help us, no help had come. The jubilant tone of his letter suggested he had been successful. How successful, we would soon see.

We had to laugh at the way in which he descended upon our house and headquarters. Dressed in fine regalia, as was his style, he was accompanied by a band of cheering officers and soldiers.

George and I met him on the front stoop. Young Hamilton, exuberant for his personal gain at the return of his friend, as well as for the national benefits, ran forward first. "He is back! Do you see? He has returned!"

"I do see, Alexander," I said. "And your joy is ours." I looked over to George and saw his eyes were transfixed upon the coming crowd. There were tears in his eyes as he spotted our dear marquis, waving his hat at us, his face aglow with shared anticipation. This truly was the return of a son.

Lafayette's band stopped in front of the house and he dismounted with a singular ease. He strode up the walk, his eyes upon only one man.

The man, first in the hearts of so many.

My George.

They embraced and, with lips to each other's ears, exchanged private greetings. Then it was my turn. He took my hands in his, kissed them with aplomb, then kissed first one cheek, then the other. "Madame, my heart cannot tell you its joy."

"There is no need, my boy. For its joy is ours."

We retreated inside, and after many exuberant greetings by the officers and aides, were finally allowed time alone in George's office.

In this place, where privacy was as dear as any provision, I shut the door, allowing us small time to ourselves.

"Well then," I said to our marquis. "Before we hear news of country, I must hear about your family. Is your new son doing well? Your wife? What a glorious Christmas present he must have been to you."

"I am most pleased to report that George Washington Lafayette is *magnifique* and basks in the knowledge he is your godson."

I laughed. "My greatest happiness is derived from the bevy of godsons named George Washington and goddaughters named for me. Did you know Patrick Henry and our own general Greene have such children?"

He joined in my laughter. "After the war, the Washington namesakes must come together and have a grand celebration."

"We are so very honoured," George said. "And your wife?"

A mischievous grin took hold of his face. "She is well, and is still very much infatuated with you, my general. That is why I keep her in France, for if the two of you were ever to meet . . ." He looked at me. "You and I would be forced to find other consorts."

"That is why I keep him here, my boy. If George were ever to visit your family in France—"

"I have invited him often, but he refuses."

George nodded. "I am too old for such travels, and my ignorance of your language . . . I would not wish to rely on the knowledge of others, and I am too old to learn."

"Too old? Nonsense," Lafayette said. "You are but . . . forty-five?"

"Eight," George said. "Forty-eight. And often seventy in feeling."

Lafayette's expression turned pensive, yet still held a degree of gaiety. "Perhaps the other news—of country—will make you feel yourself again?"

George's eyes lit up. "Please."

Lafayette sat forward in his chair, his hands clasped upon the edge of the table George used as a desk. "I am most happy to inform you that after meeting with the king at Versailles, he has agreed to send . . ." With a smile he looked at me, then back at George and said, "Six thousand French troops, supplies enough for fifteen thousand American troops, *and* a fleet of French battleships to put those British Regulars to the test as they dare harass American ports."

George sat back in his chair, his mouth agape. "Oh, my dear boy . . ."

Lafayette sat erect and pointed a finger upwards. "Together we shall, by God, conquer these troops who dare to oppress your freedom."

As handshakes and embraces were exchanged, I noticed the marquis was correct. George did indeed look his old self again.

Hope will do that.

<hr />

In June I returned to Mount Vernon—what was left of it. Oh, we had the land, the constant, blessed land, but the potential it had once shown was forced into dormancy while the war raged on. It appeared exhausted.

As was I.

This time, upon returning from winter camp, I did not spring back to life as quickly. A weariness pressed upon me, as though I wore a heavy blanket upon a hot day.

And it was hot. The heat was so invasive the sky could no longer hold its blue but gave it up to a washed-out version of itself.

Which mirrored my own condition.

Jacky and Eleanor came to stay awhile, as Eleanor was once again in the midst of a difficult pregnancy. Each morning Jacky tried to cheer me by reminding me I had received word Marie Antoinette— the empress of all France—was sending me a "valuable present" as a token of affection for my contribution to the Cause. "Do you think it will come today, Mamma?"

I attempted to play along and oft said, "Surely today."

Little Betsy and Patty played guessing games as to what it was.

I was most happy for what it stood for—our alliance with France. That *did* bring me joy. As did the news that helping our Cause had become a point of patriotism *and* fashion in France. Benjamin Franklin, doing his best in French circles, was apparently quite the celebrity, and his fur cap—considered the quintessence of wild America—was oft copied by French men of fashion.

When news came that the ship which carried my gift from the empress had been sunk by the British off the New York harbour, Jacky grieved more than I.

Although I *would* have liked to have known what it was. . . .

One morning, before dawn, began a day that added to my melancholy.

I was awakened by a scream.

I sat erect and listened again.

"Aaahhhhhh!"

"Eleanor!"

I grabbed my dressing gown, descended our private stairway, and ran up the front stairs and into the blue bedroom they used when in residence, a room that shared a wall with mine. I was greeted by my son, his face pulled with fear.

And fresh screams.

I hurried to the bedside and took Eleanor's hand, holding it to my breast. "I am here, dear girl."

She opened her eyes but a slit, and in them I saw a fear that was far keener than the fear I had seen in my son's countenance. As a mother she knew, she *knew.* . . .

I turned to Jacky. "Has Dr. Rumney been sent for?"

"Hours ago."

"This has been going on for hours? Why did you not call me?" *Why did I not hear sooner?*

"You have been so tired. Eleanor did not want to disturb you until—"

I looked at my dear daughter-in-law. "You did not disturb. I am here. For you. Always." I nodded to a maid who had poked her head in. "Fresh water in a basin, please."

Eleanor's neck stretched taut and she bent her legs as another pain took her prisoner. "Argghhghhh!"

God, please get Dr. Rumney here in time!

———✦———

Twin girls.
Twin girls born.
And died.
Why, Lord? Why?

In my grief and weariness I had to keep busy or retreat to a place within myself where nothing good could live. I had to think of those who suffered even more than I.

And so my thoughts returned to the soldiers, always to the soldiers whose sacrifice made all other miseries dim. Although it was but autumn, the months would fly by, and once again I would travel north to George, to join him and the troops in winter camp.

Unless of course, victory was ours before that time.

I planned for the journey.

As with my other journeys, I would not go empty-handed. And this time, knowing from hard experience clothing was much needed, I decided to plan ahead for the need. Although the sewing circles of our winter camps were useful, they were limited. I had to get other women, in other colonies, involved.

I contacted female acquaintances in Philadelphia and Virginia and initiated a relief fund for the poorest soldiers, to help their families as they did duty for God and country. Esther Reed, the wife of the governor of Pennsylvania, was of great help. She and other ladies went door to door asking for money. Some loyalists became so annoyed by their insistence they gave money just to be rid of them. Esther and the others were very aggressive and nailed signs all over the city, advertising the drive. I saw one, which said: "Our ambition is kindled by the fame of those heroines of antiquity, who have rendered their sex illustrious, and have proved to the universe that if opinion and manners did not forbid us to march to glory by the same paths as the men, we should at least equal, and sometimes surpass them in our love for the public good."

I admired such tenacity *and* the fact the women went further than collecting money, by purchasing linen and making the shirts themselves. I gave six thousand pounds toward the effort, and our own Lafayette made a contribution in his wife's name. Some other

Frenchwomen gave offerings, and many women, compelled by such generosity, sold their jewelry in order to give. A total of ninety thousand pounds was earned. Esther insisted on sending it to me instead of George or any other male in charge. It was not that they did not trust them, but . . . they wanted to make certain the money was used for clothing. "And we want you to be our heroine, dear Martha. You take the glory for all of us."

I did not wish for the glory, but was humbled by their trust and effort.

On this morning, I sat in the back parlour, needle in hand. I had my best sewers there—both Negros and other servants. If only I could get Eleanor to join us. She was so despondent over the loss of her babies she rarely walked a step farther than she needed, or lifted a hand but to place it upon her heart or cover a quiver of her lip. The three girls always approached with wariness, their eyes searching their mother's countenance for any indication she was open to their presence.

I was just tying off the thread after embroidering my name in a finished shirt—a tradition started during the drive so the soldier wearing it would know we were with him in spirit. When I looked up I found Eleanor in the doorway of the parlour. "Come in, dearest. Come join us. Your stitches have always been so capable. We can use the help. Too soon it will be November and I will be leaving for the North."

She smiled, which was such a shocking gesture I was not certain she had heard a thing I had said. "Eleanor? What is it?"

She put a hand upon her abdomen, and with a gasp, I knew what she was going to say. I found my head shaking no, even as she formed the words I was nervous to hear.

"I am with child again."

Every woman in the room, Negro, servant, and white, looked to one another with a trepidation tinged with joy, wariness, and fear.

Eleanor noticed. "Did you not hear me? I said I am with child—"

"Again," I said. I let the word hang as a pure fact, neither good nor bad. I forced a smile and rose to embrace her. While I had her frail frame in my arms, I mentally chided my son. I knew a woman's duty to her husband. I knew that duty was not a chore when a couple loved one another as Jacky and Eleanor loved, but Eleanor had scarcely recovered from the birth of her twins. . . . Pregnancy never came easily for her, much less when she was in such a weakened state. I too had given birth to four children in quick succession—within five years.

"I am so happy," she said with her chin against my shoulder. "So is Jack. He does long for a son."

I cringed. So that was it. Eleanor had given birth to six daughters, three who lived. Jacky's intolerance with her recovery was due to this eternal quest for an heir?

I let Eleanor go and looked into her eyes. "I do wish Jacky would pay better attention to the children he has before taking measures to father another."

She stepped away from my gaze and sat in a chair, retrieving the stitching I had set aside. Her finger traced my autograph upon the neck facing. "He is a good father."

"He is too lenient." I hesitated. I had heard accounts of Jacky's fatherhood that alarmed me, and had spoken with him about them, as best I could. They were beyond Eleanor's knowing—for her own good, considering her continually precarious health—and yet . . .

"If you are speaking of any tall tales told by our Betsy, then I am disappointed. She is but a child."

"A child who is being used as a party attraction."

The way Eleanor drew back her head, the way she blinked, told me she was not in full knowledge of what went on while she was safely upstairs at Abingdon, abed with illness.

I looked to the other women in the room. Their eyes revealed curiosity. But this was family business. "Go now," I told them. "Thank you for your assistance. If you wish, you may take your sewing with you."

They left, albeit reluctantly. I could hold no certainty they would not position themselves nearby in order to hear. . . .

That could not be helped. In truth, knowing how servants talked, I would have been surprised if they did not know the story of young Betsy from Jacky's servants who traveled back and forth with the family to Abingdon.

"Please sit, my dear," I told Eleanor.

She did so, but I could tell by her stance her defenses were raised. "If you are going to tell me Betsy sings for Jack's friends when they visit, I know that. I have heard that."

"Did you know he stands her on the dining table to sing?"

Her brow furrowed.

"Have you listened to the words of the songs he and Dr. Rumney have taught her?"

"No . . . her voice, though good, is light. I only hear her sing, not what she sings."

I looked to the doorway. It appeared we were alone. "They have taught her bawdy songs, Eleanor."

She looked to her lap. "They are not *so* bawdy."

I was appalled. "So you do know?"

Being caught, she reddened. "Jack assures me no harm can come from words she does not understand." She raised her chin, strengthening her defense. "He said he has no boy and Betsy must make fun for him until he has."

I sucked in a breath.

She stopped any words I had to say with a hand. "Betsy much likes the attention. She struts up and back upon the table and sings her voice fully. E'en the servants clap, and all the men laugh and give her high praise."

I closed my eyes at the thought of it. "She is too much in her father's care. He does her no favours by subjecting her to—"

"I cannot help that I have been ill. I too would like to be more available to my daughters, and do my best to direct them as a mother should. But when I am not well . . ."

It was not her fault. She was ill because of my son's attentions. Her wishes as to her daughters' upbringing were pushed aside, overrun by Jacky's will and pursuit of pleasure. Since I had not been able to curtail these traits in my son when he had been under my own roof, how could I expect her to do more?

"I try, Mamma. I do try. But Jack is so headstrong and . . ."

I patted her hand, making amends. Yet the guilt of what she endured—what my granddaughters endured—lay heavily upon my shoulders, for Jacky had become the man he had become because of the boy I had let him be.

If I had it to do over again . . .

— FIFTEEN —

I left for New Windsor, New York, for winter camp, reluctant to leave my family, who might—might—have benefited from my presence. And yet there was another reason I left Mount Vernon with reluctance.

Things were not going well for George or the army. The British had made inroads in the South and held Charleston and were threatening North Carolina. George had not garnered any great victories in the North. And there had been a blow set upon him that I knew had the capacity to break him: one of his generals, his friend, had betrayed him, had betrayed the country. General Benedict Arnold had betrayed us by planning to surrender West Point to the British. His plan was foiled, and Arnold escaped to a British warship, but George took it personally. How could a hero of so many battles, a man whom George considered one of his best and most accomplished generals, change sides and plan a campaign that would lead to the loss of American lives?

How could he give up?

Actually . . . considering the situation, the utter frustration of each year set upon year, problem set upon problem, with no end in sight . . .

No. I could not condone such an act. Ever. To do so would be to negate all the sacrifice and suffering that had thus transpired.

My job, as I entered winter camp, was to do my best to buoy the spirits of the men, and of my man.

We women were doing our part. Sarah Bache, the daughter of Benjamin Franklin, and a chairwoman of the Philadelphia sewing effort, sent my husband 2,500 shirts, and a circle of women in New Jersey sent 380 pairs of newly knitted stockings. With humility, George accepted these offerings.

With desperation.

Winter was as bad as ever, supplies worse, and Continental money now worthless. We had neither a coin in our treasury nor credit to obtain one. There were reports of many skirmishes in the South and the fighting of one ethnic group against another. In addition, citizens who were tired of having their property taken by soldiers fought to keep it or hid it away. Loyalists did not help matters when they banded together to aid the British. And mutinies . . . soldiers in the North, having had enough of the bad conditions, revolted against their own. It was as though fighting was high on men's minds and they were determined to do it, one way or another.

Regarding our fighting against the British—George had appointed Nathanael Greene to be in charge of our southern forces. He had some success with cat-and-mouse tactics. We annoyed them with small battles, then withdrew. They followed us deeper into the wilderness, and we annoyed them some more. This pulled the British away from their supplies upon the coast and exhausted them, but did little to offer the benefits of true victory.

Deserters from both sides were plentiful, and there had even been an attempt upon my husband's life.

And the French, who had given us such hope with their offers of help? Their warships sat in the harbour mute. We were told it would take a year before they would be ready to give true aid.

The truth was, neither side could claim it was winning. Both were merely surviving. Barely. We had heard rumours that back in England, Parliament was growing weary of the fight. We prayed they would say "Enough!" and call their soldiers home. That is all we wanted. Retreat. Just leave us alone to build this new country of ours that had barely had a chance to begin.

Many nights, while lying in each other's arms, George shared his despondency with me, the despondency he dared not share in public. On one particular night he shared something more.

The wind howled, and the moon cast a bare lightness. We huddled together in the darkness and I settled against his shoulder, waiting to hear what had been lain upon his heart during the course of the day.

"I should not be leading them," he finally said.

He had expressed such doubts before. "Of course you should. You are a brilliant leader, a fine general, a—"

I felt his head shake no against my hair. "Remember when we were courting? When I had been deemed a hero of the war against the French?"

"You were a hero."

He shook his head again. "I was not. Remember I mentioned a time that brought me shame?"

My thoughts slid back over twenty years. To the few—but detailed—conversations we had before our marriage. At the time George had intimated there was some moment in his time as a Continental colonel that brought him shame. I had not thought of it since.

Obviously, he had.

"I seem to remember something."

He hesitated, and I listened to his breathing, which grew heavy as the memories returned. "It was November 12, 1758. Remember after our engagement how I reenlisted for one last try at Fort Du Quesne? I wished to redeem myself from my humiliation at Fort Necessity?

Although I had left the Continental Army behind me, I still wished to be seen as capable as any British officer."

"Thank God they never commissioned you," I said. "How different things would have been if you had felt a loyalty to them instead of—"

His silence indicated it was not the time for such hindsight, however true.

"I apologize. Please continue."

"Bad weather was upon us and Brigadier General John Forbes, my superior, indicated we should halt the campaign against the French for the winter. We were about to do so when we heard a French raiding party was close by. He had not thought much about the ability of my men until shortly before this time, and I was eager to convince him of our worth. So when he ordered me to take one thousand Virginians and take care of them, I was quick to go, though in truth, his orders were given in a snide way, as if the entire thing were an annoyance and he did not want to be bothered with it by sending his own men."

"He does not sound like a good officer."

"He was like most British officers—confident in their own troops and wary of ours. He may have been arrogant, but I was cocky. Of the two, on that particular day, mine was the worst trait."

I waited for him to continue.

"Realizing this was my chance to prove our troops had worth, I divided the men into two groups, waited until the French raiding party was resting, and attacked. We were victorious and took many prisoners. But then, during our celebration of victory, in the twilight, more men came out of the forest, muskets raised, surprising us. And so we fired. And fired. And . . ."

I heard him swallow with slow difficulty.

"In horror I realized we were firing upon our own men. We were killing our own! I rode between them, yelling for them to stop. Never was I in more imminent danger by being between two fires, knocking up with my sword the presented pieces."

"Oh, George."

He nodded. "Fourteen of my men were killed and twenty-six were wounded. All because I did not have control over my command as I should have."

I did not know what to say. "I am so sorry."

"As I have been, all these years."

"But you are a better soldier now, a better commander."

"Am I?"

His doubt made me sit up and look down upon him. "You are commander in chief of the entire American army."

"I have the position, but I am hardly successful. Do you realize I have only fought nine battles, and of those, have only won three?"

I had not realized that. I always thought of my George as victorious.

"Other American generals are more capable in battle than I. The men believe in me, believe I can lead them to victory. But there is no evidence of that. They believe in the dream of a man, not in my true history. They should not have put me in charge."

"Nonsense!" I pointed out the window toward the army camp beyond. "Do you think those men out there are keeping score? They look to you for more than wins and losses; they look to you for inspiration."

He raised his forearm over his eyes and sighed. "They may be led, but they will never be driven."

"Exactly. You are their lead—"

"This whole thing has become more a test of political endurance than a war."

"Indeed it has. And who better to remain faithful to the Cause, to get the men to remain faithful during appalling conditions, than a man like you."

"A man who has been humiliated in one battle and shamed in another."

"A man who is but a man. A man who loves his soldiers and the

Cause they fight for with his whole heart. A man who keeps this
Cause alive. A man who refuses to give up."

"Perhaps I should give up."

I shoved his arm away, needing to see his eyes in the pale moonlight. "Do not ever say that. Ever!"

His eyes were so troubled, so burdened.

"You are the man this country needs, at this time, in this place.
God placed you here. Many believe that, including you and me. Do
you now question the Almighty's plan?"

He smiled: a wistful smile, an indulgent smile, but still a smile.
"I will try to do better, dear lady."

I patted his shoulder and gave him a kiss. "You do that," I said.
Then I laid my head down once again. George pulled up the covers
and tucked me in where I belonged.

⚬⚬⚬

'Twas a day like many others in New Windsor. The winter was
surrendering to spring. I had just come back from visiting sick soldiers,
and had set up our sewing circle with some of the wives in a back
room. George and his men were in meetings. I heard a courier come,
but took little note of it. George received much correspondence. I had
learned to be patient. If there was a letter from home, a soldier had
been instructed to bring it forthwith.

Periodically, I glanced toward the door of the room, hoping for
some news of Jacky's family. Eleanor was due to deliver any day. As
soon as the muddy roads were passable, I would go home to be with
them.

I did not expect to see George at the doorway.

Upon seeing him, the ladies fluttered. Although all had oft danced
with him and supped with him, and though their husbands were like
family, they still deferred to his presence.

I stood, suddenly afraid. He did not interrupt his day for no strong reason, and during war, such reasons were more likely bad than good. And with Eleanor in such a tenuous state . . . "What it is?"

With a short bow to the other ladies present, he said, "If you please?"

His desire for privacy added to my nerves. We stepped into a back hall.

"What is it, George?"

He pulled a letter from his coat. "A letter from Lund."

I sucked in a breath. "Is Eleanor—?"

"Eleanor is fine and awaiting her confinement. But Mount Vernon . . . The British have come up the Potomac with the intent of burning the plantations."

My heart stopped. My head shook no, no, no, no . . .

He put a hand upon my arm. "No, dear. Let me ease that fear. Mount Vernon has been spared."

I flung my arms about his waist. "Praise God!"

He gently pulled my arms away. " 'Tis how it was spared that causes me great pain."

I took a step back. Thoughts of Jacky's family, dealing with such fear, made my heart feel weak.

George shook the letter between us. "When the British vessel docked at our home, many of the Negros fled—ours and those belonging to Lund. In an attempt to save Mount Vernon, Lund boarded the vessel, brought the officers refreshment, and told them he would provision the ship if they would return our Negros and leave Mount Vernon unscathed."

"And?"

"They agreed."

I allowed myself to let out a breath, but even before its full expulsion, I took another. "But our neighbors . . . many have had their homes burned because they would not capitulate to the enemy. For Lund to save our home by giving aid . . ."

"The damage he has accomplished—"

"The miracle he has procured on our behalf, George."

He leaned against the wall and rubbed the space between his brow. "It would have been a less painful circumstance to me to have heard that in consequence of his noncompliance with their request, they had burned our house and laid the plantation in ruins. He ought to have considered himself as my representative, and should have reflected on the bad example of communicating with the enemy, and making a voluntary offer of refreshments to them with a view to prevent a conflagration . . ."

"He did what he thought best. We left him to manage—and protect—our family and property. He has done so in the best way he could ascertain."

"But not this way. Never this way."

A soldier peered down the hall at us, then retreated out of sight. George was needed.

Which was the problem.

I stepped closer to my husband, my voice for our ears alone. "Although I grieve the extent of action in which Lund has chosen, I applaud the result. The thought of returning to Mount Vernon after this war sustains me, sustains you, and allows you to do the enormity of work which has been thrust upon your shoulders. And as for myself—speaking in pure selfishness—I am relieved to know that once it is time for me to leave this place, I still have a home to return to."

George stood erect and nodded once.

I pressed my hands upon his arm, turning him toward his office. "Now, leave me. Leave *this*, knowing that Providence has chosen it, and we, as in all things, have no right to complain or question why."

He reached back and placed a hand upon mine. "I am so glad you are here, dearest."

I kissed his hand, and with a gentle nudge, sent him back to work toward saving our country.

I opened the box and gasped. "Lemons! Limes and oranges. A pineapple and sweets!" I looked up at George from my sickbed. "Such delicacies."

He dug through the boxes, picking up a bottle of what looked to be a medicine, and some tea. His mouth was shaped into a grimace.

I held a lemon to my nose and inhaled with great pleasure.

George's look did not change.

"Why the sour look, George? We have not seen such luscious items for years."

He put an orange to his nose and took in the sweet scent. But then he tossed it back in the box. "We cannot keep it."

I cradled the lemon against my chest. "It was not sent to *us*, but to *me*. I think it is very kind of Mrs. Mortier to send these items to cheer me and make me well. I have been abed for nearly a month with this jaundice, George. The fruits will help."

"You are recovering well enough on your own."

No thanks to anyone but the Almighty. "I will share. I promise."

"Mrs. Mortier is the wife of the British paymaster. She is the enemy."

"She is the widow of the paymaster. She has suffered in this war. And she does not send this gift as the enemy, but as a woman offering aid to another woman. She sent the package and letter under a flag of truce. Surely we can honour that."

"You cannot keep any of it, Martha. You cannot. If word got out . . ."

It could do damage to the Cause.

For one brief moment I wished to pitch the Cause and enjoy my lemons.

But I could not. Duty ruled me now, as it always had, as it always would.

With one last whiff of the lemon, I handed it back. "Write her a kind note, will you, George? You can word it to cause no offense, yet keep our honour precious."

He studied me a moment, wondering if I was offering sarcasm. I lay back upon my pillow and let him read between the lines. The aroma of the fruit lingered as he had the boxes taken away. Lingered but alas did not remain.

As I suffered, so did George, but for another reason.

He stood before the mirror one morning, his mouth open, his large hands trying to arrange the implements of torture that lived in his mouth.

His teeth had always been his detriment and were getting worse. Soon after we were married I had offered him the use of my home-made tooth powder, showing him how beautiful it made my own teeth. And he had used it but to no great result. For whatever reason, his teeth continued to decay. Over the years he had ordered many of them removed and replaced with false ones of bone or ivory. They were set into the sockets of the original teeth, and held in place with wires that gave him great pain.

With a sigh he stood erect. "These blasted things. I cannot get the wires to stay in place. They cut at my mouth."

"I thought you sent a letter to a dentist in Philadelphia, requesting some pinchers to help bend them."

"They have not arrived as yet." He turned to me. "Your fingers are smaller . . . will you try?"

Of course. I got out of bed and did my best to bend the wires so they would cause the least harm. But seeing his mismatched mouth, and seeing the gray of his remaining teeth . . . it seemed inevitable they too would have to be pulled.

No wonder my husband did not smile often. I grieved he should have to suffer so, on a continual basis. Did the war not cause him pain enough?

"There," I said. "Is that better?"

He moved his mouth about. "It still . . . but yes. Better. Thank you, my dear."

If I could have given him my own teeth, I would have.

Truly.

I returned home from New York in late June, not completely recovered from my illness, but eager to be home. I spent my fiftieth birthday on June twenty-first on the dusty road. A milestone.

I did not feel fifty—most of the time. But most importantly, I did not look it. Although vanity was not a virtue, I admitted to owning such a vice—at least to some degree. It brought me great joy when people mis-guessed my age. Although no one would mistake me for a woman in her thirties, I was often guessed at five years younger. As the years progressed this became more important to me. Odd how as a young woman one desires to be thought older, and soon after, one wishes for the appearance of youth to linger as long as possible. Men have no compunction regarding age and are allowed to do so with grace, while we women are forced to fight the process. It is not fair. Not fair at all.

But it was what it was. And I was what I was. Fifty and going home to meet my newest grandchild, born April 20, 1781. After giving birth to six girls, Eleanor gave birth to a son: George Washington Parke Custis. I found Eleanor in a weakened state, and the boy also a bit sickly—probably because Eleanor could not nurse him well. The wet nurse she had used before, Mrs. Anderson, had come to help. And if a babe could be made well by his grandmother's hugs and kisses, then I did my best.

By fall he was healthy enough to be nicknamed Mr. Tub, though we also called him Wash or Washy. He was the apple of his sisters' eyes and they gave him much attention. Watching them fawn over him, I was reminded of the closeness Jacky had experienced with his little sister, Patsy.

Dear Patsy. I often walked down the hill to the family crypt and sat with her. Although I would have liked her here—she would have made a doting auntie—I was glad she had not been here to suffer through the war. Would she have been strong enough to endure it? Or would it have led her to an early death in its own way? Perhaps it was better for her to have gone so quickly, at a family meal, during happier days.

I did not let my thoughts linger too long in such what-if's. For I was home, and wallowed in that joy.

Yet . . . on the night of September 9, I had just checked the doors and was headed up to bed when I heard horses approaching.

My first thought was: *the British?*

I hurried up the front stairs and called to my son. "Jacky!"

He appeared at the top of the stairs, having stoked the bedroom fires against the chill of the night.

I did not need to say anything, for the sound of the horses had grown louder. He hurried down the stairs, took up a musket, and moved into the parlour to look out the window.

"Papa?" Little Betsy called from the stairs.

"Shh, child," I said. "Get back in the room with your mother. And shut the door."

I retreated to the parlour and picked up the fireplace poker, wishing once again I had learned to shoot a gun. I would not let them take us without a fight. I would not.

I moved toward the window next to Jacky. "How many?" I asked.

Suddenly, he started to laugh—which I thought was an odd reaction to danger. But then, I too found my emotions change from fear to glee.

I ran to the door and flung myself outside as my husband leapt from his horse.

"You are here? You are here!"

He enveloped me with his embrace and swung me around. "Hello, my dearest. I have missed you."

He set me down and I took a step back. "Why? How? Is it over?"

He looked to the other horsemen—that I had not even noticed in my joy at seeing him. "Soon," he said. "Hopefully soon."

I recognized Billy Lee, George's faithful valet, and David Humphreys, one of his aides, as well as a half dozen men I did not know.

David dismounted and tipped his hat. "A pleasure to see you again, Mrs. Washington." His eyes scanned the exterior of the house. "And in far better surroundings, that is for certain."

"I will give you a fair tour tomorrow, David," I said.

"It appears I will need a tour myself." George's eyes grazed over the changes he had ordered but had never seen.

At that moment Jacky came through the door with Eleanor and the girls. "Poppa!" Jacky said, falling into his father's arms.

"My boy, my dear boy." George released him in order to see the rest. He kissed Eleanor on the cheek, and then looked upon the grandchildren he had never seen. "It appears you have been busy indeed."

"Are you Grandpapa?" Betsy asked.

George knelt down to greet them. "I am. And you must be Betsy."

She nodded. "This is Patty. And this is Nelly."

"Such lovely girls you are."

He stood and saw Mrs. Anderson coming out with his namesake, five-month-old Wash.

Jacky did the honours. "And this," he said, taking the baby in his arms, "is George Washington Parke Custis."

I was thrilled when little Wash smiled at George, who held out a finger that Wash was quick to take.

"Glad to meet you, little man."

My eyes filled with tears at the homecoming. But at the whinny-ing of a horse, I realized our guests were waiting.

"Come in everyone, come in. Welcome. Welcome home."

Over the next few days our guests, which included French gen-eral Chastellux and Viscount Donatien Marie Rochambeau, head of French forces in America, took over the dining room. The large two-story room (which George deemed perfect) had been constructed in his long absence. I was pleased to put it to such good use, finding pleasure in being hostess to these patriots, feeding them, coddling them, and making them a home in lieu of the homes they had left behind years before.

As for our own years that had passed . . . George had not been to Mount Vernon since May 4, 1775, when he had left with a group of his contingents to attend the Second Continental Congress in Philadelphia. He had left here as a simple representative, and over six years later had returned as the commander in chief of the American forces.

Forces on the verge of victory?

That very outcome was planned upon our dining room table.

Although I did not sit with the men as they strategized, I was allowed to hear plenty during meals, and from George in our time alone. It seemed the British general Cornwallis had grown weary of Nathanael Greene's cat-and-mouse war in the South and had taken over Williamsburg, but had since moved his army of six thousand to nearby Yorktown, where he had set up a camp and fortifications.

Finding out this news, George and his northern generals had come up with a plan that—if successful—would surely be considered brilliant. The plan started when George pretended to be getting ready to attack New York City, where the northern British troops were centralized. As hoped, the British had moved their reinforcements by land and sea north to stave off the attack. Meanwhile, George sent one hundred cannon, and the combined French and American troops—eighteen thousand strong, the largest yet—south to surround Yorktown. And upon the sea, we would receive the aid of Admiral Comte Francois de Grasse, who was sailing from the West Indies to help. The plan was to have him block the York River where it entered Chesapeake Bay, providing Cornwallis and company no escape.

I brought the men a fresh batch of scones and winked at Jacky, who sat under the windows, taking it all in.

General Rochambeau was speaking. "Time is *essentiel*," he said in heavily accented English. "Admiral de Grasse is only ours until the fifteenth of October. He is concerned . . ." He turned to one of his aides. "*La saison des ouragans?*"

The aide translated. "Season of hurricanes."

George nodded. "He has promised us twenty-nine warships, three thousand troops, guns, and over a million pounds—in cash."

The aides made whooping noises.

George laughed. "Such an offer must be accepted, yes?"

I left the room with an empty plate and a heart made lighter by my husband's laughter—and grand plans for a great victory. *The* victory that might end the war?

It was my fervent prayer.

<hr />

"But Mamma, Poppa, I wish to go along."

Eleanor spoke first. "No, Jacky, I need you with me. We have four children. I am not well. You have not gone to war before. Why now?"

"Because it is nearly ended." He turned to George. "Is that not true, Poppa? I hear you and the others talk about this upcoming battle as if it will bring about the surrender of the British. I wish to see. I wish to be a part of that."

I was glad when George closed the door of the family dining room. I too did not want the other soldiers to hear Jacky's plea. "Yes, we hope for surrender," he said. "It is not guaranteed by any means. We are simply in a good position and will pray Providence smiles upon us. But it is still war, Jacky. And you . . ." He glanced at me. "You are not a soldier."

"I know how to shoot. You taught me how to shoot."

"Shooting game and shooting a man—who is shooting at you—are very different."

Jacky seemed to accept this because he said, "Then give me some other job to do. Can I not be one of your aides? I just wish to be *there*, helping the Cause."

It was my turn to speak. "It is dangerous *there*."

Jacky pounded a fist upon the table, making the teacups titter. "It has been dangerous here!"

I could not argue with him.

Jacky pushed his chair from the table, nearly toppling it. "I will go! You will not prevent me from being a part of this victory. I refuse to have the war end and not be able to say I helped the Cause of freedom."

"But Jacky . . ." Eleanor said.

He glared at her, at all of us. "I am going."

He yanked open the door, leaving us to the jostling of his wake.

"George?"

He fingered the handle of a cup, then pushed it away. "I admire his desire. I understand it."

"I do too," I said, "but that does not mean it is prudent for him to leave his family to help at this late date."

"He wishes to help. That is admirable."

"I do not wish him to go," Eleanor said.

George put a hand upon hers. "I believe he is going whether any of us wish him to or not."

He was right. We all knew Jacky. Jacky did what Jacky wished to do.

"So," I said. "Can you give him a duty that will keep him safe?"

George pondered the air above our heads. "I *could* make him an aide. Give him messages to deliver. Keep him busy far away from the fighting."

I sighed with relief. "As long as he is safe."

His look was stern. "There is no complete safety, Martha. You know that."

I nodded, understanding. I had traveled during wartime. I had camped near the soldiers, I had held their hands and listened to their anguish.

Suddenly, Jacky popped his head in the door. "Mother, could you put together some sort of uniform for me? I do not fit in, dressed as a civilian."

I looked to George, who shrugged, then back at my impetuous son. "I suppose I could find something."

Jacky practically glowed with excitement.

Oh dear.

⸎

I only had the pleasure of my husband's presence for three days. On September 12, he and the others—including Jacky, dressed in a navy coat and tan breeches, with the sash of an aide-de-camp across his chest—said their good-byes. The men were in high spirits. George had even sent a message to Lafayette, who was already in Yorktown, saying, "I hope you will keep Lord Cornwallis safe . . . until we arrive."

I did not care about the safety of Cornwallis. Only of my own men.

Eleanor cried, but I would not allow my own tears to be shown in public. I kissed my son and my husband, said adieu to the other soldiers, French and American alike, and sent them on their way.

"God be with you!" I called after them.

And keep you safe.

And bring an end to this war with a great victory.

⸺∞⸺

"Another letter! A letter!"

Betsy ran into the parlour, where her mother had been playing the pianoforte. All music stopped as she brought the letter to me.

During the month since the men had left for Yorktown, this had become a daily ritual. I praised my husband for realizing our need for fresh news, for supplying us with a constant supply of letters.

Our first letter had come from Jacky, sent along the journey. Apparently, wanting to show off his new soldier status, he had stopped to see relatives in New Kent. Although I am certain my mother and siblings were glad to see him, his need for approbation made me cringe, and I could only imagine George's reaction.

Foolish, foolish boy.

His later letters revealed sights I am certain he wished he had never seen. Apparently the slaves that had left their masters to fight for the British had been ill used. They had been put to work digging the trenches at the Yorktown fortification, in horrible heat. When they were finished, the British decided they had no further use for them—as well as no provisions for them, many of whom had brought their families—and so set them free.

In the woods far from their homes.

With no way of providing for themselves, earning a living, or for some, even communicating.

There were also rumours the British had sometimes infected slaves with smallpox and sent them back into our lines in hopes our soldiers would contract the disease. Jacky wrote us a letter about all this, stating he had looked for Mount Vernon slaves, but had not found any of them. Instead he had seen scores of slaves dead in the woods, their bodies putrefying in the heat.

But beyond that horror was the news that militarily things were going well. On September 28, our combined forces of French and American soldiers lay siege to the British fort at Yorktown, with the French fleet under Comte de Grasse barricading the sea. We had them! It was merely a question of time before they would run out of provisions and give up. Each day we prayed Cornwallis would *not* receive help from the north, nor new ships from England. I wondered if others even knew of his predicament.

Again, we prayed not.

Jacky eventually sent exhilarated letters stating how he was assigned to deliver messages to our officers. He felt well used, and we breathed easier.

As far as our other military "sons" . . . as victory seemed imminent, George gave each the honour of leading a brigade. On October 8, our artillery broke through their inner fortification. Then, as George sat upon his white horse and watched, it transpired before him. He watched as Colonel Alexander Hamilton captured two British redoubts and Colonel John Laurens, a third. His heart was full of pride as he saw Major General Marquis de Lafayette lead a bayonet charge that was so fierce and full of ardour the British soldiers fled in terror.

There was heroism from many fronts. George wrote that the patriot governor of Virginia, Thomas Nelson, had a lovely home in Yorktown. General Knox, the head of our artillery, asked Governor Nelson where it was located within the city so we could avoid shelling it. The governor's reply? "As the finest house in town, it will surely have been assumed as the British headquarters. Fire away and destroy it, if you please."

I unfolded today's offering from the front. It was from George. I scanned it quickly, as I always did, wanting to save Eleanor and the children undue worry if things did not go well. But this time . . .

"Mamma, please. You are practically grinning. What is the news?"

"The letter is dated October 19 and reads, 'I have enclosed a copy of a dispatch I have just sent to the president of Congress. Revel with me, dearest Martha, as we celebrate this great victory.' "

"Victory?" Eleanor said.

I noticed a second sheet and read it aloud:

"Sir, I have the honour to inform Congress that a reduction of the British army under the command of Lord Cornwallis is most happily effected. The unremitting ardour which actuated every officer and soldier in the combined army in this occasion has principally led to this important event, at an earlier period than my most sanguine hope had induced me to expect."

"They won?" Eleanor asked. She hugged little Wash close.

"It appears so." I returned to George's letter and read for her and the children.

"I have just witnessed the surrender of eight thousand British troops. They filed through two lines: one of the smartly uniformed French soldiers, and one of our rather bedraggled American forces. The band played 'The World Turned Upside Down.' Very apropos.

"Some of the king's men were weeping. But our men did not gloat—though they had every right to do so. Before the parade, I rode up and down between the two lines and warned them to be gentlemen. I told them, 'History will huzzah for us.' To their credit, they abided by my wishes. The only cloud to the event was that Lord Cornwallis did not attend, claiming illness. He sent his second-in-command to hand over his sword. At first he attempted to give it to General Rochambeau, who refused to accept it, saying: 'We are subordinates to the Americans. General Washington will give you your orders.' But then, as he approached me—may all forgive me for this act of pride—I rejected the sword and had this British second-in-command surrender it to mine, General Benjamin Lincoln.

"It is a great victory, Martha. Whether it mean the end of the war is not known. But its significance is great. I hope to be home soon to celebrate with all those I love.

Yours always,
George"

I stood there, staring down at the letter. "It is over."

"Is it?" Eleanor asked. "Poppa said he is not certain."

"I am certain. I feel it." I took a seat beside her, held her hand, and together we gave thanks.

I stood in the kitchen and gave the servants instructions. "Scour the orchard for every apple you can. I wish to give George a plentitude of apple fritters and pies when he comes home. And peach tarts. And my Great Cake. And ham."

Addie laughed. "We have not had any ham since '79, mistress."

She was right. My desire for a grand celebration had overridden fact. "Do what you can."

"When do you expect the men?" she asked.

"I do not know for certain. But we must be read—"

Eustis burst through the door. "Mistress! Another courier has come."

He handed me a letter. It was dated the twentieth of October.

Dearest Martha and Eleanor,

I am saddened to tell you Jacky has been taken seriously ill with camp fever. He forced himself to remain at Yorktown to witness the surrender, but has since been removed to your family's home in

Eltham. He is much weakened, Martha, and I fear the worst. Go to him at once. I too am planning to come as soon as I am able.

I am so sorry. So very sorry. My heart grieves.

George

"No!" I ran to the house, that one word accompanying me. Hounding me.

No, no, no, no, no.

PART III

· THE COURSE OF DUTY ·

~ Sixteen ~

My son was dying.

Even as I stood in the doorway, peering in at him, I could not fathom it. Surely God would not take this last child of my womb.

Surely He would.

Although Eleanor, Betsy, and I had left Mount Vernon with the greatest of speed, it had still taken us two days to travel to my late sister Nancy's home in Eltham, some twenty miles from Williamsburg. The home in which we had oft joyfully stayed was now a house of death.

Eleanor had not left Jacky's side since we had arrived, and I feared for her health and mental state. As for my son, his eyes—sunken and shadowed to look nothing like the vibrant boy we had sent to Yorktown just six weeks previous—were locked upon his wife, a tether of love connecting them even as the cruel spoiler loomed close. I had told Eleanor prayer would save our boy, and we had done our best to appeal to God for a miracle.

He had not gotten better.

Had God not heard us? What good could possibly come from taking this young man away from his family?

As Jacky's condition worsened in spite of my intent, my prayers turned bitter. *Have you not taken enough men during this awful war? Must you take this one too? Have you not taken enough of my children, my family . . . must you take this one too?*

"Grandmamma? I came to tell you that—" Five-year-old Betsy tugged at my skirt.

I gently shut the door and led her away from such a scene. Although she had been in to see her father, she had not recognized him, and my greatest wish—other than the miracle of complete recovery—was that she would remember her father as he had lived, not how he had died. "What is it, little one?"

"Grandpapa is here. He just rode—"

George! I hurried downstairs to find George removing his cloak and hat. I ran into his arms. "Oh, George. What are we to do?"

He held me close but offered no words.

There were none to offer.

⚬⚬⚬

John Parke Custis, my dear boy Jacky, died at eight o'clock in the evening, on the fifth day of November, shortly after George arrived. That God had granted my husband's presence upon this awful time was of some—but little—consolation. There is no consolation in a parent outliving a child.

We buried Jacky the next day. As we walked away from the grave-site, with George offering his arms to me on one side and Eleanor on the other, my husband tried to fill the awful silence with consolation as best he could.

"Jacky was not used to the awful conditions of camp life. The food was bad, the sanitation . . . there is disease on both sides from the death that invades a battlefield."

"I do not wish to hear it, George. I do not." Death was death. I did not wish to hear excuses or even good reason.

"I wish to hear it." Eleanor looked up at her father-in-law. "I need to hear it all."

She surprised me. "Continue, then."

We turned out of the cemetery and walked toward the Bassett home. The November day was overcast, as if it too mourned a light gone out.

"The sickness overtook him very quickly," George said. "There was little could be done to stop it. And he knew, he *knew* he was dying. But on October 17, when Cornwallis asked for a cease-fire and a meeting regarding the terms of his surrender, Jacky—through sheer will—rallied. He was determined to be present for the final ceremony. He insisted on being put upon a horse so he could see it, but was too weak, and was moved to a nearby carriage. We must take comfort in knowing he witnessed our great victory."

"But why did you not send word sooner?" I asked. "If he had been moved to Eltham sooner, then perhaps—"

"I did not know he was ill," George said. "Soldier friends of his told me later that he did not wish for me to know. He knew I was consumed with the battle and he did not want me distracted from the fight. The illness overtook him so suddenly, in mere days, and I was not told until he had been taken to Eltham and . . ."

I leaned my head against his upper arm as we walked. "I know you loved him as much as I."

"I did. I would have given my life for that boy." His voice was tight.

"If only he had not insisted on going to war, he would still be with us. He would still—"

"No!" Eleanor stopped walking, forcing us to halt with her. She turned toward us, her gaunt face flushed. "Although I did not wish to see him go, although I argued against it because I selfishly wanted him with *me*, I am glad he had a chance to be a part of the fight. He was not a soldier—we all knew that—but I also know he was as much a patriot as anyone, and our Cause was dear to his heart. That he gave his life working in e'en a small way toward the completion of that Cause makes me very proud."

The girl humbled me. I began to cry. As did she.

George wrapped his mighty arms around us, and there we stood, in the cold, cold day, clinging to what we had and what we had lost.

———⊗———

"You should go back to your troops," I told George. "Now is a time of celebration, and by your own words, there is still much to do."

"No," he said, not for the first time. "I will accompany you, Eleanor, and Betsy safely home."

"But—"

He took my hands in his. "For years you left the comforts and safety of home to come to me each winter, offering me joy, support, and encouragement. You have shown yourself to be a superior wife in all ways. Now it is my turn to offer *you* support and encouragement. No, my dearest. Other generals can handle what is left at Yorktown. For now my place is with you."

I could only nod and gratefully accept his offer.

———⊗———

I wish I could have declared the war ended, but it was not. Not officially. The British were still in control in New York and in the South. Until all agreed it was time to concede . . . until the last soldier was sent home, George could not abandon his post beside them. He was tied to his position as commander in chief.

And I was tied to the position of the wife of the commander in chief.

And grandmother, and mother-in-law, and sister, and . . .

Once again, I was torn. Eleanor was devastated by Jacky's death and was overwhelmed by the needs of her four children as well as the business of their home and the lands of the Custis inheritance.

What was left of it. For in spite of our advice, Jacky had misspent and mishandled much, leaving comparatively little. The practical side of me wondered if eventually he would have lost it all.

Yet what *was* left needed managing. We asked my brother Bartholomew to help—and he agreed to handle the property issues. But he would not help with the children—claiming ill health. Or total fear. Four children beneath the age of six . . . 'twas a daunting task for even the most able-bodied.

How odd that Eleanor found herself in the same position I had been subjected to upon Daniel's death. The similarities were eerie: we both had been widowed after seven years of marriage, both had four children, though I had already lost my two youngest, I had been twenty-six, and she, but twenty-three. And both were responsible for vast estates. The difference was a matter of health. Eleanor had never been afforded a chance to recover from one birth before becoming with child again. She was weak, where I had been strong.

She was overwhelmed. We ached with the need to do something to help.

And so . . . George and I offered to take responsibility for the two youngest children, Nelly, age two and a half, and Wash, just crawling. Eleanor was not happy about the arrangement but was relieved. She saw the wisdom in taking only the two oldest, who were more deeply attached to her. Wash was being wet-nursed by Mrs. Anderson at Mount Vernon, anyway . . .

And I was getting a second chance at raising a boy and a girl. I thanked the Almighty for second chances.

It was not just Eleanor and the children who needed my care. My sister's daughter Fanny was nearly thirteen and motherless. I had promised Nancy I would care for her, but up to now, the situation had not presented itself. Then there was my sister Elizabeth, who had been widowed in 1776 and left with two sons—one born but ten days after his father's death. Both sons died of the fevers, hurling her into deep pain. She remarried in 1779 and had a daughter—another

Fanny—but I worried for Elizabeth for reasons of her own. Her new husband drank, and I feared his physicality when in that condition.

George's sister, Betty, now widowed from Fielding and in charge of their many children, often visited—though we approved of her plans to gain income from starting a school for girls in their home. Then there were the orphaned children of George's ne'er-do-well brother, Samuel. He had married five times and had died, leaving his fifth wife without funds, a new baby, and three boys and a little girl by previous marriages. George was the only brother who could help keep the children out of foster homes, or even sold into bondage. Jack Washington had too many children of his own, and Charles—the youngest Washington brother—drank to drunkenness.

And George's mother . . . his mother who never saw the good in anything her son accomplished and complained to all who would listen about how she needed money. She even appealed to the Virginia legislature for a bill of assistance! We assisted her plenty and she wanted for nothing, but appreciated less. Neither George's great victory at Yorktown nor the loss of Jacky elicited a comment within her letters. I believe it would have killed that woman to say something nice, to tell her son, "Well done, George." May God forgive me, but as long as she was provided for, I was quite willing to let her stew in her bitterness away from me. That she developed a cancer in her chest . . . could bitterness cause illness?

Everyone needed something from us, and we truly wished to accommodate them all. But it was impossible.

I sat in the dining room, organizing the family letters about me, trying to find a way to satisfy each request. I set a blank page before me, ready to make a list of who should come stay with us, who could be looked after elsewhere, and who—

George entered the room, a letter in hand. "We need to leave, Martha. Congress wishes to meet with me in Philadelphia, and then we must travel on to winter camp in Newburgh, New York, and—"

We? No.

I could not do it. Not again.

I gathered the letters in my hands and waved them in front of him—setting the many against his one. "I have my own congress, my own army who needs me here, George. Nancy's children, Betty's, Samuel's, Elizabeth, and her girls . . . not to mention Eleanor and our grandchildren."

He looked blankly at me—which infuriated me.

"Do you not remember we agreed to take Nelly and Wash as our own? Financially and physic—"

"Of course, but—"

"In the past few years everyone in our family has suffered loss. Their loss is our loss, and if we can help them, then we must help them. It is our duty."

My last statement seemed to cause him to stand more erect. "Duty is what I am trying to fulfill, Martha. I need to finish what I—what we—started." His face softened and he came close, placing a hand upon my shoulder. "I have already sent word *we* are coming, dearest. The men will be sorely disappointed if I come back alone."

George knew my weak spot. The soldiers.

He cupped my chin. "It will all be over soon. I promise. And once it is, we will return here together and help all who require our attention."

I looked down at the letters. Our family would always need us. The need of our country was finite and would end soon.

"All right," I said. "I will leave Mount Vernon this one last time."

Winter camp was not the same. Our military sons had dispersed. Lafayette had gone back to France, Hamilton traveled to New York where he planned to run for Congress, and Laurens joined the fight in the South with General Greene near Charleston. We missed them, but took solace in the fact that, unlike Jacky, they were still alive.

For a short while. Our hearts were further broken when we heard Laurens was killed by a British party foraging for food. I had been certain *if* death had found him during the war, it would have been related to his recklessness and absence of fear, not this meaningless chance meeting in the woods. We added his death to our list of griefs.

In spite of my desire to help family who needed help, leaving Mount Vernon was for the best. To wander the halls with the ghosts of dead children . . . it was not healthy. And though I never understood why God took any of them, I became reconciled to the verity that God was God and I was not, and He was not required to explain His mysterious ways. For even in the midst of many sorrows, both personal and communal, I had also been witness to many miracles. Did I have a right to question Providence about the bad while accepting the good as deserved and appropriate? As His child, I was as a slave. I had no rights, no say, and no control. And as the Almighty was the master of all things, I had to trust Him in all things. Not an easy task, but one both George and I strived to attain.

The largest miracle was our victory. In hindsight, there was no logic in our success. Everything—every thing—was against us. We were a gaggle of rebels with a notion things could be different. Better. That we chose to fight to achieve those changes—against the most powerful nation in the world, a nation that held the most powerful army and navy—belied common sense.

Yet somehow God, in His infinite wisdom, chose to hide that one fact from our eyes and hearts, and nudged us forward. *Go ahead. I know this seems impossible, and it is—without my help, it most certainly is. But I am with you. I will see you through this toward the creation of a new nation, under God, indivisible, with liberty and justice for all.*

Although impatient while waiting for the final decree, George did not sit idle. He spent much time reading. After meeting so many well-read and educated French officers, his shame over his lack of formal education was rekindled, and he absorbed the classics and books on government and agriculture.

I often teased him about it. One day when he was reading, I lifted the book in his lap to see its cover. "*History of the Life and Reign of the Czar Peter, the Great*? Is it a rousing read?"

"More rousing than Cicero's *Orations*."

"I have no doubt."

He took off his newly acquired spectacles and rubbed his eyes. "There is so much I do not know, Martha."

"And so much you do. When you are done with your self-education, I would wager you will be the most learned man in all America."

"You would lose that wager."

"I *can* guarantee at this moment there is not another being in this land reading this tome."

He held the book to begin again. "Then I shall be the *one*."

While George read, and with fewer soldiers for me to visit and comfort, the house in Newburgh seemed overly restrained and . . . odd. The largest room was the odd dining room which boasted a low ceiling, seven doors, and but one window. And more than those oddities, it held strangers. For as our military comrades dispersed, our guests at dinner came more to gawk and say they had supped with the Washingtons rather than having shared an evening as friends. Although George was quite gregarious and funny with those he knew, with these strangers he generally held his tongue, leaving me to banter on and on, drawing them all into witty conversation. It left me weary.

Christmas dinner, in 1782, was especially exhausting and frustrating. I had been home for the summer—in all hopes George would join me, but in November, he asked me to come north again. And though the last trip north had supposed to be the *last* trip north . . . I went again. I could not help myself. I was his and he was mine and that was that.

During this Christmas holiday we wished to be home with our family, yet were stuck far away, accomplishing little but waiting for others to agree on the terms of peace. Our table, in this dining room that left much to be desired, was full of young officers and their wives, all smiling in a dim sort of way, as if they were too overcome with the occasion and company to speak.

I had learned long ago the best way to keep conversation flowing was to ask others about themselves. I had just asked Colonel MacGregor's wife about her children when George suddenly stood.

"If you will excuse me a moment?"

With that, he left the room, left those present looking after him, and then to me. Although I had no inclination George was not feeling well, I felt the need to check. I also rose—to a great clatter of chairs as all the gentlemen rose with me—and said, "Excuse me. Let me check on the general."

The house was not large, and I found him without effort in the room he used as his office. He sat at his desk, quill in hand, his spectacles perched upon his nose.

"What are you doing? We have guests."

"I am writing to Lund."

"Now?"

He pointed to his mouth. "I cannot chew properly. My teeth . . ."

"This is not a new problem, George. And what does this have to do with—"

"I have just remembered where I left my two foreteeth—in a drawer in the secret locker of the desk which stands in my study. I need Lund to carefully wrap them and send them right away."

A laugh escaped and I covered my mouth—too late—with a hand.

" 'Tis not funny." He pointed toward the dining room. "Our guests can see my distress. I know it. I also know they will leave here and tell all who will listen how General Washington chews like a cow."

"A cow with bad teeth."

At his look, I went to his side and kissed the top of his head.

"Finish your letter, then come back to the table. I will have dessert served. It is a flan that is easily eaten—even by old men with bad teeth." I gave him another kiss, this one to his aching mouth. "Happy Christmas, my love."

"General!"

He continued to put on his coat.

I disliked when he would not listen to me. I moved in front of him and yanked upon his lapels. "George, you should not go!"

He put his hands upon mine and peered down at me. "I must. The soldiers have legitimate grievances. Most have not been paid in years."

"But they threaten violence."

He patted his pocket. "I have written a few words to say to them that hopefully will bring a calm end to this issue."

I was not so certain. Spurned men in need of money wanted cash, not consolation.

I did not stray from the house, even though the harsh winter of 1783 had finally released its bonds. I consoled myself with writing letters home, but paused at each sound of horse outside, or footsteps within.

Finally, the sounds of each held the results I waited for, and George returned from his meeting with the soldiers.

I rushed into his arms. "You are safe!"

"You expected otherwise?" He handed his hat to the servant and led me into the tiny parlour.

"The rebellion, the mutiny . . . yes, I too feared harm."

He sat in the large wing chair he had claimed as his own the past eighteen months. "I will admit to a bout of nerves as I entered.

Although most offered respect, I could see their discontent ran deep. And so, I stood before them, and realizing I could not read my notes without my new spectacles, had to pause to retrieve them. I must say I felt quite feeble in doing so, embarrassed at the evidence of my age, but then . . ." He smiled. "Who would have thought this one act could have had more power than my words?"

"I do not understand."

"Neither did I, but when I set them upon my nose and retrieved my notes from my pocket, I was moved to say, 'Gentlemen, you will permit me to put on my spectacles, for I have not only grown gray but almost blind in the service of my country.' And with that I could see the tension in the room diminish. I quickly said my little speech and left those in charge to arrange a compromise with Congress. I have heard both sides have agreed."

I shook my head, once again amazed at the ability of my husband to charm, appease, and inspire.

He slapped his hands upon his thighs. "Now. What is for dinner?"

The year was a blur. Perhaps it was because I did not return home that summer. Due to my own bout with illness, I stayed with George in New York—which was a blessing—but I found my lack of time at Mount Vernon sorely distressing.

Yet life went on, no matter where we laid our heads, with some occasions for celebration and some for grief.

In the spring we received word a third child had been born to Lafayette's wife, named Virginie, after our dear state. George continued to entice his French son for a visit. Also from France was news in April that a treaty of peace was finally agreed upon in Paris, though it would be months before it was signed.

Closer to home, there was news from Mount Vernon. Belvoir, the dear home of our neighbors, the Fairfaxes, was no more. Through accident it had burned to a point beyond renewal. George was especially grieved by this news, as some of his fondest memories as a young man were intertwined with that fine house, now rubbish. We wrote to George William and Sally, long in England, and offered the use of our home during a rebuilding, but they informed us they would stay in England. They also told us they had not received many of our letters during the war, as they were watched and suspected as spies. The inequities of war . . . That we would never see them again grieved us deeply.

But then there was news of a better grain. Eleanor remarried! His name was Dr. David Stuart. It had been two years since Jacky's death, and we were pleased that without the strain of constant pregnancies, Eleanor's health had improved. Yet in all honesty we did not find much about Dr. Stuart worthy of her. He was poor and serious in manner—although he did carry the wealth of a good education. But to see her marry a man so opposite of our vivacious Jacky . . .

I wondered if Eleanor agreed to the marriage in order to facilitate a manager for her holdings, as well as a father for her children. I suppose I could not blame her. I was in such a position after Daniel died. Survival can be the greatest instigator of affection.

As the year dragged on, my thoughts focused upon *our* survival. Being stagnant and of little use, especially when we knew there was much to do at Mount Vernon, was the subject of many discussions. And then, adding to our desire to move our lives along, came certain rumblings. . . .

I first heard of it at the market, while buying summer fruit.

The woman polished the apples I had purchased before setting them in my basket. "So, Lady Washington. Do you think your husband will accept?"

"Accept what?"

"The throne."

I offered a laugh. "The throne of what, may I ask?"

The woman's eyebrows rose. "Why, of the United States. People are talking about him becoming our king." She spit on one of the apples and rubbed it with her apron, then got a twinkle in her eye. "That would make you queen, I would say."

I took the basket away from her, done with this discussion. "I will state quite clearly—and you are encouraged to spread the word—I have no desire to be queen, and the only thrones my husband and I desire are the chairs beside our fireplace." I nodded my good-bye.

She called after me, "If not 'im, then who's to lead us?"

I did not know. But it was not our concern.

⌇

George and I took an evening walk in our new temporary home in Princeton, New Jersey. Congress had moved there after soldier mutinies for back pay raised tension in Philadelphia. When they moved, and with the British finally sailed out of New York City, we were summoned close. It was a hundred miles closer to home, but not close enough. In spite of the lovely autumn there, I knew back home the trees along the Potomac were putting on a stunning show—without us.

We walked in silence, as we often did when finally alone. My arm through his, my sleeve rubbing against his, the folds of my skirt brushing against his leg . . . plenty was being said between us.

Then suddenly we heard, "General Washington!" A man who was sweeping the stoop of a baker's shop rushed forward and bowed. "Milady."

We nodded. "Evening," George said. We kept walking.

It was as though that one word of simple greeting opened a gate. The man ran after us, ran in front of us, forcing us to stop. I held George's arm all the tighter.

"My brother was killed at Cambridge," the baker said.

"I am sorry for your loss," George replied.

My heart softened and I eased the tension on my husband's arm. "What was his name?"

"Joshua Caddy, milady. A fine man with a wife and two babes."

"Are they doing well?" I asked.

The man began to answer, but then his eyes darted around us, making us turn. Coming toward us from all sides were many others, most from the shops along the street.

The baker took a step back and called out to all, "Look here! We have the mighty General Washington and his lady! Right here!"

The crowd surrounded us, pressing forward, slapping George on the back, pulling at his hand to shake it, pulling at my free hand to take into theirs.

"I was at Bunker Hill."

"My father fought at Trenton."

"You are so tall!"

"Lady Washington, you held my hand at Valley Forge."

George wrapped an arm around my shoulders, trying to protect me from the surge. What had been one man was now twenty, and though I could not see through the crowd, I imagined more running to see the commotion—and become a part of it.

"George . . ." I whispered.

He nodded and addressed the crowd. "Gentlemen, ladies, we truly appreciate your well-wishes, *and* the evidence of your devoted sacrifice to our Cause, but—"

"Huzzah for General Washington!"

"God bless Lady Washington!"

Raucous cheers enveloped us. Overwhelmed us. Smothered us.

I found it hard to breathe.

My heart beat too fast.

I needed to get away.

I tugged upon his arm. "Please, George . . ."

Having the advantage of huge height, he began walking through the crowd—back the way we had come. I latched on to him like an additional appendage, burying my head against his arm.

We broke through and began to walk faster. Blessedly, the crowd stayed behind, caught up in their own revelry. But one shout ran after us, assailing us . . . "Three cheers for King George!"

—∞∞∞—

"But you must address it, George," I told him, once we were safely back to our residence—I could not call it *home*. There was only one home. . . .

"It is just idle talk," he said, pacing before the fire. "They do not want a king. No one wants a king again."

"But they do. They know no other way. And you are their choice."

He shook his head. "There are other men who long for power. Franklin, Jefferson, Adams . . ."

"No one swarms about *them*; no one adores them. No one wants them upon an American throne."

His head shook back and forth, his brow furrowed. "I just wish to go home and be a farmer again. Be with my family."

I went to him and halted his pacing. "You must tell them that. Tell Congress; stop these rumours and inclinations before you are put in a position where it is impossible to say no."

"I am not certain they will listen."

"Figure a way to make them listen. We must go home, my love. We must be away from all . . . this. I admire their enthusiasm and am glad we are appreciated, but I cannot endure being unable to take a simple walk with my husband without being assaulted by well-wishers. My only consolation was that no one rang church bells or set off cannon to honour our walking by." It was not an exaggeration. Americans were in a celebratory mood, and when they knew we were passing through their town on the way from here to there . . .

"You know I also prefer small company to large," he said.

"I do know that. But in order to attain and retain the benefits of ever enjoying small company again, you must tell all who will listen that you will not be king."

He shuddered. "To even make such a statement sounds presumptuous."

"It is the term of choice, my dear." I adjusted the ends of his cravat and patted them flat. "Remove yourself from the possibility, George. Some way."

He nodded. "Yes. I will do it. Some way."

⁂

We received the news in early November 1783 that the peace treaty was finally signed! It was over! George ordered the army disbanded. Eight years. Eight long, interminable years.

On one morning soon after, I awoke to find George gone from bed. He was an early riser, and yet it was not near dawn. I wrapped myself with a shawl and tiptoed downstairs. He was not in the parlour, nor in the dining room.

His office?

The door was ajar. I pressed it open to find him at his desk, busy with paper and quill.

"What are you doing awake?" I asked upon entering. I closed the door behind me and pointed to a clock on a shelf. "It is but two."

He put his quill down, took off his glasses, and smiled. It was the first time I had seen him smile in months. "I have a solution to the king issue."

"I am most glad to hear it. What is your solution?"

"Sit, sit, and I will read it to you."

I sat before his desk and marveled at the look of ease that resided upon his features. It did not matter what words he had written on the page, for obviously, they were the right words—for him.

He adjusted his glasses, held the page before the candle, and said, "This is what I will say to Congress, and to all who will listen." He cleared his throat and began. " 'Happy in the confirmation of our independence and sovereignty, and pleased with the opportunity afforded the United States of becoming a respectable nation, I resign with satisfaction the appointment I accepted with diffidence. A diffidence in my abilities to accomplish so arduous a task, which however was superseded by a confidence in the rectitude of our Cause, the support of the supreme power of the Union, and the patronage of heaven.' "

He looked up for my approval. "Thanking God. Yes, yes, 'tis very good. Continue," I said.

As he read the words, I studied him, studied this man who was now recognizable to all the nation, who had joined the quest for independence buoyed by the eager intentions of youth. That independence had been achieved—largely through his dogged efforts . . . for him to so humbly resign all he had earned. Although I was not an expert at history, I could not bring to mind any who—possessed with such power—had given it away.

He was still reading: " 'I consider it an indispensable duty to close this last solemn act of my official life, by commending the interests of our dearest country to the protection of almighty God, and those who have the superintendence of them, to his holy keeping. Having now finished the work assigned to me, I retire from the great theatre of action; and bidding an affectionate farewell to this august body under whose orders I have so long acted, I here offer my commission, and take my leave of all the employments of public life.' " He lowered the paper. "Is that good enough? Do you think it will make them leave us alone?"

I put a hand to my mouth, squelching a combined sob and laugh. "It is lovely, old man. Lovely in words and intent. And lovely to my ears." I bypassed the desk and went to him, finding a place in his lap.

"As you commend the interests of the country to the protection of almighty God, I commend the rest of our lives to His care."

"Amen to that." He bent his head against my chest. "We are going home, Martha. We are finally going home."

⁂

Renewed by his intention, I went home without my George, letting him have his last hurrah before Congress with decorated barges, cannon salutes, cheering crowds, and even a ball where he danced with each and every woman there—'tis said there were three hundred—allowing them each to "get a touch of him." Let them touch all they wanted. He was mine and had promised me his presence by Christmas.

By tomorrow at the latest.

Although I trusted my husband's word, I knew he was in the hands of others who cared not one whit for our Christmas, nor that a house full of family awaited him here. I had heard Congress was meeting especially in Annapolis, awaiting George's communication, but hoped they would not delay because some dignitary wanted George to come to dinner or some band wished to play an extra song in his honour. It was my turn.

Mine.

As Christmas Eve darkened, Nelly—to be five come spring—sat upon her knees on a chair by the window. My sentry, watching for her dearest grandpapa.

My memories returned to her father, also aged five, peering out a window in Chestnut Grove, waiting impatiently for the coming of the same man—my beau, George Washington. . . .

"Come, little one. You have been there all day. It is near bedtime."

"But you said he was coming," she said.

Two-and-a-half-year-old Tub jumped up and down beside his sister. "Gampapa. Gampapa!"

I took him into my arms—which, with a weight worthy of his nickname, was no small feat. "He will be here."

"Do you prom—?"

Nelly stopped her question and looked outside. "A horse! I hear a horse!"

I moved the curtain wider, for I too . . .

And then I saw him, riding hard and fast toward us.

"He is here! He is here!" I yelled. I ran out the front door and down the few steps to the drive. I waved feverishly and he waved back, fairly leaping from his horse into my arms.

"Hello, my dearest. I have missed you!"

"You are here."

"I am home."

⁂

We were a happy family—a large family—to my great delight.

I was at my best with children around. To have a house full of surrogate daughters was my greatest pleasure. And my pretty little boy, Tub, Washy . . . I doted on him as I had doted upon Jacky. I could not help myself.

He, in turn, doted on his grandpapa. He loved to dress like George, in coat and hat—to which I added a jaunty feather—walking next to him, his entire tiny hand encasing but one finger of his grandfather's.

Fanny, my sister Nancy's only daughter, aged seventeen, was with us, as was George Augustine, the son of George's youngest brother, Charles. He had been an aide to our dear Lafayette. He was not well, and suffered from a horrible cough that made us fear consumption. George sent him to the West Indies in hopes of a cure, but he returned to us not much better. Yet he was a good young man, and George had hopes of handing over the managership of Mount Vernon into his control. Someday. After twenty years in that position, Cousin Lund spoke of getting his own land. And Fanny . . . if I could read my young girls correctly, Fanny had hopes of marrying George Augustine. 'Twould be an agreeable match.

Niece Harriot—three years older than Nelly and daughter of George's late brother Samuel—also came to live with us. To our dismay she was a wild child with horrible grooming and deportment, the result of being brought up in a household torn by the constant upheaval of five marriages and a father who was lazy in work *and* in the bringing up of his children. We paid for two of her brothers to go to boarding school, and the oldest brother—at fourteen—worked, and stayed with his stepmother—who had a young child of her own. I hated to admit defeat, but I was often overcome with Harriot's inability or unwillingness to take heed to my instruction, and occasionally— needing a reprieve from my frustration—I sent her to Fredericksburg to stay with George's sister, Betty. Since opening a school for girls in their home, she seemed quite capable of dealing with surly children. Though she too sent Harriot back when she had had quite enough of the challenge.

Our two older granddaughters, Betsy and Patty, who lived at Abingdon with their mother and new stepfather, Dr. Stuart, came to visit frequently. I was very conscious of making certain my babes, Nelly and Washy, maintained a bond with Eleanor. Especially since she quickly became pregnant with more children—and began to suffer the same weakness that went along with that particular condition.

I thrived in the chaos of children.

George . . . did not.

I did my best to allow him quiet when he was in his study—his domain that was not to be breached without invitation.

He was overwhelmed by the task of revitalizing a plantation sorely strained by eight years of war. We did not blame Lund. He had done his best, and had tried to follow our instructions, but it is a truth uncontested that the eyes of a master—in residence—cannot be equaled by any other whose heart may not be so deeply entrenched in the land. We loved Mount Vernon. Others only worked there.

Lund had also been forced to deal with the deprivations of war. Money ran out. Workers left. Slaves ran away to join the British. Work stopped. Inflation negated any profit, and Mount Vernon had become a plantation desperate to make ends meet within its own needs and could not even think of looking beyond itself toward trade.

Our finances were in dire straits.

"We are in trouble, Martha," George told me one morning as I brought him coffee in his study.

I turned the cup so the handle was easily accessible. "It will be all right. It always is."

He put a hand upon mine. "No, Martha. We have no money."

I blinked at him, uncomprehending. "Then we shall sell crops and make some."

"The land has not been tended well for years, the equipment is in disrepair, the workers have grown lax and have forgotten everything they had been taught. If pressed, I am not certain about the whole issue of slavery. I have seen the benefit of workers in the North producing more because they have the incentive of pay. Yet I do not know how to change hundreds of years of tradition when we have no money for wages and need the workers." He took a new breath. "The worth of our property has been cut in half. And our markets . . . England has no wish to buy from us, so we must start anew and find new buyers. Somewhere. In addition, we owe Lund eight years in back wages. Toward *that* debt, I have given him several hundred acres and a little cash." He looked out the window. "Acres I have."

"Indeed. You should be very proud. Eight thousand acres at Mount Vernon and twenty thousand in the Ohio Valley."

"Twenty thousand acres full of squatters and unpaying tenants. Acres I have, cash, I do not." He looked at me. "Did you know I had to borrow several thousand pounds from the governor of New York before we left? And he is not our only creditor."

My stomach tightened. I did not know. I did not wish to know. "Perhaps you should have taken pay for your position as commander in chief."

He sat back in his chair, looking defeated. "I could not renege on my offer. Expenses only. That is what I told Congress when I accepted the job."

"But times changed. You had no idea it would last for eight years. You could ask them for back pay."

"I cannot. There are soldiers waiting for such pay. I cannot press in front of them and demand my due. They need it more than I."

"Do they? You said we have no money."

He did not speak.

I tried to think of ways to help. "What about your wartime expenses? Have you applied for those?"

He pulled a page from the bottom of a stack to the top. "I am doing so. I am also asking them for compensation for your expenses."

I was surprised at this. "Do you think they will pay?"

His eyes were tired as he took my hand. "I could not have done my job without you by my side. Your presence was a requirement."

I squeezed his hand. "I was happy to be there."

Most of the time.

He pointed to the paper. "The entire amount of your expenses is only one thousand sixty-four pounds—for eight years. To postpone the annual visit home I contemplated between the close of one campaign and the opening of another—to never get home even one year . . . I feel this expense is incidental and the consequence of my self-denial. Your self-denial. You offered great service in our winter camps beyond companionship and encouragement to myself. The soldiers . . . your comfort and aid to them was invaluable. Without your nimble fingers sewing and sewing and sewing . . . and the supplies you brought north from the stores of Mount Vernon . . . even when we had little to give, we gave what we had for the Cause. I do not think they should deny me one hundred thirty pounds a year for such a—"

"Shh," I said, disliking the flush in his cheeks. "It will be all right."

He stared down at the papers spread before him. "I am not certain how."

"God will provide, as He has done until now."

George did not respond.

"He will, George. We must believe it so. He spared us and our home. There must be purpose in that. Mount Vernon will prosper again. I know it."

"I only hope I am here to see it."

What? My heart skipped a beat. "Are you not feeling well?"

He shrugged, then held out a hand and began counting upon it. "We must face facts, my dear. My father died at forty-eight. My grandfather at thirty-seven. My half-brother Lawrence died at thirty-four, and Austin at forty-two. My brother Samuel was just forty-seven. The men in my family die young. At fifty-two I have outlived them all."

"But—"

"Sometimes I feel all there is left is to glide down the stream of life till I come to that abyss from where no traveler is permitted to return. It is as though I am now descending the hill I have been fifty-two years climbing. Though I am blessed with a good constitution, I am of a short-lived family—and might soon expect to be entombed in the dreary mansions of my fathers." He sighed heavily. "But I will not repine. I have had my day."

I stood there, unable to speak—for a moment. Then I found my voice. "Stop it!" I said brusquely. "Stop such talk right now."

George looked shocked at my outburst.

I put my hands upon my hips. "What? Did you expect me to meekly agree with you? Agree your life is all but over? Concede to death without a fight?" I poked a finger into his shoulder. "You, who mocked death more than once, are now willing to surrender? What kind of man are you?"

He opened his mouth to speak, but I did not let him. "You are no man I know. I refuse to tolerate such conversation. You will not speak of dying now or ever!" I pointed to the mass of papers upon his desk. "You will not leave me with all *this* to handle, and a house full of children, and the stream of constant guests, and the crops, and the workers, and the full completion of the wings we had built upon this house in our absence. When would you like me to do all *this*? Shall I get up at two and wander about the house and grounds in the darkness, hoping, by some miracle of God, I have time enough and strength enough to get it all completed? I will not have it. I will not!"

He leaned back in his chair and a smile escaped. I allowed his amusement because I knew he had listened to my words. He always listened . . . whether he would heed my requests was variable.

I decided upon one more action before the moment passed. I reached for his hand and pulled. "Come with me."

"But I have work—"

I held fast and did not give him option. He removed himself from his chair and let me lead him to the outside, to the covered veranda that had been built the length of the house on the river side.

He stepped over a pile of scrap wood being used for various fixes. "Martha, I have seen the progress of the repairs. I do not—"

I stopped before a bench I had seen the workmen rest upon. "Sit," I commanded.

"Sit here?"

I pressed upon his shoulders until he succumbed to my wishes. "Now move over. For I wish to sit beside you."

" 'Tis a bit cramped," he said with a smile.

"I will assume you refer to your own girth, not mine?"

"Absolutely."

Once we were settled, I linked a hand through his arm and with the other pointed to the Potomac beyond. "Is it not beautiful?"

"Yes, of course. Which is why I am so adamant about finding wise solutions to our problems." He began to rise.

I yanked him down again. "The first solution to any problem is to count our blessings. We are home. We are together under our own vine and fig tree. All else is incidental. "

I felt his body relax. For the first time, he truly allowed himself to gaze upon the sloping green before us, the gray of the river below, and the mass of trees edging its banks. He raised his face to the sky and closed his eyes. "We *are* blessed. . . ."

Remember that, George. Above all else, remember that.

George found me in the dining room finalizing the table for three o'clock supper. "Who is the couple in the parlour?" he whispered.

"Mr. Quarrier from Richmond and Miss Eliza Tomkins from Philadelphia."

He raised an eyebrow, awaiting more explanation.

"I do not know them either. Apparently Mr. Quarrier had a nephew who fought a battle somewhere, at some time, and was just passing by and wished to pay his respects to General and Mrs. Washington." I adjusted his fresh cravat. George always returned to the house from his rounds across Mount Vernon at quarter to three in order to freshen himself for supper.

"Strangers."

"Until now, yes."

"Are they staying the night?"

"They have given such indication."

"But the house is full."

"Which is why it is a good thing we are having extra bedrooms put in the attic." I brushed a speck off the tablecloth. "Last year we had six hundred seventy-seven overnight guests."

"You counted?"

"I did. And with only half a year gone, we appear to be testing that mark for this year. Perhaps if we put a shingle out, 'Washington's Inn,' and charged a fee, our money problems would be over."

"A hefty fee," George said.

"As for now, I am having pallets set in the hall."

George looked over his shoulder toward the parlour, but leaned low for my ears alone. "Mr. Gordon does not look to be the sort who is used to a mat on the floor."

"If his tastes deem him otherwise, then I will ask him to go elsewhere—and pay for his lodging and sustenance." I straightened a knife and spoon just so. "The expense of guests, George . . . they all believe we have a great plenty."

"And are willing to part with it, at *their* will."

My thoughts sped to the rigid schedule I had been forced to implement in order to take myself through the day-to-day regime of constant guests. "The authoress Catherine Macaulay and her husband, William Graham, are coming tomorrow." I took a step closer and lowered my voice. "Much younger husband, I have heard. She is forty-seven and he, but of age."

George shook his head. He did not like gossip. "Will you have a pallet made for them, my dear?"

I picked up a stack of extra napkins to take back to the pantry. "Unless a guest leaves, or you are willing to give up our bed."

"I choose the former, my dear. Unless you will relinquish your spot beside me?"

"Do not tempt me. The way you awake in the morning, so suddenly, with a rush . . ."

"Old habits from the front. I still awake ready to confront some wartime essential."

"Weary we are, and relaxed, we are not." I found his eyes. "Will we ever be allowed to relax?"

He kissed my cheek. "The perils of fame, my dear."

"I thought with fame came fortune," I replied.

"Alas, only in novels."

Seventeen

Knowing the children needed education, we hired a tutor, William Shaw, who was also assigned to help George with clerical duties. But as Mr. Shaw preferred pleasure to work, and though we gave him many chances, we eventually let him go on his way. Tobias Lear from New Hampshire took his place and proved very satisfactory. Finally, I had someone who could truly help me and not aggravate our arduous days.

Being spring, Tobias took the children to the back lawn for their lessons. Spring was the best time of year at Mount Vernon. I relished the fresh air and had the doors and windows flung wide.

"Done!" In one motion, eight-year-old Nelly set her pencil upon her portable writing desk and handed her paper to Mr. Lear, who looked it over intently.

Soon he proclaimed, "Perfect, Miss Nelly. Once again, perfection."

I set down my mending and applauded from my chair on the terrace. "Well done, dear girl." I looked to Harriot, who was lying on her back, using the desk as a pillow. Hopeless. Utterly hopeless.

And Wash was not much better.

"Master Wash? What did you get for your sums?" Mr. Lear asked.

Wash bit the end of his pencil, looked at his sister, then flipped the pencil, sending it end over end till it stuck like a thrown knife in the grass. "Twelve, fourteen, eight? What do I care for numbers? I want to go to the wharf. The herring are coming in and I want to watch."

Mr. Lear cleared his throat and looked toward me. "Would you not wish to cipher how many fish were caught and in how many nets?"

"Tons and tons. That is all I care." Wash ran to me, at six, still small enough to crawl upon my lap. "Do not make me learn numbers, Grandmamma. They hurt my head."

I looked to Mr. Lear, who awaited my response. "Numbers are important, Wash. Especially when you take over Mount Vernon. Your grandpapa uses numbers all the time and—"

"But that is ages and ages from now. Let Nelly do the numbers for me. She does not even have to try."

It was true. Nelly had an avid penchant for learning that was sorely lacking in her brother. No matter if it was writing, mathematics, geography, or French, Nelly excelled.

And Wash did not.

His little fingers played with the locket at my neck. "Please, Grandmamma? It is too fine a day to be thinking."

Although pretending to do otherwise, Harriot had been watching the entire exchange with interest. She chose this moment to sit up. "I will go with him, Aunt Martha. I will watch over him."

He leapt from my lap and they were gone, down the hill toward the river. Mr. Lear shook his head, though out of respect he did not look at me. I knew he did not understand my indulgence of Wash. In truth, *I* did not understand it. Why was I incapable of being stern with young boys? If I was not careful, Wash would turn out as flighty and void of academics as his father had been.

I also felt Nelly's eyes. Although I loved her every bit as much as her brother, she had to notice my inability to be stern with him while I held her to high accountability in the domestic lessons I offered toward her womanhood.

She looked back to Mr. Lear. "Can I learn about Spain today, Mr. Lear?"

"Certainly. Let me go back to the house and get my geography book and I will show you some beautiful maps of—"

Eustis burst through the door nearby. "Mistress Washington! Come quick! Mrs. Washington is having her baby!"

Fanny.

I ran inside.

⸙

Fanny's baby boy was now two weeks old. Her husband, George Augustine—although his cough and consumption were worse—took great joy in this new babe.

But the boy was not well, and Fanny was weak, and George Augustine was also in bed. My days and nights were consumed with care for them. So much so my husband worried o'er my own health.

"You must get some sleep, Martha," he said as he intercepted me in the hallway outside their room.

"I must get these linens to them," I said.

He sidestepped, blocking my way. "Have we not had enough death in the family of late? My brother Jack, your mother, your brother, Bartholomew?"

"We cannot bar death at the door, George. It will come when it wills."

He held a finger to my face. "But we need not be reckless. We cannot mock good health any more than we mock death." He took the linens from me. "Now go. To bed with you."

"But you need rest too."

"I will join you shortly."

I did as I was told, but feeling as usual—neither sick nor well—I could not sleep. I rarely could sleep. The to-do's, should-do's, and could-do's of life prevented it.

—————

The baby died.

A pall of sadness spread over the house like a shroud. Even the children seemed to sense that now—above all other times—was the time to be quiet.

The constant stream of visitors sensed nothing and continued to invade our home.

Oh, to be anonymous again.

—————

"Can they not do it without you?" I asked George.

He checked the straps on his horse. "They could. But I have given too much, spent too many years to let others create a system of government without me. We need a government with separate branches that work together: executive, judicial, and legislative. There should be power available to each, yet power that can be checked by the other." He stopped his work—and his discourse—to look at me. "We are creating a nation unlike any that has ever existed, Martha. We must find a way to unite thirteen disparate states into one mind. We must get it right."

I tried to think of some other reason, some way to get him to stay. My eyes fell upon the stable to my left, to a plow being readied for a field. " 'Tis time for planting. Unless all miraculously agree and make quick work of it, you will be months away. You will miss the growing season. You are needed here."

He too looked toward the stables. The plow toppled, and he took a half step in its direction, then stopped himself. "I have to do this. It is my duty."

There was nothing I could do to stop him. "You promise this will make it done? Once the government is established, you will let others do the work and come home to me?"

"I promise."

He kissed me, mounted his horse, and rode away.

I would hold him to that promise. I would.

———— ⁂ ————

Tobias Lear snapped the latest newspaper against his knee. "It appears New Hampshire will ratify soon."

"They will be the ninth." George Augustine buttered a piece of bread.

Eleanor's husband, David Stuart, reached for the jam. "Nine will make the Constitution real."

General Knox wiped a crumb from his chin. "Real *and* vital."

"I am very aggrieved," my George said as he passed the butter along, "that our own Virginia has not chosen to ratify. I should ride to Williamsburg and give them a piece of my—"

I rose from my chair. "There will be none of that." I proceeded to gather the ten newspapers that littered the table. "I am sick to death of politics. Who has said what, who has done what. For ten months I have endured little else as one by one the states ratify."

Lucy Knox fluttered her hands. "But it is ever so exciting."

I gave her an appalled look. I could usually count on her for lively—interesting—conversation. For her to defect to the side of politics . . .

"Well, it is," she said.

"North Carolina and Rhode Island say they will not ratify until a bill of rights is created," Tobias said. "The Constitution details the rights of the government, but the rights of the people need attention also. I do not oppose such a thing, but—"

With great drama I dropped the stack of papers to the floor, inches from the grate of the fireplace. I struck a match and held it aloft. "Though it be June these papers *would* make great kindling. What say you, gentlemen? A roaring fire on a hot day or a new conversation?"

"Sorry, my dear." George held his hand toward me. "Come back and sit down. What would you like to talk about?"

"I know." Henry leaned his three-hundred-pound frame closer to the table. "Let us discuss how George will be our first president."

Lucy clapped her hands. "Oh, George. Really?"

"There has been talk," Tobias said. "The government requires a man respected by all sides." He turned to George. "The fact you were unanimously elected president of the Constitutional Convention speaks well of your chances at the—"

My mouth had fallen into a gape. It was my turn to address George. "President? You?"

He rose from his chair and started toward me. "Now, Martha. It is not a certainty by any means. And there are others—"

"No, there are not," Henry said. "Not any in high contention. 'Tis nearly a sure thing."

President.

So much for retirement.

"If you will excuse me."

I left the room.

⚬≋⚬

"Martha. Please open the door."

"Can you not respect my privacy, husband? I am busy."

I sat in one of the necessaries that was nestled among the tree-lined serpentine walk that edged our circular drive. I had no need for its particular function but only for its solitude. The smell was unpleasant, but after rushing from the house I could think of no other place where I could be absolutely alone.

George being named president would not ease this deficiency.

"Please, Martha. I want to talk to you, to explain, to ease your fears, to—"

I opened the door and took a breath of fresher air. "Ease my fears? Which means you are not considering it?"

He pulled me out, closed the door, and placed my hand in the crook of his arm. He walked me down the row of trees, away from the house. He turned into the gardens. Three slaves weeded nearby. "Leave us," he said.

And we were alone. I sat upon a bench. I did not much care if he sat beside me or not. "So? How long have you known of this?" I asked.

He chose to stand, putting his hands behind his back. He also chose to look over my head, into the garden.

Wise man. My eyes would have burned into his in a way most uncomfortable.

"There was talk last summer at the convention that *if* the Constitution was ratified, a president would need to be chosen. A charismatic figure who—"

"What about Franklin? Adams? Even Jefferson? Choose one of those who enjoy the limelight. Someone who has experience in Europe, for wouldn't a president need to have such connections?"

"Although I have not traveled outside this country, European heads have come to me. Have come here, Martha. Stayed in our rooms, supped at our table."

"I know. I have washed their sheets and gotten up at dawn to make certain their bread had risen."

"Lafayette has told us France is in turmoil. There is a revolution brewing there. They have enough to worry about to care about our attention."

"But perhaps they will need our help as we needed theirs? Tit for tat. A president will have to deal with such decisions. If you are president, will you volunteer to fight over there, in aid of the French cause for freedom?"

"No, no, Martha. I promise—"

I stood and placed myself inches from him. "You promised before! When you rode away to the convention you promised you would let others do the work of the new government."

He tried to capture my hands in his, but I would not let him and pushed away to my own space along the path. "You are fifty-six years old, George. Too old to start something so new, so encompassing, so stressful. Your joints ache, your teeth are practically falling out of your mouth, you are going deaf, and your eyesight is weak."

"I have spectacles now. They help."

I stomped a foot and tears of frustration escaped. "This is not about spectacles! It is about there being a limit. Have you—have we—not sacrificed enough for this country?"

He looked to the sky, his white hair a striking contrast to its blue. "We have sacrificed beyond measure, my dear. We deserve to live here in peace. And honestly, I am finally seeing results in our hard work here at Mount Vernon. It has taken years to repair it from the ruins of war, but it is nearly whole again."

My words came out as a sob. "Then stay here and finish the work."

He took a deep breath and swallowed with difficulty. "There is work to be done for all, in developing the country to find its true destiny, in helping it become a great nation. Are there men more capable than myself? More versed in politics? Wiser, better men? Certainly. But as the commander of the army I became a tie that bound soldiers from all states and backgrounds. There is no other man who has that experience, nor who has loyalty to all states. I unified men before; I can do it again." He moved to take my hand and this time, I let him. "My largest fear is that without a strong leader from the very beginning this nation will fracture into thirteen sovereign states. The government we are on the verge of establishing will dissipate like fog upon the river, and we will be as we were before, thirteen instead of one. In short, my dear, dear wife, I fear if I do not accept this position, all our sacrifice—e'en the whole of the revolution—will be counted for nothing."

I clenched my jaw and shook my head in short bursts. " 'Tis not fair, George. 'Tis not fair that one man take on such repeated burdens."

He pulled me close. "*If* this position comes to me, I know it will be accompanied by a feeling not unlike that of a culprit who is going to his place of execution."

I pulled back to see his face. "Then—?"

He pulled me close again. "That being true or not, I must say yes, Martha. The country calls and I must answer its voice."

And I?

I wished to plug my ears.

Nine months had come down to this day. In the time it took for a baby to gestate and be born, so came the birth of the presidency.

We had heard that on April 6, 1789, the votes of the electoral college had been assessed—and were unanimous.

My husband had been elected president. The first president of the United States of America.

You would have thought nine months was time enough for me to accept the notion, to resign myself to that fate, but like a new mother who upon seeing her baby born realizes she still does not have a name for it, so it was with me.

I had no name for my emotions. They encompassed me completely yet left me blank and vacant. And a good part of me parlayed the absurd notion that if no one came and fetched George away, if I could keep him here at Mount Vernon all to myself, somehow they would forget their decision and leave us to grow old in solitude and tranquility together.

It was a stupid notion. A fantasy with no basis in logic or fact—or destiny.

Yet even though I knew someone *would* come to make the announcement official, even though I knew someone *would* come to officially call him to the capital city of New York, my heart and stomach still clenched when I spotted Charles Thomson riding up to the house on April 14.

Charles Thomson, who had been the secretary of Congress from the time before the Declaration of Independence, who had so meticulously kept a record of all that was said and done during those assemblies. Charles Thomson, a friend with whom we had oft stayed when in Philadelphia.

But this was not a social call.

Charles dismounted with the loud "Oomph" of less agile bones. As his horse was led away he walked a few awkward steps toward the front door, low moans accompanying each footfall.

I looked at the clock. It was half past ten. George would be in the fields until quarter to three. It would be up to me to entertain our guest—a responsibility I usually met with little effort. Yet today . . . when I knew what news he bore . . .

I removed my apron, tucked stray hairs beneath my cap, and opened the door for him. "Charles, how nice to see you."

With effort he climbed the few steps to the door. "Martha. 'Tis good to be here. My body does not appreciate such rides anymore."

I invited him in and settled into the west parlour. I ordered coffee and scones and wondered if he would mention the news or avoid it.

He chose the latter—which was agreeable, yet awkward. It was as though we both knew a vast secret yet had silently agreed to talk around it. As we chatted I wondered how I was ever going to sustain the conversation until quarter to three.

And yet . . . I did it. Blessedly, Charles was an easy conversationalist. He asked about our family, and I asked about his. We reminisced about the early days of the revolution, and I let him tell me rousing stories about his escapades with the Sons of Liberty. The children came and went, needing this and that, so the hours sped by in a way that was most relieving.

And then, George showed up early—at a quarter to one. Had someone sent word of our guest's arrival? Or had he somehow known? After a quick handshake, George retired upstairs to freshen himself, but returned with great speed, and much out of breath.

"Well, then, Charles. How nice to see you."

The tension being so long extended, Charles rose, reached into his pocket, and handed George a letter.

Had I been of less stable constitution, I would have descended to the floor, for certainly I did forget to breathe, and certainly my heart pronounced a new unnatural rhythm.

George looked to me, then to Charles, then to the letter. I saw he too had trouble breathing, and let several breaths come and go before he opened it.

He read aloud:

"Sir, I have the honour to transmit to Your Excellency the information of your unanimous election to office of President of the United States of America. Suffer me, sir, to indulge the hope, that so auspicious a mark of public confidence will meet your approbation, and be considered as a sure pledge of the affection and support you are to expect from a free and an enlightened people. Signed, John Langdon, temporary president of the United States Senate."

George looked up. "So it is."

Charles laughed nervously and clapped him on the back. "So it is."

George looked to me. I knew this was an important moment, not just for the country, but between us. Now was not the time to let my fear, my pride, my frustration, or my anger intrude. Now, as always, he needed me beside him, to support, love, and encourage.

And so, in spite of the turmoil I felt within, I stood on tiptoe, kissed his cheek, offered the best smile I could manage, and repeated what had already been said, "So it is."

Three little words that spoke volumes.

It was April 16, the year of our Lord 1789.

George was leaving today. Two scant days to make arrangements for our household to move two hundred miles. Although we had known for ten days of his election, I had not let myself acknowledge the finality of the decision until Charles Thomson had come with the letter. And so, I was not ready to leave on the sixteenth.

And so, George was going without me.

The very thought issued fresh pain.

That morning, he did not arise at four as he had done on every morning of our thirty years of marriage. And I did not rise soon after.

But we were awake—if we had ever slept.

He lay upon his back and I cradled myself beneath his arm, my head intent upon the beating of his heart.

We said nothing to each other, our embrace speaking for us, until the sun came through the windows and we heard the house come to life as children and servants started the day.

Finally, I felt his muscles tense and I knew our time was over. "We *will* come back here, Martha."

I nodded against his chest. The tears I had been so successful in saving cut through my armor. "I will miss us *here*. I will miss you."

He sat up, taking me with him. "You will have me. We will be in New York City together."

I shook my head. "Together or not, I will miss you, George. I will miss *us*. Just us."

His forehead furrowed, but then he grasped my meaning and nodded.

And all had changed.

Had been forever changed.

— Eighteen —

Ten years later
December 1799

I sat at the bedside and watched as the blood seeped from my husband's arm into the bowl set beneath it. This was the third time George had been bled. His face was ashen, and his breathing was much laboured, as the infection in his throat worsened.

"Will *this* help?" I asked Dr. Craik.

Before answering, he looked to the other two doctors who had been called: Dr. Elisha Dick and Dr. Robert Brown. Their faces were pulled in panic. I saw no hope in their eyes. Finally, Dr. Craik said, "I do not know."

" 'Tis quinsy," Dr. Brown said, with a thick Scottish accent.

I started to nod, then remembered how my first husband had died of such a thing. And now George?

No. I would not let such a thought . . . George had had quinsy during the war, and though he had come close to death, he had recovered. George had always been susceptible to sore throats. That he had succumbed simply because he had arrived home later for supper . . .

The weather two days ago, December 12, had been disagreeable: snow, hail, and cold rain. But that had not kept George from riding out on his rounds. Though it *had* contributed to his arriving home late for three o'clock supper.

"My apologies," he had said to our guests as he entered when we were already at table.

"You are soaked," I said. "Go get into some warm clothes."

"No, no," he said, brushing the damp from his breeches. He winked at Bryan Fairfax, George William's brother, back visiting from England. "You have come such a long way. I have already missed too much news of George William, Sally, and your family."

And so he had sat in his damp clothes until bedtime. "You will catch your death," I had told him.

The words haunted me. . . .

The next day George had suffered a sore throat but had returned to his work, wanting to oversee the extraction of some trees. Suppertime had found him without much voice. His secretary, Tobias Lear, had seconded my insistence that he take something for it—I had many fine remedies at my disposal—but George had refused, parlaying his usual "Let it go as it came" philosophy. We had a nice evening by the fire with Tobias, with me checking regularly on Nelly—who had given birth to dear Frances Parke Lewis two weeks previous, and who was not well and confined to bed.

I had gone to bed first, with George working late in his office. . . .

He awakened me in the dark of the night, saying, "I cannot breathe well."

I threw off the covers, going to get help, but he pulled me back toward him. "Not yet. The fires have all gone out, and with you so recently ill . . . wait until morning."

I hesitated, but he patted my spot beside him, holding the covers aloft. I climbed back to bed, and we huddled in the dark cold of the night.

I dozed but awoke when I heard his breathing turn raspy. I felt his head. It was burning with fever. "You are worse!"

George barely opened his eyes but managed a nod. When the

servant came in to start the morning fire in our room, I sent her away. "Go fetch Mr. Lear! Quickly!"

That first moment of panic seemed like a lifetime ago, and yet it had been but a day. Since then the doctors had tried their best, to no avail. I had even prepared a tonic of molasses, vinegar, and butter, but George choked on it, unable to swallow. Purges were tried—calomel— but it only added to my husband's suffering.

Dr. Brown stroked his chin. "I so dislike making it up as we go along."

His words brought me back to the eight years George had spent as president . . . *we* had perfected the act of making it up as we went along. Kings were a known commodity, but presidents? I closed my eyes, remembering the intense pressure to get the image of the office right. Some thought us too down-home and plain, and others accused us of trying to be royalty. The constant pressure to please had worn on us. I lived a very dull life as the wife of the president and knew nothing that passed in the town. I never went to any public place; indeed, I was more like a state prisoner than anything else. There were certain boundaries set for me which I could not depart from, yet when I could do as I liked, I was obstinate, and stayed at home a great deal.

Beyond it all I was determined to be cheerful and happy in whatever situation I found myself because I had long found the greater part of our happiness or misery depended upon our dispositions and not upon our circumstances.

I now looked upon George and those hovering around him. I did not like *these* circumstances. Not at all. No determination of a positive disposition had any power against what was playing out before me.

"Mr. President," Dr. Brown said in a whisper close to George's ear. "Please try to be strong."

In spite of myself, I smiled. At the title, not the instruction. Our position had been so new no one had known what to call us. *His Serene Highness, His Excellency, His High Mightiness.* We had finally grown weary of the debate and had decreed George was Mr. President, and I was Mrs. Washington. So there.

We had also had to make up our duties as we went along. People were insistent upon seeing us, so I had Friday drawing room gatherings, and George had Tuesday levees, and Thursday we had official dinners. In order to shoo people away, I had to be stern and rise promptly at nine, saying, "The general retires at ten and I always precede him." I truly believe without such a statement people would have kept us occupied indefinitely.

Then there were the soldiers who came to our door, first in New York and later in Philadelphia, when the capital was moved. I had such a heart for these men who had served so well. They meant no harm, but asked after the health of "His Excellency" and wanted to thank me for some kindness they remembered during the times I was at winter camp. I often answered the door and allowed them to speak of those times past, then sent them to the steward's room for refreshments. If possible I gave them a small gift, along with my greatest wishes for health and happiness.

Although many said I should not have allowed them access, I could not turn them away, for I remembered our times at winter camp with an odd fondness. Although the times had been overflowing with stress and deprivation, compared to the superficiality of the presidency, my days in the latter were lost days. In camp I had been allowed to do some good; as the president's wife . . . I counted the days until we could be home.

It seemed like only yesterday we had returned to Mount Vernon. I did the sum in my head and realized it would be three years come April. How had the eight years in office dragged with excruciating slowness, while the three years spent at home seemed only a day?

At home George had his fruit trees, his plans to rotate crops and expand the plantation. As during the war, Mount Vernon had not prospered in our absence. Our niece Fanny tried, along with her husband, George Augustine, but it was too much for her abilities, and her husband was too ill.

I thought of the deaths and births that had occurred without us at home. My mother-in-law had died, never appreciating the status her son had attained. And George Augustine had died seven years ago, leaving Fanny to remarry with our own Tobias Lear—who had also lost a wife to the yellow fever epidemic that scourged Philadelphia during our first years as president. But alas, Fanny had never been strong, having contracted the consumption from her husband, and she too passed on. Then Fanny's father, Burwell Basset died, and George's sister, Betty. . . .

But there had been happy occasions too, though not achieved without stress. We had taken Wash and Nelly with us when George became president, leaving Betsy and Patty behind with their mother and her husband—where they stewed with jealousy over their younger siblings. I truly believe this jealousy was the reason both married young—Betsy to a much older man. Plus, 'twas hard for them to witness their mother's constant string of progeny, and odd to have their own babies born while step-siblings were being born alongside. I became a great-grandmother times three. . . .

We tried to give these two granddaughters special times, but it was never enough. Or equal. To my great pleasure, Nelly thrived at our side, and often helped me with the socials. She continued her studies and became a charming, accomplished young woman. Through her I saw the girl Patsy might have become. . . .

I cherished the daily devotions we took together. As I cherished her devotion to George and me. Yet she was almost too devoted. I feared she would never marry. When Lafayette sent his son to us—George Washington Lafayette—to get him away from the chaos in France, it was said to be the perfect match. But Nelly would have none of it, alas, looking for a young man more like her grandfather.

We were relieved to find him in George's nephew, the son of Betty and Fielding Lewis. Lawrence was a good man, and we were pleased when they were married at Mount Vernon. This home was made for weddings. . . .

I let my gaze turn toward the doorway, remembering last February

22, George's sixty-seventh birthday and their wedding day. George had worn his old Continental Army uniform and given the bride away by coming down the staircase. The couple were married in the front hall just after the candles were lighted. Nelly wore a veil covering her face because Lawrence had once seen her behind a lace curtain and had commented on her loveliness. Ah, the romance of youth . . .

My thoughts turned to Wash. Ah, the fickleness of youth . . .

Wash was his father's son, more interested in girls and pleasure than schooling and responsibility. He had been kicked out of Princeton. I sighed, as I always did when thinking of my grandson. It was my fault. I had done Wash no favours. Even at the age of sixty-eight I did not understand why I could be so effective with the girls in my charge yet be incapable of raising boys to worthy adulthood. Though Jacky *had* made strides to be responsible. At the end . . .

I looked to the wall, to the stitching my dear Patsy had done for me so many years ago, before her untimely death. Such a delicate girl, so often ill, so often suffering. And yet—though it was difficult to say so—I had come to realize that if Patsy had lived, I would have been obligated to stay with her at Mount Vernon. I would not have been able to join George at winter camp. I would not have been able to help him and help the soldiers. Nor perhaps, would I have been free enough to help the other young women who had come into my life.

I would never know, but I took peculiar comfort that her death had provided others with my help. O'er the years I sought many such answers for life's blows, some satisfactory and others not. . . .

A servant came in and collected the bloodied cloths that littered the room. So much blood. I knew nothing of anatomy, but certainly such loss would weaken a man, even a man as strong as my husband.

If he would die . . .

Such a blow I could not bear. I bowed my head, repeating the prayers that nailed me to the bedside. *Please, almighty God, please spare this man. I love him—*

I opened my eyes when I heard George's voice, raspy and strained. I stood by his head, stroking it. I took his hand. "Yes, George?"

He smiled at me but turned his head to the doctors. "I feel myself going. I thank you for your attentions, but . . ." He paused in an attempt to take a breath, to swallow. "I pray you to take no more trouble about me. Let me go off quietly; I cannot last long."

Then he turned to me. Our eyes met. I swallowed my tears. I would not let him see them. I would not say words in the company of so many, but I spoke them with my eyes: *I love you, George.*

He nodded ever so slightly, then said, " 'Tis well."

He closed his eyes.

And was no more.

I, too, was no more.

My husband was dead. George was dead. My partner for forty years was no more.

I was alone.

I did not cry.

People swarmed about me, their shock and devastation evident. Nelly even got out of bed to comfort me. "If only Wash were here."

Wash was off with Nelly's husband, checking on the Custis estates in New Kent.

I heard little Parke fussing in the bedroom, seeking her mamma, who had left her in the late of the night. Although I appreciated Nelly's effort, I quickly returned her to her room. I needed her well. I could not endure more loss.

I could not endure this one.

I let others do what had to be done that night. I sat in the family dining room and . . . I do not know what I did besides sit. My mind could not comprehend and so left me, as though it had business elsewhere.

People came.

People went.

People spoke to me.

People were silent.

And people whispered. And worried. *She does not cry.*

I would not allow myself the privilege. Or the comfort. For once surrendered, I feared I would plunge too deep to ever recover. Two of my brothers had drowned. I felt as though I was on the edge of knowing the feeling, their final feeling. . . . I could not begin the descent lest it envelop me.

People told me, "You should rest. Go to bed."

I put them off the best I could, needing the house to be quiet more than I needed rest. That I had been forced to share my husband in death as I had constantly shared him in life angered me. Why could they not have left me alone with him for but a minute? For an hour, so we could have said our good-byes? Why had I been but one of many at his bedside when death arrived?

I lingered downstairs while others ascended to bed. I coasted from room to room, straightening this figurine on a mantel, squaring a chair just so. Meaningless motions meant to distract me until the house was mine.

Just mine.

I stopped my nothingness and listened. Silence.

I took a deep breath, drinking it in. Then, with a nod of confirmation, I ascended the private back staircase that led to our bedchamber. It was my turn to retire—not sleep, for I knew sleep would allude me as it had always done during so many other times of grief.

I stood at the door, my hand upon the knob. The room we had shared lay on the other side. The chamber that just hours ago had held my husband on his deathbed.

I started to turn the knob, but then . . .

I stopped myself.

I shook my head.

No.

I could not enter this room that was meant for two, that was our one private sanctuary amid a public life.

I would not enter.

Ever.

Ever again.

Then where would I go? The bedrooms were full: Nelly, Tobias, the doctors . . .

I turned round, my eyes spotting the tiny steps that led to the attic. At the moment no one was up there.

It beckoned me.

I held my candle aloft, lifted my skirt with the other hand, and went up, up to the attic. Up to the top of the house. I walked through the first empty bedroom toward the hall. I had my choice of four rooms. The bedroom looking out back, on the opposite end was often Wash's room. I would not intrude there. I looked toward the room above Nelly's. There was comfort in that, being close to my dear granddaughter, yet separate.

I opened the door. The moon came through the garret window that overlooked the front drive. It invited me to enter.

I complied.

It was a spare room, with white walls, a sloped ceiling, a small bed, and a few chairs. "What more could I need?" I said aloud.

There was no fireplace, but a stove in the corner. A cold stove.

Good enough.

I pulled my shawl tighter about my shoulders and stood at the tiny window.

Mount Vernon lay before me: the circular drive, the bowling green, the rows of trees so lovingly planted. The outbuildings, kitchen, servants' hall, the north lane leading to the spinning room, the salt house, the gardener's house. And the south lane leading to the wash house, the smoke house, the stables and—

And the family crypt below . . .

The crypt where George would be laid.

The crypt that held Patsy, and George's brother Lawrence, and George Augustine, and . . . the crypt that held so many who had gone before.

And now George, the only relative I had ever chosen.

Suddenly, the image of a grand dining room came to mind. In it were Patsy and Jacky, Fanny, George Augustine. . . . They were all dressed in fine garments of white, edged in gold and silver. And they were smiling, coming forward to greet the newest arrival.

George.

There were grand greetings and many hugs as he was welcomed into the heavenly fold.

"Come, Poppa. I have made your favourite Indian cakes," Patsy said.

"And I have brought some of the best Madeira," Jacky said.

I smiled at the thought of them together once more, laughing and eating and sharing. A jolly affair. As good a gathering as any I had ever done?

"We will see," I said.

And we would. For I would join them soon enough, when God so deemed. At that time I would take great pleasure in taking over the hostess duties. And at that time, I imagined George being the first in line to meet me. I would rush into his arms and he would greet me as he had done so many times after being apart.

Hello, my dearest. I have missed you.

And then I would hook my fingers into the lapels of his coat and pull him down to look at me eye to eye . . .

And I you, old man.

Death no longer mocked me.

Not with the promise of seeing my family again.

In that, I would be victorious.

— Epilogue —

Martha never again entered the bedroom she shared with George—or his study. She lived in the garret bedroom for over two years until she died on May 22, 1802. Martha was never the same after his death, her heart truly broken. And in one last act—perhaps her only act—of rebellion, she burned all the letters they had exchanged over the years as if saying to the world, *You will not have* this *part of us.* Only three have ever been found. . . .

There are two quotes, written upon her death, that would have pleased her. One, from the *New England Pledium*:

> She was the worthy partner of the worthiest of men, and those who witnessed their conduct could not determine which excelled in their different characters, both were so well sustained on every occasion. They lived an honor and a pattern to their country, and are taken from us to receive the rewards—promised to the faithful and the just.

And this more personal tribute from her dearest granddaughter, Nelly:

> I had the most perfect model of female excellence ever with me as my monitress, who acted the part of a tender and devoted

parent, loving me as only a mother can love, and never extenuating or approving in me what she disapproved in others. She never omitted her private devotions, or her public duties . . . she and her husband were so perfectly united and happy. . . . After forty years of devoted affection and uninterrupted happiness, she resigned him without a murmur into the arms of his Savior and his God, with the assured hope of his eternal felicity.

It is said that without George Washington there would be no United States, but without Martha, there would be no George Washington.

In his eyes, she was truly his "other self."

—⊶⊶—

"And God shall wipe away all tears from their eyes;
and there shall be no more death, neither sorrow, nor crying,
neither shall there be any more pain:
for the former things are passed away."
Revelation 21:4

DEAR READER

I challenge you to name a single child who has ever worn a Martha Washington costume for Halloween.

Can't think of one? I can. Take a gander at me (photo on the left), Nancy Young, 1962.

And here is my mother (photo on the right) in a Martha Washington costume, circa 1934. Two of us, in Martha costumes? And

then I write a book about her? The desire to connect to Martha must be in the genes.

When I dove into the task of giving a voice to Martha's life, I didn't expect to be so . . . impressed. I admit to originally knowing only the basics: she was short, plump, had the odd name Custis attached, and was the wife of the first president of the United States. End of story.

Beginning of story. Or rather, a tiny part of the story. Because during the first half of her life there *was* no United States. The thirteen colonies were populated by loyal British subjects, and Martha's life was more about being a wife and mother than caring about politics. Like most of us today, Martha went about her business without thinking too much beyond the small scope of her world.

But then everything changed and she was thrust into a rebellion that—if not for the determination and courage of its participants, and the divine intercession of the Almighty—could have turned out far differently. Although I'd learned the fundamentals of this Revolutionary War period in school, I was embarrassingly ignorant in regard to the depth and breadth of the story. Now, although I am more knowledgeable, I feel unworthy. For what have I ever done to deserve the sacrifice of these patriots? I live the life they planted for me, enjoy the fruits of their labor, and breathe freely through the gasps and groans of their courageous risk. What risk have I ever taken that comes close to theirs? What gives me the right to live as I do?

They gave me the right. *All* my rights as a free woman were ignited through their vision, struggle, and resolve. I've taken so much for granted. . . .

I often think of the life Martha and George could have enjoyed if there had been no Glorious Cause. Eight years of war and eight years of the presidency could have been sixteen years of peaceful bliss shared at Mount Vernon, under their own "vine and fig tree." Yet without their sacrifice, I could not live now, in peaceful bliss, under *my* own vine and fig tree.

None of us could.

In the process of discovering this country's roots, I discovered my own. In the 1970s my mother put together a family history. She noted that one of my ancestors—Jonathan Tyler—fought in the Revolutionary War. And so, on a trip to New England last year, through an amazing stream of non-coincidences, I found his grave and discovered that his family—my family—was one of the founding families of Piermont, New Hampshire. I left that tiny town girded by a profound sense of belonging, as if a foundation had been erected beneath me. My relatives have been in America since 1638, a fact that strengthens me—and makes me proud.

That's what I wish for you, dear reader. I hope Martha's story will nudge you toward finding your roots and your purpose, reignite your gratitude to God for all His gifts and blessings, and open your eyes to His work in the world beyond your own front door.

And then . . . I want you to go out and do something amazing and courageous. Under God.

Nancy Moser

FACT OR FICTION IN
Washington's Lady

As a novelist, my forte is making things up. Yet while writing *Washington's Lady*, I strove to discover the *facts* about Martha Washington's life and the birth of this country. In a historical novel of this kind, I "scene-out" true-life events and try not to change them. Unfortunately, there are often gaps in the information and I have to do what I am loath to do: guess. Ah me, it can't be helped. Below is the truth as I know it and instances of where I was forced to fudge. I hope the list adds to your enjoyment of the book.

- The Wollaston paintings of Martha, Daniel, Jacky, and Patsy are undeniably strange. Martha's and Daniel's facial features are very similar. In fact, Wollaston was known for repeating the same body, merely adding a new head—with only a few changes there too. Odd, odd paintings.

- The scene in Chapter 1 where Martha confronts her father-in-law-to-be is my creation. It's not known for sure how she won him over (only that she did), but his beloved garden seemed the one place where John Custis might have been approachable. I believe Martha would have seen that and acted on it to achieve her goal. Especially since Daniel was scared to death of his father and couldn't bring himself to face him.

- A note about the letters in the novel. Nearly all are real letters. You probably noticed the odd spellings in some of them. At this time in history there was no standardized spelling and people spelled and punctuated as they wished. Martha was a horrible speller. For this book we made a decision to correct the bad spelling if the letter was read aloud, but if it was silently read, we left it as is (or as *was*). Even people's names had variations in spelling. For instance, the children's Scottish tutor was sometimes Magowan and sometimes McGowan. And the music teacher was Stadler or Stedlar. In both cases, I chose the latter spelling. I also incorporated many quotes from letters into dialogue. The real words always got first dibs.

- The scene in Chapter 1 where Martha destroys her father-in-law's possessions is wishful supposition but based on this: historians found sixteen wine goblets, rare delft tea bowls, and hand-blown wine bottles—one with John Custis's seal defaced—in the well at the back of his Six Chimneys home in Williamsburg. Considering Martha and Daniel would have had access to his house . . . I couldn't resist giving Martha the chance for a little revenge.

- Fort Du Quesne became known as Fort Duquesne (Du-cane). This site is now Point State Park in downtown Pittsburgh, Pennsylvania. The park showcases a brick outline of the fort's walls.

- Martha's engagement ring: it is not known what the ring looked like, or if it contained a pearl, but it cost 2.16 British pounds, and George had it specially made in Philadelphia.

- The delivery of Daniel's tombstone to White House is my doing, but the tombstone and its inscription are real—as is the italicized detail in Chapter 3 regarding Martha's order for it.

- It is a sad fact that the names of women are often lost in history— even when they had famous relations. For instance, in Chapter 4, I mention: "The siblings of George who were able to attend traveled a distance to be with us: his half brother Austin and his wife, John Augustine and Hannah, and his dear sister Betty and her husband, Fielding Lewis." Austin's wife's name is not known. How sad. Another note, about Betty's husband, Fielding Lewis. Meriwether Lewis, famed explorer of the Louisiana Purchase (the Lewis and Clark Expedition), was a first cousin, once removed of Fielding (Meriwether Lewis's father and Fielding Lewis were first cousins). Fielding also was the first mayor of Fredericksburg.

• Regarding Sally Fairfax and George . . . There is a dispute over whether there was an affair. I don't believe there was. Both had too much to lose. There is an odd rumor that George William Fairfax encouraged the relationship, wanting George to father a child with Sally because he needed an heir to get Lord Fairfax's money. After all, he and Sally had been married ten years with no children. I find this farfetched, interesting. . . and impossible if one is to believe George was the cause of the childlessness between himself and Martha. Another rumor was that George William and his sister Anne (Lawrence Washington's wife) had mulatto blood, which is why George William did *not* inherit from Lord Fairfax in 1781. It is also one author's reason why Anne was allowed to marry the lowly Lawrence Washington, who had little to offer a rich family like the Fairfaxes. They were afraid no one of position would want to marry her with her mixed heritage. Again, farfetched but interesting. The truth is, we will never know.

• Jacky's writing on the wall is my creation, but Martha's inability to punish her children—and the consequences and conflict it created between her and George—is real.

• The locket Martha gave George . . . I do not know when she gave it to him or who made it, but it is said he wore it all his life.

• Regarding George and Martha not having children. Although logic leans toward it being George's problem, there is evidence he blamed Martha.

• In Chapter 6, George gives Martha a music book called *The Bull Finch*. This book still exists, with a 1759 date and her name inscribed. The song she sings ("The Gift") is a poem by James Thomson, a Scottish poet. I don't know if it was ever a song, but I made it into one. At the time, music books often supplied only the lyrics, which were then attached to familiar tunes.

- The incident that caused Jacky to be left behind in Chapter 7 is fictitious, although Martha did travel one time with only "little Pat" and did worry when she heard "doggs barke," as per a 1762 letter she sent to her sister Nancy.

- The Stamp Act might seem rather inconsequential to us now, but John Adams reflected that the "child of Independence" was born in the minds of the colonists because of it. The Stamp Act started the ball rolling. . . . And "Liberty and Property" was the phrase the mobs repeated. Jacky's hanging incident with Patsy's doll is fictional, but the information about the effigies and tax collector protests is real.

- In Chapter 8, George's list of Jacky's weaknesses is his own words: "He must learn that life is not only dogs, horses, guns, dress, and equipage."

- Martha's Great Cake served sixty and was more like a fruitcake than our image of cake. The recipe can be found on the Mount Vernon Web site.

- When George began to get involved in the rebellion, Patrick Henry said this about George's thinking process: "It was slow in operation, being little aided by invention or imagination, but sure in conclusion." He was a careful man.

- The 1772 painting by Charles Wilson Peale is one of the best known portraits of Washington. Peale would become the favorite portrait painter of both George and Martha.

- To expand from Chapter 9, some tidbits about Patrick Henry: His wife, Sarah, whom he'd married when she was sixteen, went crazy after the birth of her last child in 1771, and he kept her confined in the basement. She died in 1775, and in 1776, Patrick Henry married one of Martha's relatives, Dorothea Dandridge. She was twenty-two, the same age as his son, John—who is rumored to have also been in love with her.

- Reverend Price's sermon (which Rev. Gwatkin wrote) in Chapter 9: a transcript of the sermon is not available, but it is known that the topic was Genesis 18. The words beyond the verse are mine. After the service the speaker organized key members of the Williamsburg community to gather provisions and cash to be sent to the people of Boston.

- The wash desk George bought from the Fairfax estate can be seen at Mount Vernon.

- Martha did say "God be with you gentlemen" as she saw off the delegates for the Continental Congress. The words were recounted by Edmund Pendleton.

- George's ardent speech to Martha while sitting before the fire in Chapter 10 is re-created from his own words regarding the situation of the colonies.

- In Chapter 10, George and Martha speak of seeking God's wisdom, and George mentions a more personal God. The Great Awakening was going on at this time, changing religion from passive and ceremonial to aggressively personal. George and Martha were always quick to assign credit to "Providence," and throughout her life, Martha had private Bible study every morning. The Washingtons were active members in many churches. Their pew can be seen (and sat in) at the Bruton Parish Church in Williamsburg.

- The article in the *Virginia Gazette,* announcing George as commander, is my creation, although the Adams and Washington quotes are real.

- In Chapter 10, Patrick Henry's famous quotation, "I know not what course others may take; but as for me, give me liberty or give me death!" was said during a speech at the Second Virginia Convention meeting on March 25, 1775, a few months before the Second Continental Congress met in Philadelphia.

- The Chapter 10 letter from George to Martha is real and combines two June 1775 letters. As stated in the epilogue, in 1802, Martha destroyed their personal letters. Yet these two survived and Martha Parke Custis Peter, one of Martha Washington's granddaughters, found them in a drawer of a small desk that she inherited from Mrs. Washington.

- The locket scene in Chapter 11 is fictional, as is the cabin. It is known that Martha spent one night away from home, not too far away, but it is not known where. I assume Eleanor, Jacky, Lund, and maybe a maid would have gone with her. And women often kept lockets containing the hair of a departed loved one.

- In Chapter 11, when Martha travels to Cambridge, she mentions having never been up north. She *had* been the twenty-six miles to Mount Airy, the Calvert plantation in Upper Marlboro, Maryland, *east* of Alexandria. Note: there is a town called Mount Airy, Maryland, sixty miles north. This is not Martha's Mount Airy.

- In Chapter 11, Martha's "beautiful country" and "very great somebody" phrases are her own.

- The army headquarters where George and Martha lived in Cambridge, the home that had formally belonged to loyalist John Vassal, would eventually be owned by the poet Henry Wadsworth Longfellow. It is currently a museum.

- Prospect Hill now sits in Somerville, Massachusetts, and in the 1870s was turned into an aristocratic residential neighborhood. In 1902 a park was created and a forty-two-foot granite tower built to commemorate the hill's historical significance for future generations. Every year on January 1, Somerville residents gather on Prospect Hill for a ceremony honoring the historic flag raising.

- I do not know if Lucy Knox was pregnant (Chapter 11), as I can find no birth dates for the Knox children. But they had thirteen (ten died in childhood), and since they had been married since June of 1774, I assume she was pregnant. As for namesakes, Kitty Greene had George Washington Greene in 1776 and Martha Washington Greene in 1777.

- "Then I peered up at him, hooked my finger in a buttonhole of his lapel, and pulled him down to my level." Martha often used to do this. She also called George *old man*, even when he was only in his forties. The soldiers found this amusing. They must have thought the couple odd in appearance: George, tall and slim, and Martha, plump and petite.

- In Chapter 12, many of the details of the British evacuation of Boston were taken from the journal of army surgeon Dr. James Thacher.

- The leather key basket and brown-and-white-checkered chair can still be seen in the Washingtons' bedroom at Mount Vernon.

- A general note: Eleanor was called Nelly by her family, but because she later had a daughter Nelly, I chose to call her Eleanor, to make the identification clearer. Also, George often called Martha *Patcy*, but again, with a daughter Patsy, I chose to ignore his nickname.

- In Chapter 12, I fudged the timeline in order to let Martha meet all three young men at once. I know Hamilton joined them March 1, 1777 (Martha arrived March 15). I do not know when Laurens' offer was accepted other than it was sometime in 1777, but Lafayette showed up in August—after Martha had gone back to Mount Vernon. He did, however, become like a son to her.

- The Oneida Indian story in Chapter 13 is true. It was only recently discovered and was passed down for two hundred years through Oneida oral history. Martha did give these presents to Polly—after George was president.

- The house of Abingdon, built by Jacky and Eleanor, is now just a brick foundation that can be seen between two office buildings at the Reagan National Airport near Alexandria. On another piece of land in the area (which Jacky purchased in 1778), Jacky's son, Wash, built Arlington House (in 1802). Wash's daughter married Robert E. Lee, the Confederate Civil War general, and the couple lived in the house for many years. After the Civil War, the house and land were confiscated by the federal government because Lee was considered a traitor. The land around Arlington House became the Arlington National Cemetery. President John F. Kennedy and his wife, Jackie, are buried there.

- The winter of 1779-80 in Morristown was the worst winter in North America.

- Martha gave what would equal $20,000 in today's dollars toward the women's charity drive to make shirts for the soldiers. Total collected = $300,000!

- The friendly fire incident detailed in Chapter 15 actually happened, and the following line is a quote from George: "Never was I in more imminent danger by being between two fires, knocking up with my sword the presented pieces." He did not speak of the incident for decades, but it obviously weighed heavily on his mind. This is the incident intimated about in Chapter 5.

- In Chapter 16, George shocked everyone when he resigned as commander in chief of the army. No one had ever willingly relinquished power like that. On his deathbed Napoleon said, "They wanted me to be another Washington," something *he* obviously could never be.

- Eleanor Custis was to be pregnant twenty times. Thirteen children lived.

- "Our own vine and fig tree" is a quote from one of George's letters and refers to his sentiment regarding their retirement to Mount Vernon. If only they could have enjoyed it longer. . . .

- In Chapter 16, visitors Mr. Quarrier and Miss Eliza Tomkins were real people who showed up without introduction and stayed overnight sometime during the year following George's death, when Martha was in deep mourning. Their audacity was not unique.

- Martha had to deal with an enormous amount of loss and grief. Added to her issues in Chapter 17 was the fact her mother and brother died within days of each other in April 1785. And George's favorite brother, Jack (John Augustine), died in January 1787.

- There are discrepancies regarding how George got the news he was president. I chose to combine two views.

- In Chapter 17 Charles Thomson comes to tell George he is the new president. Beyond being the secretary of Congress, Thomson designed the Great Seal of the United States and also provided the first American translation of the Bible from the Greek.

- George and Martha's granddaughter Betsy felt so insecure and desperate for attention she changed her name to the lofty sounding *Eliza*. She became a very difficult woman.

- When Nelly got married, she wore the first bridal veil in America.

- George's last words as stated in Chapter 18 are what he actually said. But in addition, just before he died, George—with a great deal of effort—told Tobias Lear, "I am just going. Have me decently buried and do not let my body be put into the vault in less than three days after I am dead." At the time there was a common fear of being buried alive—as sometimes comas were indistinguishable from death. Martha and Nelly did not attend the funeral.

I could mention more items, but this is the gist of it. I wish to thank the following biographers for their insightful books, which were invaluable: *The General and Mrs. Washington* by Bruce Chadwick, *Martha Washington: First Lady of Liberty* by Helen Bryan, *Martha Washington* by Patricia Brady, and *The Unexpected George Washington:*

His Private Life by Harlow Giles Unger. I also want to thank my editor, Helen Motter, whose passion for history equals my own, Dave Horton at Bethany House for believing in me and my "ladies," and my agent Janet Grant for always being my champion.

May the main *fact* of this book be that it brought you a deeper appreciation of this country and the people who sacrificed so much toward its creation.

Discussion Questions for *Washington's Lady*

1. Martha gave up a lot to marry George, moving from the county of her youth to the foreign locale of Mount Vernon, moving from being the wealthiest widow in Virginia to the wife of a struggling farmer. Why do you think she took the plunge with George?

2. Although we often disparage "women's work" and look upon women of the past in pity or call them weak for not wanting more, women in America during Martha's time were often relieved to be "stuck" doing the domestic tasks in the house. It was a step up from the tough position of their mothers and grandmothers who worked in the fields and woods *with* their husbands, carving out a life in the wilderness. Discuss the roles of women in history. Are we better off now or were we then? How? Why?

3. In Chapter 4, Martha and the children move from White House to Mount Vernon. It is a poignant moment that is interrupted by little Patsy falling off the carriage seat, a distraction Martha sees as an odd blessing. *Sometimes it was best not to think too much until the peak moment of sentiment was past.* When have you been spared an emotional moment until a later time when it was easier to endure? Do you ever consciously seek a distraction to attain such a delay of emotion?

4. Martha longed for more children. How did she handle this

disappointment? Did she handle it well? Why do you think she and George had no children?

5. Martha chose to keep her enemy close by becoming friends with Sally Fairfax. Do you think this is generally a wise move? Or is it asking for trouble? If the Fairfaxes had not moved back to England, what do you think might have happened?

6. The tension caused by Martha's inability to discipline her children, and her unwillingness to let George be a true father to them, had dire consequences in her son's life. Martha knew she was wrong but couldn't seem to stop herself. Have you ever been in, or witnessed, a similar parenting situation? What were the results? What is the solution?

7. At first, the Washingtons were hesitant to join the dissension against their mother country. What do you think was the turning point for them—what made them willing to sacrifice life, liberty, and property for such a dangerous long shot?

8. George's mother, Mary Ball, never acknowledged her son was worth a whit, yet Martha enjoyed the full support of *her* family. How do you think these parental attitudes affected them?

9. Throughout her life, Martha suffered enormous loss through the deaths of family and friends, not to mention the death and suffering of the soldiers she visited. It's said God won't give us more than we can handle. What methods did she use to get through it? Did they work? Why do you think some people are asked to handle so much suffering?

10. Many times, Martha showed great bravery—on the roads north, protecting Mount Vernon from Dunmore . . . What in her life prepared her for this attribute?

11. Martha was a willing hostess, yet at winter camp she was forced into the role of intercessor by the wives of soldiers, and later was thrust into the role of wife of the new president. All the while, she just wanted to be home. Do you agree with her view? Or do

you think she should have done a better job dealing with her public position?

12. In Chapter 14, Martha was given a gift of lemons, oranges, and other delicacies from the wife of the British paymaster. George told her she couldn't keep them because the giver was the enemy and it might damage the Cause. *For one brief moment I wished to pitch the Cause and enjoy my lemons. But I could not. Duty ruled me now, as it always had, as it always would.* Duty was the driving force for many people during this time of history—duty toward country and family. How does our sense of duty differ today— toward country? Toward family? Is duty a lost art?

13. Many of the founders of this country were against slavery, yet they didn't know how to fix the problem without creating more problems. What aspects of today's society do you disdain? What are your solutions? What are the new problems that accompany your solutions?

14. Many of George's actions reveal a dichotomy between ambition and humility. Do you think his various examples of humility (such as resigning his position after the war) were real or a part of a larger plan to gain position? What do you think about his choice to wear his uniform to a meeting of Congress when they were making some personnel decisions? What about his French and Indian War exploits—how did ambition and humility enter into his choices?

15. Martha and George went to great lengths to cure Patsy—to no avail. And yet, later in life, Martha realized if Patsy had lived, Martha would not have been free to join George at the winter camps during the war. Have you ever recognized such a hindsight revelation in your own life?

16. It's been said that without George Washington there would be no United States, but without Martha, there would be no George Washington. How so?

17. The great sorrow Martha experienced at George's death broke her (can you blame her?), yet she found solace in the thought of being together again in heaven. When have you found peace in this promise?

18. This nation was created "under God." God intervened in many ways. Name some of the places where you see His hand. Where do you see God's hand in the world today?

Mᴏʀᴇ Bɪᴏɢʀᴀᴘʜɪᴄᴀʟ Fɪᴄᴛɪᴏɴ Fʀᴏᴍ

Nancy Moser

A Woman Ahead of Her Time...
Forgotten by History

Young Nannerl Mozart's life seems to be the stuff of fairy tales—traveling and performing before kings and queens with younger brother Wolfgang. But when she grows up and loses her prodigy appeal, what will become of her talent and aspirations? In a world where women's choices are limited, can her dreams survive?

Mozart's Sister by Nancy Moser

Be Transported Into the Mind and Life of Jane Austen!

In the first novelization of Jane Austen's life, award-winning author Nancy Moser draws from Jane's own letters, family accounts, and detailed biographies, infusing life into the wit and mind of the literary world's most beloved heroine.

Just Jane by Nancy Moser